INNOCENT UNTIL HIS FORBIDDEN TOUCH

CAROL MARINELLI

EMERGENCY MARRIAGE TO THE GREEK

CLARE CONNELLY

MILLS & BOON

First published in Great Britain 2022
by Mills & Boon, an imprint of HarperCollins*Publishers* Ltd,
1 London Bridge Street, London, SE1 9GF

www.harpercollins.co.uk

HarperCollins*Publishers*
1st Floor, Watermarque Building,
Ringsend Road, Dublin 4, Ireland

Innocent Until His Forbidden Touch © 2022 Carol Marinelli

Emergency Marriage to the Greek © 2022 Clare Connelly

ISBN: 978-0-263-30095-6

08/22

MIX
Paper from
responsible sources
FSC™ C007454

INNOCENT UNTIL HIS FORBIDDEN TOUCH

CAROL MARINELLI

MILLS & BOON

PROLOGUE

Ten years ago...

BEATRICE DID NOT arrive at the convent unannounced.

It had taken her a long time, not only to save the airfare from London, but to receive a response to her repeated requests to meet with the Reverend Mother. She had been told her journey was unnecessary and that there was nothing more she could be told regarding her circumstances...

As she walked up the hill for her midday interview, Beatrice consoled herself with the fact that even if there was nothing more to glean about her mother then she would find out about her dear friend.

They had been abandoned three weeks apart and had been as different as two babies—and later two children—could be.

Alicia, dark and vibrant; Beatrice her pale, timid shadow.

They had been such unlikely friends. Yet, for whatever reason, Alicia had taken a battering ram to her heart and insisted they were better than friends—more than sisters, even. In fact, she'd often declared, they were twins!

Aged eleven, Beatrice had been awarded a scholarship and sent to an esteemed boarding school in Milan. Beatrice had shivered in terror, but Alicia had tried to be brave, and they had sworn to stay in touch. Alicia had even told her to work hard and get a good job so they could be flatmates someday.

It had been a glimpse of the future that Beatrice had held on to. The scariest part of being abandoned had always been the thought of what might come after they left the convent gates—but they would have each other.

Alicia had barely been able to read, certainly hadn't been able to write, but it hadn't deterred Beatrice—she had written regularly. And then, just as she'd got her bearings in Milan, she'd been sent to a small abbey in Switzerland for language immersion. There had been no other children and certainly no teenagers or any chance of making friends there. The order had been strict, but occasionally she'd be granted permission to call the convent in Trebordi. To no avail. They'd never brought Alicia to the phone, saying she was in prayers, or with friends, or in detention.

Any excuse.

Alicia had always tended towards melodrama, and Beatrice had guessed they didn't want to deal with the upset her phone calls might cause. She'd begun to wonder if Alicia had even received her letters, and had vowed to return in person as soon as she could afford to do so.

Her final two years of school had been in England, where she'd been labelled standoffish rather than shy. Aloof. Cold.

It had been the same in her first year of university...

While her English was excellent, in those first getting-to-know-you exchanges Beatrice had always remained a beat behind. Her sense of humour had been lacking, and sarcasm truly wasted on her—by the time she'd worked out that people were joking it was too late.

She hadn't been able to get past even the first questions—*Where are you from...? What do your family do...?*

She walked on and lingered at the baby door, where she had been left as a newborn some nineteen years ago. She thought of her mother's fear and loneliness. She too had grown up feeling exactly that.

Scared.

Lonely.

She'd had Alicia though, Beatrice reminded herself.

Having rung the bell at the gates, she smiled, a little bemused, when it was Reverend Mother herself who came to let her in.

'I'm so excited to be back…' Her words, for once, tumbled out. Beatrice felt the heat on her cheeks and the glow in her heart as she walked the familiar path to the convent.

'What time is your train?' Reverend Mother asked, walking briskly. 'You are going back to England tonight, yes?'

'Oh, no, I'm planning to stay in Trebordi for a week or two,' Beatrice replied, hoping Reverend Mother might extend an invitation.

As they climbed the stairs to her office, Beatrice found out that was not to be.

'We cannot have all the children we've ever cared for using the place as a hostel…' She was terse, but softened it with a smile. 'I have to be like a cat,' she explained. 'I am kind to the kittens, but soon it is time to stand back and allow them independence—force it at times.'

'I *am* independent, Reverend Mother.'

'You are on a full scholarship at university?'

'I am.' Beatrice felt a little insulted, but was unable to show it. While grateful for the scholarship, she had worked hard for it. Still worked hard. She'd found a job at a chemist's in England, and now… 'I work as a translator in a hospital in the evenings and at weekends.'

She took a seat in Reverend Mother's office, keeping her smile in place and taking out her notebook and pen.

'Child, you can put those away. There is nothing more I can tell you.'

'Perhaps…' Beatrice held firm. 'But I remember that Alicia had gold earrings pinned to her baby suit. *Segni di ricooscimento.* Signs of recognition. I have read that should a mother return she can identify her child that way.'

'Beatrice, I have told you. For you there was nothing.'

'There must have been something,' she replied. 'A page of the bible…?' She had been told her mother was presumed to have been a tourist, attending the festival that came to Trebordi each year—especially given that Beatrice was so blonde. 'Perhaps a trinket from the festival.'

'Beatrice, if there was anything I would have told you.'

'A nappy?' she asked, tears stinging her eyes, embarrassed at the thought that she had been left uncovered and naked. Discarded. 'Something?'

'This doesn't help anyone,' Reverend Mother scolded. 'Beatrice, you have had an education most people could only dream of. Let it go.'

'No,' Beatrice said. 'I won't. I worry for my mother. If something dreadful happened to her, then I want her to know I understand. And if she was young and scared, I want to tell her myself that I know how it feels to be scared and alone. I love her, and so of course I forgive her.'

'It's not healthy, Beatrice. I have seen many children devote too much time trying so hard to get to the past that they ruin their future.'

'Well, I want to know my history. I will stand at the baby door every year, and I will be here each year for Alicia's birthday too...' She saw the flush on Reverend Mother's cheeks, and it was there in that office that Beatrice learned how to be direct. Although she was usually timid, she found out just how tough she could be. 'Did Alicia even get my letters?'

'Of course.'

Reverend Mother wouldn't lie, surely?

Only Beatrice felt sure that she was, and her pale blue eyes narrowed in suspicion as she was repeatedly stonewalled.

It took everything she could summon for her to confront the Reverend Mother. 'I don't believe she did.'

'Please show the respect you were taught.'

'Reverend Mother, I respectfully ask you, where is my friend?'

Reverend Mother responded with silence.

'Well, if you won't tell me, I'm going to ask around the village. I have enough money to stay at the bar.' *Barely.* 'I might go and visit Signora Schininà.' She was the woman who ran the brothel. 'She knows all the gossip, and her son was close to Alicia…'

'She's dead.'

'Well, I'll just ask someone else, and I'll keep asking—'

'Child…' Reverend Mother interjected. *'Non destare il cane che dorme.* Do not awaken the sleeping dog.'

What sleeping dog?

Why did her very presence seem to cause such unease?

Surely foundlings returned here all the time in search of their history?

'I'm not leaving Trebordi until I have answers.' She closed her notebook and put her pen in her bag, sat aloof and defiant even as her heart pounded in her chest. 'I will go to every shop, knock on every door…'

Reverend Mother stood, clearly flustered. 'Please wait.'

Beatrice sat for what felt like an age. She waited an hour, perhaps two, for Reverend Mother to return. Eventually she stood up and went to the window, staring not at the ocean but at the playground of the little school she'd attended. Alicia would clamber on top of the climbing frame to wave to her friend Dante as he boarded the bus to the school in the village. They'd been ten! Then her loud companion would round up a group of girls and play complicated games while Beatrice resisted.

Despite the happy promise of her name, she'd been a guarded child, who had loathed playtime and dreaded the bell and the scrape of chairs as the girls raced out. Serious and prim by nature, she had felt too old for games even at five, preferring to sit by the water taps, simply not knowing how to join in.

Alicia, though, had been so bold, confident and sunny.

She'd happily peel off her dress to swim in her knickers in the river, and had held hands with boys in the village—well, with one. There'd been no swimming in the river for Beatrice. She would emerge from the bathroom fully dressed each morning and undress in there each night, always so private and shy...

It vexed her that she'd been left naked. Exposed.

Beatrice turned as the office door opened—but not to show the round, familiar face of Reverend Mother.

'Sister Catherine.' Beatrice gave her a tight smile, assuming she was here to explain the delay, or offer refreshments, perhaps.

'I have been told you have questions.' Sister Catherine gestured for her to sit.

'Many,' Beatrice said. 'Were you here when I was found?'

Sister Catherine was a very nondescript woman—not just in looks, but in the bank of Beatrice's memory. Dark hair peeked from her habit and dark brows arched over brown eyes. She'd been a little mean, but not dreadfully so. More... indifferent. She had taught Latin, and Beatrice had been the star of that class, but on her own merit.

Sister Catherine hadn't been particularly encouraging. Just... Nothing.

And then Beatrice found out that she was her mother.

'I was plain, like you,' she said, 'and cheerless too.'

Beatrice said nothing, just stared at the features that were, she could now see, a dark version of her own. How had she never seen it? How had her own mother been in plain sight and she hadn't known?

'I did have one curiosity, though...'

Nothing dreadful had happened to her. It had been nothing but a curiosity she'd wished to satisfy before committing to the church.

'I used to help my mother clean the cottages where the tourists stayed. He was a widower. He had been married for thirty years and he missed his wife dreadfully. He was here from Germany for a quiet vacation.'

'So he wasn't here for the festival?'

'No!' Sister Catherine scorned the very thought. 'He was a historian—and he liked to live in the past too. He said I reminded him of his late wife when she was young.'

'He took advantage?'

'No, I was twenty-five and he was handsome indeed.'

Beatrice's past was being given to her rather like a history lesson—with little emotion, just a small summing-up. Two weeks of sin and then she'd repented.

'I was a novice when I realised I was with child, and...'

'Scared?'

It would seem not.

'Beatrice, I knew what I wanted to do with my life, and I knew that you would be taken care of...'

'Did Reverend Mother know?'

'Of course not,' she said rather harshly, and it was that part that shrivelled Beatrice's heart.

Reverend Mother noticed *everything*. Nothing got past her. And yet Sister Catherine's pregnancy somehow had. Beatrice's very birth somehow had. Clearly she had not done anything to alert Reverend Mother.

'It was when you turned ten, or around then, that Reverend Mother called me in here. She said the similarities were striking and could no longer be ignored. In truth, I couldn't see it. We are both petite, but you are so blonde...'

How could she not have seen it? For now Beatrice felt as if she were looking in a mirror. Or at one of those apps that aged you, but not much...just a little. It showed her what she'd look like with dark hair and dark eyes...

She searched for a memory of them both—a stolen moment, an extra treat, a bedtime story... Finally she found one—only it wasn't endearing.

One day the bell had gone for the dreaded playtime and she'd pleaded to stay in and read quietly.

'Andate a giocare fuori.' Sister Catherine hadn't even looked up.

Go and play outside.

Beatrice's voice, when it came, was hoarse. 'I used to climb out of the window and go to the festival, searching for you.' Then she would wake screaming and wet and she and Alicia would sneak down to the laundry to wash the sheets. 'I used to go every night when the festival was in town.'

'The festival has gone now,' Sister Catherine said. 'And so has your friend.'

'Where?'

'I don't know.' Sister Catherine shrugged. 'You have your answers. I have been honest…' She spread her hands, as if asking what more she could want. 'There's nothing for you here—just trouble for me if you stay. Beatrice, you have been fed and cared for, given an education I could never have afforded…'

But not loved.

Not for a single second.

Instead, she had been hidden in plain sight, and then when it had become inconvenient, she had been moved on.

'You didn't wrap me… You didn't cover me…'

'I knew you'd be found.'

Beatrice discovered sarcasm then. 'How caring of you.'

She left and took a local taxi to the train station, vowing never, ever to return. So appalled was she by the answers she'd found, she gave up on finding Alicia too. Instead, she sat on the train and cut her mother from the one photo of the convent inhabitants she had from her childhood, and then she decided to change her surname from Festa to Taylor.

Cut, cut, cut.

She snipped her mother into tiny pieces and refused to shed so much as a single tear.

Beatrice knew then why she was so emotionally frozen. She hadn't developed a heart of stone, she realised. Rather, she'd inherited one!

And now Beatrice Taylor would use it to her own advantage.

CHAPTER ONE

'*SIGNORA, ALLACCI LA cintura di sicurezza*. Fasten your seatbelt.'

The captain apologised for the rough air that had accompanied them, and the storm cells that had meant their flight path had taken them over Sicily.

Bellanisiá was, Beatrice decided as they commenced their descent, just a little too close to Trebordi for comfort. And she wasn't sure she even wanted the job.

Liaison Aide to HRH Prince Julius of Bellanisiá.

It was a newly created role for a newly appointed heir.

The brief was simple: tidy up the reprobate Prince's image prior to bridal selection.

Her career was PR. She cleaned up the images of fallen celebrities, MPs, sportsmen, or whoever needed her detached aloofness to help them navigate whatever mess they'd found themselves in. Affairs, dramas and lies—Beatrice just waded her emotionless way through it all. No one would guess that the brittle woman who could face press or cameras and address sensitive topics with ease had never so much as been kissed. Or that she'd struggled to make a single friend.

She worked on three-to six-month contracts and was successful enough to be approached for work through word of mouth rather than having to seek it out.

The secret to her success? Beatrice didn't care. And she told all her clients just that—she wasn't their agent, nor their wife, mother, psychologist…

While a royal wedding was an attractive enough incentive to have sustained her through three panel interviews,

Beatrice herself now had doubts that she was suited to the role.

Deference was not on her impressive list of attributes. And, judging by the lengthy list of protocols she'd been forwarded just to meet with the arrogant Prince, deference was a prerequisite.

It was *his* life that was in chaos, Beatrice would politely remind him, not hers.

Their flight path, though unsettling, had offered an enticing view of the Kingdom of Bellanisiá. A beautiful archipelago of islands in the Ionian Sea, it looked from the sky as if pebbles had been skimmed between Sicily and Greece. Each island was unique, but all existed under one rule.

In preparation for her first interview Beatrice had done some research online, and had caught up with Prince Julius's life.

A wild child...

A surprisingly happy teen compared to his very formal elder brother and elder sister...

And as an adult...?

He'd studied archaeology, followed by a stint in the military, and should now have an honorary PhD in brunettes—tall brunettes, widowed brunettes, curvy brunettes—all beautiful, all devoted. He had looks, charm, and all the benefits of being second in line to the throne.

Hetaerae were allowed—basically long-term trusted mistresses—as well as a wife, but Julius selected his own short-term company on his extensive travels.

Sitting in her temporary flat in London, about to finish her latest temporary job, Beatrice had topped up her hot water and lemon and read all she could on the maverick Prince.

He disappeared for months on end on archaeological excavations, then returned for duty and to party. His life, though, had swerved out of the fast lane and careered into the emergency one when his elder brother Prince Claude had died, suddenly and unexpectedly, a year ago from flu.

Prince Julius had returned to reside at the palace, where not only had his passion for archaeology been put aside, but his short-term relationships had halted and become...well, not relationships. All his flings now seemed to be with exes.

There was nothing tawdry—just gossip. He partied hard; he worked harder. From all she could glean, Prince Julius had not only taken on the role and responsibilities of his late brother, but the Queen had also retreated from duties, and he was picking up the slack.

Even after three interviews, she knew little more than the fact that the palace wanted to curb his ways and plan his wedding.

Beatrice had had several questions of her own. 'He's opposed to women in the line of succession?' she'd asked at the third interview.

Beatrice had felt her chin meet her neck and her mouth gape at the cheek of that when she'd first read it, but the tone of her enquiry had been polite.

'That's not your concern,' Phillipe, Head of Palace Protocol, had informed her.

'Actually, it is—if I'm trying to update his image.'

'That changes with the next generation,' Jordan, the Prince's PA, had responded. 'Things move slowly here.'

Indeed, it seemed they did. So slowly that when Beatrice arrived at her hotel, the receptionist informed her that the dresses she needed pressing wouldn't be returned until later that night.

'I have a meeting at the palace at two,' Beatrice said in swift Italian. 'I would like it taken care of now, please. Thank you.'

After a quick shower, she clipped her blonde hair back, put on a slick of pale lipstick, and topped her crisply pressed grey shift dress with a darker grey jacket for a neutral look.

Neutral.

When she'd been a translator, her aim had been not to draw the eye. Now, given the status of most of her clients, her aim remained the same.

A car collected her, and on arrival at the rear of the palace there was a rigorous checking of her bag and pockets, and her phone was retained.

Then she was given another tutorial on protocol, and also informed, at a pre meeting the Prince meeting, that her car today was an exception and there was a shuttle bus for most palace staff.

Beatrice had by then decided she did not want the job.

She was led down a glass passageway to a very plush office and told that, should she get the role, her own office would be two floors down.

Of course.

She awaited this unsuitable heir who was being prepared for the altar.

Beatrice already knew he was handsome, but she was expecting him to be...well, *petulant*, as well as wrung out from the effort of balancing his workload with his rather decadent ways.

He was fully thirty minutes late.

'Seriously?' His deep voice carried ahead of him, speaking in Italian, and then he walked in. 'I do not need a PR strategist.'

'A liaison aide, sir,' his companion murmured.

Beatrice stood, as she'd been instructed to do, but when he entered the room every assumption she'd had was wiped out.

Prince Julius brimmed not just with authority but with health and energy. It was as if some force field had entered the room.

She dealt with alphas both male and female at the top

of their game—or rather, when they were about to come crashing down from it.

Not he.

He was, quite literally, stunning.

He stunned.

So much so that although the main language here was Italian, followed by Greek, Beatrice spoke in English, the language she'd last been working in from the country she had flown in from.

'It's a pleasure to meet you,' she said, and then added, because she'd been told to do so, 'sir.'

'Likewise,' he said, though his eyes said otherwise.

In truth, he'd discarded her on sight. Certainly he had not registered her features.

No doubt, like so many, he had just briefly surmised that the petite blonde in her smart grey shift dress did not have what was required to deal with the intricate details of his complex life.

God, he's tall, Beatrice thought, almost relieved when he gestured for her to take a seat.

It was more than his height—he was the most immaculate man she had ever seen. His hair was black and glossy and cut to perfection. His silver-grey tie was knotted and perfectly so. From his citrussy scent and manicured nails to his porcelain-capped teeth and black eyes, he looked as if he'd just stepped off a magazine cover, or a director had shouted *Cut!* while shooting a film about—

Beatrice swallowed. She did not want to pursue that line of thought. The issue was that at most interviews she found so-called alphas to be much less in the flesh.

He was so much more.

Just too good-looking.

The unrufflable Beatrice put the flutter in her chest down to nerves.

He was royal; it must be that.

Staff were standing to either side of him, and he'd frowned as he read the bullet points of her résumé. 'Sicilian?'

'*Si, tuttavia—*' Beatrice responded in Italian but he halted her.

'Let's stay in English,' he suggested. 'I need the practice; mine is a little rusty.'

He glanced again at her résumé, presumably at her list of rather impressive clients, and then looked up at his PA, Jordan, whom, like the others, Beatrice had met at the interviews.

'No.' He shook his head. 'I really don't want my name attached to any of these people...' His top lip curled a little.

'Sir...' Jordan nodded in understanding. 'Ms Taylor is here more to assist with the press interest and your image in the lead-up to bridal selection.'

'I agreed to a reset.' The Prince turned his head and glared up to a man Beatrice knew to be one of the King's aides. 'Not to being policed.'

'I certainly won't police anyone,' Beatrice interjected. 'Sir.'

Everyone stiffened when she spoke uninvited. Well, all apart from the Prince. He glanced up, and those black eyes met hers for the first time. She put the flutter in her chest down to butterflies.

With the wings of bats.

'You studied Classical and Modern Languages...' He frowned at the details of her career path and mentioned one of the embassies she had worked in. 'You worked as a translator there?'

'Yes, sir.'

His lips pursed a fraction. Possibly he was recalling a scandal around that time that had shifted the course of her work.

'You were a hospital and then a court translator prior to that?'

'There should be a reference there, concerning my clear and accurate translations.' Somebody coughed, and Beatrice realised her omission and added, 'Sir.'

Gosh, how was she supposed to discuss scandals and such if she had to bow and address him so formally at all times? While she *wanted* a royal wedding on her résumé, in order for her to do her work well there would need to be a lot of straight talking involved.

He rested his hand on his chin and pressed a finger to his lips as he read the brief pages her lengthy résumé had been condensed down to for his perusal.

'I think this might be an issue.' He looked up at an advisor. 'If Ms Taylor translated at this embassy...'

'I have to agree, sir,' said Phillipe. 'I've made my objections clear.'

There were...political issues between our countries.

It was Beatrice who answered. 'They are more than happy to provide further references. They know I won't be a fly on anyone's wall, sir.'

Again, he met her eyes.

Beatrice held them.

'Do you have any questions for me?' he asked.

'Several.' Beatrice nodded. 'The first being how frank am I allowed to be, sir?'

'*Allowed?*' His eyes narrowed at the implication.

'For example, if I took the role would we be able to speak one to one?' Beatrice asked.

'Of course,' Prince Julius responded. 'In fact let's do so now.'

Beatrice wasn't sure if she was nervous as she stood up, for she so rarely was. Yet her heart was beating faster in her chest, as if she were climbing stairs rather than descending them. French doors were being opened by a servant, and she felt an unfamiliar hesitancy before stepping outside.

He was a prince, Beatrice reminded herself. A prince she

was about to confront. It was natural to feel nervous. However, nervous felt like the wrong choice of word.

It should be a relief to step outside after the rather hostile atmosphere indoors, yet her tension felt heightened out in the soft afternoon breeze and in surroundings so tranquil they should calm her.

'I apologise for the tension back there,' he said. 'You would be the first member of the palace team who is not from Bellanisiá.'

'I see.'

'There are centuries of tradition here—ancient laws from many cultures, many languages spoken. I assume you already know that?'

'I've read as much as I can of the kingdom's history.'

'Then you will also know that I've enjoyed the bachelor life. However, given I am now heir to the throne, it's time for the leopard to change his spots.'

He wasn't a leopard.

Nor a cheetah.

Not even a growling lion.

It was like walking beside a giant black panther and being told by his gushing owners that he was completely tame.

Nor was he cute—and he certainly wasn't particularly friendly.

'The lake is beautiful,' Beatrice said, unusually tentative in her approach. 'It's like winter…'

'Lago Lefko,' he said.

White Lake, Beatrice thought. A mixture of Greek and Italian. She could see why it had been named as such.

It was surrounded by white willows, silver birch, even the stones around it were white, and glinted as if covered in frost. It even felt as if the temperature had dropped and she shivered slightly.

'I almost expect my breath to blow white. Even the

birds…' There were doves in the trees and Japanese cranes on a central island.

'The doves were introduced when my parents married.' He pointed to the cranes, making hearts with their necks. 'They were a gift when Prince Claude was born, and the white swans were for Princess Jasmine.'

'And you?'

'I beg your pardon?'

'Were birds introduced when you…?' She suddenly realised that he had perfectly understood what she had said. 'Sir.'

'Peacocks,' he told her. 'White, of course.'

Beatrice looked around.

'They're always off preening. You will soon hear them.'

He spoke politely, yet he was removed and distant. There was a wall between them that she doubted would be dismantled even on commencement of her job, for she had seen how formal his staff were.

'So, you have questions?'

'Yes. It was the one-year anniversary of Prince Claude's passing last week.'

'Indeed.'

'And from my understanding it is now considered time for the country to look towards happier times.' She trod gently, out of politeness and also because it was beyond anything she knew, but she did try to put her client first. 'Is marriage something you want?'

'It's necessary.'

'I understand that, but I'm trying to gauge your thoughts and—'

'You won't get my thoughts, Ms Taylor. Are you always this direct?'

'I am.' She was. 'And I don't see how we can have the conversations it will be necessary for us to have if I have to constantly bow and call you *sir*…sir.'

'That's your issue to deal with,' he told her. 'I prefer to keep things formal.'

He was awful, Beatrice decided.

'I *will* tell you that my future wife will have her own country's interests at hand when she makes her decision to marry me. It will be a very mutually beneficial partnership and it will be celebrated.'

'And love?'

He managed a wry laugh at that. 'I don't need that sort of complication.' He turned his head to her. 'Would you bring *your* partner to work?'

Beatrice had never had a partner, and even though she might be delving into his private life the Prince wouldn't be getting a whiff of hers. 'Of course not.'

'Or to a business dinner? Or on a business trip?'

'No.'

'Precisely.'

'I don't sleep with my colleagues, though,' Beatrice added. 'Or have their children.'

'You're a commoner, Ms Taylor. I am not.'

She could have cheerfully pushed him into that lake. She doubted she'd be offered the job now, let alone take it.

'There was an incident a few weeks ago…' Beatrice chose the latest example. 'And an apology issued by the palace.'

'How would you have dealt with it?' asked the Prince.

'From everything I've read, it seems that a good time was had by all.' She sounded tough. And liberated, even. Which she was. Just not on a private level. It was much easier to discuss other people's wild ways when they were so alien to her own. 'I didn't see your need to comment.'

'I didn't.'

'Well, the palace did,' Beatrice pointed out. 'There have been denials and apologies as far back as I can see. On your behalf, of course.' She glanced over at him, and then upwards; he really was very tall. 'It's not how I'd have played it.'

'It's not a game, Ms Taylor. And, yet again, you are to address me as *sir*.'

'Of course.' She gave a tight smile. 'I'm just trying to get a clearer picture, sir.'

'Well, currently I seem to be being portrayed as some sort of prodigal son returning—though without the celebration.'

'By whom?'

He stared ahead.

'The palace? The King?' she probed.

He didn't respond directly. 'I make no apologies—however, they continually do. On my behalf. The press also drags stuff up, hoping if they push…' He gave a tight shrug. 'It is not the best way to go into a marriage.'

Normally her clients were pleading with her to fix their problems, but not him.

'Well, if you're to spare the embarrassed blushes of your future bride it would help if things were toned down. Your lovers seem to adore you,' Beatrice said. 'There's no specific scandal, as such. Just… You spread your affections generously, sir.'

'There hasn't been a lot of affection,' he admitted. 'Not this past year. But my—' He halted; it was clear Prince Julius did not discuss his private life with anyone. Even the woman who might be hired to shine it up. 'I've agreed to lie low for a couple of months prior to signing the Document of Intent.'

'Well, that's a start. But the palace, in my opinion, has to stop apologising and issuing statements. If I got the job, everything would have to go through me…'

It wasn't out of forgetfulness that she failed to add *sir*—more that a family of black swans were passing. They stood out against all the other birds in and around the lake which were white. The proud parents had six grey signets behind them, with one more peeking out beneath the mother's wings. They were so cute that if she hadn't been at an interview Beatrice might have rummaged in her bag for a cereal bar to feed them.

The Prince looked at the source of her distraction. 'The two black swans were introduced when Prince Claude passed away.'

'That cygnet is too big to still be on its mother's back...' Beatrice couldn't help but smile as the cygnet turned its head as they sailed past. 'Cute, though.'

'You like birds?' asked Prince Julius, and resumed walking.

'I do,' Beatrice admitted.

'Actually, I have a question.'

'Of course.'

'Does it bother you?' he asked. 'Saying something one day, then being proved a liar the next.'

Beatrice paused, unsure if he was probing her about her latest client, who had rather scandalously been caught cheating *again*, but his question had been casual and she could only hear the note of curiosity to his tone. Still, for the sake of confidentiality she kept her answer a mixture of vague and truthful. 'It doesn't bother me.'

'No?'

'They're not my lies, sir.'

'True.'

'As well as that, I don't...' She was about to give him the spiel she often gave to clients, but refrained. Probably, Beatrice told herself, because he was royal.

'Please...' he invited.

It was an odd moment. The low glare of the morning sun over the white lake gave the appearance of an icy winter, and yet the peacocks were calling as he had said they would. Screeching unseen.

'Go on,' he said, prompting her with her own words. 'As well as that…?'

Very well, then. Beatrice stopped walking and so did he. She stared up at him. 'On a professional level I'm involved, and I do my best, but on a personal level…'

His eyes narrowed more in anticipation than in question, waiting for her to elaborate.

'I don't take things personally.'

He frowned.

'I'm objective. I'm not…' She took a breath and told him what she told all her clients. 'I don't care what you get up to.'

It sounded harsh, yet it was the reason Beatrice was so good at her job. And the reason for her utter detachment? Well, that was not for potential employers to know. It was not for anyone to know.

Beatrice was close to no one.

'Well,' Prince Julius said, 'that makes a refreshing change.'

To her surprise, she was offered the role.

So Beatrice left London to take on the three-month position in Bellanisiá and signed a lease on a furnished second floor flat there, with a small balcony that looked over the marina.

In her first month there she started to take her evening meal on the balcony, looking out at the expensive yachts and sailing boats, as well as the fishing boats. Cannons were often fired, as if at random, which made her smile. In her second month Beatrice bought a bird feeder, and found herself taking breakfast out there too.

She was growing fond of the place.

Working at the palace was incredible—and not only that, Beatrice found she actually enjoyed taking the shuttle bus to and from work. On her way she always sat to the left, because the views were incredible there, and on her return to the right.

The locals didn't seem to care which side they sat on—they were, of course, more used to the views—and they carried on chatting, or reading, or dozing as the shuttle bus inched its way through the town, picking up palace staff.

There was an all-encompassing mix of designer shops and bazaars and famous fashion houses, as well as florists and bookstores and a gorgeous central square, with government buildings, monuments and houses of worship.

The job was interesting in itself, for there was a lot of pressure from within for the Prince to make haste and marry. A lot of Beatrice's time was spent going head-to-head with his aides, and even with his own team—who were, to her mind, too keen to please the King.

The simple brief to tidy up his image in preparation for marriage, was not so easily executed.

Now, with three weeks to go on her contract, the slurs in the press kept coming, and Prince Julius appeared no closer to signing the Document of Intent, than he had at the commencement of her work.

And Beatrice had found herself dealing with a very unfamiliar issue.

She liked her boss.

Or rather, she had her first ever crush.

And very inconveniently it was on HRH Prince Julius of Bellanisiá!

There had been signs, for those bats had remained in her chest, and sometimes when she met his eyes it felt as if those peacocks were screeching unseen, but she'd simply ignored her unsettled feelings. But taking the shuttle bus to work one morning, as they'd approached the square, she had found her eyes drawn to the stunning central church, with its glorious dome and endless steps.

It was where the royal wedding would take place…

Where Prince Julius would marry.

Her lips had pressed together and a surge of hurt, or perhaps covetousness, had risen in her chest as it had dawned on her that the bats residing there were actually wings of forbidden desire.

Beatrice had hurriedly looked away from the church, but the feeling had not abated.

Instead it had remained.

More accurately, it had grown.

It was so unexpected.

So unfamiliar that she would have done anything to speak with a friend.

It was so disquieting that on her birthday she returned to the place where she'd been born—hoping for what, Beatrice didn't quite know.

Trebordi hadn't changed much in a decade.

Standing on the headland, she held on to her straw hat to stop it from flying away. Until that moment, Beatrice had thought she'd changed. She had changed her surname, her identity, built a career, conversed mainly in English... yet deep down, Beatrice knew she hadn't changed at all.

Here she stood, on her twenty-ninth birthday, staring at the convent in which she'd been raised and she was still as scared and as lonely as the little girl who had grown up there.

More so, even.

She'd had Alicia then.

And now she was more desperate than ever to find her.

Beatrice yearned for advice from her friend. But she didn't know where to start looking, or the reception she might receive even if she found Alicia.

After all, it had been Beatrice who had changed her name from Festa to Taylor. It was she who had broken off all hope of making contact. And she was still bitterly ashamed of the reason she had done so.

Beatrice stood watching the nuns starting to file out of the convent, heading towards the village for Saturday night gelati.

They had a better social life than she!

She stiffened as two particular nuns walked out through the convent gates. Sister Josephine had aged, and walked a little more slowly now, but it was Sister Catherine at her side who caught Beatrice's attention.

She watched as they passed the baby door, where she'd been left, naked and unwrapped, with the umbilical cord still attached.

They were so deep in conversation that they passed it without so much as a glance. Certainly Sister Catherine didn't notice the slight woman who was watching them, almost willing her to linger, to acknowledge the box, to cast a glance around and see if her daughter was here on her birthday.

Nothing.

'What the hell are you even doing here, Beatrice?' she asked herself, and headed straight back to the rental car that had brought her there.

Beatrice would not be heading into the village.

She was done.

And on the flight back to Bellanisiá Beatrice made a private vow that next year, for her thirtieth, she would go somewhere wonderful. She would make friends and drink Birthday Girl Martinis, which she'd heard about but never tried. She would kiss someone and make love, even if the thought terrified her. She would do anything not to be as cold and as unfeeling as the woman who had birthed her.

Beatrice could feel the snap of her own thawing, and it hurt, but she was determined to do it.

She'd hire a gigolo if she had to.

It was when she arrived back at her little flat on the marina that she broke down.

Oh, she hadn't gone to Trebordi hoping for words of wisdom from her mother—that was a joke—but she ached for a friend, a true friend, to give her some gentle advice.

And yet she had fled.

She stared at the one photo she had from her childhood, desperate for Alicia, who'd always known that behind the façade she was terrified.

In truth, she needed someone to tell her it was just a crush. That the way she felt now, at twenty-nine, was just her catching up on the teenage years she'd missed out on.

More than that, though, she wanted common sense.

But, given she'd stalled at the first hurdle in her search for Alicia, Beatrice had to settle for her own advice.

So what if she liked the Prince a little more than she should?

It would never go anywhere.

He was unattainable.

Impossible.

Safe.

CHAPTER TWO

'*SIGNORINA...*' THE DRIVER greeted Beatrice as she boarded the shuttle bus with her cup of coffee.

As she made her way down the aisle, a woman Beatrice recognised from Catering commented in Italian that she was rarely late.

'*Meglio tardi che mai*—better late than never,' Beatrice responded, hoping she hadn't noticed her red eyes as she took her regular seat, second from the back and to the left.

It had become a habit.

'Beatrice?'

She glanced up, and the woman who had commented on her being late tapped her security lanyard. Beatrice nodded her thanks, because in her haste she'd forgotten to put her own on.

Then the guards boarded the bus for an ID check, and that delayed things more.

By the time she disembarked, though still easily on time, she felt as if she were running late, and she walked briskly through the rose garden and past the lake, then took the steps down to the basement offices.

'There are reports surfacing about a party aboard Prince Julius's yacht.'

Once—just once—Beatrice would have liked to make it to her office before being hauled into whatever scandal the Prince had created. This particular morning, though, she would have also liked to top up her concealer and hide her swollen eyes before facing the world.

She should never have made the short journey to Trebordi, Beatrice knew. Now she felt unsettled, as well as perturbed, and thanks to the evidence her tears had left on her features she felt exposed.

'Thanks, Jordan,' she called to the Prince's overly involved, constantly overwrought PA. 'I'll take a look.'

'Beatrice, wait.' Jordan came out of her downstairs office to further enlighten her. 'Prince Julius is—'

'Oh, please!' Beatrice called over her shoulder, forcing herself to become the aloof, say-it-as-it-is woman she'd been hired to be. 'He's gorgeous, single, and happens to have a sex-life…'

Her voice trailed off as she stepped into her own office and it dawned on her that Jordan had been trying to warn her that she had company.

Royal company.

'Good morning, Beatrice.'

Damn.

There, leaning against the wall, wearing jodhpurs and boots and a very serious expression, was Prince Julius himself. Utterly calm, with his shoulders resting on the wall. But his pose was one of observation rather than relaxation: his arms were folded and his long booted legs lightly crossed.

His glossy ebony hair was messy, his jaw unshaven, although she knew that soon the slight disorder would be righted and he would be polished, groomed and shaved. But for now she dealt with well over six feet of testosterone in jodhpurs, boots and a shirt that suggested he'd exerted both himself and his horse to the full this morning.

Oh, it hadn't been nerves she'd dealt with on first meeting him—not even butterflies, for there was nothing floaty or fluttery about this. Those bats were flapping their wings in her chest again, and she willed them back to their cave. To please hang there quietly and let her get on with her work.

'Your Highness.' Beatrice gave a tight smile.

He didn't return it.

She refused to blush over her comments, or even apologise. After all, it was nothing that Beatrice hadn't already said, either to him or during endless strategy meetings with both his and the King's aides.

'Sir...' Jordan came rushing in as Beatrice put down her work bag and placed her coffee on the desk. 'I can only apologise if we were speaking out of turn...'

'It's fine,' Julius responded. 'Carry on with what you were doing, Jordan.'

As Jordan backed out, Beatrice removed her jacket and placed it over the back of her chair, then faced him. 'To what do I owe the pleasure, sir?'

'I thought we'd addressed the matter of titles,' Julius reminded her. 'We're in your office now.'

God, why had she insisted on dropping titles? He'd agreed that when they were in her office or out walking, as they sometimes were when discussing the more sensitive subjects, she could call him by his name.

Oh, how she ached for strict protocol now. To call him *sir*, to be in his upstairs office, to be groomed and prepared rather than have him land here just after 8:30 a.m.

She felt unprepared—and not just because of her puffy eyes. There was something else. For the first time in her life it *mattered* to Beatrice that she stood there in trainers instead of smart black ballet flats and had her hair scraped back—not that she would be correcting any of those issues with Julius there.

Beatrice closed the door and opened up the blinds, then took a seat.

He did not.

Julius remained leaning against the wall, but not slouching; she doubted a man as elegant as he even knew how to slouch. He just leaned his broad shoulders upon it and watched her. Clearly he was less than impressed by her words on arrival. She could feel the tension in the air.

Fire me, then, Beatrice thought. It would probably be easier.

She chose to reach for her coffee, but after taking a sip pulled a face. 'I knew it.'

He sighed his impatience. 'I don't have time to wait for you to get another.'

'No. It's not that. It's this new cup. It's supposed to keep it warm for up to two hours…' Her voice trailed off as he frowned. What would he know about insulated cups and the shuttle bus for palace staff?

Or it was possible he was frowning because he'd just noticed her swollen eyes.

She reached for a tissue to save herself. 'Excuse me,' she said. 'Allergies.'

'Allergies to what?'

'Personal questions!'

She flashed him a tight smile and then reached into her bag and took out her notebook and pen, as well as her work phone, which she turned on.

'Ooh,' she said, as numerous alerts pinged in. 'You have been busy over the weekend.'

Still he leant against the wall. 'You don't check it at all, do you?'

'What do you mean? I have it on all the time,' Beatrice said, scrolling through the messages, and then added, 'during work hours.'

Her strict adherence to her own rules were, in this client's case, more for her sanity's sake. Constant updates on Julius and his bedroom shenanigans she so did not need! Although, Beatrice conceded, there hadn't been anything too scandalous of late—indeed, he'd kept to his side of the deal and lain low.

His past was another matter, though… Without any new

scandals to splash across their front pages, the press were digging up old ones—and there were plenty!

Nessue Respetto!

No respect. That was the subject matter of one of the many articles starting to download.

'"*Re Dezante!*"' Beatrice blinked. 'Dancing King?'

'I'm delighted my brother died, apparently. I am dancing on his grave at the chance to be King.'

She took up the file on her desk, bracing herself for whatever delights awaited. It had never bothered her till now. She'd looked at intimate shots of other clients rather as if she was searching for her horoscope at the back of a magazine, but she knew her lips pursed when the pictures were of him.

There had never been anything sleazy—Julius, even at his most depraved, had always ensured the drapes and luxury suite doors remained closed while he had his wicked way. It was just the odd image that particularly irked—that had Beatrice lying awake at night, frowning into the dark, pondering new mysteries.

Who would kiss someone's feet on a beach? All that sand. Yuck. Why would anyone want to kiss a foot?

Beatrice gave herself a mental shake and reminded herself to keep her face relaxed. She considered adding antacid to her coffee cup, to save her from the burn that hit her sometimes.

'Should I prepare to be shocked?'

'You seem completely unshockable, Beatrice.'

She tried to be, but not this morning…

Re dezante, indeed. Or *principe dezante*—because he wasn't yet King, but this prince could certainly dance.

Gosh, she had never so much as considered that he might.

In the photo he wore black trousers and a black shirt and black boots, and the woman he held was being dipped so low that she was almost lying on the deck of his yacht. Her hair was splayed out on the deck in a puddle of brunette curls and waves.

Beatrice had been anticipating something dreadful, appalling, yet the sight of him fully dressed and just *living*, while she'd spent her birthday weeping, seemed to ram home the fact that it really was time for change.

She blew her nose, to give herself time to school her reaction. She was so jealous of her, the beauty in his arms, and not even for the fact that it was Julius holding her…

It was her abandon. Her trust in the hands that held her.

'You didn't drop her, did you?' Beatrice's voice was croaky as she attempted a joke. 'Are there going to be air ambulances and medics…?'

'What?'

He sounded bemused by her question, and Beatrice reminded herself that quips were not her forte, so she got back to the remaining photos.

No, he hadn't dropped her. There were others dancing too, but the camera had been trained on him, and Beatrice's attention moved to the next shot. The woman was back on her feet, their bodies were locked together, her thigh lifted onto his, and she saw how his hand held her hip. She flicked to another picture, and another, and another…

She wanted to shift in her seat, because she felt discomfort in a place there should not be any. She wanted to rearrange her bra because it felt a size too small all of a sudden.

How could a picture of a fully dressed man do this to her?

Beatrice didn't know.

Yet it did.

He did.

At night, she slept with her hands above her embroidered quilt, as the nuns had insisted. She lay like a lady, desperately wanting to be a woman, fighting the feelings he evoked night after night.

Now, though, those feelings had not only crept into her evenings and mornings. They were following her into work—rather like the white peacock who startled her some mornings and provided an unwelcome escort, trailing his feathers behind him…

Make it stop, Beatrice thought.

The Prince's scent was not that of the stables, but citrussy and fresh, and she felt as if there must be a neon sign over her head with an arrow pointing to the effect he was having on her. She dared not look up, so she stared at the images instead.

'Did they get any photos after…?'

She felt a little shaken, which was exactly what she had been hired *not* to be.

'After…?' he checked.

After the extended foreplay, she wanted to say, but thankfully remained silent.

'God, no. It was nothing like that. We were just dancing,' Julius said, and Beatrice wished she could question his choice of the word *just*, because the images were so sensual and graceful and compelling. 'Admittedly,' he added, 'I don't know how we got onto Latin American, but clearly we did…'

'Clearly.'

Now she had another thing to add to her thirtieth birthday. Even if she didn't go through with it, Beatrice wanted to add dancing to that phantom list for that phantom night.

She tried to haul her mind from Cuban-heeled boots and all the other things she'd never done, yet which somehow Julius had made her consider.

And she didn't quite know why.

Arrogant, haughty, cutting—that didn't even *begin* to describe him.

He was so *unrepentant*.

So contrary.

For he could be so rigid and formal, yet conversely so at ease with himself.

And so damned sexy too—which was the very reason she was employed, after all.

And, although he was supposed to be lying low, they could hardly ban dancing—although Beatrice did have one genuine concern.

'These are seriously good photos.'

'Thank you.'

'I mean they weren't taken on a phone. These are professional shots. How did anyone get close enough to take them? Where was your security?'

'There were boats all around. My mistake.'

'Well, I don't see any issue. It just looks like you enjoyed your weekend.'

'The issue is…' There was a pause, a rare beat of reticence, before he spoke on. 'They weren't taken at the weekend.'

For the first time since meeting him she sensed his discomfort. 'So?'

'These were taken on the first anniversary…' He paused. 'Of Claude's death.'

She thought back to the wooden, formal man she had met at her final interview, then looked at the photos, and struggled to reconcile the two men. Perhaps she was starting to know him better…

Know him?

A tiny bit. Enough to understand that these headlines hurt him, even if he would never admit it.

'Okay.' Beatrice looked again at the pictures, with this new information on board. 'So, these were taken on the anniversary of Prince Claude's death.'

'Yes, I attended a formal service that morning—though apparently I was faking my solemn mood then.'

'So, you're only allowed one emotion a day?'

Beatrice raised her eyebrows and he gave a silent, mirthless half-laugh, as if relieved that she got it.

Lately, she did.

Beatrice herself had only used to feel two things: cold and lonely.

Now she felt as if she were juggling a hundred or more emotions and feelings, while trying to find her old favourite: cold. That way she would be able to see objectively what they were dealing with.

She turned to her computer and tried to access the files of photos taken on the anniversary of Claude's death.

Limited Access.

'What's wrong?' he asked as she gritted her teeth.

'I have to go upstairs to access the archives.'

Her security clearance at the palace allowed for little more than a schoolgirl doing a project; it was easier to go online along with the general population. She found a couple of shots of that day: the Queen looked her usual poised and elegant self, though the black jewels in her diadem sparkled far more vividly than her tired eyes; Princess Jasmine, Julius's older sister in a rare public appearance, was hidden behind a black veil and holding her daughter Arabella's hand, and the King…he was austere and sombre. But then, from what she had gleaned he'd always been austere and sombre, as well as scathing, where his youngest was concerned.

As for Julius… He stood on ceremony, but behind those dark eyes, who knew what went on?

Sometimes, lately, Beatrice felt as if she did, just a little.

Most of the time, lately, she wanted to.

Wanted to know.

Yet now, seeing a photo of him taken just a few weeks ago caused her to frown, and she looked over to where he stood. He'd lost weight in the weeks she'd been here. Not a lot. It was almost indiscernible. But he certainly had.

There was also a new tension to his features that hadn't been present even on that sombre anniversary.

She looked back to the photo and found herself nibbling on her bottom lip as she thought.

Was the soon-to-be groom having pre-selection jitters? Certainly he hadn't signed the Document of Intent that would kick things off, and even she could feel the pressure building from the palace for him to do so. Or was he just antsy from being forced to leave his normal life behind?

Julius broke into her thoughts. 'It was careless,' he admitted. 'I was just…'

'Just?'

'I suppose the term would be *letting off steam*.'

'I get it,' Beatrice said.

Last night, as she'd wept, it had felt as if a valve had been released—just a touch. She'd quickly turned it back to closed. Only it felt as if she hadn't quite managed to secure that valve, because the steam seemed to be hissing out despite her attempts to shut it off completely.

'I don't dance, of course, but—'

'You don't dance?'

'No.'

'At all?' He sounded surprised.

'No, but what I meant…' What *did* she mean? She didn't dance. 'I'm saying that I understand that we all have our outlets.'

Beatrice's outlets were studying languages and embroidery…

Julius peeled his broad shoulders from the wall and came and took a seat on the other side of her desk. He looked at her as he stretched out his legs.

'Why don't you dance, Beatrice?' He remained curious.

Can we get back to the photos, please? she wanted to beg, but Julius seemed intrigued by her little slip.

'I was never taught,' she snapped. 'Were you?'

'Absolutely.' He nodded. 'We had lessons in the ballroom…'

'The three of you?' Beatrice couldn't stop herself asking.

He nodded. 'We had costumes and everything.'

'Did you hate it?'

'Not at all.'

She'd expected him to grimace, to pull a face, but he surprised her. Many times in their short history Julius had surprised her, and he did so now.

'I loved it.' He leant back in his chair and clasped his hands behind his head, resting there as he thought for a moment. 'Claude and Jasmine loathed it…' He smiled to himself at the memory. 'My father was worried I liked it a little too much!'

Beatrice resisted the smile that ached to spread across her face and reminded herself that she was cold and impassive as Julius spoke on.

'As well as ballroom, there was *syrtaki*, tarantella… Oh, and there was *horon*.'

'Horon?'

'It's a folk dance, from the Black Sea. My mother's side…' He raised his arms and dropped his wrists. 'Like Irish dancing with your hands in the air. Great fun.'

Her lips started to spread, and then of their own accord they parted, and she didn't know how to take it off, this smile that remained on her face.

This was the part of Julius she didn't understand, because at times it felt as if he *chose* to make her smile. Sometimes it honestly felt as if he'd made a decision to remain in a conversation with her in order to challenge himself to put a smile upon her face. Then, when he succeeded, when there was no doubt the smile on her face was a genuine one, he returned it.

It was as simple and as un-noteworthy as that. Yet there was something else she couldn't properly explain…something indefinable.

It was not just that he *chose* to make her smile but that on a day like today, when she felt so out of step with the rest of the world, when she felt she must surely be the most unlovable person ever, somehow he *found* her smile.

And returned it.

When it had faded, he asked, 'Is everything okay, Beatrice?'

'Of course.' She nodded, removing her eyes from his and trying to remember where they'd left the conversation. 'What about Latin American?'

'Sorry?'

She gestured with her palm towards the spread of disturbingly erotic photos gracing her desk this morning.

'Ah, I believe I had one-on-one tuition for that. That really is filed under "Limited Access".'

'You're dreadful,'

'I try to be.'

She felt his eyes upon her and looked up from the images of him dancing to the darkest eyes, which had narrowed just a little. Beatrice reminded herself that she was at work—that he could have been dancing naked on the palace balcony and her job would be to fix the situation.

Back to the issue.

'Okay… Prince Claude's anniversary coincided with the start of the Hellenic celebrations?' She cross-checked the dates.

'It did.'

'So that's why there were so many boats all around?'

'Yes.'

'Have you discussed this with Security?'

'I'll deal with that side of things. All I want from you is to know how best to respond.'

'Of course. Is it a tradition that you go each year?'

'No,' Julius dismissed, then added, 'Claude did, though. It was his favourite thing.'

'That's good. Could it be that you wanted to honour his *joie de vivre* by going in his place?'

'Don't go there,' Julius warned. 'I won't use him as an excuse. And anyway...' he mused with a mixture of pensiveness and affection. 'There was not a lot of *joie de vivre* to Claude. He really was rather staid.'

She glanced up at the shift in his tone. He'd confided in her!

Beatrice wanted to stand on her chair and point! To call her missing friend to help her name this feeling.

Beatrice would have liked to understand this moment, because these rare insights felt like something so precious, so rare—like nothing she could find out from her colleagues or hours on the computer...

'Actually...' Julius too seemed to realise this veer from the norm, for he added, 'Don't go repeating that!'

'That' felt as if it was just for them. But she blinked herself out of any delusions by looking again at his beautiful dance partner and reminding herself that he would be married soon. And anyway, she had no idea about men.

None.

Just the dreadful ones whose chaotic private lives needed her ice-cold touch.

And so she gave it now.

'I suggest "no comment" to the photos.'

In her time here at the palace she had held fast to her strategy, and there had been no comments nor apologies made following any tabloid pictures of the Prince.

'Actually,' Julius said. 'In this instance I'm not sure.'

This was a rare moment of indecision on his part. So

rare that Beatrice had actually never seen the doubt that now flashed over his features.

'*Does* it merit an apology?' he asked.

'No.'

'A response?'

'No.'

'Because if it does…'

'Julius, no.' Beatrice was adamant, almost cross in his defence. 'You've lost your *brother*. If dancing helps, then please…' she raised her hands '…sign me up for the classes…'

'Thanks.' He gave a half-laugh at her honest and unusually passionate response. 'I always forget you're Sicilian.'

'Oh, believe me, I try to.'

Beatrice wanted to take that back. It wasn't Sicily she wanted to forget—it was one woman. She knew he'd seen that little flash of venom, but thankfully he politely ignored it as she dived into her work bag.

'I should have some…'

'What?'

'Antihistamines…' Beatrice knew there were none there, and nor did she need them; she just wanted to hide for a tiny second. 'I must have left them at home.'

'That's not like you.'

No. 'Well, leave everything with me.' She gave him a tight smile and really hoped he'd take the cue and leave. She had never felt less together at work than she did this morning.

But he did not get up and he did not leave. 'They're going to keep serving this stuff up,' he said.

'The press?'

'Whoever… The longer I leave it, the more this stuff will appear to undermine me.'

'Undermine?' Beatrice frowned. 'No…'

Oh, no! Undermine? Under *him*, more likely! That would

probably be the thought flickering across minds this morning. But, no, this photo wouldn't damage Julius, if that was their game.

'I don't think you have to worry about that.'

'Well, you can expect a lot of this kind of stuff to keep appearing until I sign the Document of Intent.' He inhaled and closed his eyes. 'Or the Point of No Return…' He looked over and gave a half-smile. 'Joking.'

But he had not been joking. His mask, too, had briefly slipped. It was the first time he had spoken of his destined future with anything other than crisp certainty.

'What happens then?' Beatrice asked, as if she were mildly curious instead of completely relieved that she hadn't found out and wouldn't, given that her contract was soon to expire. 'It was all supposed to be happening before I left, but…'

'I sign the Document of Intent, it goes to counsel, and after about a month or so I find out who they've chosen.'

'Do you have any idea who?'

'None.'

'None?'

'It could be someone from a country we're aligned with, or one with whom we need to broker better relations. My parents' union was heralded as one of the country's greatest, even if no one here had heard of her country prior to the marriage. My mother is the most esteemed queen consort in centuries… So who knows?' Julius shrugged. 'And then, once the decision is made, the marriage will take place within a month, assuming all parties are agreed.'

'Do you get to meet each other beforehand?'

'Of course. The families will dine together a week before…' He put up a hand to show it wasn't a certain thing. 'Depending on her country and their traditions, of course.'

'You'll speak the same language?'

'Not necessarily. My parents didn't. Hey, there might be

a position for a translator when your contract...' He halted, just for a fraction of a second, but then shrugged. 'Well, given your skill set...'

Sometimes she thought she was imagining things, but that little pause had felt as if it contained a wealth of information. That he might find the idea of Beatrice joining him on his honeymoon as an appalling thought as she did.

It was by far more sensible not to dwell on it.

'My mother spoke only Romeyka when they were first married, and my father's never quite mastered it. Nor me. And I'm supposed to be addressing her family at the end of the week, when I visit.'

'Well, if you need to practise I'm good with languages. Not that one, but I know some of the sounds.'

'I'll be fine.' He rejected her offer to assist and got back to the question. 'After the wedding, there'll be a month on Regalsi, so we can get to know each other...' He must have seen her frown. 'It's one of the tiny islands—just for royals.'

'What's it like?'

'I've never been. It's for honeymoons and hetaerae and such...'

'Mistresses?'

'We don't use that word here,' he warned with a shush and a smile. 'Regalsi's a place for serious relationships—and *that's* why I've never been.'

It bemused her a little. Julius, from all she could see, had had longer term relationships, but though he spoke of his exes politely, even fondly, there had never been one considered serious enough to join him at formal functions, nor, it would seem, to take to Regalsi.

Julius interrupted her thoughts. 'I have to say, with the way my schedule is, an entire month off is starting to sound tempting.'

'That's not very romantic.'

'It isn't about romance. It's about a partnership.'

He turned his head at the sound of a voice outside her door.

'Knock-knock?'

'It would seem you have a visitor,' he said to Beatrice, and called for Jordan to come in.

And this morning, when she wanted only to hide, Jordan came in carrying a cake lit with candles and the rest of the team all shuffled in behind her.

'Cake?' Beatrice was startled.

'Palace cake,' Jordan corrected.

So that was why he'd hung around making small talk. And that was why he hadn't wanted her to go and get more coffee. He was being polite.

She smiled as Jordan placed on her desk the prettiest cake she'd ever seen. It had a meadow of flowers delicately piped on it, as well as…

'My name!'

'Of course.'

There was no 'of course' about it.

A birthday cake with candles and her name on it was a first for Beatrice, and very overwhelming.

Growing up in the convent, there had been a simple square honey cake for supper on the children's birthdays, and that had felt like such a treat.

She watched as Tobias, Julius's private aide, placed two cards on her desk and listened as Jordan explained.

'It was made especially by the head pastry chef. Technically, we only do it for permanent staff, but…'

'Well, that will never happen.' Beatrice offered her usual smart response just as she saw Jordan notice her red eyes.

'Gosh, you really celebrated at the weekend, didn't you?'

Was she so removed from everyone that Jordan assumed she must have a crashing hangover from partying because it had never occurred to her that she might have been crying?

'Come on, Beatrice,' Julius snapped. 'Are you going to cut it?'

'Of course.'

She took up the knife and aimed it at the cake.

'Candles first,' Julius warned.

'Oh, yes…' She puffed them out.

God, she was useless—so useless that after a couple of dreadful attempts at slicing Tobias rescued the knife from her unskilled hand and took over.

'How was your weekend?' asked Despina, who was head of social media for the Prince. 'You went home, didn't you?'

'It was fine,' Beatrice answered.

'Did you catch up with your family?'

'I guess…'

'So,' Tobias asked, 'how was Sicily?'

'Windy,' she responded, and searched for anything she could think of to deflect the questioning. 'How's Esther? You've got the ultrasound today, yes?'

Beatrice knew what she was doing. Tobias's wife was pregnant, and there was nothing better to halt an unwanted question than to invite someone else to speak—especially someone looking forward to being a father.

'Yes! We should find out what we're having…'

Tobias chatted happily on, and out of the corner of her eye she watched as Julius went to reach for the last piece of cake, then reluctantly checked himself.

'Does anyone want this?' he offered, clearly still hungry from riding and ready to take the last of the cake and get on with his busy day.

'I do,' Beatrice said.

He halted.

So did Beatrice. Because suddenly there was something wrong with her voice. Something that made him look over.

No one else seemed aware of it, but it caused him to screw up his very straight nose just a fraction at being thwarted and rather petulantly take back his hand.

'Of course.' He nodded and shot her a look that somehow caused her stomach, as well as an area lower, to clench. 'After all, it's your cake.'

'It is,' Beatrice said, and somehow held his gaze.

'Enjoy!' Jordan half laughed and half scolded as he went sulking out of her office, but Beatrice just stood there, wondering what had happened. For a second there it had felt as if there was no one else in her tiny office.

Just one last slice of cake and him.

Oh, God, had he thought she was flirting?

Had she been?

Had he?

Had they?

Beatrice didn't know.

She had never tuned in to such things—let alone had to tune out. Before arriving here she'd thought that flirting was all batting eyelashes and bumping into each other at every turn, but it would appear that the opposite might be the case. They usually seemed to sit or stand as far from each other as possible. Something had happened there, though…

As the rest of the staff wandered out Jordan closed the door behind them and her smile disappeared. 'Beatrice, you have to be more careful.'

'With…?'

Had she noticed? Was she going to be told off for flirting with the Prince?

No, it was her words on arrival that she was being chastised for, as Beatrice quickly found out.

'How was I supposed to know he was here?' she asked.

'I was trying to warn you. This is *his* residence…' Jordan closed her eyes in exasperation for a brief moment. 'I know he doesn't usually come down here, but you have to be more guarded with your words.'

'You're not,' Beatrice retorted.

As his PA, Jordan was Beatrice's main source of information and, Beatrice thought, rather indiscreet.

'The door is closed, Beatrice,' Jordan pointed out, and then asked for the Prince's take on the photos. 'What's he going to do about them?'

'Nothing,' Beatrice said, and opened up a window. 'God, the place is going to reek of the stables…'

'I don't smell it,' Jordan said. 'Mind you, Stavros used to work there…'

Beatrice knew only too well that Stavros, Jordan's husband, had worked at the stables. Jordan talked about her marriage so fondly and freely that Beatrice felt as if she had already met him!

Still, it wasn't the smell of the stables that she wanted *out*; it was the scent of Julius that she wanted to gulp *in*. It felt as if there were a fire behind her, truly. But there were no alarms, no ladders against the wall, no passers-by to wave to for help. Nothing to show or recount.

Even Jordan was oblivious. 'I think, in this case, he ought to at least consider an apology.'

The fact that Julius had wondered the same thing would remain with Beatrice. 'Well, I don't think it's necessary— and I'll tell the King's aides the same.'

'This won't go away,' Jordan warned. 'Look, I'm only saying this to you,' she said, which Beatrice didn't believe for a second, 'but I've heard a whisper that they're discussing sending him to rehab.'

'Why on earth would they even suggest such a thing? He's the healthiest person I've ever met.'

'It's a battle of wills,' Jordan said. 'Julius won't go, of course, but he might agree to sign the Document of Intent if they threaten him with it. Honestly, you'd think he'd have more sense than to go out partying on the anniversary of his brother's death. It's not a good look.'

'He was probably just trying to get through the day.'

'And the night.' Jordan rolled her eyes. 'In his usual fashion, no doubt.'

'Well, at least he's lying low now. This is all old stuff.'

'Old?' Jordan checked. 'Claude's anniversary was in June—just a couple of months ago.'

'I meant it was before my time.'

The thought afforded her too much relief. One day—today, tomorrow, who knew when?—she would be sitting here looking at images of Julius and his current lover and discussing more recent scandals.

Better that, though, than looking at an image of his chosen bride.

'I should go,' Jordan said. 'Enjoy!' She gestured to Beatrice's slice of cake and her cards. 'I'd better get on.'

'Jordan?' Beatrice halted her. 'I don't like this gossip about rehab.'

'Of course not. That's why I told you about it.'

Oh.

With Jordan headed to the more sumptuous floors above, and everyone gone from her office, Beatrice stared at the near empty cake plate and the candles that had been lit for her. She was still a bit stunned, because she just didn't do birthdays. Avoided them.

She opened her cards—the pink one first. It was signed by all the Prince's team.

Hope you had a brilliant time celebrating!

That was the general theme. And they hoped that her trip to Sicily had been amazing. That was the other.

The Big Thirty next year, Jordan had reminded her, and added a smiley face.

And then Beatrice took up a letter opener and carefully sliced open the big creamy envelope with her name written on it in Jordan's handwriting, and pulled out the most exquisite card.

It was a beautiful black and white shot of the Prince's

residence with the White Lake in the foreground. It deserved to be in a frame on the wall in its own right.

She opened the card and saw the flash of his scrawl above his printed name and title, and then she glanced at the piece of cake.

Why did it have to be like this?

It was a simple crush.

On HRH.

It was purely physical, but her body—which knew nothing about men—seemed to be coming to life around him. She was flustered at work…perhaps for the first time.

Thank goodness she could now gather herself in private.

But suddenly he was back!

'Beatrice? Actually, those pictures seem to be turning into an issue. I'm going to have to meet with my father's aides later.'

'I can do that,' Beatrice said. After all, she did it most days. 'You've got enough to be doing.'

'No, I'll meet you up there when they call for me.'

She nodded.

He was turning to go and then he glanced to the last remaining piece of cake and then to her. For the first time ever both his gaze and a slow smile combined and homed in on her.

It was like being invited to witness a private viewing of the sun.

No wonder her services were required.

No wonder he had caused so much trouble.

'Just take it,' Beatrice snapped.

Julius didn't wait to be asked twice. He walked over and picked up the piece of cake and took a bite.

Her insides felt as if they were melting faster than the cream he licked from those decadent lips before walking out with his prize.

Oh, why did it have to be like this?

CHAPTER THREE

'THE PALACE ARE *insisting* on a response,' Jordan told him.

'Well, they can keep on insisting.' Julius shrugged.

They were upstairs in the office with the door closed. Second only to Tobias, he trusted Jordan, for though it was never spoken out loud she knew the real pressure he was under.

'I'm just relaying what I've heard, sir.'

He nodded. 'Beatrice is on it.'

'Hungover to the back teeth,' Jordan retorted. 'I'm sorry about this morning, sir.'

'Drop it,' Julius said, rather than point out to her that she'd been crying.

He'd easily seen that his usually very together liaison aide was unusually reactive today. Her lips were chewed, her nose red, and she'd been nattering on about cups and such when usually she barely said an unnecessary word.

A family drama, perhaps?

Or a relationship break-up, maybe?

He didn't get involved with the personal dramas of his staff. If he did he'd never get a single thing done. Well, he tried not to get involved. God knows, he tried.

The same way he'd tried not to notice her red eyes.

And tried not to be irked that he was something confined to her work bag and taken out on her arrival at the palace on a Monday, like a schoolteacher with his homework.

He'd tried to make inane small talk with her as agreed, while Jordan gathered the rest of the team and brought in the cake, but he had started to slip away from small talk.

That would never do.

He did his best to be present for team birthdays, but

would usually grab one slice of cake and then go. Yet he'd
seen she was struggling, standing there as if not knowing
quite what to do instead of blowing out the candles and slicing. So he'd moved things along. She'd sounded surprised
by the direction in conversation.

It had quickly become evident that cutting cake wasn't
one of Beatrice's talents; in fact her knife skills were so bad
that Tobias had relieved her of cutting duties. But at least Julius had managed to scoop up one of Beatrice's attempts—a
big slice—and then watched as she'd deflected questions.

Beatrice, Julius had found out, revealed nothing about
herself.

Ever.

He made small talk with strangers, was skilled in negotiations, but he'd got nowhere with Beatrice. She was im-
penetrable.

Beatrice had not brightened either the walls of her office
or her desk with personal touches. Whether she worked upstairs in his main offices or down here, everything personal
was returned to that vast bag at the end of the day and no
traces were left.

She didn't wear perfume; in fact, her choice of soap and
shampoo was even a little carbolic in nature. Like…anti-
septic.

Warding off germy men? he mused.

But then this morning he'd found out that she didn't
dance.

And that sometimes she cried.

He read women, adored women—that was the reason
she was here, after all—and a lot of his time was spent de-
flecting advances—hopefully nicely.

Beatrice had made no advances.

And nor would he.

She was staff, so of course it was impossible. Though

that would be remedied in three long weeks—and he would be away for one of those, thank God.

Also, he did not want to add to the poor opinion she clearly had of him, or be like those creeps she had worked for in the past.

Plus, soon his bride would be chosen.

Ah, that!

What had always been a necessary duty now felt like a weight—a weight he would like to discard, at least for a night.

Preferably with the woman hired to clean up his image.

He'd seen how she held herself back from all the team; she even ate lunch at the lake instead of in the staffroom with everyone else.

She'd revealed nothing.

Not a sign, nor a clue.

And then, out of the blue, she'd denied him cake...

'I do.'

It hadn't been the words—nor even the delivery.

And no one else had seemed to hear it quite as he had.

Oh, they had no doubt heard her teasing tone alongside her usual assertiveness, because they had laughed. And yet no one had seemed to catch what was bubbling beneath the surface.

The shell of his ear had felt as if she had just leaned in and whispered a promise.

Those two words had hit him where it should hurt, and yet they had felt at light and as potent as the stroke of an intimate finger—so much so that he had felt himself tighten in response.

He was rarely mistaken. She'd made no further advance, given no other clue, and yet he *almost* knew.

And he would find out.

In three weeks' time Beatrice Taylor would leave the palace.

Perhaps one discreet liaison with his liaison aide before he joined the monogamy club…?

'Sir?' Jordan's nervous swallow alerted him and he looked up. 'Is this latest revelation perhaps…'

'Because I haven't signed the Document of Intent?' He said it for her. 'I would think so.'

The publication of those photos was no accident; the pressure was all from within.

'Sir, do you remember I suggested offering Beatrice a full-time role here?'

'Beatrice isn't going to stop them.' He shook his head. 'No.'

Hell, no.

She was the damned reason he hadn't signed it. He would like to get to back to business—certainly not offer her a permanent role. On the permanent staff? Always there? Always by his side?

Yikes. God, no.

'Julius.' Jordan actually snapped his name. 'If Beatrice was permanent then she'd have clearance, and at least she'd know what you're up against.'

'And what would that change?'

'Please…just listen.'

And because it was Jordan's responsibility to deal with such matters, he had no choice but to listen as she pointed out how much more smoothly things had been going since Beatrice's arrival. That it had been Beatrice who had sat through many, many meetings arguing his case, without him there.

She added, 'Even though I'm a little loath to admit it.'

'Loath?' Julius checked. 'You were the one who pushed for her selection.'

'I did.' Jordan nodded. 'And she's great at her job.'

'But…?'

'I do have my reservations… Take this morning.'

'Yep.'

He got up from his seat and looked down at the lake, listening to Jordan's brusque summing up of his icy, albeit efficient liaison aide.

'And she's not exactly a team player,' Jordan said. 'But that's not your issue.'

It was, though.

Julius felt as if Beatrice *was* on his team.

Beatrice Taylor was exceedingly good at her job.

Why the hell *wouldn't* he keep her on?

He knew why.

She was the coldest, most direct, private and prickly woman he'd ever met—but she could also be suddenly kind.

It hadn't been long after her arrival at the palace that he had found that she fascinated him. He'd found himself leaning against the window, pondering a problem, and had noticed her tipping some crumbs into the lake and one of the gardeners dashing over to scold her.

Julius hadn't really noticed then; it had been but an idle observation. It was the next day that he'd looked down and watched her open a container and wave at the gardener, who'd returned her wave.

He'd found himself smiling.

Not just that day but a little more often since then.

He'd noticed that her eyes were more grey than blue, and framed with blonde lashes.

Julius had chosen to ignore the fact that he'd noticed.

But Julius wanted her to stay—after all, he could really use her skill set.

Practically, he knew he wouldn't be able to tolerate anyone else glimpsing his private life without it feeling invasive, and he knew by objecting he would be denying her the chance of an excellent promotion.

But privately?

There was no room for private.

No room at all.

And, as if to serve as a reminder of exactly what was at stake, when he looked down now it wasn't Beatrice by the lake. It was his sister Jasmine, feeding the birds with Arabella. He adored his niece, but she was so loud and so spoilt he thought she'd possibly put him off having kids for life!

He loved them, though.

And his father knew it.

It was a Sword of Damocles that his father held over Julius's head and with which he ruled his family.

Perhaps it was time to stop thinking primitive thoughts and get on with fulfilling the role he'd been born to—well, not born to, but born *just in case* to…

'Let me think on it,' he said now.

He had enough to deal with today, Julius realised.

The King was currently meeting his aides. Then the aides would discuss the situation, and then they would call him in.

'Sir, I've moved things around. The meeting is at three,' Jordan informed him, and then added, 'It's just with the aides.'

Julius nodded. All too soon it would be with the King.

Julius's dark mood now had nothing to do with his liaison aide.

He called Beatrice and said, 'I want you to come up with a bland response to these latest photos. I'll meet you in the Great Hall at three.' Then he added, 'Don't be early.'

He would not be bullied.

CHAPTER FOUR

HE'D DANCED! Yes, on the anniversary of his brother's death...

It was a minor infringement in the scheme of Julius's rather more decadent deeds. In driving terms, Beatrice would have likened it to the equivalent of a blown headlight, yet it was as if his staff were preparing for an appearance in court for vehicular manslaughter.

'Can I read the response?' Tobias came in half an hour before they were scheduled to meet.

'Sure,' Beatrice said, and handed him the paper.

'This is the press release?'

Beatrice nodded.

'No.' He shook his head. 'It says nothing.'

'That's the whole point, Tobias.'

Poor Tobias should be heading home to his pregnant wife, but it was clear he was conflicted and anxious as he re-read it. 'It needs more work.'

'Fine.' She gave him a tight smile as he scurried off.

Beatrice stared at it for another five minutes, added a comma and then deleted it, then got on with other work until Jordan called down.

'The King has just left so they're almost ready.'

'Sure,' Beatrice said. 'Julius said to meet him there at three.'

'Head over now, and call me if anything happens?'

'Anything?' Beatrice checked as she reached for her jacket.

'If they ask for scribes or...' Jordan sighed. 'Just keep me up to date.'

It was a good ten-minute walk from her office in Julius's

residence to the palace. Beatrice considered using the catering passage, as she had before on occasion, but Julius had been insistent that she not be early.

So she walked through the glass passageway, but immediately regretted it, for as she came into the main palace there was the King—so like Julius—standing there, looking up at a portrait no doubt of his late son.

Damn.

She knew he would not notice her, so she put her head down as she passed and was duly ignored. She descended the grand staircase and arrived in the Great Hall to find Julius not there and Tobias pacing.

He pulled her into an archway and brought her up to speed. 'They've just called for refreshments,' Tobias said. 'We could be here ages. You might get that royal wedding on your résumé sooner than you think.'

'All because he…danced?'

'You've seen the headlines.'

'Are you saying the wedding could be announced today?'

'If he agrees.' Tobias was seriously rattled. 'You know why you were hired. They want him married and producing heirs.'

Yes, she knew, and although it all felt very different now from when she'd first been given the brief, Beatrice was a professional, and when she worked she was always calm.

'Tobias, they can hardly drag him up the aisle kicking and screaming.'

Suddenly Julius was at her elbow. He must have heard her because he said, 'I don't kick.' He pointed a finger. 'And I'd certainly never scream. Watch your words.'

Watch your finger, she wanted to retort, but then he decided to do that without her instruction.

He was suited and clean-shaven and just too beautiful for a Monday afternoon.

'Have you got the response?' he asked.

'I have.' She handed him the very brief statement only because she knew the palace had insisted on one. Otherwise they would put out their own. 'I've kept it bland.'

'I like bland,' he said, and read it out loud. '"Prince Julius enjoyed partaking in the commencement of the Hellenic Festival and celebrating our rich Greek heritage." Perfect,' he said. 'We'll go with that.'

Tobias, it would seem, wanted a little more of an apology in there. 'Perhaps wait till the meeting, sir?' he suggested.

'Aren't you supposed to be off now? An ultrasound or something? I think Esther needs her hand holding more than I do,' Julius said. 'Go.'

Beatrice could see that Tobias was torn. This really wasn't about a night of dancing, she was fast realising. It was a push to get the reluctant Prince to instruct the palace to select a bride.

'We're finding out what we're having today,' Julius said once Tobias had left.

'Sorry?'

'That was a little joke, Beatrice.'

She frowned.

'I meant we'll all know tomorrow if it's a boy or girl. The royal *we*…the office *we*…' He gave in, clearly remembering that Beatrice didn't joke. 'Tobias is worried,' Julius admitted. 'Apparently they're discussing a stint in rehab for me in there.'

'Where did he hear that?'

'It doesn't matter.'

'Well, it does, because I'm hearing it too.'

'From…?'

She shook her head.

'I have an ear in the stables…' he said. Then, 'Why does that make you smile?'

'It's fine. I think we might have the same ear.'

Clearly Jordan had confided in both of them. Beatrice

must have let her initial worry about Jordan's loose lips show on her face, because he added, 'It's okay. Seriously, you don't have to worry.'

Beatrice said nothing.

'You have to know who to trust, Beatrice,' he told her.

'I do,' Beatrice responded. 'And I've never let myself down yet.'

'I love your constant cynicism, Beatrice.'

'You're relying on it,' she told him. 'While I might be "Limited Access", I know there's more going on.'

'Very well. The palace want to let it be known that I haven't been dealing well with Claude's death.'

'No.' Beatrice shook her head. 'Absolutely not.'

'I agree. It's just a threat so that I'll relent.'

'Relent?'

'I've told them I won't marry on the orders of my father. I don't like being told what to do. It might get a bit heated in there,' he warned. 'And by "it" I mean me.'

She had never seen him nervous, no matter what the scandal—and there had been many. He was usually insolent or arrogant. But he seemed different this Monday afternoon.

She looked at his jet-black hair and the dark brown eyes and the sulky mouth as he examined the portraits that lined the Great Hall; he arched his neck, which she had noticed was his habit when he was tense.

'Julius…'

'Not now,' he said.

'Let me speak first in there.'

'No, thank you.'

He went and sat on one of the polished benches and stretched out his long legs, then he nodded his head at her, indicating for her to join him.

'I'm fine standing, thank you, sir.'

'Please sit,' he said.

It would be far easier to stand—especially as her heart

was thumping in her chest—but she perched herself a suitable distance from him. And as she took her place on the bench, she was assailed by a memory.

It was so sharp that she felt almost transported back to happier times—not that they'd felt happy then. She remembered two little girls sitting on a bench, waiting to see what Alicia had done. The memory was so vivid that Beatrice let out a small, almost silent laugh.

'What?' asked Julius.

'It's honestly nothing.'

'Distract me,' he said.

'I was just thinking how I used to sit outside Reverend Mother's room with my…' She faltered, unsure what to say, because she rarely got as far as saying this.

'With your…?'

'Well, we called each other twins, but really we weren't even related.'

'Oh?' He looked over. 'Good friends, then? Or, as my niece would say, *best* friends?'

'Yes…' Beatrice smiled. 'We were.'

'Arabella has just fallen out with hers.'

'Poor thing.'

'I have to say, from all she's told me, it sounds very fraught.'

'She's spoken to you about it?'

'Loudly.' He nodded. 'And then tearfully, when I pointed out she was in the wrong.' He put his head back on the wall behind him. 'Thankfully I've always avoided all that.'

'Didn't you ever have a best friend?'

'God, no,' he said.

'Oh.' She couldn't imagine her childhood without Alicia—or rather, she didn't want to imagine how it might have been without her friend by her side.

He removed his head from the wall and stared ahead.

'If I had I might have spilled palace secrets or something dreadful.'

'Well, I guess there is that to consider.'

'Not really. I doubt my niece and her little friend give a damn about the future of the monarchy.'

He was cross; she could feel it.

And she was nervous about going into the meeting, Beatrice realised.

For him.

There was so much more going on than she was allowed to know. Her 'Limited Access' truly limited her access, and there was no one here who was going to enlighten a temporary employee.

It was Julius who broke the strained silence. 'So,' he asked, 'was it your attitude?'

She frowned, confused by the question.

'I mean, was your attitude the reason you were hauled in front of Reverend Mother.'

'I was the star pupil, actually,' Beatrice corrected. 'It was more a case of guilt by association. Alicia was always in trouble.'

'So, you were the good twin?'

She nodded, but then thought for a moment. 'Actually, even though Alicia might have been the naughty one, she was far nicer than me.'

'Nicer?'

'Yes.'

'Nicer?' he checked again.

'I could be mean. Well, according to Alicia.' She shrugged, intending to end the introspection, but found she lingered there. 'I was jealous, maybe.'

'Of...?'

Many things—from Alicia's gold earrings to the ease of her smile and the way she made friends with strangers.

How, even if Beatrice had been the so-called 'clever one', Alicia had always known what to do.

'She had lovely gold earrings.'

'Oh?'

'Turns out I'm allergic to gold.'

'No?'

'Yes, I come up in welts. Still, she was right; I could be mean.' She shrugged. 'You know what girls can be like.'

He didn't, particularly. But he would like to know what this woman was like. There was a potentially life-changing meeting ahead of him, but it was forgotten for now.

For Beatrice truly fascinated him.

She was seriously beautiful. Yet it was not immediately obvious that her beauty ran deep beneath the surface too. He hadn't seen it at first.

In truth, it had irritated him that he'd needed to employ her in the first place. The necessity of employing someone to handle his private life had naturally irked him. It had, at first, felt like an invasion. Yet she was brilliant at her job. Rarely did he have to meet with his father's aides now; he had started to comfortably leave all that to Beatrice.

Julius liked how she'd said upfront that she didn't care what he did and that his private life was his own. He liked her impassive features and the fact that to her he was like a phone to turn on, on a Monday—a schedule to arrange in her notebook.

When had his irritation started to grate on him in another way?

How had it shifted so that he wanted those lips to part and smile, or to hear her laugh?

When had the gap between Friday and Monday started to stretch…?

When had he discovered it was *her* private life that he wanted to dwell upon?

He wished he had paid better attention to her résumé, so that he could better understand how the very English Beatrice was in fact Sicilian. Her well-schooled voice, her education, told him she came from a well-to-do family...

Julius wanted to cheat. When Jordan had discussed offering Beatrice a full-time position, he had wanted to ask for her file. But he hadn't.

Julius found he wanted to hear it from her own pinched lips. He wanted the prim and uptight Beatrice to open up a little to him.

'I'm going to find out what's causing the delay,' she told him, but he shook his head.

'Don't.'

She swallowed and sat back down.

'So, you were the star pupil at a convent school?' he asked.

'Yes.'

'Was Reverend Mother strict?'

'She was nice.' Beatrice shrugged. 'She knew everything—well, we thought she did.'

'Were the other nuns strict?'

'Sister Josephine had it in for Alicia.' She looked up. 'Thankfully, I left before Alicia hit puberty...'

Please leave it, she begged. Her cold, cold heart was slowly filling up and she didn't know what to do about it. *Please hurry up in there...*

'You left...?' he asked.

'I got a scholarship. Languages.' She revealed nothing that wasn't on her résumé, but she did add a slight personal touch. 'I loved Latin.'

'Yuck,' Julius said. 'Were you the teacher's pet?'

'Sister Catherine didn't have favourites.'

The feeling in her heart was getting painful now, and she wished he would stop.

'I can find you a word game on my tablet if you're bored…'

'I'm not bored. Just curious. Taylor…' he mused. 'That doesn't sound very Italian.'

'No.'

'What would that be in Sicilian?' Julius thought for a moment. 'Tagghiari?' he offered. 'Or Sarto?' He said the Italian word for tailor and when she still gave no response, he moved on. 'So, your parents…?'

'I really don't discuss my private life, sir.'

'No, you don't, do you?' Julius said. 'Yet you get a front row seat to mine.'

'It's my job,' she retorted, simultaneously regretting her standoffish tone. It was what she was always like. Not just with Julius, but with everyone.

It wasn't working today, though.

Despite what he'd said at the interview, it *was* a game, Beatrice realised. Just not one she'd thought she'd ever play. It was a grown-up game, and the exchanges were little slivers of personal information. Tiny pieces that built up with each little reveal—and her pile was building.

Memories.

Opinions.

Private thoughts.

Despite her constraints, each day he brought a little more of himself to the table, and she scooped it up while putting little down herself.

Yet, she'd just told him about Alicia, and that felt like an awful lot.

'Sir…'

He shook his head and got to his feet. 'Here we go.'

'I apologise for keeping you waiting, Your Highness.' Phillipe, Head of Palace Protocol welcomed the Prince. 'Everything is in place.'

There was a table of grim faces, and the men all stood as they entered. Beatrice took her place amongst them and looked down at the folder containing the agenda, waiting for Julius to take his seat so she could read it…

But Julius did not take a seat.

'Sir?' Phillipe motioned to a chair. 'Again, I apologise for the delay. There was rather a lot to get through.'

'Then you'll be pleased to know that this won't take long,' Julius said. 'Don't ever keep me waiting again.'

So it wasn't the prospect of his bridal selection that had been winding him up; it was far more straightforward than that—and now he let them know exactly what he thought.

'I have taken on the workload of my late brother, my sister, who is raising a young family, as well as my mother, your Queen, who is deeply grieving.' He picked up the agenda and tore it up. 'I'm going abroad at dawn on Friday, and yet you think I have time to sit out there—'

'Sir,' Phillipe was brave enough to interrupt. 'These pictures need to be addressed. They are rather—'

'I suggest you stop there,' Julius said, and thankfully Phillipe took that advice and snapped his mouth closed.

'What was your King doing that night? Or your Queen? Do they have to report their actions?'

An aide to the King spoke then. 'The King knows how upset his people are—'

'Bring me one of them,' he challenged. 'There are no baying mobs out there. Know this: I celebrate my brother's life and I mourn his passing, and how I do that is my choice.'

He clearly did not need Beatrice there to hold his hand.

'There's your response,' he said, and threw her bland words on the table. 'Don't you get that every time you apologise for me you undermine my future reign? And whoever put the possibility of rehab on the table would have been marched out through the door if they were working in *my* household.'

He looked at every person in turn, marking their cards. They all looked suitably awkward and not all were able to meet his eyes.

'Don't forget—sooner or later I *shall* be King.'

He swept out, and Beatrice quickly gathered up her bag and papers, but as she stepped into the Great Hall, she halted—for Queen Teiria stood there.

She was a striking woman.

Always had been and always would be.

Today she wore a red velvet robe, and a headdress with tiny jewelled coins on it. She had passed on her beautiful black almond-shaped eyes to her children, Beatrice noted.

'Julius.'

She didn't even glance in Beatrice's direction. She was there to speak with her son. He suggested they take a walk, or have a late-afternoon tea.

'I don't want tea, Julius.' She stared up at him. 'You do know a king has to put duty above all else?'

Beatrice stood back, her head down, awaiting Julius's smart retort—perhaps pointing out that he wasn't yet King, or that he was currently doing the 'duty' of most of his family—but he said nothing.

'You have had so much leeway, Julius. I have fought for that—just as I have fought for all my children. It's time to remember the promise you made.'

Beatrice looked up and she saw that the usually very confident heir's complexion was tinged grey.

'I have never been more serious, Julius.'

Suddenly, so too was the Prince.

There was no witty retort, no shrug, just silence.

It was Queen Teiria who broke it. 'No more delays.'

She swept off, and of course Julius offered no explanation to Beatrice. He seemed to have forgotten she was there.

But then suddenly he turned. 'Thank you,' he told her. 'I won't be needing you for the rest of the day.'

Dismissed.

CHAPTER FIVE

WHAT PROMISE HAD been made?

Beatrice called Jordan on her way back, as arranged.

'I heard,' Jordan said, by way of greeting.

Beatrice wasn't sure if she was talking about Julius's meeting with the aides or what the Queen had said. 'Well, I'm just letting you know.'

'Thank you,' Jordan said.

They spoke about the press response, and also the need for a lovely, wholesome picture of their prince.

'Can I have access to his diary?' Beatrice asked as she arrived back in her office. 'I want to sort out an interview and photoshoot, and I want to see the rest of the anniversary photos and footage myself.'

'You'll have to come up.'

Beatrice held in a sigh. She needed the computers upstairs to access his diary, even though she could only type in requests which Jordan had to approve. The passage and stairs to Julius's private offices and residence were seriously starting to irk her, but reminding herself it was just for a few more weeks she started the trek.

And then halted midway.

Only three weeks left. And he would be away for one of them.

In truth, it wasn't the stairs nor the limited access that frustrated her now.

Nor even the fact that Julius drifted into her office from his residence on occasion—or, worse, stood there all gleaming and reeking of cologne on his way out.

It was simply that in three weeks she'd be gone.

It was strange to stand on a staircase and realise that for the first time ever she felt a little at home.

It wasn't just him. It was the islands, the people, the palace, her little flat and balcony. How she was starting to know the people on the bus, and how the barista remembered her order.

Jordan, Tobias, even gossipy Despina… All of them were starting to feel like colleagues rather than people who happened to work where she had landed temporarily.

The odd staffer at her last job might have remembered to ask if she wanted to come for a drink once or twice, but here everyone was waiting to hear Tobias's news—Beatrice included…

Stop it.

She took the last steps and found Jordan in a foul mood—so that helped Beatrice feel better about soon leaving the palace! She practically hammered a limited access code into one of the computers for her.

Good.

And no Julius.

Extra-good!

'Are you going to be at the Flower Festival the Saturday after next?' Jordan asked in a grumpy voice.

'No,' Beatrice said.

Jordan ignored her. 'It's a strict dress code,' she informed her.

'For a flower festival?'

'No, to get into the royal marquee,' Jordan said. 'You can bring a guest—just make sure they know about the dress code.'

'I'm not really big on festivals.'

'Beatrice, all the staff will be there,' Jordan pushed. 'I'm going to try and get there.'

'You only fly in that morning,' Beatrice pointed out. 'Surely you'll be exhausted?'

'A little… But Princess Jasmine is the royal patron and it would be nice to give her some support.'

Beatrice was tight-lipped. Perhaps if the rules weren't so rigid here then it would be Princess Jasmine who was off to Oman and South East Asia, rather than giving a speech at a flower festival.

That wasn't really what was upsetting Beatrice, though. It was the fact that she was starting to be invited to things, yet soon she'd be gone.

'Beatrice, I know you're a temp, but it would be nice if you could make *some* effort to be sociable.'

Beatrice gritted her teeth and resisted reminding Jordan that they weren't all devoted to the palace. That it was their prince's being so actively 'sociable' that was causing all their headaches right now.

'Beatrice…' Jordan spoke more nicely now. 'I really think you should try and get there. Honestly, the colours…'

'What colours?'

Beatrice stiffened at the sound of his voice.

He invited himself into any conversation with such ease! How did he do that?

'I'm trying to get Beatrice to join us at the Flower Festival.'

'Don't do it.' He shook his head. 'Not with your allergies.'

Jordan changed the subject. 'Beatrice wants you to do a photoshoot in the stables.'

'No,' he flatly refused.

'It's a really good journalist,' Beatrice said, 'and I think—'

He ignored her and took a bottle of Limoncello from a small freezer.

Jordan gave a nod. 'Just a small one.'

'Beatrice?' he politely offered.

'No, thank you.'

His grey tinge had gone and there was no trace of the

storm that had hit him this afternoon. He didn't have a Limoncello either, but poured one for Jordan, and then the two of them went and sat on their oh-so-cosy seats and went through his schedule for the upcoming trip as Beatrice tried not to listen.

'You'll need a gift for the daughter,' Jordan said.

'Oh, no.' He shook his head. 'I'm serious. Otherwise I'll end up with two brides.'

Apparently there was a poem he had to learn in Romeyka, and, no, he hadn't managed to look at it yet.

Actually, it all sounded completely exhausting, Beatrice thought, watching footage of the family on the balcony after Claude's funeral as she tried not to listen in. A night in his mother's hometown, then two nights in Oman, and then on to South East Asia and then back—all in the space of a week.

'Back in time for the Flower Festival,' Jordan said to him, although Beatrice rather felt it was aimed at her.

'Please…' he scoffed, and Beatrice found she was suppressing a smile. 'I'll be in no mood for company by then.'

Diary closed, Jordan stood. 'Have you heard from Tobias, sir?'

'I have,' Julius said. 'How about you?'

'Yes,' Jordan said. 'I've been sworn to silence.'

'And me.'

Ha-ha-ha…

They shared their little laugh and Beatrice wanted to poke out her tongue at their friendliness as Jordan said goodbye to him. Instead, she turned back to her video and watched as the royal family all walked back into the palace from the balcony, the King reaching for his wife's hand and her brushing it off.

Whoa!

Beatrice rewound.

Oh, yes, she had!

'I'll see you tomorrow, sir,' Jordan said.

'No doubt.'

'Oh, before I go…' Jordan stopped. 'No. It's nothing.'

'You know I hate that,' Julius said. 'Say what you were going to say.'

'Very well. Have you got that book?'

'Book?'

'The one I lent you.'

'Oh, I thought it was a gift.'

Beatrice found herself looking over, enjoying the very rare sight of Julius squirming.

'No,' Jordan said. 'I told you it was a loan.'

'I'll get on to it.'

'You haven't read it, have you?' Jordan said. 'Sir…?'

'Jordan, I *have* read it.' He must also have seen her disbelief. 'I have—along with all your endless and very personal notes in the margins. We used to get fined if we did that at school.'

She smiled. 'You've never paid a fine in your life, sir.'

'I'm just letting you know that I did read it.'

'Did it help?'

'It did—thank you. I'll get it back to you.'

He pulled a face when she'd safely gone, and swore under his breath, but then he must have remembered that Beatrice was there and he half turned his head.

'She keeps asking for it.'

'Oh?'

'I think I might have tossed it into the ocean.'

'You threw her book into the sea?'

'It annoyed me.' He took out his phone and called Tobias, asking him to call the staff on his yacht to have another look for it. 'Honestly, never lend me a book.'

'I won't. What was it about?'

'It was a patronising book on grief.' He rolled his eyes

and then came over and perched on her desk. 'What are you watching?'

'Footage of Claude's funeral and of the one-year anniversary memorial service,' Beatrice said. 'Your behaviour was impeccable.'

'Thank you.'

'So this book you borrowed and lost…?'

'It was awful. As well as that there were all the notes Jordan had made in the margins. Believe me, I'm not going to go into detail, but it felt like I was reading her diary.'

'She's very—' Beatrice stopped. She herself might be cold and friendless, but she didn't gossip.

Julius smiled. 'If she talks too much then it means she likes you. She's so indiscreet—but only in here. Anyway,' he added, 'I don't think her magical book applied to me…'

'Because you're unique?'

'Actually, yes.' He gave her another smile. 'It said that I'm to "talk about the departed",' he quoted. 'But every time I do they all bow and lower their eyes.'

'Oh.'

'You don't, though,' he said. 'Honestly, that's probably why I caved.'

'Caved?'

He nodded.

'What else did the book say?'

'That I should try not to make major changes or big decisions for a year. Well, that wasn't going to be possible. I immediately became the heir. I was hauled back here, given more staff…'

He was right.

'What else?' she asked.

'That I should let people know how I'm feeling.' His smile was tight.

Beatrice, whose social skills were so dire she couldn't even manage the thought of a flower festival, would usually have given an equally tight smile in response, closed down the computer and wished him goodnight, but instead she took a breath.

'You can,' she offered.

'Please…' He rolled his eyes at her offer.

How rude! He hadn't even noticed that she was trying to be nice.

'So, I threw the book in the sea.'

'Get her a new one.'

'Should I?'

'Say you made a lot of notes in her copy and underlined some bits. Perhaps say something about privacy…'

'Yes!' He was delighted by her solution. 'Could you do that now, please?'

'I'm not your PA.'

'No, but it's *for* my PA.'

He smiled as he got his way and her fingers typed out the search and purchase of a new book for Jordan.

'Done,' Beatrice said, and told him how much he owed her.

'I don't carry cash.'

'Transfer it, then.'

'I'll call Tobias and ask him.'

'Leave him alone.' Beatrice actually laughed. 'Oh, my God, you're…'

She didn't know what. Incorrigible? Annoying? Spoilt? She tried all of those words, but as she reached for her bag it was other words that sprang to her mind, and they should *not* be springing to her mind—at least not with him so close.

He moved away from the desk, thank goodness, and went to the decanter to pour a whisky for himself, as he sometimes did.

'Do you want one?' he asked, as if suddenly remembering his manners.

'No,' Beatrice said. 'I mean, no, thank you. Sir.'

They were in his office now.

And, despite the polite refusal, she very much did want one. It felt like a whisky kind of night.

Whatever that meant.

'Are you sure?' he checked.

'Quite sure. I had one too many Birthday Girl Martinis at the weekend—' She tried to make a joke, but he cut it off at the neck.

'Beatrice, can we stop with the hay fever and hangover excuses? We both know you'd been crying when you came in this morning.' When she neither confirmed nor denied it, he made his point. 'So—no, thank you, to your offer to hear how I'm feeling. Clearly it's a one-way offer!'

'That's unfair.'

'Is it?' He looked at her, and there was no repentance, no apology or taking it back. 'Okay, if we're going to talk, why don't you go first? Why were you upset this morning?'

She sat there and didn't speak. Couldn't speak.

'Okay, let's start with an easier one: how was your weekend?'

Beatrice said nothing.

'So I was right. You don't actually want conversation?'

She did.

Badly.

So badly that finally she nodded.

'The friend I was telling you about this morning...' She raked a hand through her hair. 'We lost touch. Completely my fault.'

'Fault?'

'My choice,' Beatrice said. 'But I know it would have hurt her an awful lot.'

'You were children.'

'It would still have hurt.'

It was too hard to explain to him that she'd changed her surname just to survive, and that in doing so had effectively cut off any chance of Alicia finding and contacting her. Nor could she tell him how essential a completely new start had felt at the time.

'This weekend I went back to Trebordi for the first time in a decade. I was hoping to find out what had happened to her.'

'No luck?'

'In truth, when I got there… I didn't actually try. I realised it's perhaps best left…' She shook her head, and for a moment it felt as if the day that had started in tears might end the same way. 'Really…' Beatrice nodded a little urgently '…it's best left.'

'Okay.'

He said it kindly.

Patiently.

She met his eyes and he gave a slight nod, as if he understood how hard it had been for her to share, even though she hadn't told him very much.

So hard.

The silence between them felt like an invitation to say more. But Beatrice dared not, or she really would cry, and so she did what she did best and deflected the conversation back to him.

'I think it might be my turn to ask a question.'

'I walked into that,' Julius admitted, then gave a short, rueful laugh. 'Go ahead,' he said. 'I think…'

Beatrice swallowed, and as she did so tasted the salty tears she'd been holding in at the back of her throat. Julius held her gaze and she found she had just one question: she wanted to ask if the eyes that held hers really were laced with desire. She wanted to know whether, if she dared to stand up and walk over to him now, he would reach for her and hold her…just for a moment. And then, after that moment, would she be allowed to give in and stop battling desire? Or was she crazy to be thinking such things?

That was her question.

Quite a long question.

She left quite a long pause as she considered asking it. And yet the whole time his eyes never left her face as she fought to be brave and voice it.

Come on, Beatrice, his eyes seemed to say.

Nothing moved. Even the hands on his watch had surely stopped, for there was not a sound she could hear—not even her breathing. So sure was she, when held by his gaze, that she almost risked asking it.

It was her own mocking voice that hauled her back. The voice in her head that reminded her of her complete inexperience and the agony of his brush-off if she was reading this wrong.

Rejection.

Oh, God.

She was terrified of it.

In *every* area of her life.

And so she blinked, hauled herself back from the dangerous edge, and searched the thick air for a question.

'What promise?'

'Sorry?'

He frowned, and then his mouth opened in a smile so incredulous, so confused, that she wondered if he'd misheard her.

'What promise was your mother referring to—?'

Even though the lights hadn't been off, it felt as if they'd suddenly come back on. Whatever spell had been cast was now broken.

'You *know* I can't answer that.'

Beatrice couldn't quite believe she had asked. Except it still felt safer than the other question.

She'd been about to step forward and attempt to kiss that angry mouth, Beatrice thought in horror. She'd been about to reveal her deep desire.

And so, rather than back-pedal, she snapped, 'Then it's *you* who doesn't want conversation,' Beatrice told him. 'Sir!'

She felt a little giddy as she walked over to Jordan's desk. She felt a curious mixture of anger, towards herself for confiding in him, horror at how close she had come to lowering her guard, and embarrassment at such an inappropriate question.

And she was determined to get back on track.

She flicked off the computer and commenced packing her bag, as she always did. She paused and looked over briefly. 'I answered the question you asked. You, sir, did not.'

Julius watched her, not in the least chastised.

Clearly she was feeling vindicated as she packed up her bag, and he tried to recall when it had first annoyed him.

Diary: close. Pen: put it in a box. Computer: put into its case. *Zip. Snap, snap, snap.* Whether in her office, or his, whether in a meeting room or sitting by the lake, Beatrice kept her possessions with her at all times. She was like a speedy little tortoise, carrying everything on her person, ready to disappear into herself or vanish without trace, leaving nothing of herself.

Well, she'd left *something*—but a tale of a long-lost friend didn't come close to what she was really asking him to share.

Was Beatrice stupid or did she really not know the basic rules of engagement? Seriously?

He asked himself the question again, already knowing for certain it wasn't the former.

Off she stomped, her bag on her shoulder. The woman who had put everyone's backs up. The woman who preferred to eat her lunch by the lake alone. The woman who shut down all attempts by her colleagues to be friendly.

She *didn't* know, Julius realised. Oh, she could handle

the press, and cut down his aides with few words, and she was brilliant to go into a hostile room with.

But Beatrice did not know the basic rules of engagement. She hadn't even known what to do with a birthday cake!

He couldn't understand it, nor even explain it, but in that moment it suddenly dawned on him that she actually didn't know the rules. And he wasn't thinking about palace protocol, or anything as complex as that.

She didn't know the basics.

'Beatrice.'

He was still irritated by her question, yet he was no longer angry—not even when she chose to ignore him and marched furiously out of the room and down the corridor.

'Beatrice.' He caught up with her just before she got out of sight. 'Wait.'

'For what?' She turned.

'We were talking…'

'No.' She shook her head. 'We weren't. I'll hand in my questions next time in advance, for your approval.'

He tried not to smile, and had to bite his lower lip to stop himself. How should he handle this liaison aide, who was actually dreadful at communication?

'Beatrice…' he was almost out of breath '…you don't go straight for the jugular.'

'What?'

'When you want to know something about another person—something awkward, or difficult, or personal—you don't go straight for the jugular.'

'I told you about my friend.'

'You did,' Julius agreed.

He knew he was on the right path.

'But I could tell when you'd said enough. I respected the fact that you'd told me it was best left. I knew there was more—of course there's more—but you asked that it be left so I didn't wade in with more questions.'

Yes, he was definitely on the right path because her nostrils pinched.

'I pulled back...' he said.

She swallowed.

'We're not in a meeting, Beatrice. You don't have to go straight in for the kill.'

His words were starting to seep in, and the worst part was, Beatrice knew he was right.

He wasn't completely right, because he didn't know just how big a part of her heart she'd shared, but her question had been beyond inappropriate. She screwed her eyes closed in bitter recall as she replayed her own words.

'Got it?' he asked, but kindly.

She nodded, took a breath, opened her eyes and nodded again. 'Got it. Be more subtle next time.'

He laughed a one-burst laugh and she felt it on her cheek. 'You still wouldn't have got an answer.'

His eyes widened at the very thought, as though there was no one—not a soul—who could have asked him that and received an answer. She had everyone's backs up, yet somehow, not his.

Never his.

He liked the distance she kept.

He liked how it amplified things when they were close.

They were—despite their half-row, despite her walking off, despite so little having been revealed—somehow closer than before.

In fact, if there was anyone he could tell his secrets, then he'd probably choose the woman staring back at him now.

He'd been waiting for her kiss a few moments ago...wanting to take her to bed and end this frustration.

Now there was a new craving.

The desire to take her to bed was not new, but far more dangerous was the desire to know her, and for her to know him better too.

He stepped back. 'I'll say goodnight.'

'Goodnight. Sir.'

'Best left,' he said, and returned to his office and closed the door behind him.

She carried on down the stairs when all she wished was that she were back there... Wished she'd been more subtle.

Yet Julius had just revealed something.

He had said she'd gone straight for the kill. And that told her that whatever promise had been made it was his agony to bear it.

She walked towards Prince's Lane, caught the shuttle bus, and tried to make sense of things as the bus hissed its way through town. Only when she got home did she remember to turn off her work phone.

Except she checked the messages first.

Not for work, but just in case there might be a message from him.

It wasn't so much that something had shifted—it was more as if something had been revealed. A tiny fault in the heavy veil between them had been exposed...a little glimmer of a light...a star that had always been there but which had previously been unseen. That was how it felt.

Not as though she was standing behind a stage curtain, peering out, more that she was sitting on the other side of the curtain and had suddenly glimpsed a scintilla of the Julius behind the royal veneer.

One, two, three... Like stars in the night sky things emerged, and she was entranced by them, far too aware.

Until the veil between them was dotted with stars—well, for Beatrice at least.

And even if she'd messed up back there, it had been worth it.

She didn't know how to describe it.

She only knew that it really felt as if it could have been a whisky kind of night.

Whatever that was…

CHAPTER SIX

STARRY NIGHTS FADED, THOUGH, and pink clouds were fleeting when you worked for Julius.

Beatrice happily hid in her office for most of the following week.

There were not many drop-ins from the dashing Prince.

He was busy doing fly-in, fly-out visits to a couple of the smaller islands and so was barely around, and even when he was, he was vague and polite.

Thoughts of that odd encounter—the kiss that had never happened and the almost-row—dispersed as Beatrice got through the week.

And it was quite a difficult week in the end, because the dancing-on-a-boat shots hadn't just lit a twinkle in Beatrice's knickers...there was glitter everywhere she looked!

Everyone, it seemed, had a story, or a photo, and Beatrice spent most of her time playing whack-a-mole with all the reports and counter-reports that has been generated, trying to keep her newly wholesome prince's image intact.

On Friday, she had no choice but to go up to his offices and access the computers, and get Jordan reluctantly to let her into the archives.

'I don't have time for this,' Jordan muttered, typing in a code for her. 'I finish at two...'

'I know.'

'It's not you,' she said. 'It's this damn "Dancing King" thing. He's been invited onto a ballroom dancing TV show...'

'He's not going to do it?' Beatrice gaped.

'God knows! Can you believe the King actually called him this morning to discuss it?'

This place!

Beatrice was cross-eyed from cross-referencing the Prince's exes as lunchtime approached.

'Who's the Marchioness?' she asked.

'Oh, my God!' Jordan gave a dramatic wince, 'Don't ask.'

Beatrice did as she was told and didn't!

Not that it stopped Jordan from telling her. 'She was seriously connected. I mean, real hetaera material...'

'A long-term mistress before marriage?'

'Oh, yes, it happens all the time. Anyway, she was newly widowed after having nursed her husband for years. There was no mourning period for the Marchioness—she wanted soirées...'

Beatrice rather guessed she was looking at Julius's one-on-one Latin American dance tutor.

'Well, at least he's behaving now.'

'He's being discreet, you mean.'

Unlike you, his PA, Beatrice was tempted to point out. Yet she was coming to quite like their chats.

'I'm quite sure Prince's Lane resembles Grand Central Station at times,' Jordan went on.

Or she *had* been starting to like their chats!

'Sorry?'

'Just before the stables...where the shuttle bus drops his staff off.'

'I know where it is.' Beatrice bristled.

'Well, there are special gates...' She lowered her voice. 'There's a tunnel that runs under Prince's Lane.'

'Why wasn't I told this?'

'Nobody's "told". It's just a piece of knowledge you acquire if you work here long enough.' She laughed. 'You haven't seen anything?'

'What?'

'I used to think the place was haunted by beautiful women in ball gowns, walking through the mist.'

'Are you saying that he has a secret passage to his suite?'

'Beatrice!' Jordan frowned at the clear annoyance in the usually unruffled liaison aide. 'He's not the only one; it's like a rabbit warren beneath here.'

Of course it was. Beatrice took a short-cut sometimes through one of those passages, if she was running late, and the morning coffee came via another... But a direct passage to his suite? No wonder he was so cocksure about 'behaving'.

She felt a fire burning in her chest and had to fight to prevent the heat rising to her cheeks. 'Well, it would have been nice to have been warned.'

But she had been...sort of. Now she looked back on it. It was in her job description, Beatrice reminded herself.

'Shh...' Jordan said, as the buzzer lit up to indicate that he'd left his apartment.

At least you got a slight warning of his approach when you were up here in Jordan's office.

Beatrice carried on working as he sauntered past.

'Ah, the Marchioness,' he said fondly as he looked over her shoulder.

'They're saying...' Beatrice wished he would get away from her shoulder '...that you broke up with her because she was past childbearing age.'

'Are they, now?' He shrugged and offered no insight. None at all.

'You are discreet—I'll give you that.' Beatrice turned her head just a bit and smiled, then got back to looking at the screen. 'Even I don't really know what you get up to.'

'As it should be,' he said.

'So, no further response?'

'Of course not.'

She clicked away from the image of the Marchioness and a much younger Prince Julius with marked relief—only it was short-lived, because he came beside her and leant on the desk.

'They're just going to keep digging...' he said.

'Well, you're giving them nothing new.' She looked up a little, and knew that she too was digging. 'Unless there is something...?'

'Sorry?'

'Well, if there is it's best we get ahead of it.'

He didn't respond. Instead he started to talk to Jordan about their crack-of-dawn departure the following morning. Except even though he was ignoring her question Beatrice couldn't ignore him. Julius's thigh was in her periphery, and his hand still held her desk, and she *couldn't* ignore that.

Thank goodness he flew out tomorrow, or she might just have to walk out on her job today.

This minute, in fact.

She wanted to nudge his fingers, to let him know her hand was close and feel the bliss of his hand closing over hers for a second...a squeeze of acknowledgement, saying that he *knew*, that they were both aware of each other, even as they did nothing, even as he chatted away...

'I might go and have lunch,' Beatrice said, and started to pack up her things.

'Leave all that,' Jordan said. 'I need you up here this afternoon. Anyway, lunch is being catered today. Tobias is doing the gender reveal...'

'Why?' Julius frowned. 'We already know it's a boy.'

'He's not expecting you to be there,' Jordan said. 'It's just us that have to act surprised.'

'We all know, though.'

'Just…' Jordan was cross. 'Have lunch with us all, Beatrice.'

'I actually brought my own in,' Beatrice said. 'I might get some air.'

Snap, close, zip.

Julius saw Jordan's eyes close in frustration at Beatrice's refusal to join in, and then open wide as Beatrice took herself off for lunch.

'See?' Jordan hissed. 'Why even try to include her?'

Julius didn't respond. Normally he didn't get involved in office politics, but where Beatrice was concerned…

'Are you going to speak with her, sir?'

'About…?'

'Well, I can't offer her a permanent role without telling her what it entails.'

'Be vague.'

'That won't wash with Beatrice,' Jordan warned. 'You know her contract expires in two weeks. She's already fielding approaches.'

'Who from?'

'I don't know. She closes her door, or goes to the lake…' She walked over to a window. 'She's on her phone now.'

'You said you had reservations,' Julius reminded her.

'Some,' Jordan admitted. 'Though they're nothing I can't address with Beatrice myself. It's your call, sir.'

He nodded.

'I'm going to pop down to the staffroom. You do remember I'm finishing at two…?'

'Yes, I'll see you at dawn.'

'I'll be here long before then. Sir, if you want me to squeeze in a formal interview with Beatrice before I leave…?'

He'd better speak with Beatrice now.

And say what?

Beatrice, you are brilliant at your job, and I can think of no one better to deal with the barrage from the press when I sign the Document of intent. However, I need you to leave so I can sign said document. And can we have one night together as a reward for good behaviour after your leaving do?

Hardly.

He glanced down and there Beatrice was, alone by the lake rather than eating blue cupcakes with her colleagues. There was a forlorn air to her that tripped some unknown switch buried within him.

She was making friends—not that she knew it yet. His close-knit team were warming to her. Jordan had even negotiated on Beatrice's behalf, prior to any offer, insisting on an attractive package in order to convince her to stay.

She would, as Jordan said, be an asset to the team.

The moral dilemma was all his.

He took the stairs with purpose, crossed the terrace with elegant ease, then slowed as he approached the lake.

'Oh.' She turned at his footsteps and went to stand up. 'Excuse me…'

'Don't get up,' he said. 'Do you mind if I join you?'

'Of course not,' she said, but he could hear her reluctance at having him invade her oh-so-personal space.

He peered into her very neat lunchbox, and then at Beatrice. He was good at this, Julius reminded himself. Small talk. Job offer. Small talk.

'You like to take lunch here?' he asked.

'I like the peace.' Beatrice nodded. 'Well…'

'Sorry to intrude.'

She actually laughed, and it was a sound so unfamiliar to him that it seemed like windchimes above them. Usually windchimes annoyed him, but not this sunny afternoon.

'That came out wrong,' Beatrice admitted, and even managed another small laugh. 'The peacocks are really noisy today.'

'Ah…' he nodded. 'Bastards.'

She turned, startled.

'They screech me awake an hour before my alarm.' Small talk was so easy. 'If I set it for five, they rise at four. If I set it for seven, they wake at six…' He glanced over. Enough small talk? Perhaps a moment longer…? 'You feed the swans?' he asked.

'The black ones.' She nodded. 'They're all fledging except that one.' She pointed to the straggler. 'He's lazy,' Beatrice said, watching as he hopped onto a little island of rushes and started calling out as his family glided off. 'He still likes to hitch a ride on his mother's back. She always goes back for him.'

'It's natural.'

'No!' Beatrice disputed. 'He should be independent by now. Cats are the same—they have nothing to do with their kittens after a few months.'

Julius took a breath. He was not here for her depressing take on Mother Nature. 'Beatrice, you know I fly out for a week in the morning?'

'Yes.'

'You're aware, I'm sure, that initially I didn't want to hire you.'

'You made that very clear.'

'Well, I was wrong. You have been a great help.' He looked over at her pressed lips and pointed little nose. 'I sincerely mean that. You've taken a lot of the pressure off my dealings with the press and the aides—all of it, really. However…'

'Am I being fired?'

'No!' He shook his head. 'We wouldn't be sitting by the

lake if that were the case. But your contract is due to expire soon.'

'Two weeks today,' Beatrice said.

She was counting the days. Dreading that final day. But also relieved that soon this slow torment would end.

Her desire had become a perpetual thing. It woke her in the night and it morphed into her dreams, and then it was intensified by day until she could not escape it.

Not even by the lake.

No, for today he'd come and sat beside her.

They saw the mother swan hiding behind the rushes as the lazy cygnet peeped loudly. They both watched as his mother tried to ignore him.

'What if he isn't strong enough?' Julius asked.

Beatrice shrugged. 'Survival of the fittest.'

'Remind me never to watch a nature documentary with you.'

She half laughed, but it faded when he asked another question—or possibly it was the serious edge to his voice that alerted her.

'What if he can't make it in the deep water?'

Beatrice turned and looked into his dark eyes and she felt as if he was asking her something. Or telling her something. Quite what, she didn't know, but it felt like an extension of their previous exchange.

Be subtle, he'd told her.

No, she corrected herself. He'd told her not to push. To tread gently if there was something awkward or difficult to discuss.

Was this related to the mysterious promise he had made?

Before, she would have frowned and asked exactly that. Now, she sat by his side and tried a different approach.

'Then he stays in the shallows, maybe?' she suggested.

'Or she still carries him,' Julius said, and they turned and watched as the mother swan relented and the little cygnet jumped onto her back.

It felt like a very important conversation.

The leaves were shimmering and the lake was rippling in the breeze, while underneath it all she was trying to understand what was actually being communicated.

'Well, for as long as she can,' Beatrice said. They sat in silence. Then, 'Perhaps I should stop giving him extra corn.'

'Beatrice, when I get back from this trip...'

He didn't actually say it, but she knew where this was leading. It was the point of her being here, after all.

She prepared her smile—a big one—and told it to wait in the wings and be ready to dash on as soon as it was required. She had been working diligently towards this moment, attempting to get this leopard to change his spots, albeit temporarily. And she'd done a good job—an excellent job, in fact.

But the smile she'd prepared must have stage fright, because it refused to leave the wings as he spoke on.

'Things are going to get rather busy...'

'You're not doing that dancing show?'

'No, although believe it or not the King is considering it—to show how progressive and modern the monarchy is.'

She gave him a look that said she begged to differ.

'Well, that's his latest turn of phrase.'

'I'll vote for you,' she told him.

'Thank you,' he said. 'I think. However, it's not that type of busy I'm talking about. My father and I are both in agreement that it's time to steer the country into happier times...'

'I see.'

'Only my very inner circle are aware.'

'Of course.'

'However, the reason I'm letting *you* know is because Jordan is going to offer you a permanent role.'

She swallowed.

'We've discussed it. She's very impressed with your work. She does have a couple of reservations, but you two can sort those out...'

'What reservations?'

'I don't get involved in all that.'

'What reservations does Jordan have?'

'I can't begin to imagine.' He smiled a black smile. 'So, I am formally inviting you...' He made a little circular motion with his hands.

'What does *that* mean?' Beatrice asked, and circled her own hand.

'That I'm extending an invitation for you to become a permanent member of my team and now it's between you and Jordan.' He stood. 'I'll leave you to enjoy your lunch.'

'Thank you,' Beatrice said, a little stunned.

She was about to halt him...to tell him no...to just...

Why halt him?

Why decline?

This was a job in a place she could actually call home, and if she didn't have this ridiculous crush then, yes, she'd seriously consider staying.

She really had averted disaster by not attempting to kiss him. If he felt so little for her that he could hire her to deal with his wedding then clearly it was all in her head.

Anyway, he was arrogant, haughty, and just so not her type.

Not that she had a type. But if she did it would not be him. Nor any man who opposed women in royal lineage. Nor a man who...

What else?

A man who pointed his finger.

But surely she should at least listen to what Jordan had to say?

Maybe it was time for a different approach.

'I wasn't expecting to be asked...' She looked up and

pushed out that smile, but had to squint a little at the sun behind him. 'I'm thrilled.'

Beatrice couldn't see his reaction because of the blinding light. She just saw his shoulders stiffen and guessed the suave Prince might be a little startled by her rare expression of enthusiasm.

'I'm flattered. Thank you, sir.'

CHAPTER SEVEN

TOBIAS WAS IN her office when she returned.

'Everything okay?' Beatrice frowned.

'I was just leaving you a cupcake,' he said. 'I know you couldn't get there, but...' He smiled. 'We're having a boy.'

'Wow!' Beatrice said.

Actually, *wow!*

His excitement was catching, and Beatrice found herself smiling as he showed her a photograph of the scan and spoke about Esther. 'She'll be at the Flower Festival...' he told her.

'Will you?' she asked.

'No chance. We don't get in till ten that morning and I'll be crashing.' He shook his head. 'But if you want company, Esther would love to meet you.'

He was kind.

They were all kind here.

And when Jordan called her upstairs a short time later Beatrice listened carefully to all that was being offered to her, amazed at the benefits package they had put together in order to tempt her to accept the permanent role.

Her choice of press officer, her own assistant, a driver to and from work and the salary... Well, she might even be able to afford the mortgage on a teeny cupboard on the marina...though not one with a balcony.

In her head she was actually thinking of marina views and weekends and coffee shops and being here!

'Now,' Jordan said, 'we have a lot to discuss.'

Yes, there was always room for negotiation. Maybe she could get that balcony after all!

But Jordan wasn't all smiles and waving a contract. 'Beatrice, before we go any further I might ask Deborah from HR to come and join us.'

'HR?'

'Well, I don't want to have to stipulate the number of events you attend, or how you present yourself—'

Beatrice frowned, and then looked down at her immaculate grey shift dress and neat flats and knew she presented herself professionally at all times. 'Do I get a wardrobe allowance for official functions? If there's a dress code…'

'Dress codes are the easy part—it's the social aspect.'

Yikes.

'I don't want to tell you to show up voluntarily and smiling…' Jordan shuddered. This was clearly a conversation she knew was necessary but which she was dreading. 'Why don't I call Deborah now?'

Julius had indeed been right.

Beatrice knew her attitude was being challenged.

'Jordan, you don't need to call HR before you speak with me.'

'The royal family is the touchstone of our culture, our calendar…' Jordan closed her eyes and took a breath. 'Take the Flower Festival—it was cancelled last year…'

'I do understand it's especially important this year.'

'It's important every year; it's a part of us as a nation.'

And Beatrice could be one of the *'us'*.

Aside from her feelings.

Were they even relevant here?

Did it even matter? Because clearly the world was carrying on, oblivious to the torch she carried for the Prince.

Perhaps it was time to snuff it out?

Bring forward her thirtieth birthday, maybe?

Make friends.

Say yes to life.

'I'll leave these with you to go through,' Jordan said, and opened up a glossy navy folder that contained the official palace staff brochure along with an awful lot of forms. 'Take your time to go through them and see what's involved. Formal training in palace protocol...' she turned the pages '...enhanced security vetting—that takes a few weeks...'

'I had that in the UK; it's still current.'

'We'll need our own, as well as counterterrorism measures. There's no way around it. You'll be working here upstairs, with full computer access, diaries, travelling with the royal entourage...'

Beatrice had a sudden image of herself at the rear of the royal jet, watching Julius and his bride. Or dressed in her clothing allowance wedding day best, but on the periphery. Stuck in a perpetual crush and never moving on.

Perhaps sometimes she'd get the evening offer of a cosy chair and a Limoncello and go home happy because he'd told her what a good job she'd done that day. Remain just a ridiculous teenager with a crush inside a twenty-nine-year-old body,

Or a forty-year-old body.

Or fifty.

Sixty?

The years would roll on and there they'd stand, both grey, on her retirement, and he'd smile and thank her for all her service, and his children and grandchildren would all be there...

'Beatrice?'

Her breath was tight in her chest as she glimpsed her possible future. One in which she remained safe for ever because she had a crush on the unattainable—which meant she never, ever had to move on.

Beatrice wanted to move on.

That was why she'd gone searching for her friend—for someone who had always understood that, despite her coldness and aloofness, she was hurting.

She was ashamed of having barely searched for Alicia. Of having turned her back on the one person who had ever loved her. Just to survive.

She could hear Jordan's voice, but it sounded as if it was being piped under water… 'We can speak when I'm back. I'm sure you'll have many questions…'

'Actually, no.' Beatrice heard her cold tone and softened it. 'I'm flattered to be asked, but I don't want to waste your time…'

'Beatrice?'

Jordan was looking at the page Beatrice seemed to be fixed on—about security checks. Little did she know that it wasn't the prospect of security checks that had Beatrice about to refuse the job offer. How could she know that it was the thought of being a part of the Prince's entourage that made her hesitate?

'I know already about the name-change. Is it that?'

Beatrice looked at her colleague…her almost new friend.

'It was flagged for a security check.'

'Of course.'

Jordan had Beatrice's file in front of her, which contained a more detailed résumé than the bullet-pointed pages that had been handed to Julius to review. She had probably known all along that Beatrice was a Trebordi baby.

'I just prefer short-term contracts,' Beatrice said. 'It was lovely to be asked, though.'

'You don't want some time to think about it?'

'I don't.'

'I'm very sorry to hear that.'

'Thank you.' Beatrice let out a breath. 'I'm terrible at social things. It's just not for me.' She very deliberately changed the topic. 'What time do you leave?'

'Now,' Jordan said, gathering up all the files. 'Can you stay up here for the afternoon? Everyone who's going on the trip is at home, and Despina finished at one…'

'Sure.'

'I doubt he'll be around,' Jordan said.

Jordan logged out of her secured profile on her computer and left Beatrice with her limited access.

'I'll be in touch all the time. Well, not at the weekend or after five!' Jordan gave a tight smile. 'I know you don't like to be contacted out of work hours.'

'You can contact me on my private line in an emergency.'

'If there's an emergency Beatrice, I doubt I'll be calling you.'

She meant it lightly—meant that a temp wasn't on the list of people to call if something dire occurred. It just hurt, this odd Friday afternoon.

'I'm out of here,' Jordan said.

She had to get her hair done, she said, and pack a suitable wardrobe… She listed off the million things she had to do in order to be back here long before dawn, so Prince Julius could roll out of bed and board the royal jet.

Well, that wasn't fair. Beatrice knew Julius worked harder than anyone she knew—including Jordan, including herself. It was just safer to let her mind linger in its current critical and scathing mode than to indulge in the fantasy that was trying to play out in her head—the one where she had a permanent job at the palace and friends who dropped in for a chat and sat on her balcony…

'I really am going this time,' Jordan said.

There was a rush of regret as Jordan headed off, and Beatrice battled an urge to call her back, to say *To hell with it, yes, I would love to stay.*

She tried to do some work, but kept getting met with 'Limited Access'.

Limited Access.

It felt like the story of her life.

It hurt.

Everything hurt today.

Finally she got into a redacted version of the Prince's diary and did her best not to notice as he came out of his apartment at five.

'Where is everyone?' He frowned.

'Gone for the day.'

'Jordan?'

Beatrice took a breath and held it in, instead of biting back the information that his PA would be back before dawn.

'Oh, yes, of course…' Julius answered himself.

She glanced up at his voice and knew he must have realised, but she tried to hold on to her safe scathing thoughts.

Only it was proving impossible. She was faced with the immaculate Prince, with his freshly cut hair, his nails buffed… Whoever had shaved him had slapped on way too much cologne. No, not quite immaculate, she was faced with the restless Prince. He had removed his jacket and loosened his tie and, presumably because of the hour, his shirt was untucked and he wore no shoes or socks.

He had never looked more incredible than he did right now. And for a man who always looked amazing, that was saying something.

Even his *feet* were attractive, Beatrice reluctantly noted.

The silence was an uncomfortable one—or was she simply upset? Ready to go home?

These feelings that were currently being squeezed out of the stone that beat in her chest hurt just as much as bottling them all up and ignoring them.

She attempted normality and passed on the messages Jordan had left, and then she got to the last one: 'Queen Teiria has asked that you speak with her before you leave.'

'Done.' He nodded. 'Thank you.'

'Are you packed?' Beatrice attempted to make polite conversation.

'I just have to polish my boots…' he said. 'They really need to shine for Horon tomorrow night.'

'Better get to it, then,' she said, and looked back to her screen. Then she realised she was again a beat too late to catch a joke. 'You're not in there polishing your boots, are you?'

'Correct.'

'Or packing?'

'Nope,' he said, taking the top off the decanter and splashing whisky into a heavy glass.

Julius glanced over to where Beatrice sat at Jordan's desk. Her hair was beginning to fall down, but it looked charmingly dishevelled rather than messy.

There was something else about her that was different too.

Just a slight sense of disarray that he could not articulate.

She wore grey, but that was all she ever wore. As if a sad cloud hung over her wardrobe, so it produced grey after grey after grey...

No jewellery, as usual.

Her slick of neutral lipstick was in place.

She just looked different.

'Did Jordan speak with you?' he asked.

'Yes.' Beatrice nodded. 'She asked me to work up here for the remainder of the day. If I'm in the way I can move down to my own office—'

'I meant,' he interrupted tartly, 'did she speak to you about coming on board?'

He added ice to his whisky, heard two chinks as the cubes clattered into his glass. He did not offer her one tonight.

'She did.' Beatrice looked back to the screen. 'I really think you should do this interview. Just puppies and ponies—'

'What interview?'

'I told you about it last week. You agreed.'

'Why would I when I don't have any puppies and I grew out of ponies more than twenty years ago?'

'It's for your new wholesome image.'

Julius did not want to discuss puppies or ponies. He wanted to know what his sullen, moody liaison aide was thinking.

'So, did Jordan speak with you?' he prompted. 'About the permanent role?'

'Oh, yes.'

Beatrice thought for a moment, and it was then that she realised there really were some advantages to keeping her private life so very private.

'There's a lot to think about—and obviously I'm going to have to discuss it with my partner.'

It felt as if a whip had just been cracked—as if the air had been sliced open. And she was the one holding the whip.

Beatrice watched Julius arch his neck, as he did when he was tense, and felt a flood of relief.

Because she wasn't imagining things.

He *did* feel it too.

Whatever *it* was.

Attraction.

Lust.

She doubted men like Julius suffered crushes.

Somehow, even if her five senses didn't really have anything to latch on to, she knew that he was working hard to contain whatever it was that kept him far over there with his whisky, rather than perched on her desk while they chatted.

It was actually a relief to know it was not just her.

Nice to glance up and see his jaw was clamped, to see him flash a polite smile. She knew it was mean—even as a little girl she had been mean sometimes... But, given that she was about to pass up a dream job, a new start, the first chance she'd ever had of a home and friends, she allowed herself a mean moment in the playground, rather than sitting scared at the water taps as she'd used to.

'I'll talk to him over the weekend,' she said.

'Of course.'

His voice had an edge—or was it a husk?—and she smiled to herself as she approved having a litter of Labrador puppies delivered to the stables for a photoshoot. The alternative was that she would cry, and she refused to do that.

'I'd better get going,' she said.

'Sure.'

She packed her bag, and finally the last zip had been zipped and the last popper had been popped and she was on her way.

'Stay out of trouble,' Beatrice said, as she often did on leaving.

'Oh, believe me, I have been.'

She should have left then. She should have just nodded and wished him goodnight. But instead she fired a little dig as she hitched her bag onto her shoulder.

'To all intents and purposes…'

'Meaning?' His eyes narrowed.

'Nothing.'

She gave a wave as she left his office and headed down the corridor—not a dismissive wave, more a *leave it there* one. She closed her eyes as she walked, and wished she'd heeded her own advice. Because her little barb had only invited trouble—had only delayed the moment when she should have been halfway out of the building.

Julius wasn't leaving it there. 'Meaning?' he repeated.

Beatrice halted. Her eyes were still closed, and she took a deep breath and forced herself to be calm. She prayed her face wasn't as flushed as it felt as she opened her eyes and turned around.

'I've heard all about the secret passage to your residence.'

'Have you, now?'

'I'm just saying, given that your signing of the Document of Intent is imminent, now might be the time to be careful.'

'And there I was thinking you were here to tidy up my image, not police it.'

'You're right,' Beatrice conceded. 'I shouldn't have said anything.'

'Then why did you?'

He watched Beatrice as she looked skywards and took in a breath. She even opened her mouth to answer, but then closed it, clearly changing her mind.

And suddenly he saw the difference he had been unable to articulate earlier.

Those pale blue eyes were obscured, as if by two black saucers, and it wasn't just lust. She was angry—so angry he could see her attempts to contain it. He actually stood there, watching her trying to reel in all her unseen emotions. Like some teacher with a whistle, she was demanding they all get back in line, back in neat order.

But order could not be restored.

'I'm going to go,' Beatrice said. 'You've got an early flight.'

'Am I being told it's my bedtime now?'

'Julius, stop.'

'Stop what?' he checked insolently, as if he didn't know what the issue was…as if he couldn't feel the charge in the air between them that would not dim.

There was not a chance in hell of her being able to endure this every day for the rest of her working life, Beatrice knew. She was angry—but not with him. She was angry that she could not escape her own desire for him. She was angry at the circumstances that had brought her to this point.

And suddenly she could no longer hold it all in. She no longer wanted to.

'I don't really have a partner to discuss things with. I was trying to find a polite reason to turn the job offer down.'

'What's the real reason?'

'Believe me, you don't want to know.'

'Believe me, I do.'

Despite her inexperience, Beatrice instinctively knew that what she said next meant either goodnight or bed…

And Beatrice wanted it to be the latter.

She wanted to be the on-the-ball, confident, sexual woman he thought she was.

Just for one night.

Just to know.

Then she would be able to move on.

And she reminded herself in that dangerous moment of indecision that she'd once considered paying a stranger for that knowledge. One night with this reprobate prince meant she could get it for free. And not with a stranger.

Yes, she was angry. And suddenly all her carefully tamped-down emotions came boiling out of her in a rush.

'I'll tell you why I'll be turning your job offer down. I am so through with looking at pictures of you all day and reading about your sex life, watching the game you play of pretending to behave—'

'No one's pretending,'

She gave a disbelieving snort and immediately wished she hadn't. But it was out now, and so were her words. 'You've got your secret velvet love tunnel and you—'

'Beatrice!' He snapped her name.

She stopped and looked at him, and no one was pretending now. His black eyes were focussed on her mouth and then he moved those eyes up to hold hers. He took a strand of her hair and rubbed it between his fingers. Though his skin had not touched hers, and her hair had no sensation, the action was so intimate and so forbidden.

He put his glass down on the table beside her, and still

she did not move. His hand cupped her cheek and they stared at each other.

'I've been told,' he said, 'by you, to be careful.'

'Yes.'

'No indiscretions. My liaison aide was most insistent…'

She should go. Absolutely, she should leave.

Beatrice knew she could remove his hand and tell him to keep on behaving; she knew she could leave if she wanted. Yet it felt as if the air in the room was shared: as he breathed in, so did she. She was rooted to the spot. Of course he must think she knew what she was doing. Possibly because right now Beatrice felt as if she did.

She already knew how to smile only for him, and she did that now…just a little. And she had touched his tie so many times when she closed her eyes and imagined him that it was almost rehearsed, and she played with the pointed end near his belt and felt the thick silk between her fingers.

'Perhaps she'd forgive one indiscretion.'

One.

He removed her bag from her shoulder and dropped it to the floor as if it displeased him.

A first kiss was supposed to be awkward, tentative, but she knew there was not a chance of him knowing that she was new to this, for there was no thinking, no anything, other than the relief of his lips brushing hers. Her head moved to one side to chase his mouth as he moved his lips to her cheek, to her eyes, then down to her neck, as though he were tasting her.

'Oh, God…' he said, as if he very much needed to.

And he moved his hands to hold her hips and kissed under her hair, burrowing at the side of her neck. His tongue was wet and his hands were steady. Beatrice arched her neck and he came up for air.

'Let's go through,' he suggested, with a hoarse edge to his voice, and then he lowered his lips again to hers and lingered there, until she parted to the slip of his whisky-laced tongue.

Beatrice sighed at this very new bliss, the slight shock of his tongue sliding against hers, the taste of her first kiss, and that sigh seemed to light something in them both. His mouth demanded more and more, his tongue parting her, tasting her deeper.

This was no typical first kiss; it was every kiss she had ever wanted. And she was kissing him back just as hard, knotting her hands in his newly cut hair and lost in bliss.

Her back was to the wall. His hands took hers from his head and held them against the wall so she was pinned there while he kissed her. He released her, but just for a second, so he could hitch her dress up and lift her so that she was able to wrap her legs around him.

Somehow he picked up her bag and started moving towards the door, and she realised he was taking her to bed. But even as they began to cross the room Beatrice began to slide down his body, and the moment she made contact with his buckle, and realised she was lodged against his erection, all those weeks of fighting it seemed pathetic—because nothing could have stopped this.

They couldn't even get to his apartment.

And now her bag was God knows where, and Jordan's desk was cleared in one swipe, and Beatrice's shoes were half off so she kicked them away.

Why, she asked herself, had she waited so long to know this, to allow this? To be on a desk with him parting her knickers as he kissed her ear, sucked her neck, and brought her closer to frantic completion than she'd imagined possible.

'Not here...'

It was Julius who was attempting to slow things down, even as she lifted her bottom to assist him in sliding her knickers off. He looked at her plain cotton multi-pack knickers and gave them no more consideration than Beatrice had when she'd purchased them. Rather he was looking at her pale blonde curls! And he'd clearly changed his mind about trying to get to the apartment. Instead he just slid her knickers down and got straight back to what he'd been doing.

'Or maybe here,' he said, parting her thighs.

He was no longer kissing her, and they were both watching him play with her shining pink lips, and as he stroked the little knot she'd long denied herself he groaned when she shivered beneath his touch.

Her throat was too constricted for her to speak, and she continued to watch him stroke her, fascinated not just at herself but at the sound of his response.

'Come on,' he said, as if she should be able to jump off the desk and walk steadily.

At the same time he was undoing his belt, and she watched as he so easily took himself out. Beatrice had never been more entranced, more scared and more thrilled, and somehow all at the same time. Her throat gave a little squeak that it had never emitted before.

He was so erect, almost indecent, that she shivered with new pleasure. Just the sight of his tip, stroking where his fingers had been, was enough to make her squeak again. She felt sick with pleasure as she touched the soft skin that belied the strength beneath. She ran a finger the length of a vein…all the way to the gleaming tip.

'Beatrice,' he warned. 'Bed *now*, or—'

'I know.'

But there was no stopping it as they both watched their flesh connect.

'Here,' Beatrice said.

Because she was scared that if her feet touched the ground good sense would invade and she might never have this opportunity again.

And then even that became impossible, for at the first nudge of him she felt impaled. 'Julius…'

'I know…' He stopped. 'Have you got any…?'

She almost laughed at the fact that he thought she might have condoms in her work bag, in case she wanted to leap on a desk and have sex with someone.

Her head felt a little dizzy and she leant on him for a moment and could hear his heart thumping in his chest. 'No…'

'Then we—' He stopped, his erection batting against her inner thigh as he paused. 'Shh…' he warned, and looked not at her, but at the room that existed outside of them, listening to the sounds of the outside world and the shudder of the lift further down the corridor.

'No one must—' Beatrice was aghast.

He put a finger to her lips to hush her, and very deftly pulled her to her feet. Then he ran two hands down her hair to smooth it. 'Shoes!' he said.

She was shaking as she put them on, while he tucked himself away.

'Go and stand by the window,' he said.

She was too panicked to listen, and instead knelt down and scrambled to retrieve the contents of the desk, which had been tipped onto the floor.

'Leave it,' he warned, but at least he retrieved her knickers and passed them to her. 'Go to the window,' he said again.

Beatrice did. She stared down at the lake, holding her underwear like a bunched-up handkerchief in her hand. It was far too hard to reconcile her thoughts, so she just stared at the water and the silver birch and the white willow, and willed herself to appear as calm as the lake.

'Signorina?'

She turned her head and gave a brief smile to the guard. He nodded back, but then frowned at the spilled folders littering the floor.

Beatrice was trying to pluck a lie from the air to explain it, but then the guard saw Julius sitting there, apparently writing at the desk, and instead he gave Beatrice a small eye-roll and left.

She heard his footsteps disappear down the long passageway towards the Prince's residence. She looked down, half dreading that her dress would be at mid-thigh, or worse.

'You look fine,' Julius said. 'I mean, you look normal.'

Beatrice did not feel in the least normal.

She felt touched and kissed and still wanting.

But it felt so much better than wanting without having been touched or kissed.

'He'll be back in a few minutes,' Julius warned.

'How do I explain the folders?'

'You don't.' Julius shrugged and carried on pretending to write, or whatever it was he was doing at the desk on which he had nearly taken her just a few seconds ago.

He'd have found out that she was a virgin.

She breathed out slowly, to control her frantic heart.

And the palace doves, even with their clipped wings, would have taken flight when she screamed—because she was in no doubt, after that very brief glimpse, that it would have hurt.

Should she tell him?

How?

Just say, *Julius, I've never done this*? Or, *Julius, I'm actually a virgin.*

Beatrice could almost picture his wide eyes and the flash of awkwardness as he realised that the one-night stand he wanted came with a hymen and might require a little more—or a little *less*—than pure passion.

No.

Beatrice glanced over to the gleaming desk, where for the first time she'd felt unashamed and had wanted to know sheer pleasure. Just that.

Right now, she could not think further than that.

'Those shoes of his are killing me,' Julian groaned as the guard's shoes squeaked and clomped along the corridor towards them.

Squeak.

Clomp.

Squeak.

Clomp.

'If he goes out to the terrace for a smoke,' Julius whispered in a low voice, 'we'll make a run for it.'

'No!' Beatrice was on the edge of laughing, but changed it to a smile for the guard, who nodded as he walked past.

They heard every shudder of the ancient lift creaking its way up to collect him, but it was made bearable as Julius silently mouthed all that he intended to do to her as soon as they were alone.

She blushed, but nodded her assent.

'Thank God,' he said, when they were finally alone. But instead of carrying on where they'd left off he held her by the waist and looked down at her. 'I'm so glad that guard showed when he did.'

'Why?'

'I've been waiting for this.'

'So have I.'

It felt as if she'd been waiting all her life.

'Here,' he said, and took her jacket from the chair and passed it over to her, as well as her bag. 'We have a meeting to get to.'

She slipped on her jacket and flicked out her hair over the collar. 'One rule,' she said as they walked towards his residence. She felt so confident, so completely sure in this moment.

One night.

That was as safe as she could get.

No let-down.

No hurt.

No rejection.

Just this one night.

'One rule,' she said again as they reached the door to his apartment.

'I'm the same,' Julius agreed as he typed in a code. 'Don't worry. I've got plenty.'

He took her hand and led her inside. She had never even glimpsed inside his private residence. The ceilings were high and the floors were mosaic tiles, split by an emerald green carpet that ran the full length of the long corridor.

It looked to Beatrice as if it ran for a mile.

'I'm not talking about condoms,' she said.

'What, then?' he asked, not really waiting for an answer. 'Wait here,' he suggested. 'I'll just check someone's not turning back the bed or something...'

'You mean your staff could be in here?'

'There's a private lift,' he said. 'They could be preparing the bedroom suite.'

'Julius, I cannot be seen.'

'I am more than aware of that.' He was a little more specific. '*We* can't be seen.' He drew her into a lounge. 'So what's your one rule?'

So he had been listening.

'Just tonight.'

She saw the slightest frown pull his brows down.

'I mean it.' She did. 'No repeats. No hiding in corners when you get back from your trip. We might get away with it once, but...'

She would not be his latest scandal. In fact, she would barely register as a blip; it was her own reputation she was guarding.

'Just tonight,' she said again.

'Don't make promises you can't keep.'

He gave her a smile that warned she might rue her words,

but she was very familiar with arrogance. She knew that even though she might want desperately to know what it was like to make love to somebody, she would be able to walk away afterwards.

'Wait there,' he said. 'I'll go and check.'

She stood there in the lounge of the Prince's private apartment and tested her heart, grateful for the rule she'd spelt out.

One night was better than no nights. And, given her job, she had no 'reform-the-playboy' illusions.

None.

She looked at her surroundings and noted the plump leather sofas and chairs, the low music playing and the papers strewn across the table.

This was his home, for there was beautiful artwork on the walls, rather than stuffy old portraits, and there were collections of photos on occasional tables that told of happier times. Family times. It was odd to see the King smiling with his children, laughing with the Queen, looking like a father rather than a ruler. Still looking smart, but somewhat more casually dressed, with his errant son.

One photo was recent—well, a couple of years old maybe—and from the gorgeous temple and the blaze of orange trees Beatrice thought it looked like Japan. And there was a photo she almost recognised, similar to the one that had graced the covers of all the glossies when Julius had been born. Except it was a *before* photo.

Claude was lying on the bed, looking bored, Jasmine was clinging onto her mother, and the King was smiling down at his very large newborn baby. They were a family. It only really hit her then.

She picked up a photo of the three siblings. She guessed Julius to be fifteen, maybe sixteen, in it. Claude's face looked so serious compared to Julius's smile, and then she looked at Jasmine. Her smile was so wide it took a second for her to see there was tape on her face and a tube that ran into her nose. Beatrice looked at the protruding collarbones and pale, veiny hands and saw that Jasmine had clearly been very ill.

Was she the little grey cygnet?

Had that been what Julius had been trying to tell her as they'd sat by the lake…?

Was this to do with the promise that had been made?

Guilt washed over her as it dawned on her that it might not be ego that was keeping him from changing the line of succession but love for his sister…a desire to protect her. He had to keep his promise and protect his fragile sister.

But why couldn't they just give him a moment to breathe, instead of bombarding him with constant demands to step into his brother's shoes and take a wife?

Beatrice jumped as the door opened and Julius returned. She turned to look at him, but now she saw him through different eyes and it was impossible to go back to before she knew.

'Hey…' he said, bathing her with his smile. 'We won't be disturbed.'

He offered her his hand, and suddenly she desperately needed it, because the emerald carpet felt like a glass bridge beneath her feet…or a suspension bridge across a vast ravine. She was clinging onto his hand, both nervous and excited at the danger of adventure and secrets…

His bedroom suite, his most private abode, was decorated in dark, inky silk, from the walls to the drapes, while the thick carpet was the colour of mist rising. French windows led to a terrace, but she barely glimpsed it, for he clicked a button and the drapes fell and plunged them briefly into darkness. Then soft lights came on, and it felt like a late summer's night with the air still holding the heat.

'Take your jacket off,' Julius said, and as she did so Beatrice found that the slight frown his request had evoked in her faded into a smile as she realised that she had not been imagining any of this.

This?

This interest.

For now, in his suite, he could watch as she hung her jacket over a chair even as he'd tried not to watch her before.

It was different now, though.

Different because his eyes roamed her body, and she liked their perusal as she delicately draped her jacket on his bedroom chair.

Different because Beatrice did not have to flick her eyes away, or deny that she was burning too.

Different because they were both smiling at each other.

She'd expected to feel shy, yet with only desire facing her Julius made it impossible for her to feel that way—as if her shyness had been erased, as if it had never existed.

'Shoes,' he said, and she slipped off her ballet flats.

She stood a quarter of an inch smaller, yet she walked tall as she went over to him.

'Your tie annoys me,' Beatrice said, and took in her hand the half-undone silk. 'It should be on or off.'

'Take it off, then.'

Whatever she wanted to do, she could, and so she took off his tie, and then undid the buttons of his shirt, looked at the fan of dark hair and the dark flat nipples. She ran her arms across his broad shoulders and down his long arms, then stretched up to kiss him. She tasted him, and explored how it felt to linger there.

He removed his shirt as they kissed, and almost growled in impatient desire as he unzipped her dress, for they were both aching for the touch of each other's skin.

No one had seen her less than completely dressed since she was a child, but he made it so nice, stroking the sides of her ribs as if they were made entirely for the purpose of being stroked like that.

'Lift your arms,' he said as he unhooked her bra, and she acquiesced to his odd request, and then shivered as he stroked those ribs until she had no choice but to rest her arms on his shoulders. Then he cupped her small breasts with his warm palms and she felt the pleasure of his interest, not just the tease of his touch.

He moved down to her hips and then cupped her bottom. He pressed his fingers into the flesh, but gently, as if testing the ripeness of a piece of fruit. He spun her quickly, she didn't quite know how, so he could feast his eyes on her bottom, and then he brought her back to face him…

His erection was pressed against her stomach, and he cupped her bottom again and rocked her against him. And of all the surprises that this experience was bringing—and for Julius there were many—this one felt the most intimate. For when he'd thought about Beatrice—and of course he had imagined what her naked body would look like—he had thought she might be a little bony. Yet in the flesh she was softer than his experienced eye had considered.

Julius felt as if he'd been let in on a secret—as if he was the only one who knew that beneath her grey, shapeless shift dresses her bottom was plump and her breasts were pert. She was soft and inviting, rather than the guarded, prickly woman she seemed to be outside of his bedroom.

Now she was kissing his chest and tasting his flat nipples, before going up onto tiptoe, and the motion was as beautiful and as rare as a thorny cactus flowering in the desert.

For they, too, flowered for just one night.

'I like this,' Beatrice said.

She was tasting his salty skin and feeling his hands roaming across her bottom, but he peeled her off him.

'Lie down,' he told her, and picked her up and made her do so himself.

His bed was as big as her whole basement office, and she felt swallowed whole by dark velvet. She lifted herself up to her elbows, so she could drink in his lean body, and the flat stomach and hips that seemed too narrow for what stood erect between them.

He was muscled, yet in subtle long lines, and as he turned away to go to his dresser she saw his taut buttocks and the power of his back, all the restrained energy he held within.

'I love your scent,' he told her, as he rolled a condom down his length and she tried to fathom that within her.

'I don't wear any.'

'You have horrible soap…'

'Ouch.' She winced.

'But then it fades and I get your scent…'

'Oh.'

'Doctor's soap,' he said as he prowled towards her on the bed and knelt over her.

She felt his eyes scan the path to treasure. First, though, he bent and kissed her shoulder.

'It's gone now.'

He lightly kissed the same breast he had so gently teased with his fingers, and then he bent and took her nipple deep into his mouth. She failed in an attempt to sit up and just lay there, swallowing at the shock of pleasure his actions had provoked.

He sucked harder, and then released her, and then sucked harder again. He took her hand and placed it on the breast he'd ignored, as if he expected her to caress herself, but when she just lay there he pinched her nipple for her and played with both willingly.

'Yes,' she said, and he kissed lower and lower, down her taut stomach which was held tight in anticipation.

'Relax,' he told her, his hand between her legs.

She'd thought she was relaxed, and told him so.

'Beatrice…' He knelt up and parted her legs, and still she was not shy.

Beatrice had never thought that she might lie there and feel hot breath on her sex as a handsome prince stroked her curls, that she might laugh as he told her that *here* she tasted of doctor's soap.

But then there was no breath left for laughing, because he'd buried his tongue inside her, his fingers caressing her thighs, so that somehow his mouth soothed her sex.

Beatrice held his head at first, but then gave in and raised her arms instead, grasping air, wishing for a bedhead or something to hold on to.

She wanted to arch her back, but he held her hips down. There was a mute protest within her, a refusal to succumb to the pressure of his mouth, and yet she was writhing beneath him.

'Julius…' she panted.

She didn't know what to do with herself. Initially she'd wanted to push him away—but she'd resisted doing so, for she liked the demand of his intimate kiss, liked the intensity of it. And as she lay there it was if she was falling backwards, as if the bed beneath them no longer supported her, and she was falling back just to experience the sensation over and over again. The flood of pleasure doused the sting of shame at her own guilty allowance of it.

He moaned, and he tasted her, and she did not know how to enjoy it. She just knew that she did—far too much.

'Julius…' His hands were at the very tops of her thighs, his tongue insistent, and finally she gave in to the pressure that was building inside her.

But it seemed it was not enough for Julius. He held her hips and tasted deeper, silently demanded more, but she pulled back.

'I want you now,' Beatrice said, her voice hoarse yet her demand clear.

He looked up to her and seemed surprised that even as she was on the edge of climax she still held her control.

And now, as he levered himself up and over her, she attempted to control his actions even more.

'Slowly,' she said.

'Don't bother,' he said, and they both knew he did not play by the rules, and she would not be dictating their pace, or denying their heat, or expecting to fool him that she had let go completely.

Beatrice should perhaps have rued her own naivety then, or considered this a reckless mistake, but it was overridden by the certainty that she had chosen well.

There was no one else she could be naked with, as close to trusting as she dared to be, and every nerve, every pore, said, yes, this had to be.

His face was wet from her sex and his kiss tasted a little of her. She gave a soft laugh into his mouth because, yes, beneath the antiseptic soap there was musk and citrus to explore.

It was a deliciously slow kiss. And her head really was falling back this time, for he'd dashed the pillows off the bed so she lay flat beneath him, hungry for more. His hand stroked a burning path down her body and parted her legs, and then he guided himself to where she ached.

'I want you so much,' she admitted.

'I want you too,' he affirmed.

He was ready to glide into her, to sink into bliss, but was met with unexpected resistance. Not protest—no, there was no protest. But he pulled back a fraction, heard her pant, and the slight cry at his second attempt to enter her.

She was reaching up to kiss him, trying to distract him, as if he should politely not notice the virgin in his bed.

He pulled his head back and realised he *was* the only one

who knew the softness and flesh beneath her plain grey shift dresses. The only one to witness this rare flower bloom.

He met her eyes and smiled a secret smile as she gave the smallest nod. 'Please…' she breathed.

Julius obliged, and seared in.

Her sob as he tore her flesh came from deep within, and yet she supressed it, holding it in her taut throat as he watched intently.

Julius gave her a slight pause as she tried to acclimatise to his slow strokes, like a breathless walker insisting that she was okay, that she could keep up, certain they were almost there.

His scrutiny was obviously too much, and as he began to move rhythmically she covered her eyes with her arm, trying to breathe through the pain. She wanted to hide, but he removed her arm from her face and refused to allow it.

Too late to hide, his eyes told her, though he did not say it out loud.

Beatrice found out that his first few thrusts had been but a gentle introduction, because this time when he pulled back, when she thought she knew what it would be like, he drove in and gave her every inch of him, and she thought she might split in two.

She let out a desperate shout.

He swore, but very quietly and rather nicely.

He wasn't being still to be nice. In fact, he told her, he was fighting not to come.

They stared at each other in incredible silence, as if trying not to disturb something. And when he resumed his rhythm, so too did the pain resume, and her moan could not be supressed—not that she tried.

As it faded he repeated his movement slowly, repeated and repeated. At first the cocktail of pain and pleasure was too heady a mix for Beatrice to make sense of, but the first bolts of pain were receding, spinning away to become pleasure as Julius's deepest strokes chased away the hurt.

He took one leg and angled it, positioning her and opening her more. It felt so good that she did the same with the other leg, so that both her knees were up. He closed his eyes and pushed in and drew out slowly, breathing hard as his features sharpened.

She wanted to watch him so badly, but Beatrice closed her own eyes—not to hide, but to lose herself in the moment, entirely overwhelmed by sensation.

'Don't stop...' she panted, because she was coming more undone with every stroke, every stretch within her, and every breath of his was a measured exhalation beckoning her on.

Her hands moved to his buttocks and up to his muscled back, and then her hips moved, as if they had decided to go it alone, for she'd given no conscious instruction for them to do so.

'Oh, God...'

She wished time would stop, so she could catch her breath, ease the taut pull of her thighs and the building pressure inside her, but then she realised how tame her cry had been. For he was the one who was suppressing his cries now, and there was no longer any measured exhalation, no slow, relentless rhythm.

It was his turn to lose control.

He braced himself high up on his forearms and began to move faster. Beatrice watched with pleasure as he pounded out a rhythm that felt as if it was building to something still out of reach. She noted how his eyes closed as he took her harder, how his rapid sounds did not equate to the intimacy of the caress taking place deep within her.

'Julius...' she whispered, and then she lifted her hips to him, felt a kind of white heat zap her spine, and gave in to the urge to turn in his arms, to escape what he'd un-leashed—a pleasure far too deep.

And yet he dragged it from her, demanded it of her, so that she was panting and spent and yet still somehow re-strained. She had resisted letting go all the way even as she'd pulsed around him. Even as she'd arched into him she'd pulled back.

'No, no,' he told her. 'No more hiding.'

Beatrice knew she was crying, but this time they were not lonely, hopeless tears. This time they were frantic ones. She had played with fire and now she was burning, for it was a pleasure that felt too acute, too much, too good to be real.

'*Vengo...*' she told him in Italian. She was coming. Almost.

They were locked in battle—him desperate to release, Beatrice on the edge and refusing to leap—but then he thrust one final powerful time and she tensed with that last push.

He shouted an airless cry that marshalled the white heat back to the very base of her spine, tapping fresh reserves as he shot into her and made her a liar—for *now* she shattered.

The intensity startled Beatrice, who was almost cross that he could summon these pulses and this energy...could coil her so tight and then hit release whenever he wanted.

At last, tension released, he stroked her stomach as if coaxing out the last from himself and from her, and then he slid out of her and collapsed on top of her. They lay in silence until the need to breathe overtook them both and he rolled off.

Beatrice knew he was looking at her, but she kept her eyes closed, gulping in air. Only now was she a little scared—she had no idea what to do, what was supposed to happen next.

Dizzy and sated, Julius lay on his side, one arm supporting his head, and watched her flickering eyelashes. It was as if she was pretending to be asleep, and it somehow made him smile.

'Beatrice...?' Usually he spoke so easily, so comfortably about sex, yet he knew she was hiding now, here in his bed, and did not quite know how to address that. 'Are you okay?'

'Very,' she said without opening her eyes.

And that was the only thing she really knew.

Just that she felt very, very okay...

CHAPTER EIGHT

JULIUS WAS VERY nice to sleep with.

As in *sleep* with.

Of all the events today, the one that surprised Beatrice the most was that instead of asking difficult questions he'd pulled her in and she'd fallen completely to sleep—and she would have remained there had it not been for the buzz of her work phone.

'Why didn't you turn it off?' he said, as her eyes opened to the intrusion.

'What time is it?' She frowned.

'Maybe ten?'

As she went to sit up and retrieve her phone he shook his head.

'Leave it,' he told her.

'It might be important.'

'This is important.'

Julius had not been asleep. He was up on one arm and his hand was warm on her stomach, drawing light circles and looking down at where his fingers traced shapes on her skin. He looked as if he was considering—quite what she didn't know.

Julius was, in fact, trying to heed his own advice and not go for the jugular. Not ask *What the hell?*

He did *not* sleep with virgins.

With one possible exception: his future bride.

He'd actually been crossing his fingers that his bride wouldn't be a virgin! If he was honest, he wasn't really looking forward to it—any of it. The wedding, the wedding night, the forced conversation, a month stuck on an island with a stranger…

That, though, was a side issue.

Such a side issue that he shoved the thought away and looked at the pale skin beneath his fingers, at the red tips of the blonde curls, visible evidence of her former virginity.

Julius did not sleep with virgins because he liked very uncomplicated sex—preferably with a lover who accepted that he could only partake in a casual relationship…one who shared the pleasure, smiled, dressed and left.

But he didn't want Beatrice to do that yet, even though she was already moving to sit up.

'I ought to go…'

'Hey…' he found himself saying. 'We should at least be able to talk.'

'About what?' she asked. 'Julius, there are so many parts of you I'm not allowed to know.'

'For good reason.'

'Well, I have my own reasons,' she said.

'If I'd known—'

'If you'd known then you'd have never…' Beatrice said. 'Do you know why?'

'Because you'd have been worried I'd get all clingy, demand more…'

He could almost feel the prickles rising on the skin that had only just now been so smooth beneath his fingers. He didn't stop her—not because he agreed, but because he wanted her to continue.

'You'd have worried that I'd want presents and phone calls, instead of just sex with someone gorgeous to whom I'm attracted.'

Beatrice paused, and those circles he was drawing on her stomach were like a beckoning…a soft caress so inviting she wanted to admit that while she was telling the truth she was perhaps possibly lying a little too.

It had nothing to do with her virginity, though. Beatrice knew she could have slept with a hundred men prior to this and she would still want more of him.

But then she swallowed, because he was the only man she'd felt able to sleep with. Not just sleep with…lie with, talk to, flirt with, smile at…

Was it more than a crush?

Or were all these lovely endorphins and the lull of his hand smudging her senses and letting her think it could be more…?

'Well, you don't have to worry,' she told him. 'I was actually going to hire someone…'

'Were you, now?'

His finger did not stop moving.

'Just to get it over and done with.'

'Over and done with?' He smiled a little at her choice of words, and it was a smile she could not read.

'I was going to have him take me out for my thirtieth and get me Birthday Girl Martinis and…'

'What is your obsession with this drink?'

'I've never had one,' she admitted. 'I heard Jordan talking about them the other week.'

'What else was your for-hire man going to do?' he asked.

She wanted his eyes to reveal anger or jealousy, but instead they were warm with curiosity.

'I hadn't decided.'

'Why not for your twenty-ninth?'

'I only just decided.'

'To get it over and done with?'

'Yes.'

'Do you know, a century ago—?'

'Don't worry. I was never expecting marriage.'

'Well, you'd never have got it. Unless you have a couple

of countries tucked away that you haven't told me about. Even then it would have to go to counsel—'

'Never expecting to be your mistress, then.' She glared. 'Your hetaera, or whatever you call them.'

'Oh, no.' He shook his head. 'You'd need serious connections to get that title.'

It hurt, but she knew he wasn't wrong.

'I don't make the rules, Beatrice. I live them. A century ago you would have had your choice of gold amulet.'

Beatrice met his eyes and even laughed. 'Well, luckily it's not a century ago—and anyway, I told you I'm allergic to gold.'

'Nobody's allergic to gold.'

'Well, I am. It brings me out in welts.' She pushed away his hand. 'I'm going to have a shower.'

'No, no...' he said. 'I haven't yet told you why I don't sleep with virgins.'

'Go ahead!'

'Because, as you know, I don't get to have close friends. Nor do I get to have relationships.'

'Come off it!' She blew a sharp breath out from her mouth. After all, she had spent the last few months dealing with the fallout of his relationships...

'Listen to me,' he warned, in a voice that told her he was completely serious. 'I don't get to be close to anyone unless it's family, or my future bride.'

'What? Now that you're the heir?'

'No.' He shook his head. 'Always. I told you. I wasn't even allowed close friends.'

Yes, he had told her that.

'I have had relationships—but not deep ones. Not a single one. I have always known that my wife will be chosen with politics in mind, and with an understanding that should the unthinkable happen she would be queen consort.'

'What has that to do with me?'

'Nothing,' he told her. 'At all.'

She swallowed.

'And that is why I ensure my partners are always very content to keep things light.'

'Well, lucky for you this virgin is.'

She climbed out of bed and he glanced down at her thighs. There was no need to point out she was a virgin no more.

'I'll have a body shower,' she told him.

'A *body* shower?'

She was not going to stand there and explain it to him. 'And then I'll get dressed and go out there and look like I'm working.'

'Beatrice, you are not going back to your desk and then getting the shuttle bus home.'

'What? Will you call your driver to take me home? I *know* him, Julius. If you could just check the corridor and make sure the guard's not doing his rounds again?'

'Are you regretting this already?'

'No.'

'I don't believe you.'

'I honestly am not,' Beatrice said. 'Though I might if we're found out.'

She made a pertinent point.

'I'm not worrying about your reputation, Julius. I know I wouldn't merit a blip even if this got out. I'm looking after my own. I get it, okay?'

Oh, no, you don't.

He lay back as she flounced off to the bathroom. He wanted to redo that conversation. But then again, best not.

It wasn't only Beatrice getting involved that concerned him.

Just sex, he'd thought, and then she would be out of his head.

Well, it had sounded like a plan.

Damn!

* * *

The bathroom was bathed in instant golden light. Midas must have touched everything in here, Beatrice thought, staring at the golden walls.

Oh, God. She'd told him her gigolo plan.

She'd been trying to convince him of how little this mattered to her, and yet somehow he'd rather deftly coaxed out that this plan had only occurred to her in recent weeks.

She would have loved to step under the full blast of the shower and pelt away her thoughts, but wet hair might be a giveaway, so she took the handheld part and rinsed her body, and tried to deny how much she liked him.

Really, *really* liked him.

Oh, God. She was in way over her head and lying through her clenched teeth.

But it didn't matter—she wasn't even mistress material! Not that she wanted to be one.

She dressed, and was surprised by the normality of her own reflection. It revealed nothing of the burn between her legs, or the ache of her breasts, and so, reassured by that, she stepped out.

'Body shower,' he said when he saw her dry hair. 'I get it now.'

She managed a smile.

'Do you want a drink, or some dinner?'

'I've had some water.'

'I can do better than the bathroom tap.'

'I know,' Beatrice said. 'But I do think it's better if I just go.'

'If that's what you want.'

'It is. Can you check the exit?'

'Sure.'

'If anyone asks I'll just say I was kept late making drafts.'

'Then they'll know you're lying,' Julius said. 'Since when do you make excuses for working late?'

True...

Walking back down the emerald carpet, she felt so different. She'd been so sure, so confident that she could handle this, and yet she felt an overwhelming temptation to turn, to go back to his bed, to be with him all over again.

'I'll see you in a week,' he said, trying to test this new normal between them.

'Yes.'

She nodded and reached for the door, and it dawned on him then that Beatrice might take this week to conjure up a family emergency, or some such.

And that would be it.

'Beatrice?' he halted her. 'I'll see you in a week?'

Beatrice heard what was beneath his question this time. He was asking if she was lying about being able to handle this. If she really had just wanted to lose her virginity on a Friday after work.

Well, as far as he was concerned she had.

The rest he didn't get to see.

Aside from that, it would be Jordan writing her reference. Not him!

'Of course,' she said. And then she had to execute the bravest part of the night as she turned and gave his taut mouth a kiss. 'It was a lovely night.'

The office was exactly as they'd left it. She should pick up the folders, really, return order to the place. But instead Beatrice just headed for the exit and took the stairs down.

The night smelt like rain, except the sky was clear. Very deliberately, she didn't look up or back, just gulped in air— and then stilled when she saw a figure by the lake.

The King.

Guilt made her jump, but palace staff knew how to be discreet and make themselves invisible, and so she took the long way round, through the rose garden, and tried to pretend she hadn't seen what she had.

'*Signorina...*' the shuttle bus driver said as he nodded in greeting.

No Cinderella's carriage turning back into a pumpkin for her, she thought darkly—just the shuttle bus home.

As the bus took her along Prince's Lane she sat with her head against the window, nodding when they stopped at the porter's lodge and a few familiar faces climbed on.

The best part was when the guards got on at the main gates for a random bag check, in case she'd pinched a pepper pot or something.

And then she felt teary.

And not just for herself but for Julius too.

Loneliness came in so many forms.

Then she thought of the King, staring into the lake and wiping his eyes, and that had her wondering if her allergies were starting again.

Kings weren't supposed to cry.

CHAPTER NINE

'Sir?'

Julius opened his eyes, which he had closed not to sleep but in order to take a couple of moments to assimilate his thoughts—or had he actually dozed off?

He glanced out of the plane window. But even orientated to the real world now, as the plane sliced through the dawn, Julius felt as if he was hurtling in the wrong direction.

'Sir?' It was the flight attendant again.

'No.' He declined the offer of breakfast. 'No, thank you.'

They were over the edge of the archipelago, where the ocean met the red sky as if the seabed was littered with fiery opals. There was Regalsi, the remotest island, with its unique red sands, far in the distance.

Looking out, Julius refused to think of his honeymoon. *Hell.* He was signing the Document of Intent soon; he'd been putting it off until *she* was gone...

Now he didn't want her to go at all.

He'd been resigned to marriage, ready to assume his duty, until she'd arrived to shine up his image.

'Do you want to go through this now?' Jordan broke into his thoughts. 'Or sleep first?'

'No, let's get it done.'

It was mainly practical—just last-minute changes to the itinerary and a speech, a poem he was supposed to read in Pontic Greek for his brother...

'You've practised?' Jordan asked.

He rolled his eyes.

'I figured it wasn't going so well when I saw you'd swiped all the things off my desk, so I found a recording of it for you to listen to...'

And the worrying part—the seriously worrying part—was that Julius wanted to reach for his phone and share a little private smile with Beatrice.

He didn't share private smiles with anyone.

Ever.

'Can you cast your eyes over this?' Jordan handed him a file.

'What is it?' Julius frowned even as he read it.

'A list of possibilities for a permanent liaison aide,' Jordan said, and then added, 'I like the second one; he's got two royal weddings under his belt.'

He nodded, and had to carry on as if he cared not at all that Beatrice had clearly declined the job offer.

It was odd to be mid-air and to register that he really did care. Far too much.

Not that she'd declined the permanent role—he'd already known that she would—what he cared about was whether she had declined it before or after going to bed with him.

Had she fired off a text just after she'd left his bed?

Was she coming back?

'Jordan?' he checked, seemingly oh-so-casually. 'I thought you were going to speak with Beatrice about a permanent role?'

'I did, but she wasn't interested.'

'So she formally turned it down?'

'Beatrice took herself out of the running. I spoke to her straight after you did.' Jordan was head-down and writing in margins. 'But, no. She prefers short-term contracts, she said.'

Julius was looking at last night through different eyes now, realising Beatrice had known all along that she was leaving. The whole 'I have to talk to my partner' thing had been purely to provoke a reaction from him.

Well, she certainly had.

He should feel played, and yet he did not.

Used? No.

He just sat there trying to make sense of last night, and

frowned in irritation when Jordan spoke on, interrupting his thoughts.

'I don't think that's all there was to it, though,' Jordan said, but offered no more.

It was hard not to prompt his PA, because he wouldn't usually take such a deep interest in a temp, but when Jordan went back to her writing it was clear that if he wanted to know more then he had no choice but to ask.

'What, then?'

'I don't think she wanted the hassle of the enhanced security check.'

Julius had *not* been expecting that. 'What?'

'Her initial clearance flagged a name-change at nineteen.' Jordan glanced up, perhaps thinking she was being scrutinised. 'But Beatrice was fully cleared for basic access, sir. There's been no breach…'

'Of course not.' He shook his head. 'What does her name-change have to do with things?'

'She was schooled in Trebordi.' Jordan gave him a look that he presumed was supposed to say it all.

'Sicily?' he said.

'She was raised in the convent at Trebordi—it's like Di Dio Bellanisiá,' she said, citing their national equivalent.

Julius felt his blood run cold.

Di Dio Bellanisiá was a convent infamous for its baby wheel, though it was maintained there now only for sentimental purposes and history, not for its original purpose. He had visited it, even spoken with some families who had a parent or grandparent who had been raised there.

Still, on occasion a baby was left there… Abandoned.

'I don't think she wanted anyone raking through her past. I can't say I blame her.' Jordan suddenly winced. 'Oh!'

'Jordan?'

'It's nothing, sir.'

'Don't do that,' he warned. 'There's nothing more irritating than someone saying, *Oh, it's nothing...*'

They'd had this conversation before, so it wasn't anything new. Usually it was caused by Julius's irritation at something Jordan had said, followed by boredom when she actually told him about the *nothing* that had suddenly occurred to her...

This wasn't nothing, though.

'I've been pushing her to come to the Flower Festival,' Jordan said. 'That was when I knew I'd be offering her a permanent role. I thought she was being rude when she said she doesn't like festivals.'

'I don't much like them, either,' he said.

'Her surname used to be Festa.'

He knew enough from his visits to Di Dio Bellanisiá and other places like it that there wasn't great thought given to the surnames of the children left there.

Festa. Festival.

What the word meant to her, he didn't know, but clearly it meant enough that she had changed her name.

'Was she okay about it?' He wasn't completely thoughtless; if it was anyone else he'd have asked too. At least he hoped he would...

'She seemed to be. Who really knows with Beatrice?'

Not he. He thought of her snapping whenever he'd broached her past, or her English surname, and then he recalled her red swollen eyes after her birthday weekend.

He realised he'd completely misread the situation—for she really had given him a piece of herself when she'd shared something about her long-lost friend. Her so-called twin, yet not a blood relation, and how she'd gone back to find her and then decided things were better left...

Julius had no choice but to leave things.

It didn't make him feel better, though.

Where Beatrice was concerned, it didn't feel best left. Even if he knew it would be far more sensible to do so.

CHAPTER TEN

BEATRICE CHECKED HER heart several times throughout the weekend, like a nurse taking a pulse at intervals, but it was beating steadily.

She dealt with casual sex and its fallout for a living, and she certainly wasn't going to fall apart herself.

She was very grateful to have a week's reprieve before facing him, though.

Work was quiet. As well as Julius being away, the King was visiting the other islands all week, and it felt like that time between Christmas and New Year, when there was only a skeleton staff and nothing really happened.

It was just quiet.

Incredibly so.

Sometimes painfully so.

While the cats were away, the mice hit the snooze button…

And then suddenly he called.

That day even the lazy peacocks were up by the time Beatrice had disembarked the shuttle bus and was walking along Prince's Lane. Then her phone rang, and she heard his voice for the first time since that night.

'Are you in my offices or downstairs?'

'Downstairs,' Beatrice lied, and stared at the peacock, daring it to screech.

'No problem. I'll find someone else.'

He rang off, and there was a tiny little spike on her temperature chart—a little flash of indignation that he hadn't so much as said hello or asked if she was okay.

It was solved by a couple of deep breaths, and then a nervous lick of her lips. Because she'd been walking with her phone in her hand when usually it lived in her bag until she arrived at work. Always.

Do not go there, Beatrice warned herself, and threw her phone into her bag.

Yet, it was true.

Be very careful what you wish for, she thought.

Beatrice might have demanded discretion, but Julius was taking it to a whole new level.

There was nothing—not a hint, not a breath of change in his texts, and nor, when he called again, in his tone.

'Please ensure there is no mention in the media of my trip to my mother's home.'

'Of course.'

'No confirmation I was there.'

'Sir.' She took a breath and then addressed the latest PR issue—though they were becoming comparatively few. 'There's a rather tasteless article regarding the Marchioness.'

'Okay.'

He rang off, and she breathed out, and insisted again to herself that nothing had changed.

It had *always* irked her, the way he just called and didn't introduce himself, nor said hi or bye.

Then, late on Friday, speaking with Jordan just before the entourage prepared to head home, Beatrice found out that the Marchioness had been sent flowers, and that Jordan had spoken at length with her to mollify her regarding the article in the press.

'She can be temperamental,' Jordan explained, and rang off.

You are not temperamental, Beatrice reminded herself, over and over.

You are not temperamental, she told herself, when for the first time she had to cancel her Saturday Mandarin lesson because she hadn't done her prep.

Which meant she'd have two weeks to catch up on.

And her laundry wasn't done, she realised as she pulled on her last pair of clean knickers.

All her routines had gone to pot.

She threw her washing into the machine and filled the dishwasher, happy to have things restored to their usual order.

Except she was doing housework in her knickers.

Selecting a lemon cheesecloth dress better suited to a day at the beach than a walk along the smart marina, she was determined to face the day.

She tied on espadrilles, put on a big hat and sunglasses, and put her headphones in, deciding it was easier to focus on Mandarin rather than the fact that Julius was due back this morning. Even if Mandarin was the hardest language to master for a Latin-loving girl.

The marina was practically deserted.

Even her favourite coffee shop was closed.

It was like a dystopian world, Beatrice thought as she took out her headphones. There was barely a soul around. And then suddenly there were cannons firing. They very often did here, only it seemed more than usual today—and then it dawned on her that she was possibly the only person in the country not at the Flower Festival.

Despite her aversion to all things *festa*, Beatrice found herself arriving there. It was nothing like the festival at Trebordi. There it was all bright lights and carnival music, but here it was flowers, and more flowers, and food.

It was relaxed too. She saw Jasmine's daughter Arabella with her best friend, and security guards following very discreetly behind them.

If she'd been staying, Beatrice would have bought some tulip bulbs to put in a pot on her balcony. Instead she bought some local beeswax lip balm from one of the little stalls, an insulating cup that promised six hours of heat for her coffee, and then decided to see if she could find some sunscreen as the sun was beating on her exposed shoulders.

During her search, she happened upon one of the Greek stalls and stood inhaling *sapoúni*. Soap. It smelt…not quite like him, but there was a beautiful bergamot note, and there was another with a jasmine scent …

Princess Jasmine! Beatrice wandered towards the stage, curious to hear Jasmine's speech, as were the women behind her.

'Bella, bella...'

They were chatting about her lovely family, and how soft-spoken she was, and then about the late Prince Claude. Beatrice really wished she'd done some of this listening before now, because their conversation had turned to Julius.

'Dear, dear, dear…'

One of them tutted, and then the other, but they started to laugh, and as it turned out they loved Julius.

So too did the people ahead of her, whose conversation she listened to next.

She heard more gossip in those few moments than she could ever have found in newspaper articles, and more affection for Julius than the palace had ever admitted.

People commented on his bachelor status, but without the frantic air of his family and aides, and she wished she could somehow convey to them that the word on the street seemed to be that he should take his time.

But if she did then it would sound as if she had an agenda. And maybe she did. Because she kept having little visions of them somehow managing to see each other, even for a short while. And then the bubble was dispersing, and she realised how distracted he made her—because she still hadn't put on sunscreen and her shoulders were starting to redden.

'What time is Princess Jasmine speaking?' she asked the woman beside her.

'No,' she was informed. 'Prince Julius.'

Beatrice wanted to correct her, because she'd just seen Arabella with her nanny, and she knew the palace schedule after all, but she just nodded and smiled and made her way to the gathered crowd.

She heard cheers drown out the music as, yes, Julius came onto the stage.

He looked fantastic and dreadful all in one. He was dressed in full military uniform, and that too was unexpected. The grey and Prussian blue check and the black boots were too much for the heat, but he was so handsome. He looked fresh and crisp, and yet she could see there was a pallor to his features, and those cheekbones were even more prominent.

'We had to ask the pilot to catch a tail wind so I could be here…' he told his delighted audience. But he was thrilled to have made it.

Oh, and the people were thrilled to see him.

As was she.

It was hard to reconcile the fact that the last time she had, they'd just been in bed together.

For a whole week she'd somehow handled his business texts and complete lack of anything else because he hadn't been there, but now he was.

And it stung.

Even more than the sun beating on her shoulders.

Come on, Beatrice, she told herself, *you played with the playboy. You invited the hurt. It was you who wanted adventure…wanted to get it over and done with…*

How she wished Alicia was still in her life, because she wanted someone to explain to her why she was waiting breathlessly for his eyes to land on hers. Wishing he might suddenly notice her in the crowd. Might give her a smile or react in some way.

But he just kept on with his off-the-cuff speech…talking

about the flowers. How from the plane he had seen every island, ablaze with colour...

'The same colours that greeted our soldiers when they returned from war.'

He spoke of the past, of how the islanders had almost lived underground in bunkers and how root vegetables had been their sustenance, and of the island's vital part in the World Wars.

He said how good it was to have their beloved Flower Festival back after its absence last year. 'I know the King has visited all the islands this week, and he insists he does not have a favourite...' He gave them a dubious look...

Julius was flirting with them.

Charmingly.

Easily.

And in such a way that all were convinced that this island was his favourite.

How easily he won them over with his teasing.

Then he spoke of Prince Claude, and the devastating flu that had ravaged the islands. And then he returned to speak of the flowers again, and how they brought a smile to people's faces and brightened the most difficult of days...

Perhaps for the Marchioness, Beatrice thought bitterly, watching as he left the stage and the crowd started to disperse.

Oh, she did not want to be feeling like this. It was supposed to be a crush, or just sex—not this lurch in her chest at the sight of him. Not those bats all flying out of their caves and swooping at the sound of his deep voice.

She was so awkward, so emotionally inept, that she'd probably have fallen for her gigolo, Beatrice tried to insist to herself. It was infatuation, lust—whatever label she could put on it.

Because it could not be anything more than that.

It just could not be.

'Beatrice!'

She turned at the sound of her name.

It was Jordan, with a suited man whom Beatrice took to be Stavros, but there was no introduction.

'Have you seen Despina?' Jordan asked.

'No.'

Poor Jordan must be exhausted, given they had only landed that morning. Her hair was all frizzed from a week of humidity, and she had an air of grim determination on her face.

'We're going over to the marquee,' Jordan said, and then frowned at Beatrice's bare shoulders. 'Beatrice, I told you about the dress code. And where's your lanyard?'

'I'm not here for the marquee.'

She so wasn't—though admittedly her shoulders were on fire and she thought some shade would be nice. But she knew she was beyond underdressed.

'I wasn't planning to come. How come Princess Jasmine didn't—?'

'It was always the plan to have the Prince, a soldier who has served in the military, make the speech. Princess Jasmine was the reserve.'

Jordan's eyes again lit on Beatrice's bare shoulders, or perhaps they moved lower this time.

'You could have at least—' she hissed, and then plastered on her official smile as Julius came over with Tobias.

It was then that Beatrice remembered she wasn't wearing a bra. Not that it mattered in terms of the *size* of things, more the ache of things, and the way her body reacted to his presence. She hated how she wanted to leap on him, but of course she just stood there.

'Beatrice.' He gave her an odd half-smile of acknowledgment.

'Your Highness.' Her mouth managed a smile. 'How was your trip?'

'Excellent,' he said. 'Very full-on.'

She should have just smiled and nodded and stopped talking, but Beatrice pushed on. 'I thought Princess Jasmine was the royal patron of the Flower Festival?'

He waited.

'Sir?' she added hastily.

There was an awful silence.

And Beatrice knew she wasn't imagining the awkwardness when Tobias, whose job it was to rescue the Prince from awkward silences, stepped in.

'Sir, I think they're ready for us at the marquee.'

'Of course.'

The group started to walk towards the marquee but she just stood there.

'Beatrice?' said Julius.

'Er…no. I just came to buy some bulbs.'

'I might have a scarf,' Jordan said, scrabbling in her bag.

'I'm really not here to go into the marquee,' Beatrice insisted. 'I just wanted to see the festival and have a day out… to offer Princess Jasmine my support…'

And it was the wrong thing to say, because they all had to stand there pretending she hadn't just mentioned the missing princess again.

Beatrice didn't know how to be part of a group—she was dreadful at it at the best of times, and obviously she was hopeless now.

'I'll leave you to it, sir.'

'I might just have a quick word with Beatrice regarding…'

She didn't hear regarding what, but whatever excuse Julius had given, Beatrice felt everyone knew it was a lie.

'I wasn't expecting you to be here,' she was very quick to point out.

'I'm aware.'

'What's going on?' Beatrice asked. 'Do they all know?'

'About…?' He frowned and then halted just for a second. 'Actually, please don't answer that. Of course not.'

'So why is it all so awkward?'

'It has nothing to do with you.'

Julius heard his own formal tone and knew it sounded like a put-down when he'd been trying to reassure her. However, there wasn't a hope of any private conversation in the middle of a public festival.

'There were some last-minute changes,' he said.

'Why?'

He halted, and they faced each other a suitable distance apart. She made the mistake of meeting his eyes, clearly believing for a second that she was speaking with Julius the man rather than the Prince.

'What happened to Princess Jasmine? She was supposed to be—'

'Excuse me?' His voice was icily cold. 'Ms Taylor, I pulled you aside to express polite regret that you've chosen not to join the household on a permanent basis.'

He pulled rank and reminded her very quickly that while they might have shared a bed for all of a few hours, that did not give her access to his life or the private actions of the royal family.

Beatrice knew she should politely nod and leave, but she was truly finding out in the middle of this festival that she was so not cut out for this. Not just the one-night stand game, but this—being spoken to as if there was nothing between them, nor ever had been.

It hurt to be a secret.

She'd been a secret growing up, and she felt the same way now.

To be standing in plain sight and yet not be one of the others—actually, she was less than the others, because she wasn't suitably dressed for the marquee.

Had she stepped off his yacht in a bikini it would have been fine, of course. But not for a member of temporary staff.

Of all the things she hadn't known about life, the worst was this: that when she'd opened herself up it hadn't just made room for joy to flood in, it had also allowed pain to come sweeping in alongside it.

She held onto it now, that pain, and stood with a rictus smile on her lips, for she didn't want it tainting the one glorious night they had shared.

'I hope you enjoy the rest of your afternoon…' Julius said, and gave her his formal public smile.

'I will.'

She nodded, fighting to control herself. His manner was just too reminiscent of the way her mother had dismissed her all those years ago.

All the parts of her she'd held in check, every single hurt and insecurity, came bubbling up, and instead of turning to go bitter words slipped out.

'Not even *one* personal text?'

'We can't be having this conversation,' he told her.

'Why not? You're just talking to your liaison aide.'

'Well, you don't look like one.'

He meant her hair, her dress, the freckles popping off her shoulders, the nipples like studs under the cotton. He was trying to convey all of that right now with his one arch comment, even while he ached to take off her sunglasses so he could better read her expression. But he couldn't do it today.

Beatrice smiled politely and nodded. And then from her

sweet lips, and for his ears only, she said the one word you should never say to the next in line to the throne.

It was recognisable in most of the languages she spoke and it began with a B.

Julius's response was supremely polite as he simply nodded.

And Beatrice had never been more grateful for her dark glasses, for it felt as if his eyes were piercing hers, and she could see the anger flickering in his jaw.

'Ms Taylor.'

What had she done?

'Beatrice!' Jordan called out. She had found, of all things, a shawl. 'Esther keeps one in the car…just in case.'

'Jordan…'

'I shouldn't have tried to force you to come.' She directed a pale tentative smile at Beatrice, and it was clear to her that Jordan had been having a nosy little re-read of Beatrice's file and basic security checks. 'But now you're here…'

Oh, please don't be nice.

She was actually appreciative of the stern doorman who directed her to take off her hat and glasses, and she put the shawl around her shoulders as she stepped into the royal marquee.

Prince Julius was not there to mingle casually with staff and their partners. His back was to her, and Beatrice's back was to him while she stood listening to Esther, who was equally excited to be having a boy as her husband, who was currently walking around with Julius.

'What have you bought?' Jordan asked Beatrice.

'Not much,' she said. 'I'm going to get some tulip bulbs.'

'You've been to the soap stall…' said Jordan.

Julius turned as Jordan inhaled the contents of Beatrice's little paper bag. He was angry, tired, turned on—and something else…

He was worried that the festival was hard for her, and that he had just made it more so.

And why the hell couldn't she have worn grey, as she always did?

Her shoulders were red—they would hurt tonight—and it would seem from the soap Jordan was now waving around that Beatrice had decided to venture away from her usual carbolic.

And that, he acknowledged, put him in the position of being able to understand how she must feel, looking through endless images of him and his dates…

He was cross, too, at her stab about him not texting her except about work—as if she didn't get how hard it had been for him to seem normal this week.

He was suddenly bizarrely tempted to have her removed.

Actually, it wasn't that bizarre, because if anyone else knew the threat she posed to the monarchy then yes, she'd be removed.

Her five-foot-two, pink-shouldered body was a serious threat indeed.

Because if he didn't do the job…

Jasmine couldn't.

This morning's anxiety attack had made that exceptionally clear.

Was he really considering Beatrice as a hetaera?

She was by far too common and his father would refuse.

Then again, so would Beatrice.

He laughed to himself like a mad man at his own thoughts.

'Sir?' Tobias hauled his attention away from yellow-frocked temptation. 'Il Presidente…'

One of his potential fathers-in-law was here, and Julius was always brilliant at small-talk, he reminded himself.

CHAPTER ELEVEN

FIVE DAYS. Just five days.

Her life felt like some dreadful Advent calendar, with no chocolate reward at the end.

She was thoroughly ashamed of herself for the way she'd behaved on Saturday. And at least some of that was because it had showed Julius that she cared.

Maybe she'd had sunstroke. Could she use that as an excuse?

Or she'd tell him she was premenstrual—which she wasn't. But she would be next week. Yes, she'd start banging on about periods and he'd back away. But then again, maybe Julius wouldn't.

Beatrice gave herself the same pep talk she'd give to one of her clients—well, except for the royal client, who didn't want one.

Just carry on as if nothing has happened. And deny, deny, deny, even to yourself, she added, as she pulled on one of her many grey dresses and tied her trainers for the journey into the office.

She bought her coffee, poured it into her new cup, and took the shuttle bus. And then she walked with purpose, fighting not to turn on her phone as she marched along Prince's Lane.

Even the peacocks seemed to know she needed a little help today, because one was up early this morning, fanning his gorgeous white tail, showing off.

'Thank you,' she told him as she passed, and even turned around to admire him some more.

And then she silently swore as she saw a van make its way to the stables.

Occhi da Cucciolo. Puppy Dog Eyes. It was written in red on the side of the van, surrounded by hearts, and it was driving down the lane. For once it was Beatrice making a panicked call to Jordan, rather than the other way around.

'Jordan, did you approve that puppy and pony photo-shoot?'

'Of course not.'

'I've just seen a van on its way to the stables.'

'Oh, no!' She could hear Jordan frantically tapping. 'No, I haven't booked anything.'

'I think…' Beatrice took a breath, remembering the burning she had felt in her soul that night. 'I think I might have messed up.'

'Then get to the stables!' Jordan snapped. 'After the flower festival, believe me, he is in no mood for puppies!'

Beatrice had never run in her life, and refused to do so now, but she did walk *really* fast along the lane, as Jordan barked instructions in her ear.

Normally, she dealt with real crisises with ease, and now she was panicking over some silly puppies.

She was turning into Jordan.

'It's fine.' Beatrice smiled at the bemused woman holding a pale Labrador puppy, and waved at the groomsman, try-ing to ignore Julius who was on top of his huge black—she glanced down—stallion.

Both man and beast were lathered up, as if they'd been working hard. The horse's tail was up and he was prancing about and stomping.

The back of the van was open and there were the pups, all in cages, barking and yapping. Of course she'd dealt with it, but it would take more than a few deep breaths to get herself under control.

'If you could take the puppies to the lodge?' Beatrice was

all efficient smiles. 'There should be someone to…' To do whatever Jordan could come up with.

'I'll direct them,' one of the stableboys said.

'Do you know how aggressive this horse is?' Julius glared down as he pulled back on the reins. 'What the hell were you thinking?'

'I thought dogs and horses got on…'

Not always, it would seem.

Beatrice stood there, watching as he calmed his excitable horse, with the help of a couple of stable hands, enough that he could finally dismount.

'It was an error,' Beatrice said.

'Oh, and I know when that error occurred.' He glared. 'He would have kicked your puppies across the yard.' He left Beatrice with that horrible vision and addressed the stallion as if he were a toddler. 'And then whose fault would that be, hey?' he asked him, oh, so nicely. 'It would be the same as those irresponsible owners who let their dogs off the leash and then blame you, my poor baby.'

'I'll go,' Beatrice said. 'I'm very—'

'No, no,' he said, with subtle warning. 'You shall wait.'

She stood there, trying to deny her own tension, until finally the stable hands led the beast away, and then he turned and his black eyes were a mix of anger and desire.

'In here,' he said, and marched her into a stable—a very large, airy one that was as immaculate as her newly tidied lounge, but a stable no less.

'Won't they think it odd—?'

'No.'

She swallowed.

'Anything you have to say?' he demanded.

'About the puppies?'

'No, no.' He shook his head. 'For calling me a bastard at a public event.'

'Nobody heard.'

'*I* heard!' He pointed his finger at her and stomped towards her. 'You wanted discretion and for me to ignore you.'

'I did.'

It was dark and very cool in the stable, but he was not.

'Why were you so angry, then, Beatrice?'

'I wasn't angry. Well, a bit…'

'Angry enough to call me a bastard because I didn't text you any personal messages?'

'No, it wasn't about that,' she lied. 'I was more than aware that I wasn't correctly dressed, without you pointing it out.'

'No.' He came right up to her face. 'I said, "You don't look like my liaison aide." How did you not get that? Do you think I would just insult you for no reason?'

'I didn't know.'

'Then you *should* know.'

He sounded insulted, and maybe, yes, from everything Beatrice knew about him she should have known that. She stood still as he lowered his head and inhaled her new fragrant soapy scent.

'You don't smell like my liaison aide either. Are you going to misconstrue *that*?'

'No.'

Great waves of lust seemed to rush towards her with his every inhalation, as if he pulled the tide in with every breath he took.

'So what happened?' he asked.

'I thought a personal text, perhaps, or that when you called you might—'

'Oh? So you wanted me to ignore Tobias and ask how you felt?'

'No.'

'Did you want me to say, *Are you okay?*' He dropped his voice to a husky whisper, and finally said the words she had craved all week. 'Or to be more considerate with my enquiry. *How are you?* Or, *Speak soon.* Is that what you wanted?'

'No.'

'A personal text, then,' he said. 'A little smiley face. So that when Jordan takes my phone to answer some message from the King she can say, *Ooh, Beatrice is on fire for you*?'

'Of course not.'

She was shaking—not with fear, but with something just as primal. 'Julius, not here…'

'Why not here?'

'Because if anyone came in—'

'You think I'm going to have sex with you in a stable?'

It felt like it. Every atom seemed to crackle. But no, again she'd read him wrong.

'I wouldn't even try, because—believe it or not—I respect my lovers and I would never compromise them.' He was insulted now.

'What do the staff think we're doing in here, then?'

'They'll think that you are being dressed down for your carelessness this morning. It would not enter their heads that I was sleeping with a member of staff. Not for a second.'

'I'm going to go.'

'No, Beatrice. We're going to do something far scarier than sex. We're going to talk.'

'I have to get to work.'

'No, you don't. And if you're asked what took you so long, just tell them, *Prince Julius needed to discuss the events of this morning.* You know how to fob people off— I've watched you do it. Many times!'

He opened the top stable door and light flooded in, but he did not let Beatrice bolt out. Instead he invited her to sit.

'Where?'

'Stand, then.'

He sat on the floor, his back against a wall and his knees up. Finally she joined him, but sitting with her back to the opposite wall and her legs stretched out and crossed at the ankles.

'I have had sex in the stables,' he told her, from a very safe distance.

'Of course you have.'

'But I was young and it was night-time.'

He gave her a brief smile, but then he was serious. 'I've heard the reason you're leaving.' He looked right at her now. 'The security checks?'

'No, it's because we slept together.'

'We hadn't when you turned down the job offer.'

'Come off it, Julius, we were always going to.'

'Fair enough,' he agreed. 'So did the security checks have anything to do with it?'

'No, Jordan just took it that way, and I let her.'

'Only, you *were* upset when you came back from Trebordi.'

'What does it matter?'

'It matters. Come on—you told me about your friend, that you went to look for her but couldn't face it. Now I've heard that when you were nineteen you changed your name from Festa to Taylor.'

'I hated the name Festa. I was named after the festival which they assumed my mother had visited, given...' She waved at her blonde hair. 'I went back and Alicia had gone—the festival too.'

'I'm sorry.'

'I told you—it was my fault we lost touch.'

'I meant about your parents.'

She was silent.

'Look, I can't imagine... I mean, God, my relatives are everywhere. There's one who was born in 1754—you can see him in the Great Hall. He looks like me...'

'Was he a prince?'

'Yes. Bonny Prince Julius, I call him. He's my doppelgänger, but in tights and with a hair ribbon...' He looked at her. 'Have you tried searching for your mother?'

'Why would I?' she lied. 'I think she made her intentions quite clear when she dropped me off at the baby door of the convent.'

'Beatrice, she must have been terrified. I've spoken with some families whose relatives were left at the convent here, and—'

'Please don't,' Beatrice said.

'Did she leave any *segni di ricooscimento*?' he asked.

He clearly had spoken to those families if he knew about signs of recognition.

'I don't want to talk about it.'

'Beatrice, she might have been—'

'Julius, I don't want your take on things. Alicia got gold earrings pinned to her baby suit. I got nothing.' She swallowed down her bitterness. 'I couldn't give a damn about my mother. Can you leave it, please?'

'Fine.'

She went to get up.

'Hey...'

Beatrice took a breath and sat down again.

'I did think of you this week.'

'Julius, I overreacted. I was sunburnt, premenstrual...'

'You should see a doctor,' he said. 'You were dropping tampons only two weeks ago.'

That was true. She'd dropped one on the way to the loo and he'd laughed and picked it up and tossed it to her, like a cricket ball. Then he'd laughed again, because she hadn't been able to catch it.

'I can't progress things between us as normal—you know that,' he told her.

'Of course.'

'I have to marry...'

'Look, I know this can't be love.'

'Of course not.' He dismissed that completely. 'We slept together once...' He pointed out. 'Anyway, I don't do all that.'

'No.'

'I did get you a gift, though—and with great difficulty, believe me. I have asked for an extension before signing the Document of Intent, and once you're finished here I would like to invite you to join me on Regalsi for a week of...'

'Of what?'

'The fun you refuse to have.'

She swallowed.

'Nowhere to run...nowhere to hide. Apparently there are lots of watersports—which I don't like, by the way.'

'No.'

'Why not?'

'You'll be taking your wife there soon.'

'Don't play the moral card here. I don't even know who my wife is going to be. So my bed isn't out of bounds even though she's going to be in it? But a whole island is?'

He made a rather good point. 'I don't think it's a good idea...' Beatrice attempted.

'So you don't want romance and a week of just us?'

Oh, she did—so badly, but then the agony would be even greater.

'There's no point.'

'There's every point,' he said.

'I don't feel comfortable when the Document of Intent is so close to being signed.'

'It might be weeks. I'm in my father's good books for once. Bizarrely, thanks to you. The dancing and the lack of apology...'

'The trip around the islands,' Beatrice said. 'That was your suggestion. And from everything I heard at the festival you're rather popular. As well as that—'

'A week on a desert island, Beatrice,' he cut in, refusing to be diverted. 'The sand is red. I saw it the morning after we…' He stopped. 'We can get it all out of our systems and hopefully we'll be desperate to escape each other by the end of the week…'

Oh, Beatrice wouldn't be—that much she knew.

'So you're offering me a week of sex?'

He looked at her.

'But no getting closer? No pillow talk…? Of all the rules your parents have put on you, that is the cruellest.'

'Hey!'

Beatrice would not be silenced. 'No, I'm going to say this—'

'You hardly walk around baring your soul.'

'I *choose* not to,' Beatrice said. 'There's a big difference between being private and being forbidden from having friends. Even all these years on, I still think of Alicia, talk to her—' She halted.

'You still speak to her?' he asked. 'In your head?'

'A bit.'

'What would your friend tell you to do?'

She frowned. 'I would *not* be taking advice from Alicia on this,' Beatrice said. 'Her childhood crush was Dante Schininà, and believe me, he was feral. They used to swim in the river together,' she said, 'and then sneak into the cemetery. His mother ran the local brothel—'

'Whoa!' He halted her and then said sulkily, 'Why didn't I get the bad twin?'

Beatrice was saved from answering by the sound of footsteps approaching.

'Think about it,' he said. Then he looked over as the door was pushed open.

It was Jordan.

'There you are,' Jordan said.

Beatrice was simply relieved that Jordan hadn't found them locked in a clinch, or seen her looking dishevelled and mortified.

She would have if Julius hadn't been so restrained. Beatrice was the one without restraint where they were concerned.

'I assume you've heard about the puppies?' Julius said.

'Sir, I don't know what happened with the diary…'

'Beatrice has already apologised,' Julius said. 'I think we can leave it now. Beatrice thinks I possibly might have said I'd do the photoshoot, though I think she might not be remembering very well.'

'Well, Arabella has heard about the puppies…'

'I promised her one if she stopped getting her nanny to do her homework,' Julius explained to Beatrice, and politely he didn't look as she stood up as gracefully as she could.

Beatrice was too discreet to flash her knickers. She stood there, all neat, dusting away sawdust and straw, and hoped she looked suitably chastised for bringing puppies to his precious stables.

Actually, Beatrice was taken aback.

He was supposed to be safe.

Distant.

It wasn't her reputation…it was her heart she was trying to guard. But he already had it. Beatrice knew that now.

'Was he furious?' Jordan asked as they walked back.

'His horse was a bit startled.'

So too was she.

It was a long day, because after the excitement of the morning it was quiet.

All the news about the Prince was upbeat and positive, and it seemed the tide was turning in his favour. Actually, it had already turned—and she knew it. She rather thought the King might know it too. How could he not?

It was so quiet that it left her time to think—about the King crying by the lake, and the Queen pushing his hand away, and a family all grieving the death of a loved one.

And Julius.

Who offered her more than she'd dared even to hope for.
Fun. Adventure. Danger. Passion.

What would Alicia say?

A week on a desert island with the man of your dreams? No strings, just pure bliss?

Beatrice did not need to guess what she'd say.

Go. Have fun. Come on, Beatrice. Do it!

But then she'd fall even more deeply in love with him.

Yes, love.

Not a crush…nor a simple attraction.

She didn't know quite how to define it, but Beatrice was scarily certain that this was love.

It always had been.

From the day he'd breezed in.

Just as he did later that afternoon.

'Here,' he said as he walked into her office. 'All that sulking was for nothing.'

It was the gift he had mentioned. And he'd clearly not just sent Tobias out to grab something—unless Tobias was into gift-wrapping—because it was a small parcel, wrapped exquisitely in red and gold and tied with a beautiful gold silk cord.

'I don't sulk.' She glanced up. 'Well, perhaps a bit.'

She was almost scared to open it…almost wished he'd forgotten her rather than bought her something as lovely as this. And she hadn't even opened it yet!

'Beatrice, I know I have a poor track record, but even at my worst I usually do flowers, or Jordan does…'

'I know. I was just…' She shrugged. 'Sulking.' It sounded safer to admit that than say what was in her heart.

'I learnt from a sultan I knew many years ago not to say I liked anything. If I did, it was immediately wrapped and gifted to me. I almost came home with a cheetah once…'

She smiled. He'd made her smile again even before she'd undone the bow.

'So, I saw this, and I thought how lovely it was. I have no idea what it's worth—please don't pawn it or whatever…it could cause an international incident. Or it might just be a little knick-knack—though I doubt it. Anyway, it was the only way I could get a gift for you. Tobias wanted to log it on the register…'

'What did you tell him?'

'That I'd lost it.'

It was a tiny crystal peacock, with white opals and possibly diamonds in its feathers. Aside from the Prince standing by her desk, it was the most exquisite thing she had seen in her life.

She held it up to the window to let it catch the light, and he stood watching her smile.

'That one doesn't screech.'

'He's beautiful. But…' she shook her head '… I really can't…'

'Oh, I think you can.'

No, she really couldn't. Because then she'd add it to the birthday card he'd signed, which now sat on her dressing table. Another little Julius memento to keep.

'I don't want it.' She put the beautiful creature back into its beautiful box. 'I think it's better that you tell Tobias you found it.'

'Beatrice…'

'Thank you for the thought.'

'It's a gift.'

'Julius, Security do random checks on our bags!'

'They're not going to check *your* bag.'

'Actually, they very often do. And how would I explain that?' She looked at him. 'Or in a week or so, when I leave, how do I go through airport security with the Prince's jewels—?'

'You overthink things.'

'I do,' she agreed. 'That is what I do. I overthink and I

overthink, and the more I think about it, the more I don't want him.'

'I saw the way you looked at him—'

'I want something I can dump in the bin a few weeks from now, when this is all a distant memory—not some jewelled peacock glaring at me. So, no thank you to your romantic gesture.'

She knew it was an insult to reject a gift—especially here, especially from the heir to the throne.

'What do you want, Beatrice?'

'I've had what I wanted,' Beatrice told him. 'Our one night. Also, I have thought about it, and I thank you for the invitation, but I will say no to Regalsi.'

'I won't ask twice.'

'If you did the answer would be the same: a flat no. You wanted no strings; I delivered it.'

'Well, you do you, Beatrice,' he said angrily, picking up the gift and pocketing it. 'Blame me, if it helps. Tell yourself I used you, or whatever, but you know that's not true…'

He gave her such a look that even as she stared ahead she felt the burn of his glare.

'You know, perhaps *I* should itemise that night, too…'

Her throat was tight as he brought her pillow talk admissions into her office.

'You got it "over and done with". Got all you wanted.'

'I did.' Beatrice stared coolly back at him. 'Not the martinis, but—'

He didn't even bother to slam the door on his way out.

And his calm exit was a precursor, because for the remainder of the week he blanked her.

Which was incredibly different from being ignored, Beatrice found out.

He was polite, occasionally friendly, often busy— completely normal, in fact. However, Beatrice found out just how precious those glimpses of Julius she'd had before really had been.

The stage curtains had been drawn again, and she had been shut out.

There were no more glimpses, and he no longer chose to make her smile.

Beatrice found out exactly how it felt to be a temp in his household.

CHAPTER TWELVE

'NO ONE KNOWS when that day or hour will come—not even the angels in heaven, nor the Son...'

That line had always made Beatrice shiver in church.

Alicia had laughed at her gloom.

Her final day had dawned and she lay there, almost tempted to ring in sick, but knowing she wouldn't.

It wasn't waiting for Jordan's reference that kept her showing up each day.

It was seeing him.

She'd kissed a prince, and instead of turning into a frog he'd stayed a prince. He'd stayed exactly who he was.

It was Beatrice who had changed. She'd been changing since they met, coming into herself in the weeks she'd been at the palace.

And it was killing her to leave.

She got through the Friday morning meeting, and the mood was a little jubilant, even, as it concluded. The Prince's trip had gone well, there had been a whole week without drama since, and his appearance at the Flower Festival had been a hit.

And not a single apology had been made on the Prince's behalf in the three months she had been here.

His single transgression Beatrice would certainly not be mentioning, because of course it was also her own, so she smiled and accepted congratulations for the newly wholesome Prince Julius and the PR triumph she had brought about.

'So what's next for you?' Despina asked as Beatrice slipped on her jacket.

'I'm mid-interviews,' Beatrice said with a wavering hand. 'We'll see.'

'Well, if the whispers are true...' Despina smiled.

Beatrice gave nothing away, but, yes, there was an exceptionally exciting role for which she was applying. She would be needing a very glowing reference from Jordan, and there would be extensive security checks...

Julius was the reason she couldn't stay. It had never been about her past.

This was not love. She'd been told that by the man himself. And, after all, what would she know about that? But whatever it was—love or infatuation—it was enough that she had no choice but to leave.

She walked through the Great Hall and went to take the stairs, but then she paused, for there was a portrait of Julius. Only, it wasn't his drop-dead good looks that halted her in her tracks.

The King had stood here when she'd seen him. Staring up at his youngest son. She'd assumed it was a portrait of Claude—from the King's stance she'd assumed grief or anguish...

'Are you coming?' Despina called.

'Of course,' Beatrice said, and took the passageway that led towards Julius's residence. It was bright, with the sun refusing to admit it was the end of summer, denying it as it shone fiercely, dispersing the tiny puffs of white cloud drifting above the glittering ocean.

Bellanisiá was looking exceptionally beautiful this morning.

Despite her smiles, and her seemingly easy chat with a colleague, it was killing her to leave.

'Ooh...' Despina said, halting and looking down on the central courtyard.

'What?'

'I'm not sure…' She took out her phone. 'Maybe nothing, but it looks like Princess Jasmine's arriving.'

Beatrice frowned. Jasmine was often here, but she looked down and saw that she wore a silver robe and a diadem.

'She must have been summoned,' Despina told her.

'Because she missed the festival?'

'No.' Despina shook her head. 'This looks official.'

She was firing off texts and reading replies, and Beatrice now saw there were three men in robes walking at a pace across the courtyard.

'Queen's Teiria has left her residence too…'

There really was something happening.

'It must be something serious,' Despina said. 'A death, perhaps…'

'Or a wedding?' Beatrice croaked.

'No.' Despina shook her head. 'They wouldn't be calling the Princess in for that. Oh, my goodness—this is what happened when Prince Claude died. What if the King—?'

Beatrice turned and saw Julius, walking with Tobias beside him. Of course he blanked her. Well, he was hardly going to stop and fill her in.

His face was so grey. And, terrible person that she was, now that she'd seen he was okay Beatrice was rather hoping for a funeral instead of a wedding. But, for her sins, she knew it must be otherwise.

'Let's watch…' Despina said once they'd passed.

'I have to get back,' Beatrice said.

Beatrice wanted to be sick as she fled to the offices, only to find quiet chaos there. Jordan was opening a cupboard and taking a jacket out of a suit holder—clearly one she kept there for just this kind of day.

'I was in the loo,' Jordan said, changing her earrings and her shoes at the same time and almost falling over.

'What is it?' Beatrice asked, still guiltily hoping that Despina was right and she herself was wrong.

'The scribes have been summoned…and the priests and masters…' Jordan held on to the desk. 'The Document of Intent.'

Clearly not even Jordan had known.

'Now?' Beatrice checked.

'Tobias just called…' someone said. 'Prince Julius has asked for a closed room.'

'So, not right now?' Beatrice checked, because, oh, she wanted to be gone so badly. She wanted this to take place on Monday, or tomorrow, or at least a few hours from now…

Surely he could have done that for her? Just that? No dates, or dinners, or peacocks, or trips to Regalsi. Her only stipulation had been discretion.

She shouldn't have had to specify that she didn't want to be here when the announcement was made, should she?

'They'll be thrashing out dates and things,' Jordan said. 'I'd better go.' She gave Beatrice a little pat. 'Well done. Looks like he's changed his spots after all…'

To all intents and purposes…

Except he wasn't a leopard; he was a lovely panther, and that was that.

It was the most awful wait. She felt as if she was watching the Vatican for smoke as she looked out on the palace, but there was nothing.

Well, Princess Jasmine had left, and the Queen had gone to her private apartments, but still nothing…

For hours.

She went into her office, just to escape it all, and then finally Jordan returned.

Beatrice looked up as she knocked and came in. 'Some last day!' Jordan said, and her cheerful greeting sounded a touch forced.

'Is it done?' Beatrice asked. 'Has he signed?'

'Hmm…' She gave a little hand gesture. 'They're meeting again at seven.'

'Is that usual?'

'I remember Prince Claude dragged it out. It's all politics now.' Jordan shrugged. 'I've heard there's to be a formal announcement on Monday, but my guess is we'll know tonight.'

'I won't.'

'Stay, then.'

'Ooh, I don't think I'd make a good wedding planner…'

'True.' Jordan smiled, only it didn't quite meet her eyes. *Be subtle*, Beatrice reminded herself. 'Are you excited?'

'Very!' Jordan nodded.

'So, do the Queen and the Princess return for the signing?'

'No.' Jordan shook her head and went to the little window, looked out on Beatrice's dreary semi-basement view.

Beatrice was certain that Julius's very loyal PA was very, very upset and trying hard not to be.

'So they just have to be there for the announcement?' Beatrice asked. 'Only, Despina said—'

'What would Despina know?' Jordan snapped.

'I think she was worried something dreadful must have happened. Like with—' She halted, as everyone did rather than say Prince Claude's name.

'I guess…' Jordan had recovered. 'No, it was just…' She pulled away from the window. 'Times are changing, perhaps.'

Or the King was showing Julius his hand.

What had Julius told her about his father's latest turn of phrase 'progressing the monarchy'? Was he threatening Julius with the line of succession?

But Julius didn't object to a woman ruling. He was, Beatrice was completely sure, simply giving his sister the privacy she craved.

'I'm going up…' Jordan pushed out another smile.

'I might go and have something to eat.' Beatrice replied.

'Do,' Jordan said. 'Then I must take your computer and phone… Like I said…some last day!'

'Yes.'

Some last day.

The lid of her new cup leaked. Beatrice found that out when she dripped coffee down herself as she sat by the lake. Then she felt a sudden frantic panic, because there were just six little cygnets today.

She cast her eyes around for the lazy one…

She couldn't see him anywhere.

The worst ever last day.

'Beatrice.'

He said her name and she closed her eyes rather than look at him. She was sitting with a very cold coffee and just a few hours left on the clock, but she was determined to see it through.

'I thought we were ignoring each other.'

'Well, I'm expected to wish you farewell.'

'Farewell, sir.'

'How's the new cup?'

'Disappointing,' she said as he took a seat by her side. Then, 'You couldn't wait till I'd gone?'

'I asked earlier in the week for more time. I thought I had it.'

'Well, clearly you didn't ask forcefully enough.'

But Julius was kind. She knew that. He wouldn't put her through this if he had a choice.

'Beatrice, I was conceived in case my brother died. I'm not complaining. I'm hardly a lamb being led to the slaughter.'

'So you want this?'

'It's not about what I want. It's about duty. It's about what's best for the country. I'm crazy about you, Beatrice, and you know it. Hell, my doctor even wants to take blood to see why I'm losing weight.'

She frowned.

'I was fine with it all until a few weeks ago...*almost* fine,' he amended. 'And then they had to hire someone to fix my image. To fix me...' He gave her a black smile. 'Please listen. I can give you one week, and I will do everything in that week to make up for the years you've hidden yourself away.'

'I haven't hidden myself away.'

'You know you have. Please, just think about it. Now you're finished here...'

'I'm not going away with a man who's signed the Document of Intent—whatever the hell that even means.' She stared ahead and spoke calmly, but her words were final. 'Delay signing and then we'll speak.'

'That's not an option.'

'What could he possibly do to you?'

'The *"he"* you refer to is the King?'

'You hold all the cards,' Beatrice said. 'It's not as if he's got many other options. He's not going to change the line of succession.'

Jasmine couldn't even make a speech at a festival. She wasn't an option here.

'We're not having this conversation.'

'I'm right.'

'Beatrice, I have always known that I was to marry. With privilege—'

'Comes responsibility,' she cut in. 'Blah-blah-blah.' She stared at him. 'I've been passed up for better than you, Julius.'

'What are you talking about?'

'Him!' She pointed skywards. 'My mother chose Him over me.' She stared at the six little swans, all happily swimming with one missing. 'I lied. I found out who my mother is when I was nineteen. She was a nun at the convent…'

'A nun?'

'Well, not when I was conceived,' Beatrice said. 'She was pregnant when she entered the convent as a novice, and I was popped into that baby box without a second thought.'

'You don't know that—'

'I do. She told me herself. Well, in as many words. I went back when I was nineteen to find Alicia, to find out if my mother had left anything to identify herself or me, and I found out the truth then. Eventually. I was a little blonde version of Sister Catherine, so I was sent to Milan, and then Switzerland. I thought it was because I was so good at languages, but really it was to get me away.'

'They all knew?'

'No. Reverend Mother guessed when I was ten or so.' She looked at him. 'Sister Catherine taught me Latin, and she made me go and play outside when I asked if I could stay in at playtime.'

'No favourites?' he said, and she knew he recalled their conversation.

'Not even her daughter. Believe me, she wasn't sneaking cuddles. She abandoned me as a baby and then sent me away at eleven. But she gave me away every day in between. I was screaming with nightmares, dreaming I was running through the fair at night, and all that time she was only a step away. So I know about duty, and what it means to protect a secret.'

He closed his eyes.

'I'm not asking for marriage,' she told him. 'I know that's impossible. But I won't sneak into your suite via a tunnel, nor be hidden away on an island or ignored in plain sight.'

'What, then?'

'I don't know,' Beatrice admitted. 'I don't think it even

matters what I say. You'll keep on protecting the Princess, shielding her, and to hell with everyone else.'

'My sister needs to live a quiet life,' he admitted. 'We always agreed that if anything happened to my brother I would step in.'

'And you have stepped in,' she said. 'And you have stepped up. Just not when it comes to me.' She stared at him then, and still did not raise her voice. She would not cry, but she would tell him a truth. 'Do you know, I really think it is love?' Beatrice said. 'Because it hurts just as much.'

'Don't even compare—'

'Yes,' Beatrice said, 'I do compare it. I'm a tricky secret. Well, you don't have to worry any more. Go and do your duty, Prince Julius. To your country and to the people you love…'

'He's King…'

'And clearly you're not.'

It was mean, and it was cold, but to hell with it all.

'You can be so—'

'Yes, I can,' she cut in. 'That's why you hired me.'

'No,' he said, 'it isn't.'

Julius looked at her in her perpetual grey and thought of the fresh air she had breezed into his life, and how the best bit of his day was making Beatrice smile.

He could see her eyes flashing tears, but still she would not cry, and he hated it that she couldn't.

Wouldn't.

He had left Jasmine sobbing, his mother weeping and reminding him of the promise made, and yet Beatrice's pinched, angry face and her refusal to bring it all to the table hollowed him.

'You don't know the half of it, Beatrice.'

'Perhaps not,' she said.

He knew he could never discuss the hold his father had on him—not to a temporary employee, nor to a lover.

'Then again,' Beatrice said, 'you'll never know even the half of me.'

He saw she was done.

'Good luck.' She gave him a smile as she tipped her cold coffee onto the ground. 'I might see you at my leaving party.'

'You won't.'

He stood, and therefore so did she.

'Sir,' she said.

And for all the world, if anyone were watching, they would think he was thanking her for a job well done.

All the passion only he saw and felt was just for him, he knew, and he watched her walk off as if nothing had occurred. She even waved to Tobias as she passed by.

Ever polite, Tobias halted, then he smiled and shook her hand, and wished her well before coming over to him.

'Sir,' he said, 'the Queen has requested lunch, and Princess Jasmine has asked that you call her urgently—'

'Tobias,' he cut in, 'they'll have to wait.'

CHAPTER THIRTEEN

Duty first.

Yes, he might have coloured outside the lines sometimes, but Julius loved his country. And now, on this most important of days, he'd left it behind.

Julius was approaching Trebordi from the sky.

Three jagged cliffs fell away to the ocean, so sharply it was as if they sliced like a hot knife through butter. Certainly, their slicing was a lot neater than Beatrice with a cake knife!

It was a beautiful, brutal place. Even in summer the wind meant a rather careful approach for the helicopter was required.

He saw the convent as they swept past it, and the hilly walk from there to the village. He saw the church, the cemetery, and he glimpsed a little of the life she had lived. This woman he might never see again.

The chopper came down on a dark flat area cut out from the trees—a scar on the very beautiful landscape.

'I don't know how long I'll be,' he said to Tobias, and took off his headphones.

'Sir.'

He felt the gravel crunch beneath his feet. This was the place where Beatrice Festa had been told she was born. He walked around, kicking a few stones. In truth, he didn't know what he was doing there...knew simply that he needed to think.

He walked through the village, garnering a few looks, but the people soon went back to their coffees—and he really didn't care.

The church was gorgeous, with rice and confetti between

the stones outside. There must have been a wedding recently, but apart from that there was nothing. No answers here.

He could hardly ask the lady passing with her dog for directions to the local brothel! Or could he? For that was where Dante's mother had worked, he remembered.

Julius thought of how cross Beatrice had been with her little wild friend who'd swum in the river and roamed the cemetery, so he wandered there, opening the latch, grateful for the shade and the soft silence.

He saw all the family plots, including the Schininàs, but there were no Festas, of course.

No wonder she had been so jealous of those earrings… those little pieces of gold her friend's mother had left.

But her mother must have been terrified, even if Beatrice was convinced she had felt nothing.

Then a spray of frangipani caught his eye. Placed on a single grave, away from the others. No, not a spray, but a wedding bouquet, the waxy flowers yellowing at the edges.

Schininà.

He looked at the dates and the inscription and wondered if this was Dante's mother. Carmella had been buried away from the rest of her family, it would seem.

He moved the bouquet, its scent still lingering as he lifted it, and saw the names on the little tag that held the bouquet together.

Dante and Alicia

Beatrice had been here just a couple of weeks ago.
A breath away from finding her friend.
'Best left,' Beatrice had said.
Had she been protecting her mother by not asking

around? Surely she could have found her friend if she really cared? It had taken him mere minutes…

Instead Beatrice had changed her name, cut herself off from the one person she had ever loved…

Taylor… Tailor…

He thought back to his hated Latin. *I cut.*

Her new name was no accident.

He replaced the bouquet and walked up to the convent. He looked at the little school attached to it, and could not fathom cutting himself off from his sister or brother.

They'd argued, they'd rowed, but he would kill for them…

Marry for them?

Julius soon found what he was looking for—an iron door in the wall, beneath it an inscription with the name of its benefactor.

The baby door.

At home the convent had a wheel, but here it was a door.

He pulled it open and peered inside, and he was certain that Beatrice must have done the same.

A part of him wished there had been time to tell her more of what he knew from his visits to Di Dio Bellanisiá; that there he had met families and heard of their pain and endless guilt…

'*Signor?*'

He turned and looked down at a nun.

'It's not a toy,' she scolded.

'*Scusi,*' Julius said.

And he understood now why they had moved her to Milan. Because a brown-eyed Beatrice was looking up at him. He saw a little pointed nose and tight lips, a slight figure, so similar, and yet… She was like a waxwork, or a dead fish lying on the deck of a boat, with nothing behind her velvet brown eyes.

Nothing of passion and terror and shame. None of the

things that made you question yourself at times. That caused you to doubt and ponder and consider or regret.

'The bell on the door rings and interrupts us. Always tourists!' She sneered a little. 'Please, show some respect.'

'Of course. It's a beautiful convent.' He looked up at the stunning Sicilian Baroque-style building, but she gave nothing back. 'Is it seventeenth century?' he asked.

'There are tours on the first Friday of the month.'

'I was just thinking...'

Julius peered at the black iron. Julius was good at small talk—well, unless any sunburned shoulders were around. He could usually engage anyone. But Sister Catherine was not here to talk.

'How lucky—' he began.

'We take care of the babies.'

'No, no.' He halted her tersely. 'I meant, how lucky I am.'

She looked at his smart clothes. 'You clearly have a privileged life, *signor*,' she said, and pointed to the donation box above the baby door.

This woman rejected conversation.

Beatrice deflected.

This woman rejected the chance to tell a tourist a little about the beautiful building. She rejected that little moment of connection. She rejected it coldly, and had done the same to her daughter in every minute of her childhood.

But to find out that this was your mother...?

No wonder Beatrice hadn't been able to walk down that hill, or pick up the phone. Even he felt the cold snub of this nun.

He wanted to say something cutting. He wanted to call her out so he could savour the moment, relish it later, let her know the pain she had caused.

He chose not to, for it was not his place.

Furthermore, he doubted this woman would care.

'Yes, Sister,' he said. 'I am privileged indeed.'

He was loved by someone who, thanks to this woman, barely dared to love anyone.

'Good afternoon,' he said, and although he wanted to add *Sister Catherine*—because he wanted to see her give that little jolt as she realised he knew her name—he stopped himself.

That was not the person he wanted to be.

He turned and left.

Julius stood on the headland and looked out to sea. He wished he could speak to his brother.

And then he paused.

No one could make this choice for him.

So he watched as the woman closed up the baby door, as she had done some twenty-nine years ago, and walked away without so much as a glance.

No, he didn't need his brother, nor his advice.

And he knew, as he had told Beatrice so recently, that with privilege came responsibility. Only there was no blah-blah-blah to it…

He smiled.

His choice was already made.

CHAPTER FOURTEEN

'ANY NEWS?' Beatrice asked when Jordan called her to come up.

'No. Julius is off somewhere with Tobias. He'll be back for the signing.' Jordan was, as always, practical. 'It's just security stuff I want you for. I need your computer.'

'Oh…' Beatrice nodded. 'Of course.'

'And your phone, plus lanyard, ID…'

'Sure.'

Beatrice took out all the items and stared at the phone for a very long moment.

She hated her parting shot to him.

Hated that she'd had to get in first…strike first.

For all her bravado, they had slept together once and never been on a date… He was hardly going to turn his back on duty or throw his sister under the bus for that.

Yet he had made her smile, had made her feel so happy and wanted. And as much as he'd been able to, he had offered her more than one night.

Could she fire off a quick text to him? What would she say? Sorry? Good luck? And what for?

Her phone would be checked—and anyway, in the grand scheme of a kingdom, what did feelings even matter?

'Beatrice!' Jordan called.

The team was gathering, and she hadn't expected anyone to come. It was a very rushed leaving do, given the events of the day, and it touched her very much the effort Jordan had gone to.

'Unfortunately Prince Julius can't be here, or Tobias, or…'

It was quite a low turn-out, Beatrice saw, but there was some good news at least.

'I was annoyed you were leaving,' Jordan continued, 'so you were only going to get a temp's gift. But Julius—*Prince Julius*,' she corrected, 'said I was being petty.'

Beatrice smiled and opened the velvet box. Clearly Jordan had chosen the gift, because it was a lovely gold bracelet.

Jordan helped her put it on her wrist. Beatrice knew there were no antihistamines in her bag, but she must have turned into a nicer person—because she didn't tell them she was allergic to gold, just smiled and said thank you.

There were also two cards.

'I might open these later,' Beatrice said, but immediately gave in and started slicing them open.

She smiled at all the lovely messages, and there was Jordan's private phone number.

'Keep in touch,' Jordan said.

'I'd love to.'

Tobias had signed it too, and wished her well, and she found she was looking forward to hearing about his baby boy.

Wow, she was almost crying—not that Beatrice showed it.

And then she opened the official card.

It was very bland, but then Julius chose to be bland when he did not want others to know his feelings. It was cream, with his insignia on it, and inside there was a typed message thanking her for her service. And his signature.

She checked the back of the card.

Surely a teeny little smile or something…?

She peered into the envelope.

'There's no money in there,' Jordan said, smiling.

'Pity!' she quipped.

And that was it.

'You'll need this for the shuttle bus,' Jordan said, as she

handed her a temporary pass after everyone had wandered off. 'And I'm really sorry to have to do this but—'

'It's fine.'

Jordan went through her bag, and it was perhaps just as well she'd known she would, or she might have pinched the top of his whisky decanter, or something equally dreadful.

There was no little peacock lurking in there, either.

'It's been a pleasure, Beatrice,' Jordan told her.

'It's been interesting!' Beatrice smiled. 'Wish the Prince well for me.'

That was all she could do.

Followed by a hug and a wave as she walked away.

Really, she'd barely been there any time at all, and yet it hurt so much to leave.

More than it ever had to leave anywhere.

Even when she had left the convent at eleven it had only been one person she'd wept for.

Now it was for love, and people, and her little home on the marina, and lakes and swans...

But there would be no final lingering there—no frantic check for the lost cygnet. Because a flash of silver caught her eye. Jasmine was coming out of the rose garden and walking towards the lake.

Beatrice changed direction and walked down the tree-lined avenue, but she kept wanting to turn and look at this woman who wanted a quiet life. And who could blame her?

Not Beatrice.

Who could blame Julius for protecting someone he loved and honouring a promise?

Clearly, you're not, she had sneered at him when he had spoken of the King.

What a horrible woman she was. And what a wonderful king he would be.

She had just wanted some time. And his father wanted a wedding *now*.

His father… Who had stood there weeping…

Perhaps he thought a wedding might somehow bring back his son, rectify things… Might pull Julius into line.

Good luck, she thought. Because even at their first meeting—before all of this—Beatrice had known he was his own man. No prodigal son returning with his head down was he… Julius had returned ready for duty.

The King might be threatening the line of succession—Beatrice could see that clearly now—but it made no sense. He loved his son. That much she could also see. She had seen it in the photos she had looked at, and in the way he had stood there staring at his portrait.

He loved Julius.

How could he not?

And then it dawned on her.

The King was trying to soothe the fretful Queen, who had lost one child and was terrified of losing another.

Oh, Julius.

She was going to be nicer and kinder, Beatrice vowed. No more sex with men who didn't want anything more than that from her.

Only, that wasn't fair.

How she hated it that it had ended like this.

She hated it so much that she couldn't let it.

She was like a ship on its final voyage. A ship that didn't quite know how to bring itself into port.

And even as she made the vow it was tested. Because she'd caught a glimpse of those secret gates to the tunnel beyond and she couldn't help but peek. One look at his secret tunnel, she decided, and wrenched open the heavy door.

It wasn't a velvet tunnel after all.

It was awful bricks and a fluorescent light that flicked on automatically.

And an intercom.

Beatrice buzzed because it was there and because she couldn't help herself.

But she got no response.

So she buzzed again, and again, and again.

He's out, she reminded herself… *Go home, Beatrice.*

But she'd walked away from Alicia, and she could not have the only two relationships in the world she cared about end on such terrible terms.

Even if he told her what she could do with her apology at least she would have made it. Told him how much better he had made her world.

So she buzzed again.

And she would keep buzzing…

Or maybe she should write a note—just a quick *sorry* and fling it under the door. But the door was awfully heavy and there were no gaps she could see.

Would he even come down here?

Stop overthinking, Beatrice thought, and took out her journal.

But then she heard the crackle of the intercom and braced herself for a curious servant—or perhaps Jordan dealt with this sort of thing… Or did Tobias deal with all those women in ball gowns?

'What?' Julius's voice was clipped and angry and she didn't care.

'It's Beatrice.'

'What do you want, Beatrice?'

'I don't know…the chance to apologise.'

He was silent.

'You will be a brilliant king and… Can I come up?'

There was a long silence, and just when she was sure he would never reply, suddenly the internal door clicked.

Beatrice pushed it open and peered in.

There was still no velvet, just more lights and brick walls, and now she walked where angels would never dare: beneath the palace to his lair.

She should be ashamed, really, but she found she was elated instead at having a second chance for a better goodbye…

Julius released the door and inhaled. He did not need this now. Not now, when he needed every part of his brain focussed.

But the best-laid plans… Beatrice certainly knew how to lay them to rest! The whole country was under her five-foot-two threat!

So he used the ten or so minutes her walk would take to prepare himself for her arrival, and then gave himself a stern talking-to in the mirror.

Do not engage.

He nodded to himself.

Politely ask her to wait.

This decision was his alone. By far too much to land on Beatrice. She must have no clue until it was done.

But then came a knock at his very private door, and in came his moody former liaison aide, blinking like a mole coming up onto a lawn.

'Gosh!' she said, and didn't try to hide the effect he had on her. 'Look at you!'

He wore full dress uniform, but she was up close this time and could really admire the deep grey and Prussian blue belted coat and boots.

'You're going out?' she asked.

'Clearly. I have a meeting. I need to leave in a couple of moments,' he snapped. 'So be fast.'

'I apologise. I was incredibly mean before—'

'What's new?'

'I would like that week on Regalsi, if it's still available. Even a couple of days if that's all you can manage.'

'You're so fickle.'

'Not usually,' Beatrice said. 'But, yes, sometimes I am.'

'What do you want to do with our time there?'

'Have fun.'

'I thought "fun" was what you wanted the night we made love.'

'We had sex, Julius,' she corrected him, using his own words, 'and you're right. I'm dreadful at fun. I don't want to be, though. I'd like some time on Regalsi with you and hopefully to leave on better terms.'

'We'll talk in a bit.'

She swallowed. 'Fine…' Deflated, she watched him check his reflection. 'I thought I'd like a one-night stand…' she said.

'You didn't like it?'

'I liked it too much,' she said, smiling, 'and then I had to go and spoil it all by wanting more.'

'More?' he checked.

'I've never done this before. I don't tend to get involved…' he wasn't making this easy '…with anyone.'

'Why?'

'Don't you have to go…?'

'Why don't you get involved with anyone?'

'I'm terrified they might not like me back.' She saw he was watching her in the mirror. 'And I'm scared that I'm cold and unfeeling like my mother.'

'You're not like her.'

'You don't know that.'

'Beatrice, there are seven swans a-swimming tonight…'

'Are there? I couldn't go over to check… Jasmine was there…' She swallowed. 'I understand that you have to protect her.'

'We can't discuss that,' Julius said.

'No.' She nodded. 'We're only about fun!' She wanted to be fun, and so she moved to wrap her arms around his neck. 'Can you bring this uniform to Regalsi?'

'Beatrice,' he said firmly, uncoiling her arms, 'I do have to go. However, you *are* very nice,' he told her. 'And I like sitting on the bench with you.'

'Thank you.'

'Believe it or not, you're getting off lightly. I'm sure you'd hate being Queen Consort.'

'I'll have you know I'd be brilliant.'

'And at being a hetaera?'

'Sitting at your knee and gazing up at you?' She shook her head. 'No, thanks. But I will be your lover for the next few nights.'

'Really?'

'Yes.'

'And then walk away?'

'Absolutely!'

He smiled. 'Did you like your leaving present?'

She held up her wrist. 'It was very thoughtless of you; I'll be covered in welts soon.' She looked at her wrist. 'But thank you. I do like it—very much.'

'No welts,' he told her. 'We only do the good stuff here. It's nickel you're allergic to.'

'Hmm…'

'So doubting,' he said. 'I really do have to go. But there's some food coming up. It will be in the butler's kitchen. Help yourself. He'll buzz. Wait till he's gone before you collect it. Don't answer any calls.'

'I know.'

'I mean it.'

'Yes.' She watched him go. 'Good luck.'

'You don't mean that,' he said.

'I do. You have to protect the people you love, and I get that.'

'You do?'

'Yes, believe it or not, I actually do. I hope you get a wonderful wife.'

'I hope so too. But there's no luck required if you're adequately prepared.' He looked at her for a long moment. 'Thank you for going against all your principles and coming in through the tunnel.'

He had to go—he mustn't keep the King waiting. Especially tonight! However, he looked at Beatrice one last time. She was still pretending to be fun, while sitting glumly on the bed.

'Hey, I found out something,' he told her.

'What?'

'I looked up that guy—the feral one, Dante Schininà. He's done well for himself.'

'Please don't.'

'Okay,' he said. 'Anyway, I really have to go.'

'You really found Dante?'

'I found out he owns a hotel in Ortigia, Sicily.' He gave her a smile. 'I'm going to be a while.'

'I know you are.' She watched him put on his cap. 'Julius, can I say one thing? Not as me, but as the person you hired?'

'You can't come to the meeting with me.'

'Of course not.' She took a breath, because she knew there were things he could not tell her—she very much understood that now. She looked at him, and knew he did not need her going for the jugular, as she usually did. 'Actually, I'll just say it being me.'

'Very well.'

'I don't have a family, but you do…'

He gave a small mirthless laugh.

'Your father is grieving…'

'Yes—grieving the fact it wasn't me that died.' He gave

her a look that told her he didn't have time for this. 'Beatrice, I have to go.'

'Julius, that book Jordan lent you…'

He picked up his sword and sheathed it in the scabbard on his left-hand side. He was clearly not going to make small talk now.

'Who does a king talk to?' Beatrice asked.

'Not his son, that's for sure.' He gave her a grim smile. 'What happened to Fun Beatrice?'

He was right; she was incapable of being bubbly for even five minutes. 'Good luck,' she said.

She didn't mean it.

Hopefully they'd choose him a horrible wife…

She was a dreadful person.

She walked out onto the terrace and breathed in the fragrant air.

She knew the slippery slope she was on.

A holiday—a week with him in paradise.

And then he'd head off and marry, because he had to, and he'd have dark-eyed babies, and he'd love them, and Beatrice knew she would have to watch from afar.

She knew she couldn't be kept at a distance all over again.

And so she decided to be happy.

Tonight.

She went into the shower and looked at her hair, which was straggly. She stripped off and stood under the lovely strong jets.

She was heartbroken, but she was living. She was in love with someone who didn't do all that, but she would have her week with him and that would be that.

Yes.

No.

Yes!

The buzzer rang and she waited for the butler to leave

before she padded out into the kitchen. It wasn't food. It was four Birthday Girl Martinis. She smiled that he could be so thoughtful. There were chocolates too, and another present. A new coffee cup from the palace souvenir shop.

Wrapped in a towel, she sat on a very smart chair and found out that he was right. Alicia had always been impossible to find online, but it took two minutes for her to find Dante. Indeed, that grubby little boy her friend had adored was now the owner of an extremely luxurious hotel in Ortigia—a very beautiful part of Sicily. Dante had done very well for himself.

It took two of the very sweet martinis before she could further look up the hotel in Ortigia and find out what she could about the owner. And then the world stopped spinning as she saw her friend smiling back at her.

Alicia and Dante.

She had missed their wedding in Trebordi by a few days…

Tears spilled from her eyes. Because had she dared to walk up that hill then she'd have heard the gossip and found Alicia…

Julius met Jordan in the Great Hall.

'I believe the King and Queen are ready to receive you, sir.'

'Thank you.' He nodded.

'Jordan, can I speak with you afterwards?'

'Of course, sir.'

It was a very long walk to the throne room, past the portraits. He paused at a couple, because amongst the dour faces were a few eyes that smiled, and it was nice to have a few rebels to relate to. And there was Bonny Prince Julius—smiling in his tights and curls…

He'd always felt burdened by his history, the traditions,

the faces that stared down from the walls, some oddly familiar in their similarity to his own.

Imagine having no one.

Imagine growing up without a thread of identity.

And then finding out the one thread you had was poison...

As always, his thoughts went back to the woman who had made it through this world for the most part alone. Finding out what her mother had done, knowing that the pain he was causing her might compare to that, had stunned him.

And that was when he had known it was love.

A very inconvenient love, as far as the palace was concerned.

An impossible love, but one worth fighting for.

And that meant being prepared to lose—possibly to hurt others, to inconvenience many. But he would do what he could because... He could not justify it logically, for it went against everything he had been taught, but Julius knew he was right.

If not, the King would be forced to choose.

'Your Majesties,' Julius greeted his parents. 'Could I ask for a closed room?'

'No,' his father said. 'There have already been too many delays, too many negotiations. It's time to proceed.'

'Then I must formally request my titles be put into abeyance.'

'Wait—' the King instructed the scribe, and Julius watched Phillipe's eyes bulge.

'No,' Julius said, 'this is a formal request. Please note it.' He looked at the chief scribe. 'And then we shall either proceed with all present or in a closed room.'

'Proceed,' the King said, challenging him to continue with all present.

'Very well. I will not be signing the Document of Intent.

I will choose my own partner, when and if I am ready, and when and if they agree.'

'"They"?' his father checked. 'Are you gay?'

'I could be.'

'Julius!' his mother exclaimed. 'Enough!'

He looked to his mother and could hear the frantic plea in her rather too high voice.

'I request a closed room,' she said.

It took for ever to clear it.

'You promised...' the King began.

'Yes,' Julius said, 'I did. But we are all older now, and your daughter is stronger than you allow for. I have spoken at length with Princess Jasmine and she is prepared to take over my duties. I, of course, have offered her my full support.'

'No. She can't do it,' said his father.

'I disagree. She will be wise and gentle. As well as that, she has a husband who, although he would prefer to stay out of the spotlight, will stand by her side when he has to. And I will stand by the other. Anyway, we've spoken. It's done.' He looked at his father. 'You wanted Claude to be your heir. We all did. But he's gone. You have a son willing to take his place—'

'With conditions.'

'With one condition,' Julius corrected. 'And if you cannot agree to that, then you have and a daughter who, though she would prefer to quietly raise her family, is prepared to step up for what is right. But you are King. You make the rules. For now,' he ominously added.

'Respect...' his father warned.

'Of course. But don't raise your children to be rulers and then expect them to sit meekly by while you dictate their futures. You have heirs—a prince and a princess. In the blink of an eye we could all be ruled by Arabella, who would be a very strong queen. Think on that when you make your decision.'

'You always have to get your way…'

'Perhaps you taught me too well.'

Julius walked over to his father, who did not flinch, and neither did he expect him to.

'Claude, like you, was born to be King,' Julius said. 'And you made sure he was ready for all that lay ahead. Jasmine never wanted it, and you made sure she never had to shoulder that burden. So you had your spare…' He looked at his father. 'A natural leader.'

'Arrogant.'

'Like father, like son.' He stared at the King. 'You should know better than to try to bring me to heel.' He looked right at his father, 'So it's up to you to choose what is best for your country and for your family. And may I say you have two excellent choices. Some rulers have none.'

'You dare walk out on your King!'

He dared. But then he heard his mother's urgent plea. 'Cenzo…'

She called the King by his given name and Julius stilled.

'Please…' she begged her husband. 'Stop this from happening.'

'Jasmine needs a quiet life,' his father asserted.

Julius turned, and he saw then the strain his father was under, how he had changed so much in a year that suddenly Julius didn't recognise him. Outwardly, he was the same—grumpy and stern—but they had smiled together before. Laughed, even.

Beatrice was right. Who did his father have to confide in? For his mother was still crumbling under the weight of grief—that much Julius could see.

'She couldn't even manage the Flower Festival!' the King shouted.

'Then why the hell would you put this on her?' Julius stared at his father. 'Do it if you must, but it's on you.' Julius turned to his mother. 'And on you too. You push and you push for this wedding to take the pressure off Jasmine, and yet you burden her with your doubt. But she is strong. You know she doesn't want this, but she is standing by me and she supports my decision. Talk to your husband.'

'Julius…'

He was done. 'I'm taking tonight off…perhaps the next fifty years—you decide. I have an important date to keep.' He looked at his father. 'You can talk to me about your grief any time, but don't ever try to bully me with it.'

He turned and walked out, and there stood Jasmine, with her husband who loved her; and he had never felt more of a bastard than now, as he saw her standing there.

Except she wasn't crying, and he had not lied. She was so much stronger now.

'You told them?' she asked.

He heard the quaver in her voice, but she smiled.

'I did.'

'Well done.'

Julius had not known he could produce tears. Not even when his brother had died had he produced them. He had sat quietly, silently, as Tobias had informed him of the awful news. But his eyes stung now.

'I went back on my word…' he said.

'No.' Jasmine shook her head. 'What if the woman you fall in love with can't have children? The threat will always be there for me, and now it's being dealt with. I have my husband, and I have my daughter.' She looked at him. 'And I have a brother who stands up for what is right.'

She looked up as her mother came out.

'Jasmine…'

'I can't stay, Mama,' Jasmine said. 'Arabella is waiting to tell me about puppy school.'

'Julius,' his father said, 'come back inside. We have a closed room. We can properly discuss—'

'I've been trying to do that for a year.'

Beatrice was right; his father was grieving. How could Beatrice, a woman who didn't have any family of her own, know more about families than someone who did?

Perhaps you did have to step back to see what was right before your eyes?

'I really can't,' Julius said. 'I have plans. I have to get home.'

The terrace looked over the lake. The night air was just a little cool and Beatrice stood there, still wrapped in a towel, unable to take in all that had occurred.

She heard the door open behind her and turned to see that it was Julius. She quickly wiped her cheeks with her hands.

'Thank you for the martinis.'

'Did you like them?'

'A bit sickly, if I'm honest,'

Beatrice didn't want to hear what had happened with his father, nor bear to hear about his future bride. There was something she had to tell him. Two things!

'I looked up that hotel and it is Dante's.'

'You mean, I was right?' Julius said as he tossed his cap onto a table and unclipped all the straps and belts of his uniform and removed the sword.

'You were. And while I was looking up the hotel I saw a wedding photo. It turns out he and Alicia got married. I called her.'

'How did that go?' he asked, oh-so-casually, and yet he could feel his heart thumping as he unbuttoned his jacket, and he understood now her hesitation and her terror.

Had she been dismissed…let down…forgotten…?

'When I returned to Trebordi at nineteen, Alicia had already gone to Milan to look for me. She struggled with her reading and writing and got nowhere…recently she approached Dante to help her and they hired people to search…'

'You're a missing person?'

'Sort of.' She nodded. 'Well, almost…' She took out her

phone. 'They thought they might have found me once. A detective sent Alicia this.'

She handed him the phone she was holding and he looked at the photo that Alicia had just sent. It was of Beatrice in her straw hat, with huge dark glasses on.

'That was on my birthday a few weeks ago,' Beatrice explained. 'They had a detective watching the convent. He had just given them the details of the hire car I used that day when I called…' She was still shaky. 'I didn't have much luck getting through, at first, saying I was an old friend, but then I called back—rather like Jordan does when she's making a reservation for you.'

'Did it work?'

'They put me through to Dante. He was cross with me at first, but then Alicia came to the phone. It was difficult for five minutes—like agony. Alicia was hurt that I'd changed my name. Very hurt.'

'She understood why when you explained, though?'

'We got past that…' Beatrice evaded answering directly. 'It was like we were children again. I mean, we just fell back into our friendship; she's still the Alicia I knew and—'

'You didn't tell her about your mother?'

'I didn't have to. She forgave me. She understood I was hurt and upset.' Beatrice could see his eyes were trying to reach hers and she gave in and met them. 'No, I didn't tell her. I don't think it's a conversation to be had over the phone. It's…'

'Delicate?'

She nodded, knowing and also admitting she had dared to open the door and had shown him the vulnerable, fragile part of her that she guarded so fiercely.

'So you have your twin back?'

'I do.'

'I'm so happy for you,' he told her. 'When will you see her? After Regalsi?'

'About that…'

She was so shy, like a tiny wild bird, and yet she came to him as though she were tame.

'I've been thinking about Regalsi…'

'Have you?'

'I've misjudged things…' She fixed him with her eyes. 'I want a year.'

'Sorry?'

'I want a year without your wedding hanging over us.'

'So what happened to a few days of fun? A week?'

'Well, I've decided that I'd like to have a lot of fun in what's left of my twenties. I'd like to get to thirty and then…' She looked at him. 'I'll be discreet, but I'm not hiding, and I won't be a secret.'

'Your twin's been whispering in your ear.'

Beatrice smiled a new smile. 'Actually, I did most of the talking…'

Gosh, to share her heart with someone who knew her, who cared, must have been so precious, he thought.

'She agrees with you. She thinks I should have fun, let go, loosen up…'

'It's not you, though.'

'No.'

'And even a year's not going to work, is it?'

'No.'

Now she was starting to cry, and he couldn't bear it.

'But I want to try…'

'Will you marry me?'

Her heart stopped. 'You can't marry me…'

'Actually, I just put all my titles into abeyance. I can do whatever the hell I want.'

'Julius!' She felt a deep-seated panic and moved to stand up, but he stopped her. 'What about Jasmine—?'

'She'll be fine. It might not come to it, but I have told my father…' He took a breath. 'You're right. I think my mother is crazy with grief. But whatever happens I'm going to marry the woman I love—if she will have me.'

'You love me?'

'I'm lovesick. Tobias told me so.'

'You've told Tobias? When?'

'This afternoon.'

'And Jordan?'

'Just now.'

'Before you told me?'

'Well, if you turn me down, they're going to need to know why I'm crying at my desk, clutching a jewelled peacock…'

He made her smile, as always. He chose to make her smile as he dealt with the scary things.

'Julius! You can't turn your back on duty.'

'My first duty is to you,' he told her. 'I mean it.'

She thought he had never looked more serious.

'They're passing up a brilliant king, but that's on them. I'm not turning my back, and I will be a better king with you by my side. That's it. So, do I have to ask again? I don't know how this romantic stuff works… Do you want to marry me?'

Then he put a hand over her mouth.

'Before you respond, you should know that there is still a very good chance you would be Queen Consort. Would you want to be?'

He removed his hand.

'I want whatever makes us work.'

'I think we can handle it either way.'

'I would love to marry you, Julius.'

'Good,' he said. 'What else? Do we go and sign something…?'

'No.' She smiled. 'That's it. We have a verbal agreement. Well, there is one more thing… You have to return my peacock…'

'No, he's mine now. And he will sit on my desk. Don't ever say no to me unless you mean it. Or yes…'

'Oh, I mean it. Yes!'

He kissed her with heartfelt emotion, and she kissed him back with the same. Then he removed the towel she'd stopped clutching with ease, and discarded it, and she wrapped her arms around his neck and breathed in his love.

She closed her eyes but could not stop the tears falling. 'I'm happy…' she said.

'I know…'

He was everything she hadn't known she wanted, and just impossible not to completely love…

'Take my boots off,' he told her.

'I can't.'

She couldn't remove herself from him, or stop kissing him.

'Stay there, then…'

He told her that his military wear wasn't designed for easy access, but she didn't care. She was kissing his neck, and his ear, and pressing herself into him.

She hadn't known that she could love so very much. Every part of her, even her heart, felt as if it were opening, and she was wet and ready as he slid into her.

'Oh…' He closed his eyes and told her how good she felt.

'And you…'

He made her unashamed. He lay back and watched her and Beatrice thought she might die with the pleasure that was building—and this time she wasn't fighting it.

All her reservations were left at the door, and she was relaxed as he played with her breasts and then held her hips as he thrust into her, and even as she closed her eyes she knew he was watching her climax.

It shuddered through her, and she felt the swell and rush of him inside her. She was giddy with deep pleasure, and so breathless…looking down at herself, and him, and watching the last beats of their union.

'I love you so much,' she told him.

'I know.'

There was a buzzer pinging over the door. 'That's the serious one,' he told her. 'The King-is-dead one.'

'Should you answer it?'

'No.'

'So we just hide here till they decide?'

'We're not hiding,' he told her. 'Tonight, at least, we're just Julius and Beatrice. We have at least one night of freedom—possibly many more. But for now no rules or protocols apply. So, what do you want to do?'

'I didn't come with a wardrobe…'

'Jordan's sorting that out for you. We can go out or stay in—you choose.'

'Are we escaping by the tunnel?'

'No. I told you—we're not hiding. It can be like a first date.'

'It actually is my first date,' Beatrice said as she looked at him. 'And I don't know what I want to do.'

'Go and have a shower, then get off to the hetaera's dressing room…' He nudged her with his head. 'You can play dress-up.'

It was a very quick shower, and she came out dripping.

'Put on a towel,' he told her. 'Jordan's waiting.'

'Oh, my God!'

'What? Would you rather wear your grey dress again?'

'No.'

She went through a door and down a rather long corridor and into the hetaera's dressing room. And finally she found velvet. Deep red velvet walls and everything wicked—except for Jordan, who smiled.

'I'm so happy…'

'And me.' Beatrice grinned and gave his very loyal PA a hug. 'I don't know what to wear. What do you wear for your first ever date? I don't know where he's taking me.'

'I do.'

And apparently it required a black dress that scooped a little low at the front and far too low at the back, black stockings, and Cuban-heeled dance shoes.

Jordan put loads of liquid black eyeliner on her as Beatrice's hand was shaking too much.

'Is red lipstick over the top?' Beatrice asked.

'Loads of red lipstick.'

A silent palace staff stood reeling as the maverick Prince and his Cuban-heeled date made their way across the passageway and down the central stairs.

'Your Highness…' Phillipe was almost running. 'The King wishes to—'

'Tomorrow,' Julius said, and he knew from Phillipe's sudden reverence and use of his title that the decision had been made.

He would be King.

He just didn't need to hear it tonight.

Tonight was time for a bar on the water's edge, with music so loud there was no chance to speak.

'What would you like to drink?' He had to shout to be heard over the heavy beat of the music.

'Whisky!' Beatrice said. It felt like a whisky kind of night.

'Right…' He took her onto the dance floor, pulled her in close. 'One-two-three…five-six-seven. Remember that.'

'What about four?'

He pulled her tighter in. 'We move direction.'

'Oh.'

'Got it?'

'No.'

It was brilliant to learn, though, and indecent to be joined at the groin, with his hand on her lower back, while she tried to count in her head.

She was dreadful, and nobody cared; they were too busy keeping count themselves. She could feel the music rippling through her, and his kisses were rough and frequent. The bar was a bit shabby and crowded, and not really a great first date location…unless you knew where the night was headed.

And they did.

But right now it was time to dance.

CHAPTER FIFTEEN

'WERE YOU NERVOUS?' Beatrice asked her bridesmaid.

'No,' Alicia said. 'But then, I wasn't marrying a future king.'

'Were you?' Beatrice asked her little flower girl's mother.

'I was so scared I almost had to be sedated,' Jasmine admitted. 'It was the best thing I ever did, though. How are you feeling, Beatrice?'

'Very sure and very scared.'

It was a serious royal wedding, and her dress was both heavy and heavenly, in rich silk the colour of weak tea. It looked dreadful hanging up, but came alive when she slipped it on.

There was no veil, because she didn't want one, and the bouquet was all white flowers, picked that morning by the lake, with one violet so dark it was nearly black— for Claude, whom she wished could stand at his brother's side this day.

Jasmine's husband wanted to stay in the background, but he was an emergency fill-in—just in case—as Julius had chosen Tobias, his very loyal aide, whose baby was due any second.

As Miss Arabella the flower girl went for one more wee, the two sisters of the heart stood alone together.

'Alicia!' Beatrice warned, because her friend was holding a gorgeous clock she had pilfered from the mantelpiece and her open handbag.

'I want a memento,' Alicia teased.

'I have one for you.'

It was a framed copy of a photo—the only one Beatrice

had from their childhood—and Alicia had never seen it, nor any others like it.

'You have a photo…' Alicia opened up the present and they looked at the two little girls on the grass, surrounded by nuns. 'Beatrice!' Alicia gasped. 'You cut her out.'

'I did.'

Beatrice had told Alicia who her mother was and they were closer than ever now.

Yes, she *had* chosen her surname with care that day, and she thought back to Julius on the bench, probing, knowing a little and wanting to know more about Beatrice Taylor.

I cut. I separate.

A necessary requirement at times in order to grow.

'Are *you* going to tell *me* something, Alicia?' She looked down at her friend's little bump.

'It's your day today.'

'And this makes it even happier. A baby!'

'Yes.' Alicia beamed. 'You are going to be an aunty, but right now…'

Today Beatrice and Julius became family.

'Bridesmaids!'

Jordan was at the door to the suite, calling for the bridesmaids and in full royal wedding mode, but a wonderful friend too.

And giving Beatrice away was the rather wild boy she'd warned Alicia about—proof that sometimes she got things wrong.

But this was so right.

The crowds were a blur, and the golden dome of the church was shining as if to rival the sun, but it all fell away when she saw his smile.

Julius was in full military uniform. Clean-shaven, he looked younger than the man she had first met.

She was a *very* composed bride. A little cold, some might say. A little too calm for such a big occasion.

But it was easy to be calm, for it was the surest walk of her life.

'Good morning, Beatrice,' he said, when she finally made it down the long aisle.

'Good morning, Julius.'

Such beautiful words to be greeted with each and every day. In bed…via text…however they were delivered, they would always greet the day that way.

Julius closed his eyes briefly as the King loudly blew his nose. He knew his father would miss his other son always, and was relieved that he was a little more able to show that now.

The bride was not misty-eyed.

Beatrice turned and handed her flowers to Alicia, smiling at her very dear friend. 'Thank you,' she said, and she smiled too at Arabella, who was behaving beautifully.

Then she turned to the man who had found her hidden heart.

The service commenced and Beatrice was deeply serious, listening intently and nodding as she heard his vows.

His beautiful voice brought a gentle calm to her soul as he told her, 'I shall love you all the days of my life.'

And she knew those days would start with a month on Regalsi…

* * * * *

EMERGENCY MARRIAGE TO THE GREEK

CLARE CONNELLY

MILLS & BOON

PROLOGUE

POWERFUL, STRONG, SELF-MADE. Alexandros Zacharidis didn't make mistakes, but this was one of the biggest of his life.

He pulled away from her in shock, a thousand emotions possessing him, most keenly, betrayal and shock.

'Cristos.'

Theresa stared up at him, all wide, amber eyes, innocent pink cheeks, passion-swollen lips.

'Alex?' She frowned, her confusion obvious. That only angered him more. How could she not understand what he was feeling? 'What is it?'

Dumbfounded, he stared back, hands on hips, magnificent naked body on display, so her blush grew darker. 'This should not have happened.'

Her lips tugged downwards, lips that had been dragging across his torso minutes earlier, lower, sensually tasting him, flicking...

He groaned softly. 'It was a mistake.'

'I don't understand.' She sat up straighter. 'What's the matter?'

'You were a virgin.' The words were hissed between his teeth, his eyes barely able to hold hers. It was bad enough that he'd slept with his best friend's much younger sister, worse that he'd been her first, and unforgivable that it had happened on the day of Stavros's burial. He cursed in his mind, every curse he could think of, while waiting for her to respond.

Her eyes dipped down, not meeting his, and he felt a rush of frustration.

This shouldn't have happened, but it wasn't her fault. At least, it wasn't *only* her fault. He'd approached her, drawn her into an embrace, held her close until sympathy and grief had turned into something else, a low beating drum that had pulled at them both.

'You should have told me.'

'I—it didn't occur to me.' The words were heavy, uneven, as though she was fighting off tears. He needed to stop, to pull back, to let this go, but hell, he didn't like being surprised, he didn't like making mistakes. This was his worst nightmare.

'Dammit, Theresa. What were you thinking, coming here with me? You know who I am, *what* I am. Why would you do this?'

'I—thought—' Her skin was pale now, whiter than paper, as she looked around the room, as if for the answers she couldn't provide.

'I asked you to my room. I thought my meaning was clear. Did you come here expecting to have sex with me?'

The brutal directness of the question should have stopped him in his tracks, but nothing could. He wanted answers; he needed to understand this.

'*Cristos*, I need to know.' He stared at her until she nodded slowly, eyes haunted.

'Yes.'

'Why in God's name would you do that? You were a *virgin*. Did you think I would welcome this "gift"? Damn it, Theresa, you should have told me you were a virgin. I'm not interested in being your first. Do you understand what this was?'

Her lips parted and now her head moved side to side, her dark, glossy hair tumbling over her shoulders. Loyalty to Stavros should have held him silent, but Alex was blinded by emotion, shock at what he'd just allowed to happen overtaking all else.

'Sex. Just sex, something I do with women all the time,

and it means nothing. Nothing. You're just a child, for God's sake.'

She flinched, and again he told himself to stop, to pull back, but an anger was rushing through his veins that he'd never known before. Loyalty was something Alex considered to be an unwavering trait, and his loyalty to Stavros was second to none. His best friend's body wasn't cold in the ground and Alex had seduced his sister?

He turned his back, stalking across the room and staring at the wall, panic rising inside of him, and a strange feeling that he might vomit.

'Get dressed, Theresa. You need to leave now.'

He left the room without a backwards glance, ashamed in a way he'd never forget for what he'd just allowed to happen. He swore that for as long as he lived he'd never think of her again, nor the weakness that had brought him to his knees.

A month after their night together, Theresa heard from Alex. It was unexpected, and completely unsettling. His voice at the other end of the line was businesslike. None of the passion they'd shared that night came through in his call, nor did the white-hot anger he'd expressed afterwards.

'How are you?'

Her heart was about to explode out of her chest. Was that what he meant? 'Alex? Why are you calling me?'

'We slept together a month ago.'

Her pulse gushed. 'And?' The word was a thready whisper.

'If there were any consequences from that night—'

The purpose for his call then became crystal clear. She closed her eyes and shook her head. 'There weren't.'

A pause crackled down the phone line and then a rumbling noise. 'I'm glad. Then it's over.'

Bitterness filled her throat. 'Was it really so awful?'

She waited, the silence pulsing between them. 'Yes, *agape*. It really was.'

He disconnected the call and Theresa was glad they'd had this conversation over the phone, because that way he didn't get to see the tears sparkling in her eyes. She stared across the room, resolve hardening in the pit of her stomach.

Stavros's death had pulled her apart, and the night with Alex had added to that, but she refused to be a victim. She refused to let her parents continue to treat her like a baby. This was her life, and she had to live it, she had to reach out for what she wanted with both hands—and what she wanted, more than anything, was to forget Alexandros existed. To forget the perfection of his hands on her body, to erase him completely from her mind and life.

Stubbornness ran through her veins, and in that moment she was glad. She'd never think of him again.

CHAPTER ONE

TESSA STILL FOUND it hard to get used to the sight of her empty ring finger, despite the fact it was twelve months since her divorce had been finalised—thank goodness, because if she'd had to spend another day legally bound to the awful man she'd foolishly married, she feared she might have curled up into a ball and never unfurled again. None the less, she stared reflectively at the empty digit as the lift sailed higher and higher, towards the top of the Athens high-rise, telling herself the butterflies in her tummy had more to do with the rapid ascent than they did the fact she was about to come face-to-face with Alexandros Zacharidis for the first time in four years—and definitely not because of the proposal she was about to make.

After all, when it boiled down to it, her proposition was practically business, and that was a language the great Alexandros Zacharidis spoke fluently. Absentmindedly, she scratched off a speck of white paint from her knuckle—courtesy of the landscape she'd been working on that morning, whilst trying to steel herself to this.

What if she couldn't get through to him? That night they'd spent together had changed the shape of her universe. Not just because he'd been her first lover, and not because it had been right after losing her beloved brother—and Alex's best friend—but because the girlhood crush she'd nurtured for Alex for as long as she could remember had threatened to explode into something else entirely.

Until reality had intervened, and he'd pushed her away so hard and so fast she was still suffering whiplash.

Her heart had been broken. Or, at the time, she'd thought it was. She was too grown-up to believe in hearts and love and shattered dreams now. A lot had changed for her since that night, her idealism included.

The doors to the lift swished open, parting to reveal a floor of polished concrete with industrial pendant lights and a desk in the centre of the cavernous space that housed three receptionists. Behind them, a stunning view of the city was framed, like a painting—but Tessa fought her artist's natural inclination to study it in detail, steeling herself to focus on the task at hand.

'Hello,' she murmured, just a little unsteadily. 'Is Mr Zacharidis in?'

The receptionist nearest to Tessa frowned, scanning her computer screen. 'Good afternoon. Do you have an appointment?'

'No.'

'Ah.' The receptionist's brows beetled. 'I'm sorry, ma'am, but Mr Zacharidis has a very busy schedule. If you'd like, I can check if he might be able to see you next week.'

But this morning's headlines were still swimming in her brain and Tessa knew this couldn't wait another day. Her father's health was fragile and worsening by the day. If her awful ex-husband kept selling stories to the tabloids, she worried about how that would affect her dad.

It wasn't in Tessa's nature to be bullish, so it was a sign of her desperation that she persisted. 'I really believe he'll make time for me.' Having attended an exclusive British boarding school, her accent was as crisp as the Queen's, and it gave the receptionist a moment's pause.

Tessa capitalised on her silence. 'Please,' she leaned forward, 'tell him I'm here.'

The receptionist's reluctance was obvious.

'My name is Tessa Anastakos.'

'Tessa Anastakos,' the receptionist repeated, as though trying to place her, and then jackknifing out of her chair as the penny dropped. After all, the Anastakos name was well-known not just in Athens, but throughout the world. 'Yes, ma'am.' She moved with elegant grace despite the fact she was almost running, towards a timber door across the foyer.

Tessa waited, and a moment later the receptionist reappeared. 'You were right.' She nodded crisply. 'Mr Zacharidis will see you now.'

'Thank you.' Despite her outward calm, the butterflies multiplied in her belly, so she felt a thousand and one things as she moved towards the door. Four years ago, grief had brought Alex and Tessa together, and in that perfect, magical moment she'd felt, briefly, healed, her grief salved, until he'd jerked away from her, obviously disgusted by what had happened. Her virginity had surprised him, but it was more than that. She was Stavros's younger sister, just a girl to him, as he'd callously pointed out whilst dressing as swiftly as he could.

Would he be any less disgusted by her proposal? Would his loyalty to her family mean he'd put aside his own personal feelings and agree to her plan? Uncertainty made her gut twist, so she pushed the doubts from her mind. If this was going to work, she had to think positively.

In preparation for this meeting, Tessa had written a thousand lists, each of them enumerating the reasons this made sense. What she hadn't done was Google Alexandros recently, so the moment the door opened and he turned to face her, she felt as though she'd been rammed by a cement truck.

Holy crap.

Her knees turned to jelly and her stomach swished and swooshed, but outwardly she remained businesslike, her features barely shifting beyond the hint of a tight smile, even as memories of that night rocked her to the core.

'Damn it, Theresa, you should have told me you were a virgin. I'm not interested in being your first. Do you understand what this was?'

He'd gripped her upper arms, staring into her eyes, as if to make her understand better.

'Sex. Just sex, something I do with women all the time, and it means nothing. Nothing. You're just a child, for God's sake.'

She flinched at the recollection, his words as clear now as they had been on that awful night. He'd been wrong, in any event. At twenty-two, she might have been sheltered and innocent, but she was no longer a child, and she had been so sick of everyone perceiving her thus.

'Theresa.' He used the full version of her name, just as her brother always had, and something in the region of her heart panged.

'Everyone calls me Tessa.' She waved a hand through the air, her bare finger again catching her eye. 'How are you, Alex?'

The mockery in his expression was unmistakable, so for a moment her step faltered, and then, when his eyes dropped from her face to her breasts, and lower, to the sweep of her hips and back up again, she almost fell over. His inspection was slow and purposeful, setting little fires going beneath her skin.

'I'm very well, thank you, Theresa.' He said her name with a whisper of cynicism and her pulse picked up a notch. Had this been a gigantic mistake? He was teasing her, laughing at her, and Tessa really wasn't in the mood for it. All of Europe was already laughing at her after Jonathan's latest tabloid splash.

She jerked to a stop, tension radiating from the lines of her body. 'If you're going to treat me like a joke, I might as well turn around and leave.'

His eyes narrowed, fixed on her face, so her heart almost stammered to a stop. He wore a navy-blue suit that had clearly been made for him, lovingly hand-stitched for his six-and-a-half-foot frame, his broad shoulders and muscular abdomen. The jacket was discarded on his chair back, and his crisp white shirt was unbuttoned at the neck to reveal the thick, tanned column of his neck. Memories of scraping her lips across his stubbled throat burst into her mind, unwelcome and surprising. Her pulse shifted into tsunami territory.

But it was his face that made everything go wonky.

When they'd slept together, she'd been twenty-two and innocent, completely sheltered from the world by over-protective parents; she'd had no idea about men and sex, despite the fact she'd attended school in her mother's native England, and college in New York. Now she was older, wiser. She'd been married, for goodness' sake, and her girlhood crush on Alex was eons ago, so her body's reaction was as unexpected as it was unwelcome.

She'd always been fascinated by the hundreds of little micro muscles of his face that moved when he felt something, the way his dark brown eyes turned an almost grey when he was angry, or gold when he laughed. And in the heat of passion his eyes closed, those long lashes fanned over his tanned cheeks, and his lips parted…

'Maybe this was a mistake.' The last couple of years had taken their toll on Tessa. She was emotionally bruised and battered and, despite the fact she was making her last stand here and now, she wasn't sure she was ready for what she'd feel if he rejected her. Or accepted!

She stood completely still as his eyes roamed her face, tracking all the changes he'd no doubt see there, boring into her caramel eyes and full red lips, dropping to her bare decolletage and the swell of her breasts, the nip of her waist and the slimness of her hips, right the way to the red-soled shoes she'd donned for confidence that morning, before returning, slowly, all the way back to her eyes. Heat followed his gaze, burning her with its intensity.

'Why don't you tell me what you came here for?' He

crossed his arms over his broad chest, drawing her attention to the muscular definition there.

'I…' Uncharacteristically, she was lost for words. She swallowed, attempting to focus.

'It's been four years,' he pointed out with cool disinterest. 'Is this a social call? Or did you come here with something specific to discuss?'

Come on, tear off the Band-Aid!

'The latter,' she assured him, her voice cool as she strode towards the seats, conscious of the way his eyes followed her the entire way. She sat, crossing her legs neatly and keeping her hands clasped in her lap.

'Then by all means, enlighten me.' He was still pushing her away, just as he had that night, holding her at arm's length, so her stomach tightened and she doubted, again, the wisdom of this plan. But the purpose was clear: for her father, and the legacy he'd spent a lifetime building, she'd do whatever was necessary.

'I have a proposition for you,' she said haltingly. 'One that's going to sound completely crazy, admittedly. Hear me out?'

He dipped his head in acknowledgement, so she fumbled her fingers a bit, aware that she couldn't prevaricate for much longer.

'Naturally, whatever I say in here is confidential.'

'Of course.'

She offered him an apologetic grimace. After all, she had no reason to mistrust Alex, but after what she'd been through with her ex-husband, she couldn't help making the stipulation.

'I have to be sure,' she muttered.

His eyes were mocking. 'Cross my heart, hope to die.'

She ignored the droll sarcasm.

'I'm serious, Alex. This is—important.'

He dipped his head, silently encouraging her to continue.

'Okay.' Her voice shook a little. She swallowed, trying to clear her throat. 'You obviously know how my parents feel about you.'

He furrowed his brow. 'Is something the matter with Elizabeth and Orion?'

Grief was like a knife in her gut. She'd already lost so much, the idea of life without her father made her uncertain and cold to the bone. 'Dad's heart condition isn't responding to medication, and another surgery—while necessary—is not without risks.' She swallowed, desperate to keep her voice level even as grief saturated the words. 'Until he can have the procedure, his specialist has instructed him to avoid all stress.'

'I know he takes his health seriously,' Alex murmured, but there was tension in his voice too, that spoke volumes for how much he cared about her parents.

'They've always adored you,' she said softly, so he took a step closer, to hear her better, and she caught a hint of his masculine fragrance. Her stomach somersaulted. 'After Stavros died, they took a lot of comfort from how often you'd call in to see them.'

He said nothing, and that silence was powerfully unnerving.

'You're a connection to him,' she continued nervously, turning her honey-coloured eyes on the view of Athens without really seeing it. 'They love you.'

'Your parents are special people.'

She lifted a hand, drumming her fingers against the base of her throat. 'Yes, they are.' She forced her eyes back to his, knowing that if this was going to work, she'd have to appeal to his affection for them.

'They always hoped we would get together,' she blurted out, finding it hard to hold his gaze but knowing it was important. 'But I was never a big fan of the idea of an arranged marriage,' she said with a self-mocking grimace.

'Particularly not with me?' he drawled, and she held her breath, something in the region of her heart flickering as remembered girlhood wishes crashed right into her, when dreams of a big wedding to Alex had dominated all her thoughts. But she'd tried marriage once—it had been a disaster.

Straightening her spine, she shook her head once. 'No.' She bit down into her lower lip, a sense of ambivalence gripping her. 'You were always Stavros's friend, not mine.'

'Except for that one night.'

Her eyes swept shut, her throat thickening so swallowing was almost impossible. 'That night didn't make us friends.'

She didn't see the way his eyes combed her face with speculative appraisal, or her heart might have leaped right out of her chest.

'Why have you come here today?'

Nerves were a writhing pit of snakes in Tessa's belly.

'I'm worried about him.'

'Who?'

'Dad.' She blinked over at Alex, and her gut twisted for the genuine concern she saw, briefly, before he concealed it behind his usual mask of determination.

'Tell me what's going on.'

'I'm—' her mouth parted, then her lips pressed together. The words lodged hard in her jaw.

'Go on.' His command pulled at her, and she realised she didn't have anyone she could talk to about this. Jonathan had made her wary; his constant gossiping to tabloids had her on a knife's edge, terrified to trust anyone. But Alex was different—he always had been.

'He's really sick, Alex. I don't know when you last saw him—'

'Not for several months.'

Was that guilt in his voice?

'Then you won't have noticed. He's lost weight. He's

tired, all the time. It's so unlike him.' Her voice cracked as she forced herself to admit what she'd known for some time. 'I don't think he has long.' The words were whispered.

Alex's frown was contemplative. 'You think? Or you know?'

Her eyes met his and her lower lip trembled. 'I know,' she whispered, standing then, moving to the window on knees that were unsteady. 'It's nothing he's said, but I can just tell. He keeps talking about Mum, about how to take care of her.' She lifted a finger and dashed at a tear before it could spill over. She'd told herself she wouldn't do this! Not here, and not in front of this man; not after how he'd treated her.

Her nerves pulled taut. 'If there was anyone else I could ask…' she said slowly. 'You have to understand, I've looked at this from every angle.'

'You need help with your father?'

'No…yes.' She sighed with exasperation. 'In a sense, yes. I…made a mistake, Alex, and I need help to fix it.'

'You're not making sense.'

'I know.' She rubbed her temples. 'My parents always hated him.'

'Who?'

'My ex-husband, Jonathan.' She couldn't meet his eyes. So much of her choice to marry Jonathan was bound up in Alex's cold-hearted rejection of her. Her entire world had then been tipped on its edge—by the death of Stavros, by sleeping with Alex and the way he'd reacted, by her parents' total and all-consuming sense of grief, which had translated into an over-protectiveness that was beyond suffocating. Jonathan had been her way out, she just hadn't realised she was jumping out of the frying pan into the fire.

'So, he is your ex-husband now. Doesn't that solve the problem?'

'If only it were that simple. Unfortunately, he's taken to blathering about our marriage to anyone who'll listen. As

I speak, he's locked away for *Celebrity Housemate*—you know, that fly-on-the-wall reality show?—and the promotional clips they're airing are all about me.'

His silence wasn't particularly encouraging.

'Every time there's an article maligning me, or our family, it affects Dad. I need it to stop.'

'Yes,' he agreed, arms crossed over his chest again. 'I can see that. Would you like me to speak to my lawyers?'

'That won't work.' She shook her head. 'I've tried it. He won't sign an NDA, as it's far more profitable to sing like a canary.'

'He's significantly underestimating your net worth, then.'

'He's trying to parlay our marriage into lasting fame and fortune.' She rolled her eyes. 'It's not his fault. He had nothing, and he doesn't want to go back to that.'

'Was the divorce settlement not generous enough?'

'I don't think it would have mattered what I gave him; he'd have always wanted more.'

Disapproval curved Alex's symmetrical lips. 'He sounds like a catch.'

He was only echoing her own thoughts, but she wasn't in the mood to be spoken down to. 'I didn't come here to appraise my husband's shortcomings.'

'Ex-husband,' he corrected factually. 'And apparently, you came here because you need my help. Tell me how.'

'I want to take back control,' she said with a small jut of her chin, quiet determination steadying the words. 'Part of the reason he's been able to blather on in the press is because I completely withdrew.'

Alex's eyes were heavy on her face, but she didn't look directly at him.

'Why? What have you been doing?'

Great question, without an answer. Her art had largely stalled, as stress about her father, her marriage, her mother, had all bundled together to paralyse her creativity. 'I never expected to get divorced,' she murmured, 'then again, I never expected to be married to someone like him.'

A sharp exhalation drew her eyes to Alex's face. 'What does that mean?'

She shook her head, lost for words.

'It doesn't matter.' The awful truth of her marriage was something she needed to hold close.

Alex tensed. 'Did he hurt you?'

Theresa shook her head. 'He didn't hit me,' she whispered, eyes moist. 'But he hurt me in other ways.' Her eyes hid from him. 'He was controlling. Angry. Jealous. Possessive. And when he felt that I wasn't paying him enough attention, he sought to destroy my confidence. He insulted me, always. Sometimes subtly, sometimes not. Sometimes privately, sometimes not. It's amazing how quickly a person can break you down, and make you lose all faith in your own abilities. And when he didn't get what he wanted, he went out and slept with someone else, then made sure I heard all about it.' Bitterness flooded her words.

'And yet you stayed with him?'

How could she explain to Alex? Her marriage had been untenable after only a few months, but Jonathan had too much over her, and the idea of divorcing him, of upsetting her parents, had kept her right where she was.

'He always threatened to do this, if I left him,' she said with soft resignation. 'I didn't want this to be my life, my parents' life, and so I stayed with him until I really couldn't bear it any longer.'

'You should have given him nothing in the divorce,' he spat angrily.

'In the end, I just wanted him to go away.' Her eyes were haunted.

'No wonder your parents hate him.'

She nodded awkwardly. 'I have put them through hell, Alex.'

'It sounds to me as though you are the one who's been through hell.'

Sympathy would be her undoing. She focused on her parents rather than allowing his words to serve as any kind of balm. 'It's been hard on them, and after Stavros, it's the last thing they need. Now, with Dad's health, I need to make everything right. I need to fix this.'

'And you have a plan?'

'Yes, that's exactly right.' She swallowed past the tangle of nerves. 'I can see a solution to everything, but I have no idea if you'll agree. It's actually going to sound very mad, I'm afraid, but there's nothing for it. No idea's too crazy, right?'

He didn't look convinced. 'Go on.'

Her stomach squeezed. *Do it.* Get it over with. 'I was wondering how you'd feel about marrying me, Alex?'

The sound of a pin dropping would have echoed through the silent room.

'Just to be clear—is this a joke?'

'No.' Her pretty lips formed a perfect Cupid's bow as she grimaced, and her eyes skittered away from him, as they'd done far too frequently during this short meeting.

He couldn't say what he'd been expecting, but definitely not this.

'So you came to my office to propose?' he demanded, wondering at the anger that was sparking low down in his gut. He hadn't seen Theresa Anastakos in years—she shouldn't still be able to invoke this kind of response in him—but there was no questioning the fact that she'd shot his senses into overdrive from the moment of her arrival, just as she had that night.

Sleeping with her had been a mistake he regretted to this day, almost as much as he did the cruel words he'd thrown at her afterwards. But the truth was, he'd have said anything in that moment to put a stop to what had happened. If he could have taken back that night, he would have. It had been madness. He still wasn't over it. Not the sex, but the fact he'd made a mistake by sleeping with her at all, and Alex didn't *make* mistakes.

Yet the desire he felt for her was unmistakable. Even now, after living with the guilt of his betrayal of Stavros, he couldn't look at Theresa without those old feelings stirring, as potently demanding as ever. But Theresa was not a mistake he intended to make twice, no matter how tempted he was.

'I know it sounds mad,' she admitted.

'Mad? It's worse than that. It's impossible.'

Her skin paled to the colour of cream. 'Why?'

'Because—' He cursed softly. 'You may not have realised this about me, but I'm hardly the marrying kind.'

'My parents think you are.'

'Your parents are far too generous in their assessment. Believe me, I could never make you happy.'

'I'm not looking for you to make me happy,' she volleyed back with urgency. 'I've already been married once and I think the whole idea stinks.'

'On this, we are in agreement.'

Her eyes met his, a challenge in their depths, so a strange tightening gripped his gut. He stood perfectly still, refusing to be moved by her request.

'You're a businessman, and I'm suggesting a businesslike marriage. We'll sign some contracts, pose for a few photos, then move on with our lives.'

He shook his head in a demurral. 'I can see why you're suggesting this, but what is in it for me?' Her cheeks flushed and an answering awareness flared to life inside of him, so danger sirens blared continually. 'A businesslike arrangement would involve us both getting something we wanted from the deal,' he continued, careful not to betray the direction of his thoughts. 'What do I get out of it?'

'Apart from making a man you purport to care about happy?'

'I care for and respect your parents, but I am too old to do anything for anyone else. What else have you got?'

She flinched, evidently not expecting this barrier. 'Tell me what you'd want.'

'Nothing,' he was quick to respond, even as his whole body tightened with a surge of powerful attraction, a need to possess her that was every bit as strong as it had been four years earlier. He closed his eyes against its power and sway, but that was worse, because his mind homed in on another point in the marriage's favour, something he could present as a term of his own.

'There must be something,' she pleaded now, sucking in a sharp breath, and her breasts thrust forward, so for a brief moment he was powerless to resist and allowed his gaze to drop, to admire the sweet swell of her cleavage against the pale dress she wore, awareness of her femininity stirring something to life inside of him.

The night they'd made love, they hadn't been Alex and Tessa. They'd been as wild as animals, driven by primal grief, so he'd torn her clothes from her body and she'd scratched his back and they'd bitten one another and made love so hard and fast that it hadn't been until he entered her that he realised it was her first time. And then it was too late, they were both too caught up in the moment, too desperate to feel the heavenly release to do anything but surrender to it completely. Everything about that night had been feral and elemental, had made perfect sense at the time, and none in the moments immediately afterwards, when he'd realised that he'd betrayed some vital bond of trust, crossing a line he should never have gone near.

'Please, Alex, won't you think about it?' For a moment,

he was reminded of Stavros, and how he would do anything for his dear friend. Guilt chafed at him. He'd slept with Theresa. Didn't he have a moral obligation to help her in some way? Because of Stavros. Because of her parents. Because of how he'd treated her in the past.

And yet, the idea of marriage was anathema to him. It always had been.

'It would never be real,' he heard himself say, the acquiescence close to agreement, so her eyes widened with triumph.

'I don't want real.'

He swore under his breath, dragging a hand through his hair. 'I mean it, Theresa. If we were to do this, you would be nothing to me. The kid sister of a dear friend. Nothing more.'

Her eyes glinted with an emotion he didn't recognise, determination clamping her features into a mask of resolve. 'As always,' she said with a terse nod. 'So tell me what you need? What can I offer to get you to say yes?'

He was alone. Utterly and completely. His best friend had died—Stavros had been more like a brother to Alex, anyway. He was the only son of an only son. There were no siblings, aunts, uncles, cousins. There was no other Zacharidis in his life. That hadn't bothered him until his father's death, and then, the idea of being an island on his own, all his life, had made something shift in his gut. The pledge he'd made, decades earlier, to stay single and childless, to do whatever he could to avoid the hell of his parents' marriage and his own childhood, no longer seemed as important as a physical need to procreate, a biological urge to see a part of himself in the world, to know that he wasn't completely alone.

No one could have been more surprised by this urge than Alex, and perhaps he might have quelled it, or fought it, over time. But here was Tessa, offering him a marriage, asking him what he would want out of that marriage... Ever the opportunist—how else did a person build an empire like Alex's?—he saw a way to turn this to his advantage, and he shamelessly prepared to take it, even as regret was already promising to expand through him, even when he knew Stavros would hate him for this.

He straightened, crossing his arms over his broad chest, aware of the way her eyes soaked up the gesture, landing and remaining on his mid-section before she reluctantly lifted them back to his face.

'You might not like the conditions I'd have, if I were to agree to this.'

CHAPTER TWO

'IF' WAS WAY better than what she'd come here expecting. In her heart of hearts, she'd been almost certain that his answer would be no, so it was a sign of how desperate Tessa was that she'd even gone through with this.

'If' was the starting of a negotiation. Her insides squished with a mix of adrenaline and anxiety.

'I'd like to hear them,' she said unsteadily.

He took two steps towards her, closing the distance and knocking her nerves sideways. Her heart stammered inside her ribcage and despite the fact she wasn't an inexperienced, sheltered twenty-two-year-old any more, for a moment she sure felt like one.

She held her breath as he came to stand right in front of her, his alpine scent dangerously addictive, so she inhaled deeply before she could stop herself, tasting him at the back of her throat and wanting... Her eyes flared wide as she immediately tamped down on her illicit thoughts. This wouldn't work if she *wanted* him. Desire was a double-edged sword; she'd felt the sting of its blade before and would do whatever she could to avoid that.

'So?' she asked, the word emerging as a husky prompt.

His smile was slow to spread, and it made her tummy feel all hollowed out.

'Tell me about the kind of marriage you'd imagine us having.'

'That's a question, not a term.'

He dipped his head in agreement.

Rather than argue on a technicality, she acknowledged it was fair for him to want to understand exactly how this would work.

'We'd have to live together,' she said haltingly. 'At least initially. Thanks to Jonathan, there's a level of public scrutiny around my private life.' She couldn't contain a small shudder. 'Obviously, I'm hopeful that will die down. At some point, I would imagine we could go back to living almost completely independently.'

'I see.'

'It would really be a marriage in name only. We'd give the media a new angle, and hopefully Jonathan's relevance would fade into obscurity. But more than that, most importantly,' her voice trembled, 'Dad would have some peace of mind, at the end of his life.'

His obsidian eyes didn't move. If he was touched by concern for her father, he didn't show it. Such was the power of Alexandros Zacharidis. He was a skilled negotiator, an intimidating executive. 'And what if I told you I'd want more than that?' he asked, his eyes probing her, reading her, so she suspected he could see all her doubts and uncertainties, and so much more.

'Which brings us back to your terms,' she pointed out, huskily. 'Why don't you tell me what they are, so we can decide if this will work? I'm prepared to be flexible,' she added, after a beat.

His eyes were gently mocking, and her insides turned to goo.

'Am I to understand you're suggesting a marriage without intimacy?'

Heat scored her nerves even as painful memories of her own marriage turned her veins to ice. Her crisp nod was belied by her stuttering voice. 'Behind closed doors, we wouldn't need to pretend we were anything more than… polite acquaintances.'

'Is that what we are?' The words held a gruff challenge.

'We haven't seen each other in years,' she pointed out

acerbically. 'I don't know if we could even say we're acquainted any more.'

'And yet you came to me and poured out your heart, begging me to help you.'

She swallowed, her throat scratchy and dry. 'Was that a mistake?'

'The mistake was in thinking the marriage you're suggesting would ever work.'

Her insides twisted and uncertainty lurched through her. 'Why wouldn't it?'

Another laugh, so soft it was as though it had been designed just for her ears, and his husky warmth floated across, teasing the sensitive skin of her neck. 'We cannot ignore what happened between us.' She could barely look at him.

'That was for ever ago,' she said, unconvincingly.

'And you think it wouldn't happen again?'

Her eyes flew to his face. He moved closer, his expression a mask of grim determination, and her pulse went into overdrive.

'I know it wouldn't,' she whispered, remembering with a shiver how total his rejection of her had been. The crush she'd harboured for him for so long, the desire he'd stirred in her, the culmination of her grief and need and wanting that had brought them together, and the way he'd dismissed her afterwards, showing her so clearly that she meant nothing to him. 'One time with you was more than enough.'

'Careful, *agape*. That sounds like a challenge.'

Her knees knocked together, unsteady and weak.

'And the problem is, even when I know you are off limits, or should be, I find myself intrigued by that challenge, desperate to make you eat your words.' He lifted a finger to her chin, holding her face towards his, so that every husky, warm breath she expelled brushed his lips like a caress. 'Do you remember what it was like with us?'

'I remember everything about that night,' she whispered, eyes sweeping shut to hide the hurt that was still layered over her heart.

'There is too much passion to ignore. I won't marry you unless you accept the inevitable—otherwise we will both be in a hell of our own making.'

She groaned, desperately tempted, and also terrified, because Jonathan had destroyed beyond repair every normal emotion and sense she possessed. She was too broken by his betrayal to even contemplate sleeping with Alex. 'How can you say that? You didn't want me four years ago, why do you think you're going to want me now?'

His eyes narrowed, his lips pursed tight as though he was physically restraining himself from speaking.

'I'm serious, Alex. What happened between us was a stupid mistake. We both regretted it,' she added, even when the words didn't ring true for Tessa. Not completely. 'Do you think anything is served by agreeing to sleep together again?'

'It was a mistake,' he agreed with a dip of his head. 'But that isn't to say it wasn't also enjoyable.'

She flinched. Jonathan's criticisms came barrelling towards her. She looked away, lips clamped tight.

'I was there, remember? You didn't seem like a man who enjoyed anything about what we did.'

His expression didn't change. 'I regretted sleeping with you because of who you are. It had nothing to do with the sex itself.'

'I thought it was "awful"?'

A frown gashed over his face. 'It was.'

Her laugh was a strangled sound. 'Lovely. Thanks for that.' Just what she needed!

'The *fact* we slept together was awful. You are Stavros's baby sister—how did you expect me to react?'

Her heart kicked up a notch as she contemplated that.

For years she'd believed his insult had been a reflection on the experience, rather than the circumstances surrounding it. 'I betrayed him. How could I take pleasure in that?'

'And now?' she pushed. 'You don't seem to have that reservation any more.'

'You're wrong,' he responded, nostrils flaring as he expelled a sharp breath. 'But I am also a realist. If I marry you, it will be to help you, and your parents, and I have to believe Stavros would want me to do what I could. But there is no marriage if we cannot acknowledge that what drove us together that night still exists between us.'

Her lips parted as she searched for how to respond. That night was still a source of too much pain. She looked over his shoulder, stomach twisted into knots. 'Are you saying you'll marry me if I agree to sleep with you?'

'No.' The word was darkly uttered. 'I'm saying this marriage will only work if you admit sex is going to happen between us, whether that's convenient or not. I don't want to go through the emotional upheaval of having you come to terms with that side of our relationship once we are married. We are two consenting adults—if we choose to indulge our bodies' needs, then that's not a big deal. As with that night, it would mean nothing.'

She pulled away from him, her heart racing, because everything he'd said was anathema to her. Sex mattered. It had always mattered to Tessa. It was a large part of why her marriage had failed—how could she sleep with a man who treated her so badly? Whom she didn't love?

'Is there anything else?' she whispered, wrapping her arms around her body.

'Are you saying you accept what I have said?'

'I'm just getting a full picture of what you want before I decide,' she corrected unevenly, body already tingling at the prospect of his suggestion.

'There is one other thing.'

Slowly she looked at him, heart in her throat.

'My father died six months ago.'

She nodded. 'I heard. My mother mentioned…' She tapered off into nothing, unsure how to offer condolences.

'After he was buried, I stood in the middle of his empty home and I realised something I should have been prepared for.' He paused, not for effect, so much as to rally his thoughts. 'I was alone.' His eyes stared into the distance. 'I have no other family. No siblings, cousins, no one.'

She didn't know what to say, nor did she understand why he was telling her this.

'My parents destroyed any thoughts I might have had on marriage as a desirable objective in life. I don't see the point to it, frankly.' Curiosity sparked in her chest. She remembered throwaway comments her parents had made over the years about his family. She'd gathered that it had been quite a volatile relationship, but she didn't know any particulars. 'Standing there, completely alone, I had to contemplate what that meant. For six months, I have grappled with my isolation in this life. Largely, this has been by choice. I have avoided relationships assiduously.'

She remembered what that felt like. Being pushed away by Alex was an experience from which she doubted she'd ever really recover.

'But something strange has happened to me since my father's death.'

'Oh?' Unconsciously, she moved towards him, fascinated.

'I have a yearning not to be alone.'

She frowned. 'So you've changed your mind about marriage, then?'

He ignored that. 'I want children, Theresa. A family. I want to have descendants to pass on my wealth to. I want…' He stared at her, as if evaluating her for a moment before deciding he should proceed. 'I want my life to matter beyond the balance of my bank account.'

Sympathy flooded her, alongside compassion, and, more terrifyingly, adrenaline and excitement, for his list of demands was filling out something inside of her, something she'd denied for a long time, because Jonathan was far from a suitable man to have children with.

'Your life does matter. Of course it does. A child doesn't make you inherently more or less valuable.'

His eyes bored into hers. 'Believe me, this is the last thing I expected to find myself wanting.'

Tessa considered that a moment. 'So what were you planning to do about it?'

'Nothing, at this stage, perhaps ever.' He shrugged, his eyes narrowing contemplatively. 'And yet, here you are, offering yourself to me on a silver platter.'

'I wouldn't say that, exactly' came the breathy response. Because no matter what words she responded with, an image was blooming in her mind and she couldn't ignore the temptation of it.

'I will only agree to this marriage on two conditions. The first is that you acknowledge the full extent of what you're asking for. Sex between us is inevitable—but can you accept that? And do you understand that I mean sex without any emotional strings?'

She almost walked out on him then. Only the thought of her father's worsening health had her hold her ground.

'And the second is that you fully understand my desire for children. If you are not on the same page, this could never work.'

Her fingers trembled. Another speck of paint caught her eye, a vibrant purple thanks to the agapanthus hedge she'd been rendering to canvas hours earlier. She ran her finger over it carelessly. It was the duty of an artist to be paint splattered, and since her divorce she'd been trying to throw herself back into her art, indulging the work Jonathan had always sneered at as being 'beneath' her.

'I realise it's a curve ball.' He shrugged his broad shoulders, moving away from her a little. 'If the idea of this marriage no longer appeals to you, then you're free to leave. This conversation never happened.'

Her smile was hollow, her stomach in knots. 'It's not that simple,' she whispered, moving towards the window and pressing her over-warm forehead against the thickened glass. Her throat was dry and her head ached. 'My parents have lost so much. After Stavros, they've never been the same. I know I'm no substitute for him.'

'What does that mean?' His tone was sharp, his voice close. She didn't move. Grief was wrapping around her, as fresh now as it had been on that day so many years earlier.

'I'm not like them,' she whispered softly. 'My mum, dad, Stav. They're all cut from the same cloth. I'm a cuckoo in the nest, an enigma. They never got me. Marrying Jonathan was supposed to be—' She shook her head, not wanting to discuss her husband then, nor the reason she'd jumped far too rashly into the engagement. 'I didn't mean to compound their sadness, but I did. I've put them through the wringer, and I just want to give them this gift—I want to do something they'll be proud of, just once in my life, before it's too late. Dad—' Her voice shook but she pushed herself to standing, refusing to show any further signs of weakness to this man.

She turned to face him, so overwhelmed by the strength of her feelings that she didn't see the emotions in his eyes, the pity in the depth of his gaze. 'I'm sure they're proud of you.'

She brushed aside his meaningless reassurance. She knew her parents, and she knew how they felt about her. They loved her, they couldn't bear the thought of something happening to her, but they valued her as an object, rather than a person all of her own. Her interests, her passions, her art, they were meaningless to her family. But that didn't change the fact she'd do anything for her parents, for the father who was nearing the end of his life.

'Yes,' she whispered. 'Let's do this.' Before she let common sense return and she backed out of the scenario altogether.

His only response was a small shift of his head. 'Come to my house tonight.'

Her eyes flared wide. 'What? Why?'

His laugh was a hoarse sound that split her heart in two. 'To discuss the details, *agape*. Don't worry. I'll keep my hands to myself—unless you don't want me to?'

Heat flooded her cheeks. Was she so transparent? 'What details?'

'Where we'll live, for starters. When we'll marry. How we'll announce it and tell your parents. These things matter.'

He was right. There were logistics to plan for. Only everything felt all wobbly. She'd been so sure this would be a businesslike marriage proposal and he'd completely redefined the borders of those expectations. Not to mention, coming face to face with Alex for the first time in four years made it impossible to forget just how much she'd used to worship him. That crush had become a source of so much embarrassment, so it was shocking to discover that she still couldn't look at him without going weak at the knees.

She couldn't have a second disastrous marriage to her name. She had to be sure they would make a go of this—and his idea of discussing the details made sense. This would work. It would be fine. 'Okay,' she said on a small exhalation. 'Tonight.'

He had expected her to refuse. He'd goaded her, challenged her, thinking she'd turn her back on this whole preposterous idea and walk away. And now that she'd accepted, he had to make his peace with it, because she was offering him something he hadn't even fully acknowledged to himself that he wanted.

'You understand the limits of this?' he pushed, just to be certain. She was Stavros's sister, and, while the lines were getting blurred, he could still control the boundaries of their relationship. He had a lifetime of experience with that, after all.

'Yes.' It was as though a switch had been flicked. Now that she'd accepted his terms, the uncertainty had disappeared, leaving determination in her beautiful face. And she *was* beautiful, he contemplated with a tightening in his groin. As beautiful now as she had been then, as she had been as a gawky, uncertain teenager and she'd smiled at him as though he was the centre of the universe.

Stavros had always been protective though. *'She's way too young for you. Don't even think about it.'* And she had been. Even the night they'd slept together, at twenty-two, she'd still been far too inexperienced and sheltered for a man like him—ten years older and far more worldly.

He'd used her.

She'd had a crush on him for years—he couldn't have missed the way she'd used to stare at him, and when she'd walked through the hotel bar, distracted and grieving, he'd moved to intercept her, drawing her into his arms because he'd needed the contact, the physical connection, the distraction.

The taste of acid filled his mouth.

He disgusted himself.

Stavros had only been buried hours earlier and there was Alex disregarding his friend's often stated warning, seducing his younger, innocent sister for his own selfish needs.

There had been other women in the bar that night, other women he could have turned to in order to slake his needs, and yet he'd chosen Tessa. He'd betrayed Stavros and Alex had never forgiven himself for that. He'd pledged he would never see Tessa again, that he'd never indulge that weakness, and he'd been right to avoid her. Only he thought of her often, not because of who she was, but because of the weakness she'd brought out in him, and how much he'd hated that. He should have turned her away the moment she'd arrived. He should have told his assistant to send her away. But he'd been curious, and wanting to see her, to see how she'd changed and grown.

Their marriage would be a gift to her parents, and so too would a child be. Surely even Stavros, then, would have approved of this? With a sound of frustration, he shook his head. There was no way his best friend would *ever* condone the marriage of Alex to Tessa. Stavros had always protected Tessa, and he knew, better than anyone, what demons pursued Alex. He knew about Alex's parents' marriage, the torment of living with a couple who could swing from wildly happy to murderously enraged in the blink of an eye, the torture of feeling that you were losing not one, but two parents every time they argued. The instability of growing up in a home split in half by emotional arguments, or vibrating with tension and silence. His parents had hated each other, but they'd hated the idea of separating even more, and so they'd stayed together, trapped in their loveless marriage, until they couldn't survive another day, and finally they had parted, both destroyed in every way that mattered by the torment they'd put one another through.

Alex had known he would never marry, from a young age, and he had told Stavros this on many occasions. Stavros had teased him, saying it was only because Alex liked to bed a different woman each night, that he might feel differently if he actually got to know one of the women he slept with. But Alex had been resolute. Sex was sex, he saw no purpose in getting to know the women he slept with— and there hadn't been any complaints from them, anyway.

But sleeping with Tessa had cheapened everything about his way of life. He'd been so angry with himself, and, unfairly, so angry with her, for being in the lobby, for walking past him, for looking at him as though he could fix everything, for understanding, as no one else could, what Stavros's death had cost Alex. Hell, he'd even been angry at her for being a virgin—a twenty-two-year-old virgin! He hadn't wanted that gift, the special uniqueness of what they'd shared. Betraying Stavros was bad enough, but being her first?

Goddammit.

They'd discussed a marriage without emotion, but Alex wasn't a fool. For Tessa had been the only woman who'd ever invoked anything close to sentiment in him—even if they had been dark emotions—and he would now have to spend a lifetime ensuring it never happened again. Feelings had no place in his marriage—they never would.

CHAPTER THREE

THE DRIVEWAY GATES opened as soon as she keyed in the security code he'd given her, and when she pulled up in front of the stunning house she noted the door was open. It was one of the best areas of Athens, and he clearly felt confident with the security arrangements in place. A quick study of the façade showed several discreet cameras, which she suspected held a live feed to some data cloud somewhere, if not a real-time monitoring service.

She stepped out of the car with innate elegance, smoothing a hand over her dress, wincing a little as the late-afternoon sun cut through her like a blade. She shielded her eyes, scanning the house with interest, noting the mid-century modern architecture that put her in mind of a Frank Lloyd Wright masterpiece, with carved balconies overlapping one another, part stone, part timber. The garden was breathtakingly lovely too. Formal and wild at the same time, the juxtaposition of conscious design elements was perfectly offset by rambling flowers and a canopy of trees that sheltered the drive. Grabbing her leather document wallet from the back seat, Tessa moved away from the car with an effort to keep her breathing steady.

She knew it might have seemed like overkill, but, having been married once before, Tessa could only go through with this if she knew she had complete control. It needed to be on her terms, and so she'd brought a sense of armour with her: a prenuptial agreement that would guarantee they could keep this marriage rational, despite the terms he'd stipulated.

This wasn't going to be anything like her marriage to Jonathan, she reminded herself, poking her head through the doorway and looking around. Besides a pair of polished brown shoes, there was no sign of Alex.

'Hello?' she called out, clearing her throat and trying again, louder this time.

There was no reply. Clutching her phone in one hand, she moved deeper into his home, the click-clacking of her sandals on the tiles making her feel reassured and in command.

If it was possible, the interior of his home exceeded the exterior. The mid-century modern features continued internally, with tall ceilings, timber beams and glass everywhere, as well as a sunken lounge conversation pit, grey carpets meeting slate floors and light fittings that were like something out of *The Jetsons*.

She wove past an Eames armchair, black leather with moulded walnut wood, and then, through large timber-framed glass sliding doors, onto a pool area that was perfectly placed to take advantage of the views of Athens. But apart from a brief glimpse of buildings and the most stunning late-evening sky she'd seen in a long time, Tessa wasn't capable of taking any further note of the details of his property, because Alexandros Zacharidis was swimming in said infinity pool, his powerful arms pulling him through the water as though swimming were as easy for him as walking was for her. Arms that had been shielded from her view that afternoon were now on full display, rippling, rounded biceps covered in rivulets of adoring water, glowing beneath the early evening sun, his skin golden—no, bronzed, like any of the sculptures of ancient Gods she'd admired at the museums. Her mouth was drier than the desert at full sun and her feet were planted to the ground, her heels no longer offering a reassuring clickety-clack as if they too were struck dumb by the sight of him like this.

As he reached the end of the pool he came to a halt, standing so his ridged pectoral muscles were on full display, his dark hair a pelt against his head until he shook it vigorously from one direction to the next, flicking droplets over the tiles, so Tessa instinctively stepped back rather than getting splashed. Her involuntary movement drew his attention and he turned to face her, a wolfish smile spreading slowly over his features.

'You came.' Was she imagining the mocking amusement beneath the benign words? Was she the only one who heard the double entendre?

He could have swum to the edge of the pool, where there was a perfectly good set of steps available, but instead Alex pulled himself out of the water right where he was, giving that magnificent body a chance to tighten as she watched, each muscle taut as he moved with easy athleticism from the water, towards a sunbed that was perilously close to her. She took several more steps backwards, eyes on him warily, tongue too thick to enable her to speak, so she simply nodded as he approached, one hand gripping her briefcase more tightly, the other almost strangling her phone.

'I'm glad.' Up close, she could see the fascinating glitter of water droplets against his even more fascinating face.

Oh, good heavens.

This was, perhaps, her worst idea ever. How could she possibly have a businesslike marriage with someone she was clearly still attracted to? What had she been thinking?

'Nice house,' she murmured, her voice strangled, as he reached for a towel and wrapped it around his neck. She tried, she really tried, to keep her eyes on his face, but standing there like that, dripping and basically naked, how could she not look? Just quickly. Of its own volition, her gaze slipped lower, to his chest, lower still to his narrow hips, and disastrously to the black shorts which were clinging to him like a second skin. Their dark colour hid most of the detail but that didn't stop her cheeks from flaming red as memories of his possession steamed through her.

'Care to join me?' He gestured to the pool, so her attention jerked back to his face, and then beyond Alex to the turquoise water. Despite her being paralysed by the strength of her attraction, the pool was tempting. The afternoon had been hot, and the water looked so inviting. But was it the water, or the idea of being close to him, barely dressed, that had her desperate to accept his suggestion?

'No,' she said quickly, frowning as she returned her attention to his face. 'We had a meeting scheduled, didn't we?'

'We did,' he agreed, his expression giving nothing away. 'But I don't think we decided firmly on the venue.'

'Not the swimming pool,' she clarified.

'Right, because heaven forbid we have fun while we discuss—'

'This isn't fun for me,' she cut in quickly. 'In fact, it's something of an emergency.'

Speculation darkened his eyes and she swallowed, aware she was showing more than she wanted to, hating the panic that curdled her voice.

'Come inside then,' he invited with a firm nod, gesturing to the sliding glass doors.

'Thank you.' She followed behind him, aware she should have more willpower than to stare at his bottom as he walked ahead of her, turning left and moving into a large, open-plan kitchen. More architectural features drew her eyes here, and she tried to focus on them rather than Alex, because she needed the momentary reprieve.

'The house is beautiful,' she repeated.

'Yes.' He withdrew a bottle of champagne from the fridge, the famous label speaking immediately of exclusivity and expense, then filled two stemless glasses before retrieving a bowl of fruit—grapes, strawberries and peeled citrus—and placing it between them. 'Help yourself.' He gestured to the fruit. 'Give me a moment to get changed.'

'Fine.' The word couldn't have come across any more curtly, and she flinched inwardly. Why the hell was he agreeing to this? He could find any number of women to bear his children. But not without emotional complications, she reminded herself after a beat. Alex didn't want a 'real' marriage, any more than she did.

And what about having his child, or children? The idea sat in her throat like gravel. All afternoon, she'd gone over that requirement of his, remembering how sure she'd been, once upon a time, that she wanted children. But day after day of marriage to Jonathan had killed that dream for her, and Tessa wasn't sure she could revive it.

She placed her briefcase on one of the barstools and reached for the champagne, taking a single sip before replacing the glass on the counter.

He returned quickly enough, dressed—thankfully—in a pair of khaki shorts and a white T-shirt, so all she had to contend with was the fascinating spectre of his tanned legs with muscular calves and the perfect covering of dark hair. So masculine and...inwardly she groaned. This was going to be a disaster.

'Okay.' He took up a matching position to hers, bracing his palms on either side of the counter, watching her with a small flicker of amusement at the corner of his lips. 'Let's do this.'

She nodded, gratitude making her heart twist. 'I've got some documents for you to review.'

'Documents?' His eyes flickered over her face with a hint of mockery, but she refused to be intimidated.

'Given our individual wealth and asset base, legal protections make sense.'

'In case I ever try to take you to the cleaners?'

Her lips tightened. 'It wouldn't be the first time.' She unzipped her document wallet with force, removing the contracts.

She hated the sympathy she saw in Alex's face. All year, people had viewed her as a victim, but that was about to stop. She was going to show everyone not only that she'd moved on, but also that she was deliriously happy—and with Greece's number-one bachelor, to boot.

He reached for the contracts, skimming the first page, turning it, reviewing the second. 'This looks standard.'

She raised her brows. 'How many prenuptial agreements have you signed?'

'None.' He glanced at her. 'But enough contracts to recognise unaltered legalese when I see it.'

'I just downloaded a standard template and modified it slightly. The gist is just that we keep what we came into the marriage with. So if we were to divorce, neither would have a claim on the other's wealth.'

'Seems reasonable.' He paused as he turned the page. 'Is there anything in here about children?'

'No.' She hesitated, feeling as though she were stepping into the twilight zone. 'I've been thinking about that.'

His expression gave nothing away, but her tummy suddenly squeezed as her nerves began to jangle. 'I know that's your condition for agreeing to this.' She spoke the words so quickly they all tripped over each other. 'And I agree to it in principle. But…' She paused, reaching into her briefcase and pulling out another document. 'There's something important we should discuss first.'

He waited with an expression that gave nothing away.

'I know your parents divorced, and that a lot of people do, and that's fine.' She missed the twisting of emotion deep in his eyes—her own feelings were taking too much space. 'But we're making a decision to get married specifically for the purpose of having children. I think it's only fair—to those children—that we agree to do everything we can to hold our marriage together. I would prefer not to share custody across our homes if we can find a way to live as husband and wife, come what may.'

'That seems fair.'

Her eyes widened. 'So you're saying you'd want to stay married?'

'Yes.' His eyes lanced her. 'My preference would also be to raise our children together.'

'What if you're miserable? Or I'm miserable?'

'Then we'll re-evaluate things. But as much as possible, we should go into this marriage with the intention of it being for good.'

Her heart leaped, and she tried not to be too pleased at the small victory. Everything with Jonathan had been a fight, all the time. She hadn't expected—or been prepared—for Alex to be so *reasonable*. Strangely, despite having spent a year fighting for divorce from Jonathan then a year recovering from it, she didn't feel at all nervous about what she and Alex had just agreed to.

As he continued to read, her cheeks flamed red, because she knew what the next section of her homemade contract dealt with.

'Sex on Friday night through Sunday night only.' It was obvious, when he lifted his face to look at her, that he was trying to flatten a smile. 'Never during the week?'

She shook her head firmly. 'I think it makes perfect sense to establish these—'

'Rules,' he supplied.

'Right.' She nodded, briskly.

'Uh-huh.' He turned the page, frowning when there was nothing further. 'There's no penalty clause.'

'I'm sorry?'

'Well, what happens if we slip up?'

'We won't,' she promised with complete confidence.

'I see.'

But Tessa had thought about this from every angle, and she knew this was the perfect way to contain the chemistry he'd referred to, to ensure it didn't boil over too much. 'This isn't a real marriage, and we're not really a couple. While I won't even attempt to deny that there's a spark between us, we're not animals, Alex. We can control when and where we act on it.'

'Of course,' he agreed, even when she had the feeling he wasn't agreeing with her at all, so much as teasing her.

She ignored the whip of frustration inside her belly. He could laugh and joke all he wanted; nothing would change Tessa's mind on this score. They had to take charge of this marriage, or it would never work.

'Do you agree to the contract?'

He ran a finger over the page and shook his head. 'It's a good start, but it could do with a bit of work.'

'Okay.' She reached for a berry, popping it in her mouth then wishing she'd resisted when his gaze followed the innocent gesture, lingering on the softness of her lips. Heat rushed through her.

'Where would we live?'

She looked around them. 'I'd actually been planning to suggest my apartment but...'

He waited, regarding her.

'I like your place. I can move in here, if that's easier.'

His eyes sparked with something she didn't understand. 'I will give you the full tour after this.'

Alarm bells dinged. A full tour would include things like bedrooms, and right now that was a dangerous prospect. 'That's okay, I can imagine,' she mumbled.

A knowing glint in his eyes showed he understood exactly what underscored her hesitation, but fortunately he didn't push it.

'We'll live here.' He made a note at the bottom of her contract. *Will.* Not *we could.* Something ignited in her bloodstream. This was happening. And even though she'd wanted this, it felt surreal and scary to contemplate the reality of becoming Mrs Alex Zacharidis. 'When will we get married?'

'Soon.'

'A week?'

'That really is soon,' she said with a shake of her head.

'I made enquiries this afternoon. I can get the legal documentation expedited.'

She bit down on her lip. What point was there in prevaricating? 'I guess that adds to the idea of this being a red-hot love affair.'

'As though we absolutely couldn't wait for the ink to dry on your divorce.'

'Yes,' she agreed, glad he understood.

'And we'll tell your parents together?'

'My parents.' She closed her eyes briefly, the main purpose for setting this in motion sharp in her mind. 'I'll call them soon. They should hear the news from me.'

'No.'

She blinked at him.

'I know your father, and he will only respect this if we do it properly. I'll ask for permission.'

She almost spat out her champagne. '*You'll* ask for permission?'

'What's the matter with that?'

'Apart from the fact I'm not an object of my father's to be given away?'

'He's traditional. It's about respect.'

'But you're *you*,' she reminded him.

'What is your point?'

'That you're the last man on earth to ask anyone for anything.'

'True, but the circumstances here are unique. My relationship with your brother, your parents… I can't ignore your father's wishes. I'll speak to him first.'

She hadn't expected this old-fashioned insistence and she had to remind herself it was just about respect of her father, nothing more.

'Good.' He turned the page of the contract. 'What kind of wedding do you want?' He peppered her with questions for the next hour, nutting out details she hadn't considered, until finally he dropped the pen and rocked back on his heels. 'That should do it.'

'Very comprehensive,' she agreed, wondering why the butterflies in her tummy seemed more excited than anxious.

'I'll have my office draft a press release tomorrow.'

'I've already done it,' she said, aware of the look on his face that spoke of being impressed. 'But what I don't have is a photo of us. It would be better if we could submit the press release with some kind of image. Do you mind if we take a selfie?'

He looked at her for several beats. 'Of course not. Mind if I see it?'

'The press release?'

He nodded once.

She reached into her handbag and withdrew a final piece of paper, handing it to him with fingers that shook slightly.

Theresa Anastakos announces engagement to Alexandros Zacharidis

'Well, for a start…' he paused '… I'll make the announcement.' He grabbed his pen and drew an arrow from his name to hers, indicating that they should swap.

'Why? Because you're the guy?' She almost poked out her tongue.

'Sure.' He shrugged his shoulders as though submitting to such outmoded patriarchal ideas wasn't innately offensive. 'And because you want your ex to seethe with jealousy. So, let's make it seem like I've pursued you, and finally won you over. How about…?' He scratched a confident line through the title. *'"Alexandros Zacharidis is delighted to announce engagement to Theresa Anastakos"?'*

Her heart did a little flutter, but she nodded curtly, as though it was an insignificant detail. 'Sounds good.'

He continued to read:

"After a brief courtship, Theresa Anastakos is pleased

to announce—"' He paused, put the lid on the pen and then shook his head.

'On second thoughts, this is way too stilted.'

'Well, what do you want me to do? How should we say it?'

He withdrew his phone from his pocket and clicked a few buttons, then let out a low whistle. 'You have a heap of followers on Instagram. Why not just announce it there?'

'Instagram?' She shuddered, the idea of social media covering her skin in goosebumps. The whole concept of social media was to put oneself out there, to exhibit and display, and beyond a few photos of artworks she'd been particularly proud of, Tessa had never taken to using the communication medium much at all. 'I'm not really into it.'

'I can see that. But regardless, you have many followers, and major news networks are bound to pick it up.'

'I guess that's more in keeping with what people do,' she agreed anxiously.

'So why don't we call your parents now and let them know, then you can post a photo and be done with it? My company will share any post you make. News will get around swiftly.'

Her heart stammered. 'So soon?'

'This was your idea, right?'

'Yeah, I just…'

She felt his eyes burning into her and had to confront the truth of their situation.

'Honestly? I really didn't think you'd say yes.'

'Nor did I,' came the swift response. 'Yet here we are, engaged.'

They stared at one another with a strange, shifting sense of fatalism, as if only now coming to grips with the fact this was really happening.

'So let's make it official.' He slid her phone across the bench, eyes on hers, holding a challenge. He was right. There was no sense putting this off a moment longer. Her parents would be thrilled, and that was all that mattered.

CHAPTER FOUR

THE MOMENT SHE hit 'post' on Instagram, events were set in motion.

She muted notifications on her phone, then turned it off when the calls started coming. First from friends, then from acquaintances, and finally from the media who, somehow, always managed to be able to get hold of private mobile-phone numbers.

After that, there was barely time to breathe. From the choosing of a wedding dress to confirming all the details in a hurry, to the delivery to her home of the most stunning engagement ring she'd ever seen, every minute of every day of that one single week jettisoned her towards this afternoon, a sunny Friday, on the bow of Alex's mega yacht, surrounded by a select handful of friends, and the only family they had remaining—her parents. Their presence as both Tessa and Alex's only blood relations underscored his personal motivation in making this marriage happen, highlighting how small their family connections were.

It was a week beset by uncertainty for Tessa. Was she doing the right thing? To launch from one marriage to another seemed like a particularly stupid idea. But then, just when her doubts almost had her convinced to abort the entire plan, she'd catch sight of her father's expression, his smile, his relaxed state, and she knew that this was worth it. If Jonathan had been her rebellion, then Alex was the path to repentance.

Some gossip rags continued to run whatever salacious detail Jonathan revealed on the reality TV show, which made it even easier for Tessa to convince herself she was doing the right thing. This marriage would put an end to Jonathan's hold over her, once and for all.

Every detail of the ceremony was perfect. Her father walked her down the aisle, beaming this time, in contrast to the stilted way in which he'd led her to the altar the last time she'd attempted this. The group with whom they'd chosen to mark the occasion were people with whom they could relax, and the ceremony itself was blessedly brief— because, as much as Tessa knew she was doing the right thing, that didn't stop her from feeling almost suffocated as the formalities went on.

The vows were recited in full, and then, out of nowhere, the reverend uttered those well-worn words, catching Tessa completely unaware.

'You may now kiss the bride.'

She startled, eyes wide and flying to Alex's face, as she grappled with this turn of events and kicked herself for not having pre-empted it. Of *course* they'd have to kiss—and look to be enjoying it.

Conscious of their guests watching, smiling, unaware that anything was amiss, she lifted a hand to Alex's chest, her fingers splayed across his pectoral muscles, as if to hold him at a set distance—or perhaps to draw him closer? There was no time to analyse her intent. A second later, his hands lifted to capture her face, one on either side, big and strong so her cheeks were completely covered and she was both trapped and caught, neither word holding negative connotations for Tessa.

He angled her face and his eyes lanced hers, mocking, questioning, and finally warning, as he dropped his head lower. His breath brushed her mouth first, warm and heady, so her lips parted of their own volition, and the hand in his shirt tightened, holding on to him for dear life. He dropped lower, his lips brushing hers, teasing her, tempting her, so she moaned, low in her throat, as a thousand memories, wishes, dreams flew into her mind.

There were so many layers to her feelings for Alexandros. As a teenager, she'd loved him—as much as any teenager could love a man. He'd been the object of all her fantasies. Every night she'd lain in bed thinking of him, willing herself to dream of him—because in her dreams, he'd never notice their ten-year age-gap or how gawky she was. After Stavros, and their night together, he'd taken on a new significance, so that she was almost lost to the power of her memories and needs, quite destroyed by the absence he formed in her life, particularly after she'd known the sweet completion of being in his arms.

His total desertion had destroyed her.

She'd been desperate for someone to make her feel whole again. She'd wanted someone to replace Alex, she'd needed to overwrite him, to push him from her mind, and then, Jonathan had appeared, handsome and flattering, fixing her bruised ego with his compliments. She'd thought it was love even when, with the benefit of hindsight, she could quite clearly see it was more a matter of Jonathan loving her family's fortune.

All her complex memories of Alex washed over her as his lips paused against hers, so she was rammed by the past, the distant past and the tangle of the unknown future, and, out of nowhere, tears threatened to sting her eyes, because she needed this marriage to fix her life, not complicate it.

Had she made a deal with the devil?

For the sake of her father, yes, she had. And now she had to live with it.

She went to pull away, but just as she did so his tongue flicked out, moving between her lips, taunting hers, duelling with it, and she moaned, because on some elemental level, despite what she'd just been thinking, she wanted this, so badly. She ached for him, regardless of how he'd rejected her in the past, regardless of how he'd hurt her.

And what kind of fool did that make Tessa?

She swayed forward, her body melding to his, and then he deepened the kiss with a swift, hungry strength, taking her and turning her away from the guests, his kiss now private and intimate, promising a thousand things that were between the two of them, and no one else.

And just when she felt ready to melt into the deck he lifted up, his dark gaze holding her dazed eyes, and his arm came around her waist for support. Their friends and family cheered, standing to celebrate the new couple, but inside, Tessa was numb.

There was no way she could control this. For the first time since agreeing to this marriage—and his terms—she realised that she was just as powerless to control her feelings for Alex as ever before. She knew how that would end…she had to protect herself.

Alex made a short speech, and then there was cake, and champagne, and finally they returned to the shoreline to allow guests to depart, enabling the 'happy couple' to enjoy their wedding night on a boat that more closely resembled a penthouse on water.

Tessa offered Alex a cool smile to prove to him, and herself, that she was calmly in control of their situation, even when their kiss had left her with a thousand doubts on that score.

'Mrs Zacharidis,' he murmured, watching her and seeing far too much.

Her lips tightened. 'I guess it's official.'

He moved closer, his hand reaching for hers, so she frowned, because they weren't really a couple and they didn't need to pretend. But when his fingers curved around hers, it felt…right. *Careful, Tessa.* She couldn't trust these feelings. Nothing about this was right—it was simply a means to an end.

'Any regrets?'

She considered that a moment, then shook her head. 'You?'

'I never have regrets,' he said with classic Alex arrogance. 'You look stunning.'

She dipped her head forward. 'Thank you.'

'I like this better than what you wore to your last wedding.'

'You weren't there.'

'No, but your parents had a huge photo by the door.'

'It's gone now.'

'I know.'

'No doubt you'll be up there before tomorrow morning.'

He laughed with genuine affection and a pang of something like jealousy hit her right in the heart. His affection for her parents was genuine, there was no doubting that. 'I'm flattered.'

'They really love you.'

Something flickered in his eyes, a look she didn't understand, and then he turned his face away, eyes chasing the cliffs that formed a wall to the shore. They were white in colour, crisp against the perfect turquoise of the sea.

'On days like this, they miss him so much,' Tessa continued, her smile slipping. 'Stavros should be here.'

'Yes.'

And then it was Tessa who was closing the distance, coming to stand right beside him, their hands held at her side.

'I wonder what he'd make of this,' she asked with a small shake of her head.

'He'd want to kill me,' Alex responded with not a hint of doubt.

'Why? For swooping in and being my saviour?'

He angled his face to hers, his eyes sparking with unmistakable intent now. 'For the direction of my thoughts all week.'

Her lips formed a perfect 'o' and she didn't dare ask—she didn't *need* to ask—for clarification on the direction of his thoughts, because her own thoughts had gone there plenty too. She'd done her level best to keep busy, but in the back of her mind the fact they were to be married, and that a whole weekend stretched before them now, was like a form of hypnosis. If she didn't use all her concentration, she felt herself falling under the spell of those thoughts, wanting, more than anything, to remember every detail of that night.

'Are you hungry?'

The question was the last thing she'd expected. She shook her head without breaking eye contact; she couldn't.

'Do you want to go for a swim?'

Swimming? As warm as the weather was, it was the last thing on Tessa's mind. 'Do *you* want to go swimming?'

His eyes bored into hers and she held her breath, waiting for him to deny it, but then, earning a whip of frustration from Tessa, he nodded slowly. 'Why not? We've got all night.'

And just when she thought the moment was over, he leaned down and kissed her with the same kind of hunger he'd shown during their wedding ceremony, as though this was the end of their time together and not the beginning, as though he could commit the taste of her to memory. It was all a lie. She knew how important it was to remember that. Alex was a very practised lover—he'd had more experience than she cared to contemplate. He was capable of turning his passion on and off at the drop of a hat, but Tessa wasn't. She was nothing like him.

'Did you bring bathers?' He asked the question right into her mouth, so the words washed over her and she shivered.

She shook her head without breaking contact with his lips. 'It's our wedding, not a beach holiday. I...wasn't expecting us to stay onboard after… I mean, after the ceremony.'

'Then we'll have to swim inside.' He lifted her easily, cradling her against his chest and kissing her as he carried her along the side deck of the yacht and through a timber door.

She didn't notice anything as he walked, navigating the corridor with ease, passing rooms that could have been bedrooms or not, until he reached a large space that had a spa bath at the front of it. 'Oh.' She tried to subdue her butterflies into order as he carried her towards it. She tried to keep hold of her sensible thoughts, and, most importantly, the knowledge that even when things looked and felt perfect, they could actually be the exact opposite.

On the edge of the spa bath, he placed her down, his eyes meeting hers with a mocking challenge as he began to unbutton her dress, reaching behind her so their bodies touched and his lips were just an inch from his.

Did he know how much she wanted to reach up and kiss him?

Did he understand what he was doing to her?

Of course he did. This was Alex Zacharidis. He knew *exactly* the impact his purposeful seduction was having on Tessa.

As he put her in the swirling spa water, she reminded herself that relaxing into this relationship would be the first step on a path to disaster, and yet she didn't make any effort to remove herself from the situation. She simply watched, heart racing, blood firing.

He shucked off his shoes and shirt and trousers before stepping into the spa in only his boxer shorts, and then he was kissing her again, this time pulling her towards him as he sat, so she straddled him, her hair falling down her back in dark chestnut waves, every part of her singing at the perfection of this physical moment.

Tessa no longer believed she had a sensual bone in her

body, so it was incredible to *feel* these responses, to know her body to be wanting him, and to feel evidence of the way in which he wanted her. After Jonathan, she'd presumed this part of her had been destroyed; feeling it stirring to life made her want to throw caution to the wind and make love to Alex, just to prove to herself that she was, in fact, capable of pleasure and pleasing.

Hunger drove her, making her ache to take him just like this, but he went slowly, slowly, chasing his fingers over her body, followed by his mouth, teasing her flesh with little flicks of his tongue then nips of his teeth, so sensual, so flirtatious, but nowhere near *enough*. Frustration made her growl because she didn't want to be taunted. She wanted to be made love to, right now. Every single one of her fantasies was barrelling through her. The week of waiting had been all the foreplay she needed.

'I want you,' she declared against his throat, grinding her hips to prove her point, shocking herself with the power of her needs and also her directness.

'That is something we share,' he grunted, rolling his hips in an answering rhythm, then moving his mouth to her breast, taking a nipple between his teeth and wobbling it before withdrawing and flicking it instead with his tongue. She arched her back as arrows of pleasure shot through her and he laughed softly, then bit down again, sucking this time, so she whimpered, because it felt so damned good and yet it was still not enough.

His touch was so sure, so confidently demanding, and yet she was tumbling out of control—and even when racked by passion, she was innately terrified as well, because control offered protection and she *had* to protect herself.

Tessa pulled away from Alex, face pink, eyes sparkling when they met his. 'But this is just sex, like we agreed in our contract.'

'Well, it is Friday,' he agreed, without missing a beat.

'Right.' The reassurance relaxed her, as much, at least, as Tessa was capable of relaxing in any circumstance like this. Her relationship with Jonathan hadn't been easy, and on the handful of times they'd been intimate he'd been so critical of her that she'd lost all confidence. It was so easy to believe she was terrible in bed. The insults he'd thrown at her when he'd turned to other women, the way he'd looked at her... The insidious voice of self-doubt was peppering her mind, so she pulled away, needing to know that this wasn't just a means to an end. 'You know I'm still on the pill, right?'

He paused, and ice infiltrated her veins, until he lifted his shoulders. 'Then this will not be the time we make a baby.' He pushed up, kissing the skin on the side of her mouth. 'But we can discuss contraceptives another time.'

Butterflies burst through her. So this wasn't just a means to an end, he wasn't using her desire for him to make a baby, yet she couldn't get self-doubt out of her mind regardless. Old habits were too entrenched, and she had too much to overcome. Yes, there was Jonathan's treatment of her, but at the root of it all, and the real reason Jonathan had been able to undermine her so successfully, was because of the way Alex had rejected her four years earlier.

The scathing way he'd looked at her, the way he'd spoken to her...

She would never forget it.

What if it happened again now? What if they slept together and then he responded in the same way? Panic exploded, so her brow beaded with sweat.

He kissed her hungrily, yet her pleasure ebbed, leaving only anxiety.

Sensing Tessa's shift of mood, he pulled away, frowning a little as he scanned her face. 'Are you okay, *agape*?'

Great. Just what she needed—kindness. From Alex. She blinked, turning her attention to the stunning view and pretending the kind of fascination that would befit someone who'd never before seen the ocean. 'I'm fine. Let's keep going.'

He made a sound of surprise, then moved, unseating her and shifting her to the tiled ledge beside him. Dark colour slashed his cheekbones, indignation carved his features into granite. 'This is not supposed to be a chore, Theresa. Contract or not, we do not have to have sex.'

Her eyes flashed to his, and her stomach tied itself completely in knots. Maybe her first instinct was right, and he *didn't* want her after all. And just like that, the sting of tears threatened the backs of her eyes, so she blinked quickly, doing her best to push them away. 'It's okay,' she said, as though it didn't matter. 'I don't mind either way.'

When he didn't respond, she blinked towards him quickly, in time to see his jaw shifting as though he was grinding his teeth.

'You're annoyed with me?' Just like Jonathan. This was a disaster.

'No,' he answered quickly, frowning. 'I'm confused by you, but that's okay.'

He had every right to be confused. A minute ago she'd been kissing him as though her life depended on it, and now she was completely devoid of desire.

'It's been a really long time for me,' she whispered, unable to meet his eyes.

'That's all right.' His gentle, kind response physically hurt her. She felt vulnerable—which she hated—and his kindness was just evidence that he saw her vulnerabilities and was taking pity on her. She almost groaned in frustration.

'No, it's not. I agreed to this. I can do it.'

'*Cristos*, Theresa, I don't want you to grit your teeth through sex. What the hell do you take me for?'

His offence was obvious. She grimaced, offering an apologetic smile before pushing up to stand on feet that were none too steady. She was a mess. She hadn't thought this through before—she hadn't been capable of thought—but as she looked around, she saw no towels and a perfectly nice floor she didn't want to saturate.

'I don't want to leave puddles everywhere.'

'It's a yacht—puddles go with the territory.'

She didn't respond. The idea of walking, dripping wet, away from him was undignified and somehow wrong.

'I'll get you a towel.' As he stepped out of the spa, the evidence of his own arousal was on display, so she turned her back, lips parted, breath burning. She was beyond confused. If he was aroused, then it was proof that he had wanted her. But maybe that was just a physical response, like sneezing when you looked at the sun.

Plagued by self-doubt, she hated herself in that moment, and everything that had happened to turn her into this. Wasn't there a saying about time healing all wounds? Maybe eventually she'd be herself again.

Alex returned with the towels, but instead of handing one to her, as she'd expected, he placed one on the floor at his feet and gestured for her to step out. She did so, not able to meet his eyes, and when she was standing in front of him he wrapped the other towel around her shoulders, making her feel warm and protected and safe. All feelings she immediately pushed aside. She was none of those things because of him. She had to find her own way to those emotions, she couldn't rely on Alex to provide them.

'Thank you.' Her gratitude was expressed crisply.

A sharp sigh escaped his lips and then he was lifting her up again, cradling her wet body to his broad chest, carrying her through the yacht. They were definitely leaving the puddles she'd intended to avoid, but she clung on to Alex, breathing in his masculine scent as he turned and walked through a door, into a bathroom that was too grand to exist on a yacht. Her family's own boat was well-appointed but this was next level.

He placed her on the tiled floor, holding her right in front of him. 'May I?' he asked, hand lifting to the back of her bra.

She couldn't look away. Eyes huge in her face, she nodded slowly, then blinked her eyes closed as he unclasped it.

He dropped it to the ground and her nipples puckered against the evening air, her skin lifting in goosebumps: not because she was cold, but because she was warming up again, finding it hard to keep a grip of the reality she so desperately wanted to have uppermost in her mind.

It would be so easy to lean forward and kiss him. To throw caution to the wind and surrender to their passion as they'd done earlier, but doubts collided with her absolute need to control the terms of their relationship, so instead she took a step backwards, looking over her shoulder. 'Is there anything I need to know about operating the shower?'

A lump formed in her throat and she looked away, conscious of the way he moved to the enormous shower and stepped inside, flicking a lever then sliding another one. 'This does temperature,' he said. 'And this, water pressure.'

'Okay, thanks,' she mumbled nervously.

'Do you need anything else?'

It was a loaded question with one answer. She needed him. But she needed, even more than that, to push the past from her mind. She just didn't know how. Marrying Alex had made sense on the day, but she hadn't realised that she'd be living with—making love to—the man who'd broken her heart and destroyed her self-esteem. She honestly believed she'd got over it, but the more the idea of sleeping with Alex became a reality, the more her fears bubbled to the surface, convincing her he'd reject her all over again. And how sharp would the sting of pain be this time?

'No. I won't be long.'

CHAPTER FIVE

THE DUSK SKY was filled with shards of light, splintered from the slow-falling sun like arrows of gold against a mauve and peach background. Stars were just beginning to spark overhead, and the air tasted of salt and summer. For the first time in years, her fingers itched to capture the scenery on a canvas. She closed her eyes for a moment, imagining the colours she would blend to distil exactly the right shade—it went beyond the colours for Tessa, it was about translating the atmosphere of that moment into a picture.

But with her eyes closed, her mind moved from the image of the sunset to the man at her side, silent and strong, haunting her not with anything he'd done, so much as just by his nearness.

Her eyes jolted open, and she turned to face him, the suddenness of the gesture drawing his face to hers. She frowned slowly, nerves fluttering inside her.

'Alex,' she said, his name hovering in the air between them, a little uncertainly. There was so much she didn't know—questions she should have asked before marrying him suddenly erupted as a volcano.

His features prompted her to continue, then he reached for his beer, removing it from the nearby counter and taking a sip.

'If…' She paused, the words seizing in her throat. She forced herself to continue. 'If we were to have kids, how would you see that working?'

'Do you mean the biology of falling pregnant?'

Heat flooded her cheeks. 'I meant the parenting, not the pregnancy part.' Though the thought of growing round with his baby was doing strange things to her equilibrium, and now the idea of children wasn't a strange, abstract concept, but a reality that was hovering just ahead of them. She could even imagine what their children might look like, with his eyes and symmetrical features and her glossy brown hair.

'We'd make it work.'

She bit down on her lip. 'That's a little simplistic, isn't it?'

'What exactly are your concerns?'

'You work a lot, right?'

He dipped his head in agreement.

'So you'd barely see our child?'

'My intention would be to scale back, once the baby was born.'

She angled her face, focusing on the disappearing sun.

'That doesn't suit you?'

'It's not that.'

'Then what?'

'I just…remember how busy my dad always was. And then Stavros. I know you're just like them…'

'Yes,' he said quietly. 'But I'm not asking you to have and raise my baby. I want children so I can be a part of their lives.'

'You keep saying children, not child. Why?'

She turned back to him just in time to catch the hint of a frown on his face. 'Why not?'

It was an unsatisfying answer, but she let it go.

'Did you have a nanny?'

He opened his mouth to respond, then closed it again. 'No.'

That was strange. 'But?' she prompted, reaching across and taking a sip of his beer, because her champagne was empty. Only just realising, he reached for the bottle and replenished her glass, his face averted from hers.

'There is no "but".'

'I got the feeling you were going to say something else.'

'No.'

'So your parents were active in your upbringing?'

He lifted his beer to his lips, taking a long sip, and she shivered because a moment earlier her lips had been on the bottle, and in a strange way it almost felt like they were kissing by proxy. Flashbacks of the way he'd kissed her in the spa sent her pulse into overdrive.

'Until I went to boarding school.'

'That was after the divorce,' she murmured, almost embarrassed by the little biographical details she had stored in her brain. As a teenager she'd been so in awe of him that she'd sat on the edge of her seat, listening to every word he said.

'A week after they told me they were separating.'

'That must have been hard.'

He ran his finger down the side of the bottle, apparently fascinated by the condensation. 'Not really.'

'You don't want to have this conversation, do you?'

'There's nothing to be gained by having it,' he confirmed, his tone unfamiliar to her, because for a moment, he didn't sound like a human so much as an automaton, devoid of emotion. But that wasn't Alex. Not really.

None the less, she let it go. 'That's a long way down the track anyway, right?'

He was quiet a moment, then turned to face her, speculatively. 'It's not essential that we conceive a child immediately, no.'

She considered that. 'How come you're not already settled down with some woman who's just as desperate to have babies with you?'

His lips twisted in a hint of amusement. 'Because until you came into my office with your very pragmatic proposal, I had no intention of getting married.'

'Why not?'

'For many reasons.'

'Such as?'

'Has anyone ever told you, you'd have made a great inquisitor?'

She wiggled her brows. 'Nope, but thank you.'

'It wasn't a compliment,' he murmured, but with the hint of a smile, so something warm zinged in the centre of her chest.

'You date women. I've seen the proof.' She tried not to think about the photos of Alex Zacharidis that cluttered the internet, beautiful women hanging on his arm, coming in and out of nightclubs, so handsome, so desired.

'Have you?'

'Photos, anyway.' She shrugged. 'And you're obviously a very attractive, successful man.' The description emerged stilted. 'I'm guessing lots of women would be interested in becoming Mrs Zacharidis.'

'Would have been,' he corrected her tense. '*You* are my wife.'

You are my wife. The words were so possessive, so insanely hot, that her spine felt made of lava.

'Who knows?' he said after a beat. 'I never considered marrying anyone else.'

Her stomach fluttered. She ignored it, focusing on what he was revealing with his very spare answers. 'Why not?'

He compressed his lips with a hint of exasperation. 'You don't give up, do you?'

'Is it some big secret?'

He hesitated a moment, then shook his head. 'It's not something I generally discuss, but no, it's not what I would call a secret, either.' He finished his beer, leaning over the bar then, staring out at the ocean. In profile, his face was determined and strong. 'My parents' marriage was a living hell. Their very particular brand of love-hate was my purgatory from birth. I learned to walk on eggshells growing up, and I hated it. I was still a very small boy when I formed an intention to live on my own, always. I didn't want to fight the way they fought. I didn't want to know the tension of moving from love and tranquillity to hatred and rage.' His eyes burned across the horizon. 'They fought, always. And by that, I mean they almost killed each other. Shouted, cursed, accused, ranted, generally destroyed one another, until they'd make up and for a few days everything would be rosy, but not really, because it was like being in the eye of the storm. I only ever knew one thing for certain: the storm would keep going. They were incapable of being together without arguing.'

'You grew up in a war zone,' she murmured intuitively, so his eyes locked to hers, his expression grim, and then he nodded.

She shook her head wistfully for the boy he'd been. 'A lot of marriages *are* happy, though. Look at my parents'.'

'Your parents are very lucky to have found each other, but what they have is rare. Divorce is far more common. Present company included.'

'Ouch.'

'That wasn't meant to be an insult, so much as an observation. I would have thought you, of all people, would understand my perspective.'

She considered that thoughtfully. 'We didn't really fight like that.' Her finger went to the champagne flute and she curled her hand around it, distracted by the popping bubbles.

'What was it like between the two of you?'

She hadn't spoken to another soul about her marriage, but for some reason it didn't hurt to imagine opening up to Alex the way she thought it might have. 'We married very quickly,' she admitted, rushing the words rather than giving him any hint of *why* she'd been so eager to accept Jonathan's proposal, how desperate she'd been to overcome the hurt and embarrassment Alex had inflicted when he'd callously rejected her, but unconsciously she pulled away from him, putting distance between them as she remembered the pain he'd caused her. 'I'd known him a little over a month, and so I wound up married to a man who was, in many ways, a stranger to me.' She gnawed on her lip, hating to remember that time.

'Why get married so fast?'

Trust Alex to pinpoint the one area she wasn't comfortable discussing.

'I thought I was in love,' she lied, shooting him a cynical look. 'Why wait?'

'It's prudent to get to know someone, I would have thought.'

'Hindsight is a wonderful thing,' she muttered, then sighed. 'The truth is, there was a part of me that wanted to escape.'

'Escape what?'

You, she wanted to shout, *and the grip you had on my every waking thought.*

'Oh, a lot of things,' she mumbled. 'After Stavros, my world felt tipped off balance.' She couldn't meet his eyes. 'I lost my brother, and essentially my parents, who were so fogged by their own grief that they refused to let me leave the house, lest something happen to me, at the same time as they barely acknowledged my existence because they were in such a daze. They've always been very protective of me, and that got a thousand times worse afterwards. Jonathan offered a way out—from all of it.'

He was quiet, considering that, but if he wondered, in the back of his mind, if any part of her decision was a reflection on him, he didn't ask the question.

'And yet you stayed married to him?'

'I wasn't miserable at first. All marriages have challenges and I thought we had to overcome ours. But some problems were too big to solve. We officially separated after two years, though we had been living basically separate lives for some time already. And then a year after that, we divorced. It was a…difficult time.'

Alex was quiet for so long she presumed the conversation had moved on, and she listened to the gentle, rhythmic lapping of the water against the boat's pearlescent sides. 'Do you still love him?'

The question zapped her, coming as it did almost out of nowhere. 'No.' A harsh rebuttal. Too harsh? 'Definitely not,' she added for good measure.

But when she turned to face Alex, there was cynicism in his eyes, as though he didn't, for a second, believe her. And maybe that was a good thing? If he believed she still partly loved her ex-husband, he'd never have reason to suspect he'd hurt her so much four years earlier, that she was still hurting from his words.

'In my experience, only deep love can cause such lasting hurt.'

She flinched, because he was right, but it hadn't been Jonathan she'd loved and been hurt by.

Eager to change the subject before he could ask anything more insightful, she said, 'I suppose we should be getting back to the marina.'

'Actually, I want to take you to Epíneio.'

'Where's that?' She immediately liked the musical name.

'My island.'

'Your island?' She arched a brow. 'Seriously?'

He nodded once, eyes returning to the sea. 'Is your ex-husband the reason you didn't have children?'

'Oh,' she chased an airplane across the sky with her eyes, 'I guess so.'

'Because it was so tense between the two of you?'

'Yeah.' There was no real need to elaborate on that. She sighed softly. 'Let's not talk about Jonathan, Alex. I don't want him in my life any more, and I sure as hell don't want him in our marriage. He's not relevant.'

She could tell, from the look in his eyes, that he didn't believe her.

Epíneio meant haven, and as his yacht drew closer to a small pontoon Tessa couldn't help thinking how apt the name was.

Even from the deck of the boat, she could see the calming quality of the place. Tall white cliffs tufted with dark green grass and spiky trees gradually lowered to form a white sand beach with a thick wall of overgrown trees, creating the impression of nature run amok, and through the busy, ancient trunks she caught fleeting glimpses of a home— too fleeting to see much detail, so curiosity and anticipation filled her belly.

It was more than the scenery though. There was something exquisitely transient about the light, and again her fingers craved the familiar grip of a paintbrush, her artist's mind analysing the textures and shapes, the colours, imagining exactly how she could capture this natural palette.

As the crew brought the boat into the dock, expertly guiding it to the pontoon's edge, Tessa stood with her elbows propped against the railing, warm breeze lifting her hair, eyes trained on the island. She hadn't seen Alex for hours. They'd shared coffee that morning, and made some necessary small talk to break up the silence. It was all so…polite. Sitting across from him, she could never have guessed how close they'd come the day before to making love. Except for the way her pulse trembled when his eyes hooked to hers, and heat seemed to be burning her from the inside out.

As the boat achieved its resting position, the crew sprang to life, throwing down ropes and leaping onto the deck, to unfurl a walkway that would make it easier for Tessa and Alex to depart.

Alex appeared almost magically at her side, and the sight of him like this caused her heart to clench. He was wearing a white shirt and knee-length shorts, with glasses tucked into the collar of his shirt and a cap on his head, so Alex was so casual and handsome that her bones turned to puddles and she almost forgot about the distance she needed to keep from him and threw herself into his arms.

Instead, she offered him a small, tight smile. 'This is very nice.'

Nice? So tepid! She had become used to keeping much of herself screened off, and it hadn't bothered her. In fact, she'd been grateful to have developed that technique, but for a moment she wanted to crack through that veneer and just be…herself.

'It's a good place to come when I need to get away.'

'And how often is that?'

He put a hand in the small of her back, simply to guide her towards the walkway, but that didn't matter. He might as well have been cupping her breasts, for the way her central nervous system went into overdrive. 'Most weekends.'

The narrow width of the gangplank brought their bodies close. She suppressed a shiver. 'Really? I thought you were out with a different woman every night?'

'And that bothers you?'

Damn it! She'd walked right into that. 'Of course not,' she responded stiffly. 'I suppose you come here with them, anyway.'

'No.' His interruption was sharp. 'Epíneio is personal. Private.'

A shiver ran down her spine, because he'd brought her here regardless, to his private sanctuary. It didn't mean anything, but something fluttered inside Tessa's belly; she felt ridiculously pleased.

From this vantage point, she could see more of the house and it forced a small sigh from her lips, because the building had clearly sat in this very position for a long time. Terracotta walls that had been rendered white were offset by a red-tiled roof. The door was painted a happy blue, and big pots of geraniums stood on either side. Everywhere she looked was a scene she wanted to capture. Excitement bubbled through her blood. During her marriage, she'd struggled with her art. Jonathan's criticism and her deeply unhappy state had paralysed her, but here, she felt inspiration at every turn.

'This is beautiful,' she whispered, the words utterly inadequate for the perfection that surrounded them.

'What about you, *agape*?' he asked with a note of determination.

Her eyes skittered to his and her heart thundered. 'You don't have to call me that, you know. No one is around. When it's just the two of us, we can be ourselves.'

'Okay, Theresa. Is that better?'

No, it was way worse, because he said her name like a whisper, and it hit her as a warm breeze on a spring afternoon, so she tingled all the way to her soul.

She was mesmerised by him, unable to look away. 'No one calls me that.'

'Stavros used to.'

Her stomach tightened. 'I know.'

'Whenever he would talk about you, he'd call you Theresa.'

Her lips twisted in an involuntary smile. 'What sort of things would he say?'

They moved from the jetty to the warm white sand, and because it was dry and uneven she almost stumbled. Alex's hand shot out, capturing her elbow, holding her close. She didn't pull away at first—the support was appreciated—but once they moved beyond the sand, under the shade of the coastal trees, she took a step to the side, her equilibrium in tatters.

'He was very proud of you,' Alex belatedly answered her question. 'He believed you were going to set the world on fire. In a good way,' Alex added, a small grin changing his face completely so the world seemed to tip off balance, and not just because of the unexpected compliment.

'Stavros? I don't believe it.'

'Surely you know he thought the world of you?'

Her lips twisted to the side. 'We were chalk and cheese,' she said after a beat. 'He was always talking about the company with my parents. The way his brain worked… I was in awe. Honestly, I didn't even know if he noticed me, half the time.'

Alex made a strangled noise of surprise and stopped walking. 'Don't say that.'

She looked up at him, his reaction unexpected. 'I loved him very much,' she hastened to add. 'I worshipped him, in fact.' She'd worshipped *both* of them. 'But I'm ten years younger, and we had nothing in common.'

Alex's chest moved as he drew in a breath, and awareness heated Tessa's veins. 'He was very protective of you,' he said, after a beat. 'He thought you were smart and determined, but far, far too kind. That your kindness would make you vulnerable.' A muscle worked overtime in Alex's jaw. 'He wanted to protect you from the worst of the world.'

That wasn't new information, and his protectiveness had driven her crazy, much of the time, but she still loved how much he'd cared. 'I miss him,' she said on a soft sigh.

'As do I.'

He put a hand in her lower back, guiding her once more along the path towards the house, and as it came into view, thoughts of anything else shifted from the forefront of her mind.

'Oh, Alex. This is stunning!' she exclaimed, genuinely moved by the perfection of the unassuming little house in the middle of an expanse of green grass. 'It's just what a beach house should be!'

She was unaware of the way his eyes rested on her face, his gaze hungrily travelling her features, reading her in a way she wouldn't have wanted to be read. Tessa was far too absorbed in the building, the geraniums and lavender and frangipani trees that formed a relaxed garden at the front, and the citrus she could see growing down the side. 'I can see why you come here so often.' She quickened her pace and unconsciously pulled away from him, moving up the stairs of the house with eyes full of wonder.

'It's an easy commute,' he said with a shrug, leaning

across her to point across the garden. 'There's space for a helicopter, and, on the other side of the island, cabins for staff.'

'How many staff?'

'It varies depending on the season. In summer, just a couple—my housekeeper and gardener. She stocks the fridge with meals, he keeps the vines from taking over.' He gestured to the jasmine that was creeping advantageously along one side, reminding her of the story of Sleeping Beauty.

She sighed, the warmth on her back and the fragrance of the garden relaxing her in a way she would usually have fought against.

'I can already tell, I won't want to leave,' she joked, moving up the steps. They were uneven from years of use, their middles gently dipping like a hammock.

'You don't have to leave.'

But she bristled against that intuitively. She couldn't let herself get caught up in the fantasy of this. Because it was so easy to see how she could stay here and relax, how the beauty of this place would convince her—easily—to let her guard down. How she could let him call her *agape* and hold her close, kiss her and make love to her, and she would start to believe that this was real. It would be so easy to *trust* him, when she knew that trusting anyone was a sure-fire way to end up getting hurt. 'It's beautiful, Alex, but it's not real life.' The words were stiff and heavy, reality tightening around her like a straitjacket.

'Then just enjoy the weekend, Theresa. Your *life* will be waiting for you, Monday morning.'

CHAPTER SIX

ALEX DIDN'T THINK of his parents that often, and he hadn't dreamed of them in years—not since his mother had died and his brain had thrown random, ancient memories into the mix, so each dawn had brought with it a sense of total disorientation as he tried to wade his way back to the right time zone and reality.

But on that night, alone in his bed on Epíneio, he dreamed of his mother, and his father, and their fights were as vivid in his mind as if they were happening anew. He dreamed of the worst night—the one when his mother had threatened to kill herself, and a twelve-year-old Alex had run from his room to find her, heart racing, chest hurting.

They'd been in the kitchen, his mother's face tear-stained, his father's resolute and unfeeling. His mother held a butcher's knife in her hands, the one she used to slice the tomatoes when they were ripe and just picked from the vines. 'I hate you so much,' she'd sobbed, lifting the knife higher.

Alex wasn't conscious that he had made a noise, but he must have, because his mother turned to face him, her eyes like a wild animal's, her body trembling with anger and shock, face contorted. Her breath was the only sound in the room, and then it grew harder and more forced as she dropped the knife onto the counter.

His father spoke first. 'Alexandros. Go back to bed.' The words were a command, barked from his body, but Alex ignored them, running to his mother and pushing her—pushing her away from the knife, trying to shake her out of the mood, trying to bring her back to him.

She was stiff, like a board, her eyes enormous, and Alex

had the strangest sense that she didn't recognise him. He was losing her, or had he already lost her?

He woke, on the second night of his marriage, in the early hours of the morning, face wet with perspiration despite the open windows that rolled a soft, salty sea breeze towards him. He could taste the tang in the air and, on autopilot, he stood and walked towards it, hovering at the window for several beats, waiting for his breathing to calm, for the images to recede.

His marriage had brought certain issues to the forefront of his mind. The dreams were an unwelcome intrusion.

He knew from past experience that he wouldn't be able to sleep after the nightmare, and so he didn't bother trying. Instead, he strode from his bedroom, wearing just a pair of boxers, into the open-plan kitchen. The full moon was high in the sky, cutting a silvery beam through the trees and across the floor, so he only flicked on the little lamp above the range hood, pouring himself a glass of Scotch in a crystal glass then resting it, untouched, on the counter.

His mother hadn't killed herself that night, but she'd planted the seed of worry in Alex's mind, and from that moment he hadn't had a single encounter with her that wasn't framed by his concern—even the good memories were tainted by his understanding of her desperation, and his apprehension of what she might be capable of. When she did, finally, end her life, it was with no witnesses, no tries, and no one to push away the knife. Which wasn't to say Alex hadn't been left reeling.

His lips tightened as his thoughts turned to his wife, and the marriage from which she'd escaped. Theresa was a very different character to his mother, but that didn't mean that staying in a miserable marriage might not have led her to the same all-consuming depression that had dogged his mother.

The idea of Theresa suffering even a fraction of that amount left Alex with a strange taste in his mouth, like acid and petroleum. He threw back a generous measure of the Scotch, then kept his hand curled around the outside of the glass, his grip firm, his body wound tighter than a spring.

Once, he'd heard his father describe his marriage as 'the dark side of the moon', but it had taken Alex's growing into a man for him to understand the meaning. Their marriage was indeed dark, but it was beautiful too, silvery and perfect, all too briefly, and so they'd both fought for those moments, for the silver and light, enduring the waxing of the darkness for the brief periods of shimmering joy, ever hopeful the latter would come to dominate. It rarely did.

His parents had let their emotions dictate their relationship.

His father he couldn't help but blame. Where his mother had clearly, he saw now, been suffering from depression and anxiety, his father had refused to get her help, and he'd refused to let her go, when the marriage was so obviously one of the reasons she was in pain.

His mother hadn't had the strength to leave.

But Theresa had.

She'd realised that the way she was being treated was wrong, that she deserved better, and she'd packed her bags and left, despite the fact that was admitting to having made a mistake. Despite the fact her bastard of an ex-husband seemed intent on continuing to mar her happiness, just because he could.

Hatred flooded Alex at the idea of any kind of person who could behave that way. Love turned to hate, hope dashed, enmity remaining. It was a common story—one he'd sworn he would never play a part in.

Which was why, as he finished off his Scotch, he couldn't help but feel glad that love wasn't—and never would be—feature of this marriage. Somehow, they'd ended up in near-perfect scenario, having negotiated terms that suited them both. True, their desire was inescapable, but even that they could tame.

Although it wasn't completely perfect, he thought, pouring another drink. This time he carried the glass out of the kitchen, onto the front porch, where he leaned against the railing, regarding the ocean. He could see only darkness, and a hint of seafoam on the tip of the rolling waves, as the milky whiteness of the moon formed an uneven line in the distance. Theresa hadn't got out of her relationship with Jonathan scot-free. Her reaction to their intimacy after their wedding had shown how much of a burden she still carried.

They'd slept together before, so he understood the desire that stirred in her veins, and all the ways in which she was a passionate, sensual woman, but now it was clear to Alex that she'd been hurt badly, her confidence shaken.

His mother had been broken by marriage, and so had Theresa—albeit in different ways. And as much as he wanted to *show* her how great sex between them would be, he needed her to get there first, on her own. He couldn't put his finger on why that was so important, but he knew it mattered, and he knew he would wait.

It was one thing to make a pledge to himself in the small hours of the morning to respect her boundaries and keep sex from becoming an issue, and quite another to be confronted by the sight of his newly minted wife in a shirt of his that exposed her tanned, smooth thighs and which clung to her body like a second skin courtesy of the fact she'd obviously worn it swimming. She lay draped over a sunlounger, face tilted towards the house, eyes closed, her dark hair pulled over one shoulder. She looked beautiful, untouchable and incredibly hot.

So much for good intentions. As all his blood pooled in a specific part of his anatomy, he walked towards her, glad his boardshorts were black and would go some of the way to hiding the evidence of his attraction. He moved until his shadow was cast over her face and then he watched, waiting. Slowly her eyes peeped open, locking to his, and a frown briefly tightened her features before she sat up, awkward and self-conscious, reaching for her towel and pinning it to her chest, as though instead of one of his business shirts, she wore nothing.

'Alex!' Her voice was croaky, her eyes huge, lashes clumped together by water. 'I didn't know you were here.'

'I wasn't. I just came outside.'

'Oh. It was such a warm morning and the pool looked so inviting, but I didn't have a swimming costume so I borrowed one of your shirts—I hope that's okay?'

Uncertainty made her voice husky, and he hated that. He didn't want her to be nervous around him.

'Of course. I'll have the housekeeper arrange some clothes for you today.'

'There's no need,' she denied quickly. 'If we go home tomorrow—'

'Monday,' he corrected, taking up position on the lounger beside her with the appearance of effortless calm. 'There's no rush. We could stay longer.'

'Oh?'

'Technically, it is our honeymoon.'

'Right.' She nodded, frowning though, uncertainty on her features. 'But that's not really necessary.'

'You said you love the island.'

'I do.'

Even as he pushed this point, he wondered what the hell he was doing. He hadn't planned to suggest they remain any longer than the weekend, but something about her inability to relax made him want to keep her here. Away from Athens, reality TV shows, ex-husbands and the real world.

'Let's play it by ear,' he said with a lift of his shoulders. 'We'll leave when it suits us to leave.'

She opened her mouth as if to argue then shut it again, pushing herself back on the sunbed and staring straight ahead, clearly ruminating.

'How's the water?' he asked after another moment had passed, the sun beating down on him, warming him to the core.

'Divine.'

'Did you try the ocean yet?'

She shook her head, turning to face him, her cheeks pink.

'Well? Shall we?'

She hesitated and he could tell her first instinct was to say 'no', so he stood, extending a hand, gently encouraging her, waiting while she waged an inner argument and then finally pushed her legs over the side of her sunlounger.

'Just quickly,' she huffed, as though annoyed with herself for agreeing. He hid a smile as they walked towards the beach, Tessa one step in front of Alex, keeping a wise distance. He suspected that the slightest touch would cause them both to burst into flame.

The water was utterly perfect. It should have been relaxing and soothing, but Tessa was far too aware of Alex to let it be either of those things.

She was on edge, just as she had been all night, lying in a big bed with crisp white sheets and the sound of the waves causing an answering rush of blood through her body, making her want to do something really stupid and go in search of him.

In the small hours of the morning, she'd craved him. Human connection. Contact. But more than that, Alex. He'd awoken something inside of her; emotions she'd long thought dormant, or non-existent. Desire. Attraction. Sexual curiosity. Feelings he'd kindled years earlier, that only he had ever managed to invoke.

Navigating them again now was a nightmare.

She'd clung to the contract she'd made him sign, to the rules she'd carved out, and tried to tell herself that it would all be okay. If they were to succumb to the temptation of sex, it would only be within the parameters she'd specified. She could still control it. Everything would be fine.

But as he hovered in the water beside her, so close she could reach out and touch him, brushing her fingertips over his naked torso and feeling the muscular ridges of his abdomen, she knew she was in way over her head.

Slowly she turned to face him, unable to resist at least that temptation. Her breath caught in her throat.

He was so…*elemental*. So tanned his skin was like mahogany, with water droplets forming rivulets over his strong arms, his dark hair brushed back from his brow, wet and catching the glint of the sun in its ends. He was completely at one with the ocean, the sky, the sun, and when he turned to look at her and their eyes met, his smile made her heart tilt off balance. She wanted to look away, but he was too magnetic, and so she let herself stare, a moment longer, just a moment, before she returned his smile, albeit curtly, and jerked her face towards the house.

'How long have you had this place for?'

If he was surprised by her abrupt change of conversation, he didn't show it. 'I bought it about ten years ago. I wanted a place to get away.'

'Why?'

He moved to stand in front of her, blocking her view of the house, forcing their eyes to meet, and her stomach squeezed, her nostrils flared as she inhaled his fragrance and trembled in response.

'I worked hard, played hard back then, too.' She remembered. She'd only been a teenager, but she'd been fascinated by her brother's best friend, by his charisma and charm, his incredible good looks. She'd loved it when stories ran about him online, or in the papers, and she could read what he'd been doing. He'd taken on an almost god-like presence to her. 'The island was removed from all that. Calm, and quiet. There were no bars here, no parties.'

'You didn't ever invite friends here?'

'No. Not my father. Not even Stav.' He moved closer, so there was only a small volume of salty water separating them. 'You're the first person I've ever brought to Epíneio.'

Her tummy flooded with butterflies and she pulled back through the water, just a step, just enough. He echoed her movement, so the distance between them didn't grow any greater.

'Why?' she asked unevenly, then, with more urgency, 'Why did you bring me here?'

A small frown creased his brow as he contemplated that. 'You are in need of a haven more than anyone I can think of right now.'

She tingled all over. 'I'm glad you did.'

'Are you?' His eyes drove into hers, pushing her to look inside her heart and be honest. 'I did wonder if you'd prefer to be back in Athens right now, blissfully ignoring me.'

'I don't want to ignore you,' she admitted with a gnawing sense of doubt in her chest.

'No?'

She shook her head, slowly, not sure what they were talking about, nor what she was conceded, but following her instincts.

He moved closer, so now they were touching, and she froze, because on the one hand, this contact was all her dreams coming true, and on the other, it was terrifying, so her body jolted, frightened by the immediate response she felt in her cells, and the strength of her need for him.

'I wish…' he said, then cut himself off, eyes holding hers, his expression inscrutable.

'What do you wish?' she prompted urgently, the warm

ocean lapping against her sides, their bodies brushing in the water, her pulse thundering.

He lifted a hand, holding it tentatively beside her arm before resting it on her shoulder, his gaze dropping to the sight of his dark skin against her fairer. 'That you'd never married him,' he said with dark honesty.

Her heart twisted sharply, but she refused to read anything into his admission. After all, they'd both said their one night together had been a mistake. It wasn't as though he was admitting some long-held unrequited love.

'He was bad for you,' Alex continued, moving his hand to the collar of his business shirt she wore, holding the fabric between his fingers. It billowed in the water, so she was secretly aware of her exposed belly, of how close to naked she was beneath the shirt, with just a flimsy pair of undies protecting her modesty. That knowledge was setting her soul on fire, dragging her closer and closer towards the desires she knew she ought to fight.

'Yes,' she said simply, because he had been.

'You deserve better than that.'

She wondered, in the back of her mind, if she should pull away from him. It would be the smart thing to do. She'd promised herself she wouldn't let things get out of control between them. She couldn't. If she surrendered to these feelings, she'd lose herself completely.

'Anyone does,' she said with a tight movement of her shoulders.

'You particularly.'

'Why?'

A frown flickered across his face and, rather than answering, he shifted closer, so his body pressed to hers, and every single inch of her was aware of the hard planes of his body, the warmth of his flesh beneath the waters of the Aegean, his skin supple and firm, hair-roughened on his chest, and covered in water droplets so she had an insatiable urge to lean forward and taste him.

'I was so angry after you left.'

'When?'

'The night we slept together.'

Her eyes widened, the change of subject unexpected, so she startled as though being awakened from a dream. 'Were you?' She dropped her gaze to the pristine water that lapped between them.

'I'd been so weak.' Her eyes lifted once more to his face, but the intensity of his stare sent little arrows of awareness through her, making it impossible to concentrate. 'Not only had I slept with you, but I'd also been your first lover. I felt as though I'd betrayed Stavros in the worst possible way.'

'You were his best friend. He probably would have been thrilled to think of us together.'

'No.' Alex shook his head emphatically. 'He was very protective of you and I was—'

'So much more experienced,' she finished unevenly.

'That's a polite way of putting it.'

She searched for a way to explain. 'That night, I was just so—sad…' Her lips twisted into a bitter frown. 'I wasn't thinking straight—'

'But I was,' he interrupted urgently. 'Or I should have been. I should have known better.'

'You were very clear that night,' she said, ice now running through her veins. 'You regretted it. You wished it hadn't happened.'

'Yes. For many years, I have felt that,' he admitted, dipping his head in silent agreement. 'But now, knowing that you went from my bed to his, I wish…'

Everything in her body ground to a halt as she stared at him, willing him to finish the sentence. 'Yes?' she said, when only the sound of water splashing filled her ears.

'I shouldn't have let that happen,' he muttered. 'I should have taken care of you…'

Her heart stretched almost to breaking point. On the one hand, she wanted to point out she was a woman of the twenty-first century, capable and in control. On the other, she wanted to push forward into his arms and rest her head on his shoulder and allow herself, just for a moment, to be cared for, as he'd said.

'Stavros would have wanted me to take better care of you.'

Her insides felt as though they were being compressed. She couldn't make sense of how she was feeling—a thousand different things at once now. 'I don't need rescuing,' she muttered on autopilot, because that felt familiar and important to tell him. 'I made my own choices, my own bed, and I lay in it for as long as I could manage. Jonathan was my mistake, and my problem to fix.'

'And our marriage is your solution,' he said quietly, scanning her face, a hint of disbelief in his question that frustrated her completely.

'It's certainly changed the story,' she said with a shrug, wondering at the flicker of something in the depths of his eyes. The news outlets had all printed photos of their wedding, the carefully selected images they'd released to announce their union.

'I'm glad.' Their eyes were locked, a strange tension buzzing between them, myriad thoughts and feelings unspoken, so despite the stillness of the afternoon, the water felt choppy.

'I would never have got involved with you back then,' she muttered, wishing that were true, pulling away from him, moving deeper into the ocean until she had to tread water to stay afloat. He stayed where he was a moment, a perfect bronzed god, his eyes watchful, his body still, and then he moved to follow her, his arms bringing him through the water with ease, until he was just a few feet away from her. He could stand easily, though.

'No?'

'You were too much what my parents wanted.' And despite the strange air of discord between them, a small smile twisted her lips.

'You have never seemed like the rebellious type, Theresa.'

'No,' she agreed, frowning. 'I'm not. Never. Except in that one way. Jonathan was my single act of defiance.' She tilted her chin. 'After Stavros died, I tried so hard to be everything I thought my parents needed me to be. I was terrified of putting a foot wrong, of failing to live up to who he'd been.' She bit down on her lip. 'But the way they tried to push me into a marriage with you...' She shook her head. 'It was too much. You were his best friend; you were, in my mind, his, not mine.'

'Even after we slept together?'

'Especially then,' she agreed, shivering as she remembered the way she'd been pushed away, the rejection Alex had put her through. 'If anything, that made me more determined to find my own way. I met Jonathan a week after we slept together, and a month after that he proposed.'

He nodded slowly, his eyes gently probing hers. 'I remember.'

Her heart gave a funny little stammer. 'You do?'

He lifted his shoulders. 'Call it male ego,' he said with a strange, throaty laugh. 'I didn't love how quickly you moved on, even when I felt guilty as hell for what we'd done.'

'You didn't exactly make me think you'd be interested in a repeat performance.'

'It wasn't possible.'

She flicked her gaze away, hating how easily he could hurt her, hating how much that night had pulled at her. She'd loved him. A childish crush had probably always been so much more, and that night they'd been drawn together by forces greater than either one of them. At least, that was how it had felt to Tessa.

'I meant nothing to you,' she said quietly. 'You can hardly have been surprised when I started dating someone else.'

'And did I mean something to you?' he pushed, picking up on her carefully worded explanation.

Her lips parted in surprise. Damn it! She'd been careless. 'What do you think? Of course, I had a stupid crush on you.'

His jaw tightened.

'But I was just a girl.'

'Twenty-two,' he pointed out.

'And inexperienced and sheltered, thanks to my parents and brother. You were unlike anyone I'd ever known. But it wasn't real, Alex. None of that was real, and none of this is real.'

'The sex was real,' he responded sharply, surprising them both.

Her lips parted as she tried to think of how to respond. But Alex was there first, his voice low and determined. 'You are my wife, and you want me just as much now as you did then. You cannot keep running from this, Theresa.'

Her eyes swept shut, the delicious sound of her name on his lips driving shards of need through her. He was right, she was running, because the alternative scared her senseless. 'We've negotiated the terms of our marriage,' she said, forcing cold resignation into her tone. 'I have no intention of reneging on our agreement.'

'That's not good enough.' She wondered at the dark undercurrent to his voice. 'I'm not going to let you sleep with me and pretend it's all because of a contract.'

She pulled her lower lip between her teeth, wobbling it uncertainly, eyes huge in her face.

'In fact, I'm willing to cancel that condition of our marriage. Forget I ever suggested it.'

The colour drained from her face. Familiar feelings of rejection slashed through her. 'You don't want—'

'What I want,' he interrupted swiftly, closing all the distance between them and lifting her in one motion, so her body was pressed to his and her legs moved, of their own volition, to wrap around his waist, 'is for you to admit you want me as a woman wants a man. Not because of the grief we shared that night, and not because of some deal we made before we were married. I want you to listen to your body and accept the desire flowing through you.'

But how could she? Tessa had been so badly burned by Alex that night, and then Jonathan had only compounded her hurt. How could she surrender to this?

Deep down, she knew that he was right, but that didn't mean there was no danger here.

She wanted him, with all her soul, and not because of Stavros, not because of their marriage contract, but because her body yearned for him on an almost mythical level, only to confess that to Alex would make her far too vulnerable to the kind of pain she was determined to avoid.

'It's never going to happen,' she denied, her voice wobbly now, her words husky.

He stared at her, long and hard, and she tilted her face, lips parted, aching for him to kiss her, even when a part of her felt as though she was breaking apart.

'Never is a very long time, *agape*,' he said with a lift of his shoulders, dropping his hand so hers fell away likewise. Her body felt flushed by ice water. 'If you change your mind, you know where to find me.'

CHAPTER SEVEN

SHE WOKE UP even earlier the next morning, the sound of the rolling waves breaking through her light sleep, so she blinked into the soft light and pushed back the covers, deciding against trying to settle again. A strange, unfamiliar energy was bursting through her, and Tessa wanted to burn it off. She dressed quickly, pulling on a pair of shorts and a T-shirt—taken from the shopping bags the housekeeper had left in her room the afternoon before—and decided to go exploring. This was a beautiful island, and a walk out in nature was exactly what she needed to shift her focus away from her husband and the way they sparked off one another.

Tiptoeing through the house as though she were a burglar, she crept into the kitchen and pressed the button on the coffee machine, sliding a cup beneath the nozzle and waiting for it to pool out. She watched as it formed a thick black liquid in the bottom, then, when it had stopped, lifted the cup to her lips and swallowed gratefully, eyes closed, experiencing the hit of caffeine with all her might.

'Good morning.' His voice, deep and hoarse, set her pulse raging immediately and she spun quickly.

'Oh, hi.' Heat flamed through her at the sight of Alex in a pair of jeans and a white shirt that accentuated his tan wonderfully. *Never is a long time.* It sure felt like it already. 'Did I wake you?'

'No, I've been up a while.'

'It's only just gone six,' she pointed out.

'I wake early.' His expression was carefully blanked of any emotion.

'I see. Well, don't let me bother you. I was just about to go for a walk. I thought I'd explore the place a bit.'

'You want to see the island?' He regarded her thoughtfully.

Why, when he looked at her, did she feel as though her whole self was fully visible to him?

'Yes.' It was easy to be emphatic in response to that question. In fact, it was easy to be emphatic about anything, other than the desire that was flooding her veins.

'Then let me show you a better way to see it.'

It was on the tip of her tongue to demur, but dammit, there was an inherent weakness inside of her, a weakness she'd always felt around Alex, that made her contemplate that for a beat. 'I was just going to walk around a bit,' she said, unconvincingly.

His expression tightened, his eyes warring with hers. 'If you want to be alone, that's fine. For my part, I'd enjoy showing you the best parts of Epíneio.'

Her heart skipped a beat. He was saying what he wanted. He was telling her he'd enjoy spending time with her. Why couldn't she admit as much?

Because he'd burned her once before. She'd offered him more than her body and virginity that night: she'd offered him her heart. Not in words, but surely in every look, every touch. He hadn't wanted her—not her heart, nor her body, beyond what that one night had been.

And yet she was married to Alex now, and they had to find a way to be together, to be civil and mature. That would take time and it would take practice. Perhaps the more she was around him, the better she'd get at this.

'You can think of me as your tour guide,' he said casually, and despite the fact she felt permanently on edge around Alex, with her nerves completely helter-skelter, she found herself nodding. After all, it would be churlish to decline.

'If you have time.'

'I wouldn't have offered if I didn't.'

Whereas Tessa had been planning to set off from the house on foot and explore at a snail's pace, Alex had other ideas. Around the back of the house there was a garage, with an off-road car, a jet ski on a trailer, and a jet-black motorbike with shiny chrome features. Her heartbeat accelerated rapidly as he moved towards it, running his hand over the leather seat then turning to face her. Her eyes lingered on his fingers and their touch of the bike; it was impossible not to imagine those same fingers caressing her with that lightness and intimacy.

Her pulse was thready and she jerked her eyes away. 'Have you ever been on a bike before?'

Her smile was wistful. 'No.'

'Not interested?'

'It's not that.'

'Ah, let me guess.' He watched her closely. 'Your family.'

She sighed. 'They're so dangerous.'

'They can be, when ridden inexpertly.'

She almost laughed. It was so like Alex, so brimming with arrogance, to dismiss the dangers inherent to motorbikes, because he had so much faith in his own abilities. Then again, it was hard to doubt him when he spoke with such confidence.

'What do you think, Theresa? Are you afraid to ride with me?'

'Are you trying to goad me?'

He laughed softly, his eyes crinkling at the corners. 'Perhaps a little.' He strode to the wall and removed two immaculate helmets, shiny and dark. 'If you don't want to ride, we can go in the car.' He nodded towards the four-wheel drive. 'You can't reach as many places on the island, but it will still give you a good overview.'

Her lips tugged to the side as she considered the options. The problem wasn't that she didn't want to ride on the motorbike, it was how much she did. Suddenly the thought of straddling the powerful machine, her arms wrapped around Alex's waist, pushed her senses into overdrive. Resisting him would be a Sisyphean task. So why, why, why did she start walking towards the bike, eyeing it as though it were some kind of irresistible dessert?

'Promise you won't tell my parents?' she joked, earning a smile from him that made her feel as though the sun were shining all its warmth directly through her.

'Cross my heart.' He walked towards her then, helmet in hand, pausing a foot or so away, before lifting the helmet towards her head.

'I can do it,' she said, though in truth Tessa had no idea how to fasten a motorbike helmet.

He ignored her interjection, sliding the safety device onto her head and checking the fit. Even when he was satisfied, he didn't step away.

'I like doing your firsts with you.' There was no humour in his voice now, only a deep, gruff intensity that flooded her body with awareness and heat of an entirely different nature to the sunshine warmth his smile had invoked.

It was an inescapable reference to the night they'd slept together, and she felt as though she'd been plunged into a river of lava. Memories assaulted her from every direction, but his words were a contradiction to the pain of those memories. He hadn't liked anything about that night; he'd made that perfectly clear.

'So what do I do?' she asked, glad he couldn't see her pink cheeks through the dark tint of the helmet.

He returned to the bench to pick up his own helmet and secure it, then moved to the bike, straddling it easily with his long legs. 'Sit behind me,' he said simply, then revved the engine to life, so the thrum of power reverberated in the pit of her stomach and she felt a rush of daring and excitement.

She was glad he wasn't looking, because the motion of getting onto the seat was nowhere near as easy for her, particularly when she tried to keep her distance from him.

'Grab on,' he said, once she slid into place behind him,

a leg on either side of his, so she was intimately aware of him regardless of how she tried to keep some small distance between them. 'Or you'll fall off,' he added over the low throb of the engine, giving her little choice but to wriggle all the way forward and wrap her hands around his waist.

On second thoughts, perhaps they should have taken the car. At least in the four-wheel drive, she'd have had her own seat, and a whole console between herself and Alex. She was opening her mouth to say exactly that when he gave the engine another rev and drove forward, straight out of the garage and onto the driveway. From that moment, Tessa's heart was in her mouth as adrenaline overtook her system.

There was a track she hadn't noticed before, because it was narrow, carved between grass, but it took them away from the house, higher up, along the edge of the island, until white cliffs formed a sheer drop beneath them, and unconsciously she held on tighter, as the terrain grew more beautiful and more threatening, as fear warred with wonder, and she had to take deep breaths to calm her wildly firing nerves.

The bike hummed beneath her, and Alex's warm, strong body was wedged at her front, so when she inhaled she caught a frustratingly light hint of his masculine fragrance and desire shifted through her at the provocation. Her hands pressed to his chest, feeling his strength and power, his muscular chest and steady heart, and as he steered, his arms brushed hers, so her mouth went dry and breathing became almost impossible.

He navigated the bike along the clifftops, far enough from the edge that she never felt in any real danger—she trusted him—but close enough to show the stunning view and death-defying drop. After circumnavigating the perimeter of the island for some time—though time no longer had any meaning to Tessa and she couldn't have guessed if they'd been five minutes or fifty—he reached a fork in the track and turned inward, taking them away from the edge of the island and towards a more wooded area. Olive trees grew wild, interspersed with citrus and bushes of geranium and lavender huddled chaotically wherever they could find land, so the grass was thin and dappled by only a hint of sunshine through the thick coverage of leaves. The temperature change was immediate, but Tessa barely felt it; her heat had very little to do with the beating sun. A movement to their right caught her attention and through the tree trunks she saw several goats, pausing in their grass chomping— another explanation for why it was so sparsely covered—to lazily regard the passing motorbike. Alex was driving with care, navigating a track that was mostly smooth but which, from time to time, presented a rock or branch, so Tessa had time to stare right back at the goats, smiling inside her helmet at their intelligent eyes and curious manner. Her hands moved of their own accord, feeling the ridges of his chest through his clothes, and she trembled because she wanted, all of a sudden, so much more.

The trees gave way once again to open grass and then another path along the other side of the island, but this time the cliffs dropped away, bringing them down to a small, perfect cove. Though it was difficult to track their progress, she'd guess they were directly opposite his home now, on the other side of the island. The patch of beach was like something out of a tourist brochure, with crisp white sand and rolling hills to shield it from view, creating the impression of being walled off from the world. The water was the sheerest shade of blue she'd ever seen, even for this part of the Aegean. He brought the bike to a stop, but didn't cut the engine immediately, so it continued to rattle between her legs, beneath her, shooting barbs of awareness into Tessa's body and making her want to act on the feelings that had been tormenting her ever since she'd arrived at his office and realised that whatever had driven her into Alex's arms back then was still between them, just as urgent and undeniable. But Tessa wasn't that woman any more. So much had changed in her life.

Despite the beating of a drum, convincing her that there was some form of inevitability here, just as Alex had said, Tessa fought that, dropping her hands away from him and flexing her palms. He turned off the bike then, and the silence, after the roaring of the engine, was almost overwhelming. Here, there was nothing but the occasional bird call and the gentle lapping of the water against the sandy shore.

'Ready?' he asked from in front of her, so she scrambled off the bike, trying to put physical distance between them as a defence against her treacherous thoughts.

'Yes, please.' Her response was prim, her face still hidden behind the helmet.

He removed his own first, and before he could reach out to do the same to hers she acted, curving her fingers around the equipment and sliding it off, relieved when it came easily.

He watched, his eyes skimming hers, and then he turned away, placing his helmet on the grass near the bike as he went. She did likewise. A few feet away he stopped walking to wait for her and she slowed a little, uneasiness coiling inside her belly.

She'd proposed this marriage because she'd wanted to fix the mistake she'd made in marrying Jonathan. Her parents had thought Alex would be the right husband for her, but they'd had no idea what had happened between the two of them. They had no idea that she'd offered herself to Alex and he'd rejected her—after taking her virginity. So instead she'd married a man they'd hated, who had subsequently dragged their family name through the press at every opportunity. Yes, she'd married Alex as a way of apologising to her parents, of saying 'you were right'. But deep down she had to admit, just to herself, that she'd also married him because she wanted to be close to him again. She'd fought that knowledge, but standing here, staring at him as the sun bathed them both in its golden light, she could no longer hide from the truth.

She'd walked into this willingly. She'd wanted him the day she'd gone to his office and she wanted him now.

It terrified her, but it also excited her, just like the motorbike ride up here. Maybe the best things in life were always complicated and multi-layered?

'Come,' he commanded, holding out a hand. She eyed it warily for a second before, with a degree of fatalism, placed her own in his, shivering the moment their flesh met. It was just a simple holding of hands, but for Tessa, coming on the back of her realisation, it was so much more. It was as though they were saying their wedding vows all over again, even more so when their eyes met and locked and she felt, right in the centre of her heart, as though something was stitching back in place inside of her.

It was the magic of this place, that was all. The island stood on its own, unfazed by humanity and heartbreak, by hurt and dishonesty.

'It's beautiful,' she said, because it was true but also because she needed to break the intimacy of their connection.

'It's private.'

And again she had the sense that his own privacy was something he valued immensely. She tilted her face to his, staring at him until he turned to look at her, his eyes lighting little fires beneath her skin.

At the edge of the beach he kicked off his shoes, waiting for her to do likewise, then taking them onto the white sand. She yelped as the heat caught her off guard. She began to hop and then Alex lifted her easily, throwing her over one shoulder as a caveman might his quarry, carrying her towards the lapping shore and placing her on the cooler, wet sand, sliding her down his body so every single inch of her was aware of every single part of him and her brain was filled with floating shards of glass, blades of awareness punctuating the perfection of this day.

There were a thousand reasons why she wanted to keep her level head, to hold on to her reasons for resisting this— and him—but there was also the beating of a drum, drawing her towards him, so the past, her marriage, their one night together, all seemed to fade into nothing—concerns carried away by the gentle drawing of the ocean, now in the custody of the deep sea beyond.

He didn't move. His body—strong, powerful, safe— stood like a sentry, but Tessa couldn't fight this any longer. She was shaking from the effort of resisting him, her whole body in meltdown. She wanted him, so badly, and that terrified her, so she could only lift a hand to his chest and press it there.

Her eyes sought his, probing him, asking him to be gentle with her, begging him not to hurt her again, because Tessa wasn't sure she could bear that again.

And yet, wasn't this paved with pain? Alex was not like Jonathan. She'd never felt anything like this for Jonathan— that was why she'd chosen to marry him. Because he was completely non-threatening. She'd never felt her senses shuttling into overdrive with Jonathan. She had never lost sleep over desire, never dreamed of him. Everything about it had been reassuringly lukewarm, until he'd started to belittle and demean her, until he'd begun to cheat on her. She knew now that her pain had more to do with the realisation she'd made a terrible mistake, rather than any hurt feelings over Jonathan's lack of love for her.

But with Alex, the threat was so much more real.

If she let herself go with him, if she *really* let herself go, and forgot the contractual nature of their deal, she was terrified she might lose her heart as well as all of herself.

Alex was a man determined not to love. She might give her heart to him, but he'd never return his own; the effects of that would be devastating.

The smartest thing of all would be to pull back from him. To push space between them, to take several deep breaths and remember that the worst thing she could do was become swept up into their relationship, to forget, even for one single moment, that this wasn't real.

'Alex…' She tried to find the words to explain, to tamp down on the sense of building urgency, but he was so close and the war raging within her felt a lot like a losing battle.

'Yes?' He was so close. Their bodies were almost as one, and the heat of the day was nothing to what they were generating. Did he feel it too? She had to believe he did. After all, he was the one who'd argued for their relationship to become physical.

And if he was disappointed by her? If Jonathan's insults held water? *You are just incredibly lacking in sex drive. Can you blame me for looking elsewhere?* She flinched, as though the words were being rained down on her in real time, and her central nervous system began to quiver, because she was enraged and filled to the brim with desire, needs flooding her, so she dug her fingernails into his chest, as though she could stem this from getting out of control, if only she held on hard enough.

'What is it, *agape*?'

She didn't argue with his use of that term. She bit down on her lip, eyes holding his, so there was nothing for it but to be completely, openly honest.

'I'm scared, Alex. I feel—' She searched for words that could describe all of her angst and fears and shook her head when they didn't come. 'I don't want to get hurt again.'

A muscle jerked in his jaw as he dropped his head, his lips brushing her hair. 'I'm not going to hurt you.'

'You don't know that.'

For a long stretch of time only the sound of wind rustling through the nearby trees broke the silence, and then, his voice, deep, gruff and steady: 'Would you like to go back to the house?'

She stared at him, frustration swishing through her at the very idea, and she shook her head. She was sick of being careful. Sick of listening to the fears that had become embedded in her. And most of all she was sick of ignoring the basic, physical needs of her body.

'No,' she ground her teeth together, aware that she was about to admit to something quite mad, and unable to care, 'I don't.'

His eyes flickered with curiosity and speculation and then Tessa was moving, no longer able to resist temptation, no longer caring for the consequences. It was impossible to think this wouldn't complicate things; it was also impossible to care.

CHAPTER EIGHT

SHE MOVED QUICKLY, as though jumping into a pool, throwing herself at him with all her body, lifting her lips to his at the same moment he wrapped his arms around her waist and pulled her against him, kissing her right back, his mouth dominating hers, claiming it and holding it. Shards of something like certainty burst through him, because something about that kiss on this beach felt a thousand kinds of right and he knew then that he'd brought her here for this exact reason. Not because he'd thought they'd have sex, but because there was something so pure and right here, that it felt like a place to be free of all the restrictions that had been dogging them ever since she arrived in his office and suggested this marriage.

His tongue duelled with hers, tasting her, flicking her mouth, as his hands drew her down onto the sand, a fierce need erupting inside of him, demanding more, making him want her a thousand times over, so he rolled her onto her back, the water lapping gently at their feet as he kissed her, tasting her sweetness and being deluged by memories of that long-ago night when a similarly urgent need had rolled through them.

She made a whimpering noise that sent his senses into overdrive, so he pushed at her shirt, gliding it up her body until she lifted her head off the sand so he could remove it altogether, revealing her beautiful breasts contained in a lacy bra. He groaned, the sight one he wanted to hold in his memory for all time. He savoured the moment of seeing of her just like this, with the sun striking rays of gold across her body, her eyes glinting with sensual heat, and then he kissed her again, running his hands over her, feeling the softness of her skin, the smoothness of her hips, before he pushed at her shorts and she lifted her hips, inviting him to remove them, kicking her legs to get them off faster, until she was wearing only a pair of briefs and a bra and his own pulse was so frantic he wondered if he might be about to have a heart attack.

But wild horses were at his back, and Theresa's frantic cries were passion-soaked and urgent, so he moved his lips to her throat, then lower, flicking his tongue over her decolletage, tasting her sweet saltiness, then to her breasts. Through the fabric of her bra, he clamped his teeth around her nipple and felt a wave of masculine possessive heat when she shuddered against him, and suddenly this wasn't enough. He needed so much more.

He pushed at the fabric urgently, releasing her breasts, cupping them, holding them, feeling their weight in his hands, rubbing his hands over her puckered nipples so she arched her back in silent invitation and he brought his mouth to hers, swallowing her cries as water lapped at their feet, gently, warm, heavenly sweet.

He was urgent, there was something wild and frantic driving him, something that was completely beyond his control. He pushed at her underpants, sliding them down her legs, his breathing forced, rushed, as he stared at her then, naked beneath him, so stunning and pale against the sand, so trusting and so completely his. He groaned, because even when this felt so inevitable and *right,* on some level it felt wrong too, because she was Stavros's sister and he'd already had to make his peace with what their relationship had morphed into. Guilty or not, he surrendered, pushing out of his own clothes quickly, until he was naked before her, his arousal straining, hard and desperate, and her eyes, so round in her delicate face, fell to it, to him, staring as though she'd never seen a man before.

'Alex,' she moaned, lifting her hands, reaching for him, her cheeks pink, her lips swollen from his kisses. 'Please.'

But right as he was about to succumb, to give them both what they wanted, reality burst into his brain, well-worn habits drawing him to a stop. 'I don't have any protection,' he hissed, cursing himself for not bringing his wallet. Her cheeks grew pinker.

'It's okay,' she mumbled, so his heart slammed into his ribs and he had to stay very still to stop from immediately lowering himself to her and taking her, claiming her, as he'd wanted to do ever since she walked into his office. 'Remember, I'm on the pill,' she said. 'And I'm clean. I've been tested.'

'Me too,' he said with relief, sinking to his knees, between her legs, staring at her as though she were some kind of magical sea creature, as though this were a dream. And perhaps it was. It felt far more likely that she'd change her mind or disappear into the ocean than it was they'd actually make love, and yet she didn't make a single move to leave.

She reached for him and this time he dropped lower, so her hands curved around his arms, drawing her to him, and he kissed her again—it felt like coming home.

He couldn't stop.

His mouth ravaged hers and she whimpered, and he felt strong and powerful and terrifyingly vulnerable, brought to his knees by the strength of his need for her. She lifted her legs and wrapped them around his waist, holding him close, and though he wanted to pull back, to slow down, he couldn't. His body was independent of him, acting of its own volition, seeking hers, so he drove into her without even realising it, only her cry and his own guttural groan heralded his intrusion.

'God, Alex,' she called his name into the sky; he loved the way it sounded on her lips, heavy with passion. Her nails dragged down his back, scoring red marks, and she lifted her hips. 'Don't stop.'

'I'm not going to,' he promised, moving inside of her, feeling her tightness, the muscles gripping him as he moved, his body racked by pleasure, his needs almost overwhelming him, so he had to slow down, even when he felt as though a rhythm had overcome him. He pushed up and watched her, watched as he moved and she reacted, understood what she loved, where she was most sensitive and he teased her there, pulling out and hovering a moment before taking her again, driving her wild, to the point of incandescence, and then she was calling his name with more urgency and he was inside of her, feeling her muscles squeeze and release, losing her control completely as he swallowed her euphoric cries into his mouth, kissing her until her breath had calmed. Then, he began to move all over again, barely giving her time to recover, stoking her to new heights of desperate need, and this time, when she fell apart, he was right with her, his own release overcoming him, so he wrapped his arm around her and held her close as his body was racked with pleasure and release, and he was aware only of the sound of their breathing, of the pleasure that had exploded around them, making him feel strangely, perfectly at peace, for the first time in a long time.

His weight on her body was its own aphrodisiac. She lay beneath him, conscious of everything in that moment. Of the warmth of the sun, the lapping of the waves, the grit of the ancient sand beneath her, the hair on his chest, the strength of his frame, the heat of his skin, the hawing of his breath, the movement of his chest, *everything*. She lay perfectly still, as though it was somehow vital to feel this and relish it, to commit it to memory, to savour these feelings. As though she was aware they were hers only for a finite time. As though she knew regret would follow.

And perhaps it would, but in that moment she could only be glad, beyond words, because it felt to Tessa as though Alex had woken up an important part of her, as though he'd brought some of her back to life again.

Mortifyingly, tears dampened her eyes and she blinked furiously to clear them, but too late.

He pushed up, his body stiffening. 'Theresa?' The way he said her name made her chest heave. She bit down on her lower lip. Emotions deluged her—which was exactly what she wanted to prevent from happening.

'Yes?' She forced an overbright smile to her face, but it was belied by the salty tears filling her eyes.

'Are you okay?'

Surprised, she dragged her gaze to his face, to his grim lips, and shook her head, pressing a hand to his chest.

'I wasn't gentle,' he muttered. 'I couldn't... I was—'

'No, God, no, Alex. That was—' She bit harder into her lip. 'Honestly, perfect,' she mumbled, heat filling her cheeks as he jerked inside of her. But concern had him moving, rolling away and then standing, his back ramrod straight as he took a step towards the beach, his back to her, his attention focused on the distant horizon. Impatient with herself and desperate for him to understand, she stood, moving quickly to his side. He didn't look at her, but she could see from the set of his face that dark emotions coursed through him.

She reached for his shoulder, squeezing his bicep, so he turned to face her, his eyes loaded with self-loathing.

'Alex, I wanted that to happen.'

A muscle jerked in his jaw, as he lifted a thumb to her cheek, wiping away the tear there. 'Did you?'

'I'm not crying because I regret it.' *Though I'm sure I will.* 'I'm crying because it was so, so good and in the course of my marriage I honestly came to believe I didn't have a sexual bone in my body. I thought what we shared all those years ago was some kind of illusion. I didn't know...'

She shook her head. 'The way you just made me feel, the way I feel now, truly, I have no words to express what this is like. I'm just… I've spent so long wondering if this part of me is dead, and now I know it's not. There's nothing wrong with me.'

His eyes bored into hers, his emotions unreadable. 'No, *agape*.' His voice was gruff. 'There is nothing wrong with you.'

She was shaking now as relief took over, a deep relief that sprung from the core of her doubts and worries. He moved closer, lifting his hands to either side of her face, holding her steady so he could stare at her in a way that made her feel as though her soul was on display for him to see and understand, and for some reason, despite her habit of keeping her innermost feelings secret and guarded, she didn't mind, in that moment. 'There is nothing wrong with you,' he repeated, a frown curling his mouth. 'You are passionate and sensual, beautiful and addictive.'

Addictive. Hardly. And yet, somehow, standing in that small, idyllic cove, it was easier to believe Alex's words above all else. Alex was making her feel *wonderful*, and that terrified her, because feeling great would lead her to relax, to trust him, to let herself care for him again, and Tessa couldn't risk that. She'd pull away soon. But right now it just felt so good to be close to him, naked and bathed in sunlight, the ocean wrapping around their feet with each decadent roll towards the shore.

'Just be sure to only be addicted to me between Friday and Sunday,' she said in a light-hearted tone that didn't quite ring true. But it was important to remind him—to remind them both—of the deal they'd struck.

He drew his brows together, not understanding her words, and then his face was expressionless. 'Right, the contract.'

She nodded, dislodging his hands. Or perhaps he withdrew them. Either way, the effect was the same. Her chest felt as though it were caving in. 'It makes sense,' she clarified. 'I don't want this taking over our lives.'

His eyes probed hers, and now she didn't like feeling seen, she didn't like how visible her innermost feelings were to him. 'You're really worried about that, aren't you?'

She parted her lips, a denial on her tongue, but when his eyes held hers, and their bodies were brushing, she could only be completely honest. 'Yes.' She looked up at him, hoping he'd understand. 'It has to be this way.'

The air between them crackled, tension zipping through her. She held her breath, waiting for him to say something, and in a small part of her mind she was hoping he'd argue. That he'd insist on their tearing up the contract and being married, for real, rather than the pragmatic arrangement they'd forged.

'If you say so.' It was what she wanted, and yet it left a funny feeling in her throat, as though something had lodged there and wouldn't break free. She ignored it. This was the marriage they'd agreed to—it was what they both wanted.

Tessa was an excellent chess player, and it was obvious Alex hadn't been expecting that. It was also obvious that he didn't enjoy losing. Tessa hid her smile behind a cup of tea, watching as his confident, hair-roughened fingers hovered over the pieces with what she could tell was an unusual level of uncertainty for a man like Alexandros Zacharidis. His dark eyes flicked to hers, his lips a flat line as he reached for his drink—coffee—and took a sip.

'I don't know how you drink coffee at this hour,' Tessa murmured, her eyes latched to the way his hand gripped the cup, his fingers so strong and tanned against the white ceramic, bringing back memories of his skin against hers at the beach that morning. Her heart rate doubled and her stomach squished. 'I'd be up all night.'

He replaced the cup at his side, returning his attention to the chess board. 'I'm used to it.'

'Late night chess and coffee?'

He made a growling sound. 'I haven't played chess like this in a long time.' Finally, he moved a piece—a clever move that bought him a little more time before the almost inevitable checkmate. 'Not since your brother and I used to sit up late in our dorm doing this, in fact.'

Tessa's eyes grew round in her face and something sparked inside her abdomen. 'Stavros taught me to play,' she said unevenly. 'He was very gifted, and never let me win.'

'I could say the same of you.'

She laughed softly. 'I'm not gifted. But I did have to get good, fast, playing Stav. We shared a competitive streak and a mutual hatred for losing, which meant our games were hardly quiet. My mother took to leaving the swear jar beside the board—he had a terrible vocabulary, when we played chess.'

It was Alex's turn to laugh, a throaty, guttural sound. 'I remember. Not that he lost often to me.'

'When did you start playing? You're good.'

'But not as good as you and Stavros,' he responded without ego, easing back in his chair and watching her, so she was glad she'd already formed a response to his move, and wasn't completely thrown off kilter by the intensity of his gaze. Beneath the loose kaftan she wore, and despite the balmy warmth of the night, her skin prickled with goosebumps.

'How old were you when you started playing?'

'Properly playing? Around seven.' Her smile was involuntary. 'But playing with the pieces? Much, much younger. As a girl, I used to steal into my father's study and take them for make-believe games. I would tell the most fantastical stories about the queen that was taken hostage and the army of pawns raised to save her, and the fights between the gallant knights, and finally the kings.' She shook her head. 'That was back when I still thought queens should be saved by their loyal, loving husbands.' Cynicism touched her lips. 'Your go.'

He made a noise of agreement but didn't move at all.

'Stav was the one who found me playing with the pieces. He wasn't cross, but he took them away, telling me they weren't dolls, that the set in Dad's office was actually hundreds of years old, and quite breakable. He said that if I wanted to touch them, it would need to be in a game of chess, not make-believe.'

'That sounds like Stav.'

Her heart squeezed. 'He was always an excellent rule follower.'

He shifted his fingers to the board, sliding a pawn across. She frowned at the unexpectedness of the move, momentarily distracted by his technique, which made no sense to Tessa. It was a play she hadn't seen before, and she tried to formulate his game plan, but he was too close, and his masculine fragrance was wrapping around her, so it was almost impossible to concentrate.

'And you weren't?'

'I was,' she responded, a small smile on her lips that was echoed on his.

'Stavros told how you would take the jars of Nutella from the pantry and hide them under your bed, and whenever your parents asked about it, you would shrug and say you had no idea.'

Heat coloured her cheeks. 'I was only a little girl then.'

'But you were cheeky,' he murmured.

'Yes.' Her eyes flickered to his. 'I liked to see what I could get away with.' She sipped her tea. 'And I really, really loved chocolate.'

He laughed, this time with more humour. 'And what about the sneaking out you would do? Stav said you had keys cut to the house when you were fifteen years old, so you could come and go without anyone knowing.'

Her eyes were huge. 'He *knew*?'

'I think your brother knew everything,' Alex murmured. 'He was always paying attention.'

'Yes.' She sighed heavily, missing Stavros more in that moment than she could bear.

'You were fifteen,' Alex pushed. 'Why not just ask your parents for a key?'

'Easy for you to say,' she responded quickly.

'Why?'

'You couldn't possibly understand the way they were with me.'

She bit down on her lip, pretending fascination with the chess board, when the game had momentarily lost interest for Tessa.

'They didn't want you dating,' he prompted, and when she lifted her gaze to his face he was frowning, as if trying to catch the threads of a memory. 'You had a strict curfew.'

Heat stole into her cheeks. 'Yes.'

'Why?'

She lifted her slender shoulders.

'They didn't trust you?'

'They didn't trust boys,' she said after a pause. 'And I guess they also didn't trust me.'

'Did they have a reason?'

She twisted her lips to the side. 'Not really. I was a bit naughty as a kid, but only with silly things.'

'Like jars of Nutella.'

She nodded, distracted. 'When it came to the stuff that mattered, I think I was pretty good. I drank from time to time, at parties, but I never had a…'

'Boyfriend,' he supplied, after a pause that made Tessa wish the ground would open up and swallow her.

She nodded.

'But you went away for college. Surely by then, you could have done whatever you wanted.'

'By *then*,' she said quietly, 'I was way out of my league. I was a nineteen-year-old virgin. I was so embarrassed. I didn't want to go out with a guy and have to tell him that I hadn't even been kissed.'

Alex swore softly under his breath, and her eyes flicked to his face as realisation dawned as to what she'd just admitted.

'Just as well you like doing firsts with me,' she said with a tight smile.

He reached out and took her hand in his, lifting it to his lips. 'I do.'

It was sweet, and kind, but Tessa felt like a gauche child again. 'It wasn't just my parents. I mean, it was mostly them, but maybe that lack of confidence and experience affected me, because I never really met anyone I felt... I wasn't...' She looked at him pleadingly, hoping he understood, but he offered no help. 'I wasn't attracted to anyone. A few guys asked me out,' she said unevenly, 'but no one ever made me feel as though I couldn't bear to say no. It wasn't hard to remain a virgin, all things considered.'

His eyes narrowed thoughtfully. 'And yet, you're a very sensual woman.'

Only with you. She stayed quiet, returning her focus to the chess board and moving a piece into position.

'Why did you marry him?'

The question whipped around Tessa, startling her. She reached for her tea, sipping it, then faced him with the appearance of calm. How could she admit the truth to Alex? How could she tell him that she'd married someone partly because she'd been running from Alex, and what she'd felt with him? 'I don't really know,' she said breathily, after a moment. 'I guess I thought I loved him.'

He moved a piece without taking his eyes from her face.

She didn't look down at the board immediately. 'But you didn't?'

She dropped her eyes to their game, considering her next move, then lifting her fingers to a piece and driving it across the board, leaning back with satisfaction at her manoeuvre.

She didn't know how to answer his question, and she didn't have to. A moment later he moved on, or perhaps simply changed direction.

'You haven't put on a show in years.'

Her gaze flicked to his. 'How do you know?'

'Your parents,' was his swift, flat response.

'Of course.' It wasn't as though he'd been waiting on tenterhooks for her next art show—it wasn't as though he'd ever been to one.

'How come?'

He responded to her move, but she was barely concentrating.

'I…' She sought one of her ready deflections but none came. With Alex, she felt compelled to be honest. 'I lost my mojo for a while there. After Stavros, my work took a very dark turn,' she murmured, not admitting to Alex that his rejection of her had played a part in that. The whole world had angered her. 'Then I was a newlywed,' she said with a lift of her shoulders, oblivious to the way Alex's expression darkened, his cheeks gashed with dark colour. 'Mum and Dad were grieving. Other things took priority.' She lifted her shoulders.

'And since your divorce?'

'I'm getting there.' She lifted her shoulders. 'I'm enjoying it again.'

'I'm glad. You're very talented.'

Her eyes narrowed. 'Why would you say that?'

'Because it's true?'

'You haven't seen my art.'

'Haven't I?'

Her heart thumped into her ribs. 'I don't know.' She looked back at the board. 'I presumed not.'

'Your parents have several paintings on the walls.'

Of course. He'd been to their house. It wasn't as though he'd been to an exhibition.

'I would like to see what you've been working on lately.'

Her eyes widened and her pulse kicked up a gear. 'I'm not sure why.'

'Because you're talented,' he repeated and then, more dangerously, 'and because you're my wife.'

Possessive heat burst between them, so much more real now that they'd slept together. He stood swiftly, staring at her face for several beats before holding out his hand. 'Come with me, *agape*.'

'But the game,' she murmured, even as she placed her hand in his and stood.

'You can beat me in the morning. There are better ways to spend our night.'

CHAPTER NINE

WALKING BACK INTO Alex's stunning home in Athens felt different now, and not just because her skin was three shades darker courtesy of days stretched out by the pool. It was different because they were home, and home brought with it a crushing sense of reality. She would have been tempted to enjoy the sanctuary of his haven, where none of the real world intruded, none of the problems, none of the worries.

But that wasn't practical.

Only she hadn't banked on how pressing the real world would feel. She made a coffee and turned on her iPad and immediately it began to ping with news alerts. With a knot in her tummy, she opened them up, flicking past the fluff pieces—announcements of her marriage to Alex—and focusing on the fallout.

Jonathan, blissfully unaware that she'd remarried, courtesy of the show's sequestering of its participants, continued to divulge secrets and lies from their marriage. There was nothing of particular importance, just gossip, but Tessa's innate desire for privacy bristled at the casual way her name was being thrown around, so when Alex sauntered into the living room some time later it was to find Tessa pink-faced and jabbing at the screen, flicking an angry email to her lawyer. Surely there was a law against the press running articles without fact-checking them first? Some of the pieces were damned close to slander.

'Problem?'

Yes. She had a problem. But being back here, in Athens, reminded Tessa forcefully of who she was, of who Alex was, and the realities of their marriage. The honeymoon was over. Now they had to get on with their lives.

'No,' she clipped in response, standing and casting her iPad aside. 'I'm going to my studio to work.' She looked around for her handbag and found it on a chair nearby. 'I'll see you tonight.'

He watched her go without evincing a single emotion. She was a free agent. If she wanted to work, of course she could. He had plans to return to the office himself, though he hadn't been planning to rush in there today. In fact, there were many other things he thought he might enjoy doing far, far more. But Tessa had been withdrawing from him ever since they'd left Epíneio. She'd read her book on the boat, made polite small talk only when absolutely necessary, and then sat silently during the car trip back to his place.

He hadn't pushed her.

Their situation was complex and the marriage new. They were both navigating it as best they could.

With a frown, he moved absentmindedly to the sofa, his hand brushing the back, where she'd been sitting, before his eyes landed on the iPad, a moment before the screen went black. But he'd seen it first—the picture of her and Jonathan with a splashy tabloid heading. Reaching for the device, he swiped it open and read the article with grimly held lips.

So her ex-husband was still spewing his disgusting nonsense? Just as Tessa had feared he would.

And their marriage hadn't stopped the stories from leaking into the headlines. His first thought was of Tessa, but very quickly his mind shifted to her father, to the plan she'd had to save her parents from any further pain caused by her idiot ex.

This wasn't working. Would it ever have worked? And if not, why had he agreed?

Then again, a quick Google search showed that the only place Jonathan's indiscreet blather landed was in the most low-rent tabloids. No broadsheet masthead was remotely interested in his troublemaking stories. Their marriage had more coverage, simply because it had invigorated share prices for both companies as news of a corporate merger gained steam.

And?

He rubbed a hand over the back of his neck, staring into space as he considered that. Orion was getting older, and his heart was failing. Since Stavros's death he'd returned to the role of CEO, but surely alleviating those pressures would be beneficial?

Would he agree to hand the reins over to Alex? And would Tessa think he was taking on too much, given the nature of their marriage?

He replaced the iPad with a growing sense of unease. The straight lines he'd planned to hold in place seemed to be starting to wobble, but Alex simply wouldn't let them. He expelled a long, slow breath, retaking a grip on reality. Nothing had changed since that morning. They were married, in a very specific kind of marriage, and her issues were still there, just as they had been before.

It was just as they'd agreed.

He showered quickly and left for the office, seeking normality and escape from the direction of his thoughts.

Tessa painted with anger. She painted with grief. But she also painted beauty and pain and the inescapable presence of both in life, the euphoria of bliss shadowed by the threat of loss. She painted Epíneio, the shoreline, with white sand beaches and frangipani trees casting a telltale shadow. It was only when looking closely that one could see the dark depth of those shadows, the ominous promise of their presence.

She painted, the light in her studio perfect, the sun streaming in through the large windows of the disused fire station she shared with two other artists, and she worked tirelessly, ignoring the painting hanging to her left, the pai of eyes staring back at her that were now as familiar to her as her own had been.

She painted under Alex's gaze, the painting she'd done in the week after they slept together, when he'd filled her mind and heart and soul and she'd yearned for him, and ached for him, and had wanted a piece of him even though she could never have him.

She wasn't sure why she'd kept the painting all these years.

It wasn't her usual thing.

She loved landscapes and still life. But his face had taken shape and she'd sculpted his features onto the canvas brushstroke by brushstroke, particularly proud of the cynical mockery she'd captured in his eyes, the derisive curl of his lips. It was how she'd always wanted to remember him—scathing. Hurtful. Because she'd known she could never forget.

Yet here she was, blissfully sinking back into a state of unawarness, allowing herself to delight in his company, to delight in him.

She dropped her head forward, into her hands, and moaned. Everything had seemed so simple, but it wasn't, and, no matter how determined she was to maintain their contractual agreement, she couldn't change the fact that he'd become a part of her all over again.

Tessa painted until the light was dim and her hand cramping, but some time after eight she packed up, diligently cleaning her brushes, sealing her paints, wiping her work surface and locking up the shared studio space, moving slowly, because in the back of her mind was a sense of dread at the evening ahead.

In Epíneio, they'd become close. Sleeping together, swimming, playing chess. The past had ceased to matter. But here, it was all around her, and the weight of that truth pressed into her like concrete.

She couldn't pretend this was simple, she couldn't pretend it was safe. Tessa had to keep her wits about her.

He was in the kitchen when she walked through the door, and the moment their eyes met her heart began to skitter and roll.

'Hi.' A deep, throaty greeting that made her stomach drop to her toes.

Her hands clasped more tightly around her bag. 'Hi.' Her own voice was breathy, hoarse from misuse. She cleared her throat.

'How are you?'

'Fine.' She cleared her throat again.

'I was just about to order dinner. What do you feel like?'

Panic skittled through her. She couldn't do this. She couldn't pretend everything was fine. It wasn't. Suddenly her head was swimming—with worries about her dad, anger at Jonathan, and most of all confusion about the man she'd married, the man who'd broken her heart, the only man she'd ever loved.

'Nothing. I'm not hungry. I—' she looked anxiously towards the hallway '—I'm going to catch up on emails in my room. Goodnight, Alex.'

He watched her walk away with a groaning sense of impatience. *My room. Goodnight, Alex.* Was she kidding? They'd spent five days living in each other's pockets on Epíneio and now she wanted to go back to separate bedrooms? To sex on weekends, as she'd originally suggested? Before he could stop himself, he began to move after her. 'Wait a second.'

Her shoulders slumped, and if he'd been thinking straight, that would have been enough to make Alex pause but his own emotions were crowding him, so it was almost impossible to comprehend hers.

'Yes?' Her voice was quiet, soft.

His gut twisted. 'You are running away from me,' he said simply, because there was nothing else he could say. He just wanted her to confirm it. No, he wanted her to explain it, too.

'I'm just going to my room,' she said softly.

'Why?' he pushed.

Her eyes lanced him and then dropped away. The turmoil in them was too much to bear. He ached for her. The Jonathan media storm might have seemed like nonsense to him, but to Tessa it was obviously painful. But didn't she understand, he could fix this? He could fix it by holding her close, by making love to her, by getting his legal team involved with the newspapers running the baseless stories. He could fix everything if she'd let him.

'I need to be alone,' she replied quietly.

'But you are not alone,' he insisted, moving closer, gratified when she stood her ground rather than moving back. 'I'm right here, and I can help you.'

She bristled. 'I don't want help.'

'Why not?'

She looked up at him, anguish in her face. 'Because this is my problem.'

'And I'm your husband.'

'But not really,' she pointed out quickly. 'You were so, so kind to marry me, and at the time I really thought our marriage would fix everything, but it didn't, and I just— need to think.'

Something shifted at his side. He felt as though he'd been punched, hard, right in the gut. 'Are you saying you want a divorce?'

Her skin paled. 'No.' She shook her head for emphasis. 'That would make everything worse. Unless you want a divorce, in which case of course I'll agree.'

He wondered at the anger writhing inside his chest. 'No,'

he said slowly. 'I want to be married to you. Your father's health situation has not changed, has it?'

She shook her head.

'Then we stick to our agreement,' he said quietly.

'Exactly.' She pressed a hand to his chest as if in triumph. 'And this *is* what we agreed, remember? Through the week, we keep to ourselves. Weekends are…different.'

He was more irritated than he should have been. 'Right, on weekends we can have sex.' He said it to provoke her. He said it because he was mad, and he hated himself for that, because dealing with his feelings was clearly the last thing she needed. But hell, she was pushing him away right when he wanted to comfort her, and Alex wasn't one to be told what to do and where to be. She needed him. She needed comfort.

Or did she need space, just as she was saying?

'Yes,' she agreed without meeting his eyes. 'Fine. But right now I want to go to my room and have a bath, and then go to bed,' she admitted, her voice quivering, so all the anger he'd been feeling, the frustration, disappeared on a wave of concern.

'Okay,' he said after a loaded pause, surprising himself with his capitulation. But Tessa was telling him what she needed; he'd be a fool not to listen. 'That makes sense. Why don't you go and run the bath and I'll bring you a glass of wine in ten minutes?'

Her eyes clung to his and the sight of tears sparkling on her lashes made him want to pull her towards him again, to wrap her up in a big hug and promise her everything was going to be okay. She didn't deserve any of this. Just as they'd come together in grief on the night of Stav's funeral, he wanted to make love to her now, to blot out her pain, to make her feel better. He wanted to make love to her because it was the *right* thing to do, because they both needed it, but he took a step backwards, because he wasn't his father and she wasn't his mother and they were capable of making decisions in their marriage that were rational and calm.

'Go on,' he said gruffly, knowing he'd change his mind if she lingered.

In the bath, she gave in to the tears that had been threatening since that morning.

Finally alone, she let them slide down her face without thinking they were a form of weakness, without worrying she was betraying herself in some vital way. It was okay to be sad. It was okay to feel completely sideswiped by the news of today.

Footsteps in the bedroom outside had her dipping her hands in the bathwater and lifting it to her face, splashing her eyes with the bubble-filled water so the telltale sign of tears wouldn't be so apparent.

He knocked on the door and waited, and the small gesture did all sorts of things to her.

'Come in.'

He held out the glass of wine, offering it to her from a safe distance.

'Thank you,' she murmured, curving her fingers around it.

'Want me to go?' he asked, with no pressure, no expectation.

The problem was, she wanted him to stay, which was exactly why she needed him to leave. She couldn't let herself go down this path. 'Please,' she said without meeting his eyes, so she didn't see the way his lips compressed at the single word.

'I'll be downstairs if you need me.'

He was doing everything right: giving her space, respecting her boundaries. So why did she feel so utterly rubbish when she was, once again, alone?

CHAPTER TEN

THOUGH TESSA COULD scarcely believe it, the next day things launched from bad to worse. A friend texted her the headlines: *Heiress Ice Queen*. An article followed full of drama and misinformation, quoting a lengthy conversation Jonathan had had with a one-hit-wonder pop star also residing in the Celebrity House, in which he'd cried his heart out about his unfeeling ex-wife, relaying minute details of their marriage, as well as many, many points of fiction. She read it with a strange sense that she was choking.

'Good morn…' The greeting died on Alex's lips when he saw her face. 'Theresa?'

She nodded, numb, unable to speak, then pulled her phone from her pocket, flicked it to life and handed it to him, the offending article on the screen. 'It's never going to stop, is it?'

She watched him at first, but after a moment the look on his face was too much to bear. She turned her back, bracing her palms on the counter, staring out at his stunning infinity pool and, beyond it, Athens.

'This guy is a pig,' Alex muttered with cold derision.

Tessa flinched. 'Yes, but he's a pig that's going to keep squealing for the rest of my life,' she said softly, the reality of that driving any brightness from her mind. 'I made a mistake when I married him, I know that, but I am going to have to keep paying for that mistake for a very long time.'

Behind her, Alex stiffened. Not if he could help it. This had gone on long enough. From the brief details he'd gathered from Theresa, their marriage had been borderline abusive. Oh, Jonathan might not have hit her, but he was coercive and a bully, and had undermined her at every opportunity. Emotional abuse was still a torment, and he was continuing to chip away at her. To see beautiful, intelligent, funny Theresa cowered by her ex-husband's indiscretion made him want to punch something. It sure as hell made him want to wrap her in cotton wool.

But hadn't she had enough of that?

Hell. He dragged a hand through his hair, two sides of Alexandros at war within him. His first instinct was to protect her, to make her feel safe and happy, and he could think of one sure-fire way to do that. But his second instinct was to give her the space to work this out for herself, because he knew that was important to her, and her independence would be more meaningful if she found her way there on her own. She'd been protected all her life—over-protected—and she'd hated it. Wouldn't she come to resent him if he tried to coddle her? Wouldn't she hate it, and possibly him, if he got involved?

He knew the second instinct was what he should listen to, but maybe there was a way to do both?

'Let's go back to Epíneio,' he said, his voice firmly insistent.

She turned to face him, eyes widened, and he knew then he'd found the right option. It was obvious that she was tempted. 'That won't solve anything.'

'Won't it?'

She shook her head sadly. 'This is my life now.'

'That's the point.' Screw it. He closed the distance between them and lifted her up, sitting her on the edge of the kitchen bench so he could stand between her legs, their gazes level. 'It's only your life if you let it be. On Epíneio, did he enter your head, *at all*?'

She frowned, eyes searching his.

He pushed on, regardless of the fact she hadn't answered. 'He is going to try to spin out the secrets of your marriage—'

'And lies,' she interjected hotly.

'Yes,' he conceded. 'For as long as there's commercial value in him doing so. But no one who knows you will take any notice. He's providing salacious gossip, it's true—'

'And I'm at the heart of it,' she moaned, shaking her head softly.

'Which is frustrating,' he was quick to agree, because the last thing she needed was to have her feelings rendered invalid. 'But you are a much better person than him. Every lie he tells, every story he sells, that hits the bottom-feeding tabloids, and every day that you stay silent, speaks volumes about his character—and yours. You have so much integrity, Theresa, whereas I doubt he even knows how to spell the word.'

She blinked slowly, then focused on a point over his shoulder. He wasn't getting through to her.

'You married me for two reasons. One of them was to drown out his stories with news of your own. The other was for your father.'

Her eyes met his and she nodded slowly.

'Every day that your father believes our marriage to be real, and us to be happy, is a gift to him.' Alex leaned closer, truth and wisdom in his eyes. 'But there is a third reason perhaps you weren't aware of. Let's call it a silver lining.'

'Oh?' she whispered. 'What's that?'

'On Epíneio you are happy, and you deserve that. Isn't the best revenge living well?'

She bit down on her lip. He was right, but what about the inherent risks of being close to him? On Epíneio she was in the most danger of forgetting their boundaries, of imagining this marriage to be real, of hoping it might morph into everything she'd ever wanted.

'Let's go there, today. Let me help you forget.' He expelled a sharp breath. 'You wanted to change the narrative? So change it here.' He pressed a finger between her breasts, feeling the steady thumping of her heart. 'Free yourself from him. As long as he can upset you, he wins.'

'It's not just me. It's my parents, my friends, and now it's you.'

'Me?'

'It's anyone who knows me, who is embarrassed by this—'

'I'm not embarrassed.' He moved closer, pressing his lips to her forehead, so angry that she could feel any of these things. 'I don't give a— I don't care what he says about you. I know you, the real you. And anyone else who does will see this for what it is.'

He felt her sharp intake of breath.

'His stories *will* lose currency. At some point the media will move on, and his fifteen seconds of fame will be at an end. Or he'll be married and divorced from someone else he's trying to exploit.' He shrugged, staying close to her. 'All you can control is how you respond to his behaviour. Come away with me. Forget him.' And then he kissed her, to show her how easy this could be, and how right it felt. He told himself this was the best, smartest option, that she was his wife, and it was his duty to help her, even as he felt something shift between them, something he couldn't explain.

Perhaps she felt it too, because she pulled away warily. 'This doesn't change anything,' she said, curling her fingers in his shirt. 'Our marriage isn't real, Alex.'

'I know that.' His voice emerged clipped and cold now, as if pushing away the tenderness he'd just shown, in a moment of weakness. 'We both know the deal.'

'Do we?' She scanned his face. 'Because the last thing I want is to get involved with anyone. Emotionally, I mean.' Pink darkened her cheeks. 'I can't give you more than this,' she whispered. 'I won't.'

'Then it's just as well I'm not asking for more,' he said

simply, honestly, even when a stitch formed in his side. 'Neither of us wants a relationship.'

She bit down on her lip. 'How do we make sure we remember that?'

'By not falling in love,' he said, as though it were the simplest thing in the world.

'That's why I want to limit our time together...'

'Let me make you this promise, *agape*,' he said, wanting to assuage her concerns. 'It doesn't matter how much time we spend together, or how often we sleep together. I will not fall in love with you, and I will make sure you don't fall in love with me. I don't want a real marriage,' he said darkly. 'I just want to enjoy what works between us. Trust me.'

Three hours later, on the beach of Epíneio, it was impossible to question his logic. All her problems still existed, but they felt so far away, and here, on this stunning island floating in the middle of the Aegean, she could *breathe*. 'Perhaps there's something to be said for running away after all,' she said with a half-smile for the man who'd rolled up his sleeves and waded into the madness of her life, to hell with the consequences.

'Definitely.' He drew her closer, one arm around her shoulders, holding her against his side in a gesture of friendship and support. At least, that was what it was supposed to be, but the second they connected, heat exploded inside her, and her body softened against him, wordlessly inviting him closer, conveying her need for him. It was a need he could stir so easily! She knew better than to try tamping down on her desire, but she held her resolution close to her heart: when they were back in Athens, she'd reinstate the rules they'd agree to. This was an aberration. A moment out of time, exempt from their agreement, because Jonathan had been such a monumental jerk. Yes, they were cheating, but it was justified.

Convinced enough to let go of her control, just a little, she tilted her face to his, and when he kissed her she smiled against his mouth, feeling, for a moment, as though everything was exactly as it was supposed to be. For the first time in years, she relaxed—in the midst of the storm that was her life, here in this haven, with Alexandros at her side, she was happier than she'd been in a long time.

He waited until she was asleep before leaving the bed, moving to the door of the room and hesitating a moment, studying her from guarded eyes, weighing up what he intended to do before he slipped from the room completely.

Alex was not a man to second-guess his instincts, and ever since yesterday morning he'd known one thing for certain: he could not sit by and allow Tessa to be her ex-husband's punching bag.

Though he thought of Epíneio as his haven from the frenetic pace of his real life, he wasn't able to escape it completely, and the office here reflected that. It was a state-of-the-art space, with two side-by-side computer screens, and all the technology he required to be able to function at his level without interruption.

He stepped inside with determination, moving towards his desk and flicking the computers to life as he reached for his phone and dialled his office, only one person in mind that he could trust with this. 'Get me Berringer,' he said, without preamble.

'Yes, sir, of course.' His assistant put him through immediately, despite the lateness of the hour, and Berringer answered on the third ring. In the background there was the clinking of glasses, the sound of laughter.

'You're busy?' he prompted.

'I have friends for dinner, it's not important,' Berringer said.

Alex pushed back in his chair. He didn't like to eat into

his staff's private lives, and yet he paid well above the average.

'I have time, sir. What is it?' There was the clicking of a door, and then the noise dulled.

'This won't take long.' Alex pushed aside his qualms about the timing of his call. He had to know this matter was dealt with. 'I need you to do something for me. Delegate, if necessary, but it must be handled.'

He proceeded to outline the list he'd come up with: threaten the television network with a lawsuit for slander, threaten Jonathan's lawyer with the same, regardless of the fact he was in the *Celebrity Housemates* complex and sequestered from communication, and include a promise for more detailed litigation if Jonathan didn't submit to a retroactive confidentiality clause. Alex had no idea if it would work. God knew he had the teeth to pursue Jonathan through all the courts in Europe, but did Theresa have the stomach for that?

He suspected not.

The last thing she wanted was more drama and attention on her private life, and if there was a big legal bust-up it would lead to that. So he had to hope the threats would be sufficient. And if they weren't? Would he go against her wishes and use his deep pockets to simply make this problem go away?

He closed his eyes and saw her face, the hurt there as she'd read the article, the hauntedness around her eyes and lips, the sense of betrayal, and he knew that, yes, he would do anything he could in order to relieve her pain. For Stavros, he had to. He owed his best friend that much, at least.

For no reason that he could think of, he loaded up the latest article and began to read, phone tucked under his ear. Just as with the first time, his blood pressure went through the roof, until he could take it no longer and jackknifed to standing, stalking across the room to the window and star-

ng out at it, his body very still. The ocean was dark tonight,
ne moon submerged by thick clouds, so even the trees were
ost in the darkness. It suited his mood to look out and see
arkness. And yet, at just that moment, the clouds parted,
nd a pure beam of moonlight split through, casting the
round in silvery light. He braced his hip against the win-
ow frame, staring out at the ocean, a frown marring his
ace. Darkness and light. Black night and moonlight. Would
ach be as beautiful without the other?

I want to show you something.'

She jolted her gaze to him, the X-rated nature of her
noughts surely written all over her expression as her hus-
and stepped onto the pool deck. She flicked some water
ver her knees, waiting for him to elaborate.

'Come with me.'

She lifted a single brow but stood, her knees a little
nsteady, and her awareness of Alex only grew when he
eached down and laced their fingers together as naturally
s if they were truly a couple.

He guided her away from the house, and down a wind-
ng, gravel path, to a small building she hadn't seen before.

'What is it?'

The walls were whitewashed, the roof terracotta, and a
arge barn door made of glass was painted in peeling tur-
uoise paint. He swished it open, and then gestured for her
o step inside. She did so, with a small frown, onto a painted
oncrete floor.

'Your studio, if you want it to be.'

Her eyes widened as she turned to look at him, and a
housand things flashed through her mind. Pleasure, be-
ause this was so thoughtful. Danger, because it was
houghtful, and if she wasn't careful she might read some-
hing into that, and excitement, because the need to paint
nly intensified when she was here.

'I have an office inside,' he pointed out. 'It only makes sense for you to have a studio.'

'That's so kind, Alex. I really—I'm blown away. Thank you.' Her voice cracked so she cleared her throat, moving deeper into the space and admiring the light streaming in through the wide doors, and then the view of the ocean she could see from the windows on the side. 'I love it.'

'I'm glad.' His voice was cool, with no hint of emotion. She stifled a sigh. On the face of it, this seemed like a thoughtful gesture, but she'd be reading more into it if she allowed that to mean anything. More likely, it was just Alex's practical brain taking over, thinking of ways she could be kept busy while on the island, so he could work guilt-free.

That dose of reality was essential, but it did take the shine off things, just a little.

When she turned back to him, her smile didn't reach her eyes. 'I'll organise some equipment when we're next in Athens.'

He nodded his agreement, waiting by the door.

'You woke early,' she murmured as they made their way back towards the house.

'Yes.'

'I thought this was your haven, where you come to relax?'

'I am relaxed.' He shrugged, his frame as rigid as a brick wall.

She threw him a sidelong glance. 'Then why get out of bed in the small hours of the morning?'

'Actually, I worked through the night.'

She blinked. 'You did?'

'You fell asleep, and my mind was racing, so I went into my office.'

She grimaced. 'I hardly slept the night before that.' She frowned. 'Actually, I'd barely slept since leaving Epíneio, but here, something about the sea breeze and the rolling waves... I could fall asleep right now.'

'Would you like me to tuck you into bed?' he offered, and her pulse kicked up a gear.

She needed boundaries…almost as much as she needed him. She nodded slowly, fatalistically, because how could she resist?

The temptation to stay in bed all day was hard to ignore, but he forced himself to, stretching and pulling away from Tessa's naked body even when he wanted to stay with one arm clamped around her waist, holding her to him.

Beyond her window, the ocean glistened, and the sky was a brilliant blue. An idea bubbled in his veins, and he didn't stop to question the wisdom of it, just as he hadn't the suggestion to come to Epíneio, nor to offer her the old guest house as a studio.

'How'd you like to hit the water?'

'A swim?' she murmured.

'Eventually. I was thinking a jet ski first.'

Her smile was spontaneous and mesmerising. 'I'd like that.' She nodded. 'I'd like it a lot.'

CHAPTER ELEVEN

HER BODY WAS pressed close to his as he surfed the coastline, tracing the outline of the island from the water, showing her hollowed-out caves dug into the cliff face, and the little stone cottages that his staff used when they were on the island, as well as grapevines that yielded just enough fruit to make a small pressing of wine, and the nimble mountain goats that had graduated to the edge of a cliff now, and were lazily chomping their way through wildflowers. Everything about the island fascinated her, and the man in front of her, whose body she had her arms tightly wound around, fascinated her most of all.

There was danger in that sentiment—it was the opposite of how she should feel—but there was something about Alex that made her want to stop time and devour him. To understand him completely—everything about him—even when she knew him on an instinctive level that defied explanation.

Jet skiing was wonderful, but when they returned to the house Alex said he had work to do, and disappeared abruptly, leaving her alone. She told herself she was glad, that their time together had to be carefully balanced, or there would be too much danger. She read for a while, then wandered into what would become her studio and imagined how she'd lay out the furniture, then, as the sun started to become almost too much, she stripped down to her bathers and stood on the edge of the pool, toes curled over the coping, eyes chasing the ripples of the water. She counted to ten, breathed in deeply then dived in, cracking beneath the surface and spearing through the water, holding her breath all the way to the other side, before pushing up and resting her arms on the edge of the pool.

'Mind if I join you?'

She bit back a smile as she turned to see Alex crouching on the side of the pool, his fingertips caressing the water.

'It's your pool.' She shrugged, hiding the fact that she wanted him to join her almost more than anything.

His eyes were lightly mocking, as though he understood the stand she was taking. He stood, eyes still on her as he stripped out of his shirt, leaving him standing in just a pair of boardshorts that did little to hide the muscular nature of his body. Her mouth felt as acrid as the desert as he walked around the pool, closer to her, his every step an inducement, a temptation, a fascination, so that by the time he'd reached her the air in her lungs seemed to crackle.

He stood directly in front of her, his hair-roughened legs and strong calves so close she had an irrational urge to pull herself out of the water and press her lips to his flesh there. Thankfully, before she could indulge that craving, he lifted his arms over his head and dived in, his body a study of strength and elegance as he swam to the other end of the pool easily. When he was halfway there she could no longer fight her body's cravings and she gave chase, moving beneath the water to follow him stealthily, eyes scanning to find him. When he changed direction she followed, no longer pursuing him beneath the water but splashing on top of it, moving faster, laughing as she got close and he slipped away, changing direction again, spinning easily in the water, his far more powerful stroke no match for hers. So when she caught him, finally, she suspected it was because he'd allowed it, but that didn't make the success any less sweet. Her fingers curved around his bicep, and he laughed, drawing her closer, their arms tangling as they splashed in the water. He was so much stronger, and yet he let himself be caught and tamed, let her body wrap around his, until she was breathless from laughing and the exertion, in his arms, legs wrapped around his waist, so close to him she felt as though they were one person.

'Hi.' She smiled, all rules momentarily pushed from her mind by the pleasure of this moment. Her lashes were clumped from the water and her dark hair fell like silk down her back.

'Hi.' He grinned back, his handsome face knocking the air completely from her lungs.

The sunset was stunning, and she was aware of it in her peripheral vision, but mostly she was aware of the man in front of her, of how perfectly they fitted together, and of how much she liked being here with him, like this.

Before the idea could terrify her, and make her pull away from him, he shifted, kissing her—wet, urgent, important kisses that spoke of time wasted and imperative needs. Breathless, she kissed him back, and as he steered them through the water she didn't argue, but let him direct them to the wide pool steps, lifting her bottom onto the edge of one so that he could kiss her properly, his body dominating easily, hers surrendering to his completely. It was a magical night, from the colour of the sky to the perfection of his possession. He peeled her bathing costume off easily, then dispensed with his own, tossing both onto the pool tiles before kissing her again, slowly at first, and then with desperate need, until she was a quivering mess in his arms. When he parted her legs and moved between them she bit down on her lip so hard she almost drew blood, holding her breath until he thrust into her, and her muscles squeezed him in welcome abandon.

They were unified by passion and need, each moving with the same desperate haste, she writhing to be closer to him, he rolling his hips until she was incandescent, the water lapping around them creating waves that rivalled the ocean's, until finally they exploded in a shared, redefining moment, clinging to one another as though that was the only way they could make sense of what they were doing.

When he pulled away a little, so he could look down at her, she saw the dark slash of colour on his cheeks and felt a rush of female power to know that for all he could drive her wild, she did the exact same to him. It was a shot of confidence and a balm to her traumatised soul. She pressed a palm to his chest, smiling contentedly when she felt the strong racing of his heart.

In the space of a week, she'd gone from thinking of herself as entirely sexless to suspecting she might actually be a little bit of a sex goddess. The thought made her laugh softly beneath her breath, earning a cocked brow from Alex.

'Something funny, Mrs Zacharidis?'

Her heart stammered and air was suddenly in short supply. 'I...'

Mrs Zacharidis. How ridiculous that it had only just hit her fully: they were married. Man and wife, for the rest of her life.

Her gaze dropped to the water beneath them as emotions too strong to interpret began to pull on her. 'I was just thinking that a week ago I would have said I didn't have a sexual bone in my body,' she said with a small shrug.

'You hadn't had the opportunity to get to know yourself properly.'

'No, I suppose not.' She lifted her face to his. 'Except for that one night, when I was just too grief-filled to realise that what we'd shared was...' She stalled, not sure she could put into words what she thought about that night, nor what it had come to mean to her during her marriage.

'Yes?'

Perfect. She couldn't admit that. It hadn't been perfect... it had been a lie. Just as this was a lie. Not the sex, though. But beyond that? Her heart beat harder, faster, more urgently, demanding that she listen.

Alex had rejected her four years earlier, and despite the fact they'd only spent one night together, it had broken her. His words had shattered her in two. She'd married Jonathan in the stupid hope that she could start to feel normal again, but it had failed, because Alex had always been there, larger than life, in her mind, her memories, her studio, and her heart.

Instinctively she shied away from any deeper self-analysis, because it would be too catastrophic if she was to start thinking she'd done something stupid and fallen in love with him. Even the idea had her stiffening, breaking away, putting space between them, physically and, she hoped, emotionally.

It was one of the things she'd come to love most about being on the island with Alex. Walking aimlessly, directionless, along his private beaches, sand warm beneath their toes, water lapping at their feet, and the sun, half-concealed by the horizon now, spread a blanket of gold from it to them, so it seemed as though there was something magical in the air. When they walked it was easy to talk, or to simply be silent, side by side, and it was natural for his hand to reach down and grab hers, to lace their fingers together in a small yet intimate contact that did funny things to her heart.

'There's something I'd like to discuss with you.'

His tone of voice was flattened of emotion but the formality of his statement had her slowing. 'Oh?'

'Your father's company cannot keep running with him at the helm.'

Oh. Relief began to throb inside her chest.

'He's not well, and there's too much pressure on him.'

'His VP—'

'Is not a man I respect,' Alex dismissed swiftly. 'And nor does your father, clearly, or he'd have handed over the reins a long time ago.'

That was a fair point.

'You know Dad. He's a control freak.'

'I understand that,' Alex said with a lift of his shoulders. 'He owes it to his shareholders—and himself—to protect his legacy.'

'What are you suggesting?'

'That I buy into the company and take over as CEO.'

Her jaw dropped. 'You're kidding?'

'You don't like the idea?'

She tucked a stray strand of hair behind her ear. 'It's not that.' She struggled to think. 'It's just, you have your own enormous business to run.'

'I can do both.'

Which would leave them very little time to share. The thought was a red herring but she pushed it away nervously, only to have a far less pleasant one enter her head. Was he doing this to avoid her? Was he already getting bored of her? Regretting this? She looked away.

'If that's the case, then you should speak to Dad. It's nothing to do with me.'

He made a noise of impatience. 'It has everything to do with you. You're a major shareholder, for a start, and secondly…'

But he didn't finish, so she turned to look at him, only to find he'd stopped walking and was staring into the ocean, his expression brooding.

'Secondly?' she prompted, surprised at the sharp tone in her voice.

He began to walk once more, catching up to her. 'I don't want you to think it's why I married you,' he said finally. 'There's financial advantage in this for me.'

'You have enough money,' she pointed out.

'Yes.'

'And I know why you married me.' Something sat hard

in her throat. She looked away. 'I get where you're coming from. You want to help Dad. I'm okay with that, of course.'

And she was, for the most part. But the undercurrent to every conversation was the sense that they were becoming more and more entwined, and that it spelled danger for Tessa. She couldn't think of Alex without a strange sensation stealing through her heart.

They walked in silence for a while, just the waves bringing soft, shushing sounds towards them, and the night birds beginning to sing their lovely, high-pitched songs, so Tessa breathed in deeply then exhaled.

'How come you got involved in shipping?' she asked thoughtfully as the sun dipped completely behind the ocean, slipping to the other side of the world.

'I had an opportunity, right out of college. I didn't want to take over my father's company.' A muscle jerked in his jaw, so she felt the emotion behind his simple admission. 'So I raised as much capital as I could, as quickly as I could— your parents were early investors, did you know that?'

She shook her head.

'And then I bought a small line of boats.'

'Which you've somehow turned into all this.'

He lifted his shoulders. 'Global logistics boomed right as I moved into it.'

'If I didn't know you better, I'd say you were being modest.'

He laughed. 'Fine, I have good instincts, and I worked hard. I worked very hard. I was determined to make a name for myself, outside of my father's money.'

'Why?'

His pace slowed, ever so slightly. 'Isn't that normal?'

She shook her head slowly. 'I don't think so. You come from old money. Your father inherited his parents' business and so on and so forth. To strike out on your own—'

'I'm Chairman of my father's company.'

'But you still refer to it as your father's company.'

'He only died six months ago.'

Sympathy shifted through her. 'I know.' She moved closer, pulling her hand free so she could put it around his waist instead, needing full body contact to convey the depth of her sympathy. 'It was so sudden.'

'Yes.' He dropped a kiss on the top of her head and brought his arm around to drape over her shoulders. Something clicked into place inside her, so despite the heaviness of their conversation, she was utterly at ease.

'But it will take me a while—if ever—to stop thinking of those businesses as his.'

'Before he—before you lost him, you were still hands-off with those companies. Why?'

'Haven't I already answered that?'

She frowned. 'I don't think so.'

He laughed, but it was a sound without humour. 'You're too damned perceptive.'

'I just have a feeling there's more to it.'

'And what gives you that feeling?'

'I can't explain it. I just…know you.' Their eyes met and her heart zinged with the power of a full-blown electrical storm. Her knees went weak. She looked away, and when he spoke his voice was distant, cool.

'I loved my father, naturally. I admired him a great deal. He was strong and smart and fiercely determined. But I also hated him, Theresa.'

She jerked her face to his.

'My childhood was spent watching him obliterate my mother's sense of self, watching them argue like cats and dogs, watching her spiral further and further into misery, and my father never doing anything to help her. I don't know why. Ego, perhaps? She needed help, and instead he fought with her, again and again. Their divorce should have liberated her from the situation, but by then she was destroyed.

Their marriage had taken its toll.' He paused, swallowing and looking out to sea. 'When she died, a part of me broke off and went with her. I knew I could never forgive him. For all the ways he treated her in their marriage, and for how he was with her after. She killed herself, but in many ways he killed her too.'

Tessa's eyes closed, her lashes hiding the tears that were forming.

'The idea of working with him, enriching his companies further, was anathema to me. He was my father, and I loved him, but it was not an easy relationship, and when he died I mourned more than just him; I felt as though I was losing her all over again, too. We never spoke about her. We never spoke about their fights, their marriage. All I knew was that she'd loved him, violently, and that love had killed her.' He turned back to face Tessa, his lips twisting in a cynical grimace.

She nuzzled closer, pressing her head against his chest, slowing them to a stop and just standing there, two people embracing on the shoreline as the stars began to shine.

'And so you see love as bad?' she murmured.

'Yes.' His smile was mocking. 'I don't see any upside to it. You open yourself up to someone, and what for? I'm happy as I am.'

Her throat worked overtime as she swallowed hard, trying to remove the taste of bitterness. 'I'm sorry for what you've been through. I'm sorry for your mother.'

'I wanted to save her, Theresa. I wanted to, so badly, but I was too young, and her needs were so difficult to grasp. I didn't know how…' He growled, his frustration obvious.

Sympathy washed through Tessa, but so did comprehension, in equal measure. 'And so you saved me instead,' she murmured as a pang of guilt tightened her chest. Because unconsciously she'd presented him with a situation he could never say 'no' to.

She'd come to him as a woman in distress, a woman who'd been made miserable in her marriage, who'd been emotionally manipulated and abused to the point she'd forgotten who she was and had certainly lost the waypoint to her inner strength. But Alex hadn't been prepared to let history repeat itself, and so he'd stepped in, to save the day. He wasn't a child any longer, but a grown man, perfectly able to be the saviour.

It all made perfect sense, and his actions were no less honourable, but she felt a strange heaviness resting in her chest all of a sudden, and she pulled away from him, forcing a smile to her face. 'Let's go back and have dinner. I'm starving.'

CHAPTER TWELVE

THE ISLAND WAS a haven, but not from Tessa's thoughts. The longer they remained, the harder it was to fight the inner knowledge she was wrestling with, the love that was taking hold of her, that scared the hell out of her, because of how vulnerable that love would make her. Neither of them wanted a marriage built on love, but she could no longer deny to herself the feelings that were stirring through her, feelings she'd always had for Alex. Why else would his rejection have hurt so damned much?

If she told him how she felt, it would be an unbearable burden.

She knew what he feared most in the world; she knew how he felt about love.

She'd heard the rich emotion in his voice when he'd spoken of his parents' marriage, of his mother's love for his father, and how that love had been her downfall. What would his protective instincts do if she told him—or even just showed him—her love?

A lump formed in her throat as she stared out at the early morning coastline, the trees almost silver in the cool morning light.

He could *never* know the truth.

She wasn't aware of Alex's approach, but the fragrance of coffee curled around her and she cast a look over her shoulder, her heart giving an enormous jump at the sight of him, dressed in a suit now—like the Alex he'd been on the day she'd proposed this marriage.

'You're a little overdressed for our island vibe,' she observed with a sideways tilt of her head.

His smile was like warm honey on her spine, and she

shivered, taking the coffee with a grateful smile that felt tight on her lips.

'I have meetings in Athens today.'

'Ah.' Another shiver, this time shaped by the idea of the city. It wasn't geographically far, but at the same time it was a million miles away from Epíneio.

He crouched beside her, tailored trousers straining across his haunches, drawing her gaze, stirring hunger in the pit of her stomach. She sipped her coffee, closing her eyes as the taste assaulted her senses.

'I'm signing some contracts, otherwise I'd have someone else handle things in my place.' He lifted a finger to her cheek, feeling the soft flesh, a smile on his lips as her own parted on a sigh.

She moved her face slightly, so her mouth touched his fingers, and his pupils dilated, passion immediately visible. He pulled his hand away; they both knew what would happen if he didn't.

She loved him. The words were bursting out of her, as surely as the waves were rolling towards the coastline. She wanted to say them. She wanted to tell him.

It was this place, she realised, eyes wide. Here, on the island, everything was simple and elemental. They were just a man and a woman, biologically programmed to be together, to want each other, and, for Tessa, to love. The heart she'd sworn would never work again was now working overtime, racing whenever Alex so much as breathed near her.

But the island magnified all those feelings. Here, there were no distractions, no reminders of who she was and the life she had to live. She was running away here, and she couldn't do that any longer.

'I'll come with you,' she said decisively. 'To Athens, I mean.'

He cocked a brow, regarding her thoughtfully. 'It's not

necessary. I'll be back before dinner—tomorrow, at the latest.'

Something panged in the region of her heart. For Tessa, the idea of that separation was unbearable, and for him, it rated nothing more than a lift of one shoulder. Nothing could illustrate their different feelings more than that.

'No.' She couldn't let herself be this woman, so completely in love with him, waiting for him to return. 'I'd like to see my parents, maybe catch up with some friends.' She pushed to standing, finishing her coffee in one gulp. 'I can get ready quickly, okay?'

Her stomach was in knots as his helicopter came in over Athens, the city bleak despite the perfect, golden morning. Landmarks she'd loved all her life, that had fascinated her for their history and culture, now felt like barbed wire against her skin. This was her real life, but she was dreading returning to it. Not because of Jonathan and whatever else he might have said during his time on the show, but because here, in Athens, she knew she would have to put distance between herself and Alex. They wanted this marriage to last, and the only way she could survive a life married to him was to find a way to coexist with the love she felt. That meant returning to the boundaries she'd originally insisted on, and those boundaries would be so much easier to enforce here.

'I'll be done by lunch. Shall we go and see your parents together?'

So much for space and boundaries. 'You could talk to Dad about taking over.'

'You're sure you don't mind?'

She lifted her shoulders. 'It's not up to me.'

Dissatisfaction was obvious in his features. 'None the less, I'd like to know you approved before I suggested it.'

'It will be good for Dad,' she said softly.

'But how do *you* feel about it?'

'Of course I approve. It just seems that you're taking on an awful lot…'

'I can manage.'

Of course he could. He was Alexandros Zacharidis, superman. 'Fine.' Her smile was overbright. 'I'll set it up.'

It was strange stepping into her parents' house with Alex by her side, and in some ways it felt completely normal. Elizabeth Anastakos pulled her daughter in for a huge hug while Orion and Alex shook hands, and then the older couple shepherded them onto the terrace, where an enormous lunch spreadhad been laid out.

'Mum, you've gone to so much trouble.'

'It was nothing,' Elizabeth said, with her usual humility. Not only did Elizabeth possess a PhD in electrical engineering, but she'd also become her father's right-hand woman, bouncing ideas off one another, and then Stavros. To top it off, she was an exceptional cook, who could make eight dishes without breaking a sweat.

'We could have brought something,' Tessa murmured, old feelings of inadequacy creeping in.

'Next time, we'll come to you,' Orion volleyed back, his skin pale beneath his tan, but his eyes still smiling with pleasure.

We'll come to you. Such a perfectly banal and domestic phrase that spoke of normality and long-term expectations. And could she blame them? It wasn't as if Tessa was planning on leaving Alex. They were married, and at some point they might conceive a child. This was for keeps.

Something tightened in the region of her heart, but she refused to let it unsettle her.

Over lunch, Tessa described Epíneio to them, and whenever she missed a detail Alex was right there to fill in the blanks, answering questions regarding the history of the island house, so she listened in rapt fascination as he spoke. But then, whenever her could hand over to Tessa he did so, deferring to her, allowing her to charm her parents with stories of the beautiful sanctuary.

As they sat back and enjoyed coffee, Tessa too full to ever contemplate eating again, Alex broached the subject of the business.

'I can see a way to alleviate your worries, but, of course, it's a big decision, and one you should weigh up carefully.' He proceeded to outline his proposal, how much he'd pay for a controlling stake in the company—an eye-watering figure—and how he'd juggle his duties across three large multinational companies. 'My father's company and my own run as well-oiled machines. I can step back from both without too much risk, while I come to terms with Anastakos Industries. Naturally, whether or not you're ready to cede control is a personal matter, for you to decide.'

'No, it's not,' Elizabeth demurred, her eyes slightly misty. 'The decision has been made for him.'

Tessa reached over and put a hand on her mother's, stroking it gently.

'You can't keep going on like this, my darling,' Elizabeth said gently to her husband, who harumphed in response. 'And if you're going to see anyone take over, surely it has to be Alex? After Stavros, I wasn't sure he'd ever…'

They were silent, and beneath the table Alex squeezed Tessa's knee comfortingly.

Another noise from Orion, this time one of contemplation.

'Our share values have already gone up at the mere prospect of this,' Orion pointed out.

'That's true. It makes excellent commercial sense.'

'And my wife is right. I'm tired. I would rather be here, with my family, for whatever time I have left.'

Beneath the table, Alex's hand curved over Tessa's knee, as if he understood how desperately she needed that support.

'I can start immediately.'

Relief whooshed through Tessa, on behalf of her father, as well as a strange, aching sense of grief. Alex was talking about undertaking a huge career shift. Superman he might be, and he'd be able to get to the point where her father's company was running as smoothly as his own, but there'd be months, at least, while he learned the ropes and came to terms with the existing commercial arrangements. Months in which he wouldn't be able to fly to Epíneio at the drop of a hat, and she'd be forgotten.

This signalled a shift, surely, in their marriage. After such a short time, the honeymoon was well and truly over.

Lunch stretched into the afternoon, but the sun was still high in the sky as they left, and Tessa, her mind spinning in overtime, couldn't contemplate returning to Alex's home just yet. She needed to make sense of things, to adjust to yet another change in the landscape of their lives.

'Would you mind dropping me at my studio?' she murmured. 'I'd like to work on something. And it would be a good chance to gather some paints for the island,' she added, though who knew when she'd be back?

'Of course,' he replied. 'Address?'

She gave him the street and number, which he keyed into the GPS.

They drove in silence, and the longer it stretched, the more she became aware of a throb of tension between them, until finally, as he pulled up, he turned to face her. 'If you don't want me to buy your family business, just say so.'

Her eyes widened. 'What?'

'You've been mulling since your parents agreed to the sale. So? You're not happy about this after all?'

'I'm very happy for them,' she promised softly, looking

at her studio as salvation now. 'You'll do excellent things with it, I'm sure.'

His displeasure was obvious, but she stepped out of the car before he could respond, saying goodbye through the slightly ajar door then closing it and walking quickly away, towards her own Epíneio— the studio.

She leaned against the doors once she'd entered, eyes closed, breathing in deeply.

Everything was going from bad to worse. The boundaries she'd wanted to keep in place were all over the place, and worst of all, her heart couldn't stay out of things. She pushed up from the door and went past her friends' studio spaces to the back, where her own area was, and sat on the stool with a frown on her face, staring at the landscape of Epíneio.

She loved it. Not just the painting, but also the island. It was—

A noise caught her attention and she looked up just as Alex strode in, his features grim. 'You forgot this.' He held up her phone.

She swore softly. Alex's being here was an invasion she hadn't counted on. This was her private space, too intimate for him to see. Too revealing. Anxiously, her eyes shifted to the painting of him, which only served to draw his attention to it, so he followed her gaze and then stood completely still, his expression inscrutable.

'When did you do this?' he asked, eventually, moving closer to the enormous canvas with its striking likeness.

She compressed her lips, the walls closing in on her as the answer seemed likely to give away so much more than she wanted to.

'Tessa?' Sensing it was important, he didn't let her get away with not answering. 'When?'

'After that night,' she said, and he closed his eyes in response.

'I see.' He took another few steps nearer. Her sense of vulnerability increased. 'While you were seeing him?'

She shook her head. 'Does it matter?'

'Why do you have this here?' He moved closer. 'Why do you have a huge painting of me in your studio?' He turned back to it incredulously. 'Why do I look as though I'm laughing at you?'

His words lashed her, but she couldn't help the small simmer of pride at having accomplished what she'd set out to with the work. 'It's just a painting.'

His eyes bored into hers and for a moment she wondered if he was going to pursue this, but then he expelled a sigh and turned his back on it.

'Shall I wait for you?'

'No, no,' she murmured, feigning distraction. 'I could be hours. You go…home.'

He cast the painting one more contemplative glance before leaving.

She added touches to the landscape, but mostly she just stared at it, and remembered. The sunlight on her back, sand underfoot, the simplicity of life on Epíneio, before she'd realised she loved him; again. Still? Making love in the water, on the pool deck, in their bedroom.

A lump formed in her throat. *Their* bedroom. On Epíneio, it really had felt like a shared home, a shared vision.

She worked until the light was gone and then decided she couldn't delay any longer, locking up the studio and moving outside. Just as she was going to hail a cab, she saw headlights across the street and her heart did a funny little patter.

'You waited?' she asked as Alex stepped out of the car.

'I had some calls to make. It was no trouble.'

'Uh-huh.' Just like that, the small shimmy of pleasure faded, because he'd stayed only because it was perfectly convenient for him to do so. *Don't read into it,* was the subtext.

Her stomach squeezed uncomfortably as he came around to the passenger side and opened the door for her. Out of nowhere, she wished this was a motorbike, not a car, and that instead of sliding into a sumptuous leather seat she was curling up behind him, arms wrapped around his waist.

On Epíneio she'd felt unconstrained, the rules of the relationship she'd established out of self-preservation had fallen by the wayside, and she'd allowed herself to feel everything without boundaries, without rules. And Alex? What had he felt?

She frowned, the light seeming to dull a little.

It was obvious that he liked her, and that he respected her. He went out of his way to make her happy. But none of that meant he loved her, nor that he would ever love her, for one simple reason: he didn't want to. And Alex was not a man to feel something he didn't welcome.

She was struck by the irony of buckling her seatbelt. It was protecting her from danger, but what about the danger that came from loving Alex as fiercely as she did? And what choice did she have?

Tessa's pulse fired up a little, as misgivings began to hammer her from the inside out. How in the world could she make this marriage work if she loved him like this, and he didn't feel the same way? And why hadn't she seen this possibility was likely? She'd walked into this marriage so absolutely certain she could control it. What a fool she'd been!

The air simmered with tension as he drove home and expertly parked the car, coming around to her door before she could open it herself.

Once inside, he turned to face her again, his expression impossible to read. Neither spoke for several beats, and then they both did at once.

'Alex—'

'Listen, I—'

She compressed her lips. 'You first.'

He nodded slowly. 'Are you okay?'

'Sure,' she said, overbright. 'Why wouldn't I be?'

'That's what I'm trying to work out. You were fine at your parents'. You say you're happy for me to buy out your father. So what is it?'

How could she explain? How could she tell him the obsessive merry-go-round of thoughts she'd been navigating since realising she loved him? It wasn't fair to put that pressure on him. Nothing had changed since he'd agreed to marry her. She couldn't expect him to love her, just because she wanted him to. He'd made his feelings clear; it wasn't his fault she'd broken their rules.

She lifted a hand to his chest, intending to say something placatory and then move away, but the second her skin connected with his muscled abdomen sparks exploded in her central nervous system.

'Alex,' she sighed, his name a whisper on her lips, a dream and a hope, even when she knew hope was stupid.

In response, he kissed her, hard, as if his frustration at not being able to understand her translated into a frantic need, his dominance overpowering Tessa, so she ran her hands over his body, aching to be close to him, to taste him and feel him.

The same needs were rampant within Alex. He slid his hands inside the waistband of her knickers, brushing his fingers over her sex, finding her flesh and teasing her, before sliding a finger into her moist core so she bucked hard against his hand, aching for more, aching for him. When he touched her like this, nothing else mattered. She felt complete, just in this moment, just for now.

He growled, low in his throat, and their clothes flew, each moving frantically to release them from fabric, to be naked together,

Stars danced in her eyes as his hand returned to her sex, pleasure burst on the tip of her tongue, and then she was exploding, digging her nails into his shoulders as sensations racked her body. Even as the waves were still rolling, not yet receding, he withdrew his hand and lifted her, pushing her back against the wall so he could thrust into her, his arousal filling her, his claim complete, and perfect. She whimpered into the curve of his neck, biting down on her tongue to stop herself from murmuring, over and over like an incantation, the words that were flooding her brain.

I love you. I love you.

But she felt them. Oh, how she felt them, right to the tips of her toes, as he moved within her and she felt the full force of that love. Their coming together was swift, their satisfaction mutual and powerful, their cries mingling as they burst into the heavens together, riding the wave, clinging to one another as though therein lay their only hope of salvation.

But as the waves of pleasure receded for Tessa she wondered if there was no hope of salvation here, but, rather, devastation.

Her first instinct had been to erect boundaries around their lives, to keep Alex at a distance. Had she known, even then, on the day she'd propositioned him, that love might be just as inevitable in this marriage as sex? Was that why she'd wanted to delineate how and when they'd be together?

Of course it was.

And that was no less important now than it had been then.

Unless…

She lifted her face, searching his eyes, looking for some hint of love, needing to know if perhaps he was fighting the same battle she was.

'Tessa?' Concern shaded his eyes.

'I was…' Uncertainty made her pause. If she did this, there'd be no going back. She could swallow these feelings and act as though she didn't have them. She could force them back to the same rigid boundaries she'd implemented in the first place, and act as though that wasn't killing her. But Alex deserved better, and she wanted more.

'You were…?' he prompted, and courage failed Tessa. She needed to talk to him, but it could wait.

'It doesn't matter.' And before he could push the matter she kissed him again, doing her best not to think about the future, or the complications she'd welcomed by letting her foolish heart fall for him.

CHAPTER THIRTEEN

As THE NIGHT wore on, the nerves in Tessa's tummy grew tighter, more frantic, so when he went to draw her with him to his bedroom she stood where she was, feet planted on the floor.

On Epíneio, they'd shared a bed every night. There'd been no suggestion of anything else. But here she had her own room, her own space, and if she was to give that up, without knowing how he felt about her, she'd be lost, completely. This emergency marriage that had been entered into as a form of salvation would instead become a silent torment, one from which she could never escape. Because she didn't want to leave Alex. Even loving him as she did, and believing that love to be unrequited, she couldn't turn her back on him. She'd sooner endure the pain of that unreciprocated love than live without him.

'I'm exhausted,' she said with a shake of her head. 'I'm going to my own room.'

He arched his brow with such mocking curiosity that she was reminded immediately of the painting. 'You think I can't be trusted to keep my hands to myself?'

Her heart lurched. 'I think you're as big a risk as I am,' she responded lightly, even though her heart was coiling tighter and tighter.

'I like it when we share a bed. Tell me you don't,' he challenged.

'I do.' She couldn't meet his eyes. 'But it's not really—it doesn't make sense.' Her gut twisted.

'Why not?' His nostrils flared. 'We are married. We were doing it on Epíneio and the world did not end.'

'That's different. The island is different.'

His frown deepened. 'But we are the same people, no?'

She pulled a face. 'Don't be difficult about this, please.'

'Difficult?' he responded, dragging a hand through his hair. 'Two hours ago, we made love as though it was essential for our very survival. Now you are saying you don't want to so much as rest your head on one of my pillows, yet I'm being difficult?'

She nodded slowly. 'That's how it has to be here.' She felt as though she were drowning.

'You're not serious? This again?'

'What?'

'The rules?'

If anything, his derisive response hardened her resolve. 'Nothing's happened to change them.'

'Everything has changed,' he responded, briefly giving her hope. She felt it flare and tried to tamp down on it, but hope was a powerful force and it rolled through her body now.

'Has it?'

'Of course.' He ran his hands through his hair in frustration. 'Look at how much better we know each other, Theresa. When you came to my office and we negotiated that damned contract, you were someone from my past.'

'A mistake,' she interjected with a hint of bitterness.

He ignored that. 'And now you're my wife.' The last word was growled with possession and heat, so her body startled, but she stood still, holding her ground.

'And what does that mean to you?'

His exasperation was obvious. 'That we are married. A team. A *good* team.'

Her heart pounded with nerves. 'That's not enough for me,' she whispered, terrified but knowing her instincts had been wrong: she couldn't put this off, even when she was scared of what he might say. Somehow, knowing he didn't love her would be so much worse than wondering if he did or not, and yet she wanted to have that answer.

'What do you want, then?' he asked, perfectly still, his expression unreadable.

She lifted a finger, toying with the strap of her dress, searching for words. 'I want…' She frowned, still so very anxious. 'I need—'

'Tell me,' he urged, moving closer, the words laced with intensity.

'I want this marriage to be real,' she said finally, eyes lifting to his.

'Did I miss something? Our marriage *is* real.'

That he could think so showed her the truth of his heart, and yet still she persisted. 'I want us to be a real couple,' she said with quiet determination.

'Again, I feel as though I've missed something. We talk with each other, we eat together, we sleep together. How is this not real?'

She frowned. 'Are you serious?'

'What did you think we were doing, Theresa? On the island there was no one around to witness our behaviour, yet still we touched and kissed and walked along the beach holding hands. That wasn't for the benefit of anyone but you and me. Because we like being that way.'

Liked being that way. 'Yes,' she whispered, 'I did like that.'

His eyes narrowed slightly at her use of a past tense.

'But it's not enough.'

'Then what more do you want?' he asked, as though she could demand a sliver of the moon and he'd find a way to give it to her.

'I want you,' she said simply.

'You have more of me than any woman ever has.'

'I want all of you,' she insisted with a shake of her head. 'I want you to love me, as a husband should love his wife.

I want you to wake up in the morning and reach for me not because your body desires mine but because your heart beats for my heart. I want you to kiss me not because you like the way it feels but because your soul has a secret it must share with mine. I want you to be my husband because the idea of being anything else is torture.'

She tilted her face to his, hoping against hope that he would admit he felt the same way, but he was very still, and very, very silent. As the seconds stretched between them, without him responding, the hope that had started to build inside her dropped as a stone would in water.

'When you suggested this marriage, you were adamant that you'd never love again.'

She closed her eyes, the response not a denial, and yet it may as well have been. 'I remember.'

'You've changed your mind?'

'You changed my mind, actually. I wanted to keep this businesslike, just as we discussed, but every day we spent together was a form of nirvana, and bit by bit I found my way back—to myself, my happiness, my truth, and most importantly to the life I want to lead.'

'Theresa.' He groaned her name. 'This is lust, not love. You were in a deeply unhappy marriage. You've never felt anything like what we share. But sexual infatuation isn't the same thing as love. Nor is friendship. Give it time, you'll see that I'm right.'

His rejection was like a rock, pelting into her belly. Friendship. Sexual infatuation. Was that all this was to him? She took a step back, drawing in a harsh breath. 'You're wrong,' she said, twisting her lips into a tight smile. 'But the fact you can even suggest that tells me how you feel about me.'

'I care about you,' he insisted reflexively. 'You are important to me, and the last thing I want to do is hurt you, but for every part of you that wants our relationship to be real,

I know I don't want that. It is everything I have avoided my entire life. I have known, for a long time, that I am someone who values independence. I like the idea of being your husband, of living with you, but as two people on parallel journeys, not entwined in the ways you wish us to be.'

Her heart slowed to an almost-stop. He could not be clearer. Grief tore through her at the finality of his words, suddenly and completely, so much worse than what she'd felt as her marriage to Jonathan had turned dire. That hadn't been soul-destroying because she'd never really loved him. Not like with Alex, who had always threatened to overwhelm her senses.

She lifted a hand to her mouth as she began to understand, only now, why his initial rejection had hurt so much. She'd been terrified. The love that she felt for him was too big, too much; it was a love that could sustain her or destroy her and now she felt the destruction raining down.

Marriage to Jonathan had taught her to conceal her feelings, and she did her best to employ those skills, looking at Alex carefully as she focused on her breathing. Only Alex wasn't Jonathan, and she couldn't keep the turmoil from the shadows of her eyes, nor could she still the breath that was rushing out of her in quick gasps.

'Okay,' she said quietly, the word heavy with her sad acceptance of his stance.

But he moved forward, catching her hands and holding them at chest height. 'Listen, *agape*, this is for your good as much as mine.' His eyes probed hers, as if willing her to understand. 'I cannot be in a marriage like theirs. Love is—a force to be reckoned with, but not by me. I saw the flipside of it and would never willingly experience that, nor would I put you through it.' He squeezed her hands.

'But how do you know we'd be like them?' she demanded. 'Look at my parents! They're happy together. Sure, they quarrel sometimes, but they love one another deeply and their lives are better for that.'

'You don't know what it was like,' he said quietly, and sympathy flooded her, because he was right.

'Are you saying you're afraid of loving me?'

His eyes held hers for a long moment, the colour shifting as he contemplated that. 'I won't let it happen.'

'What if it's already happened?'

But he was withdrawing from her. Not physically, emotionally. She could see it in the tightening of his features, the bracing of his shoulders. This was a fight she couldn't win. Childhood had a way of shaping you, sometimes beyond remedy. As a little boy, Alex had seen too much, his heart had felt too deeply, and so he'd closed it down, bit by bit, and there was nothing she could do about that. Not if he didn't dare try.

'You were right in the first place.' He spoke with the appearance of calm. 'Having sex has complicated things unnecessarily. If I had known that sleeping together would make you believe you loved me, I would never have—'

She swore under her breath, interrupting him. 'I don't *believe* I feel it, I do feel it. It's fact, not fiction. And as for *allowing* us to sleep together, I don't think either of us could have stopped it from happening. Just like I couldn't help but love you. Honestly, Alex, I wonder now if I haven't loved you this whole time? That night we slept together it wasn't just physical. Something transformed inside of me, something so big it was terrifying.'

She hesitated, because she'd never planned to tell him this, but now the words came bursting out of her. 'Do you want to know why I did that painting of you?'

Curiosity sparked in his eyes. His nod was deliberate, slow, his gaze intense.

'I couldn't get you out of my head. The things you said to me…' She lifted a hand to her chest and clutched it there, as though she could somehow ease the awful, gutted sensation in her core. 'You destroyed me, Alex.'

'I was—'

But she wasn't ready to be interrupted. 'You broke my heart,' she groaned. 'I loved you then. I'd always loved you. It was easy to think it was just a crush, but now that I know you better, I understand my feelings more. I loved you, and I turned to you when I needed you—not sex, *you*—and you told me it meant nothing, that you wished you could undo what we'd shared. I was devastated. I felt like such an idiot for spending that night with you. And so I painted your face exactly as it had been then, so laced with scorn and disdain, and I made myself look at it every day, to remember never to be such a trusting idiot again.' She swallowed. 'It didn't work though.'

He was very, very still, watching her with a look in her eyes she didn't recognise. 'Did you love me when you married him?'

She dropped her head forward, tears filling her eyes. She'd come this far. 'Yes.'

'So why marry him?' he demanded.

'Why not? You'd made it clear you didn't want me, and I needed to get you out of my damned head somehow.'

He swore under his breath, then pressed his back against the wall, as if needing support. 'All this time,' he said slowly, the words heavy with realisation. 'I've been blaming him for your insecurities, for hurting you, for damaging your confidence. I've been blaming him, but it was me, wasn't it? I'm the one who broke you apart? I'm the one who hurt you.'

A tear fell down her cheek; she dashed it away.

'It was an awful time in my life,' she groaned. 'It's not your fault.'

'Damn it, don't make excuses for me. Don't excuse me. I don't deserve it.'

She flinched.

'Stavros had died, my parents were heartbroken. I wasn't thinking clearly. I needed—'

'A friend,' he groaned, hitting his palm to his forehead. 'At the very least, I owed you that.'

Oh, how much his friendship would have meant to her! 'None of this matters now,' she whispered, throat thick with emotion. 'It changes nothing.'

'It changes *everything*,' he retorted, the words half-yelled. He stared up at the ceiling, his face unreadable. 'You can't love me.'

She felt sympathy for him then, for how even the idea of love was shutting him down.

'Why not?' she demanded, even as a part of her lay dying.

'You can't,' was all he could say. 'Promise me you won't.' It was a demand, not a question. She wanted to deny that, and in her heart she did.

But she loved him enough to prioritise his needs, to understand that he was almost at breaking point.

'I'll stop saying I love you,' she whispered. 'But not feeling it. It's not something that can be turned on and off.' She'd laid it all on the line, but there was no ultimatum, no threat to leave him. Even when there was no hope of his returning her love, she knew she would stay with him, in his orbit, because it was better than living without him. What kind of fool did that make her?

'So now do you understand why I need to sleep in my own room?' she asked, neatly bringing their conversation full circle, and this time he didn't argue. She waited, hoping, even then, but he said nothing, and after a few moments she turned and left, another small tear rolling down her cheek as she stepped from the room.

Over the coming days, Alex realised that there were some things in a marriage that could be worse than his parents' arguing. Silence.

Not companionable silence, but heavy, burdened, painful silence, and smiles that were as fake as the lawn at so many houses. He had felt both from Theresa. He knew the silence was not to punish him, but because there was nothing else they could say.

The easy flow of conversation had disappeared, and any time he went to speak the words dried in his throat, strangled by his inability to give her the one thing she wanted. As for her smiles…they were an effort. They showed her attempts to keep things even between them, a sign that she wanted to persevere with this marriage even when it fell so wildly short of what she wanted and, hell, what she deserved.

Every moment was agony. He ached for Epíneio. Not just the home, the beach and the breeze, but for how things had been there—so easy and free. He ached to make her laugh, to make her cry with pleasure, to hold her so close he could feel her breath through the walls of his chest. He ached for her.

And yet he kept his distance, because his own needs paled in comparison to hers. He wouldn't hurt her again. Knowing the pain he'd inflicted all those years ago cut him to the core. He'd been such a bastard to her. He couldn't think of it without a deep, mortifying sense of shame. He'd been angry with himself, but he'd lashed out at her. He'd punished her because he'd wanted her so badly. He'd pushed her away, knowing he'd betrayed Stavros and needed her to go, to understand the finality of what he was saying, but he'd destroyed her in the process, and he'd never forgive himself for that. It was remarkable that she had.

As the weekend came around, he thought of their original deal, and the fact she'd agreed Friday through Sunday would be different. He thought about clinging to that lifeline and reimposing those terms, but almost as soon as the idea formed, he dismissed it.

A clean break was better.

If they wanted to salvage their marriage—a marriage that was just a friendship, really—he had to resist temptation. He had to resist Tessa, even when every part of him was yearning for her.

It was the longest month of Tessa's life. Every day she counted off, wondering at what point this would start to get better? She'd always believed in the power of time to heal all wounds, but each day that went by crackled like radio static and, if anything, the pain she felt grew deeper. A week after she'd told Alex she loved him, Tessa had thrown herself into her art. Ten-hour days had stretched to twelve, and then to sixteen. Some nights, she slept on the sofa at the studio rather than go home. She focused all her energy on a large-scale scene, working tirelessly to perfect the details, losing herself in the colours and design.

It helped—barely, but a little. There were even some moments of the day when she was able to put Alex from her mind, but never for long, and the more time she spent estranged from him, the more she craved him. His painting hung across from her, and her eyes flicked to it often, as a talisman, a reminder of what she needed to recover from.

Being home was worse. There, she could feel him. Smell him. See him. It always caught her by surprise, when she'd walk into the kitchen and find him making a coffee, or go to dive into the pool and realise he was already there. For the most part, she would simply turn on her heel and leave the room again, pretending she hadn't realised he was there.

It wasn't because she didn't know what to say to him, but rather that she was scared of pleading her case once more. Of telling him that they could go back to the way they'd been—that she'd never again burden him with her love.

There were many things that led up to it, but in the end it was one thing in particular that made Alex snap. There was the fact that Theresa, always slim and athletic in build, was now far too slender. Her clothes had grown loose and her eyes haunted. Had she realised? Was this on purpose? He knew it wasn't. She simply wasn't eating regularly enough.

She was also working too much. Several nights a week she slept at the studio, though not well, if the bags under her eyes were anything to go by. His own sleep patterns were nothing to boast about. When she didn't come back to their home, he found it hard to sleep—one ear was always trained on the door, listening for her. And when she did come home it was worse, because he lay in bed perfectly aware that they were separated by only a single wall. If he strained, he could hear her when she turned over in her bed, and so he spent a ridiculous amount of time lying there, listening for her movements, and wishing he could reach out and hold her tight.

At least her ex-husband had got the memo and ceased his campaign of misinformation and slander. The lawyers had written a conciliatory response accepting the warning and Alex had reiterated his threats to sue Jonathan to blazes if another word was said about Theresa. At the time, he'd thought the damage Jonathan was doing to her was the devil and he'd done whatever he could to ease her pain. He hadn't realised that he would become a far worse instrument of heartache to his wife.

Guilt stormed through him, and something else too: dread.

He had thought this marriage would be the perfect mix—the exact opposite of what his parents had shared. He had entered into it with a cool head, and yet it had all gone downhill so quickly. Was there any hope they could turn things around? He felt as though they were living in their own war zone, and yet they weren't fighting. They were… nothing. The void of their relationship was almost impossible to accept.

Alex ran a silver fountain pen through his fingers as he contemplated that, his expression grim. A moment later his phone began to ring—it was Tessa.

'Theresa?'

'Um, is this Alex?' An American voice reached his ears, and a trickle of dread ran down his spine.

'Yes. Who is this?'

'My name's Beth. I work at the studio, with Tess.' His eyes swept shut as instinctively he felt something change in the air around him.

'Yes?' The word was clipped.

'She passed out. She didn't want me to call you, she says she's fine now, but she's pale and I thought—'

He gripped the phone tighter, standing. 'I'll be there immediately. I'm calling a doctor—she might get there before me.'

'She seems okay now,' Beth murmured, clearly not expecting this whirlwind response. 'I don't know if she needs—'

'I want a doctor to see her to be sure. I'll be there soon.'

He was already in the lift, and as soon as the doors pinged open on the ground floor he began to run to his car. Suddenly, the idea of there being any distance between them was like eating fire. He couldn't stand it. He needed to be with her, and to hell with overthinking that. To hell with everything.

CHAPTER FOURTEEN

'I TOLD YOU, I'm fine,' Tessa muttered, considerably *less* fine now than she had been a moment earlier, before Alex had burst into the studio, midway through the doctor he'd sent drawing blood from the crook of her arm.

'Doctor?' Alex turned his attention to the middle-aged woman with the reassuring bearing. 'What's going on? How is she?'

'Dehydrated,' the doctor replied without lifting her gaze, removing the needle and pressing a cotton ball against the skin, stemming the blood droplet. 'Beyond that, I won't know until I get these results.' She lifted the three vials of blood and then slipped them into the pocket of her lab coat, only then making eye contact with Alex.

'But you suspect something is wrong?' Alex demanded, not looking in Tessa's direction, so she had a moment to stare at him, and she took it, drinking in the sight of him while he was distracted, allowing herself to commit every detail to memory. It had been weeks since she'd properly looked at him, longer since they'd touched. Her heart did a funny little palpating thing and she let out a soft groan.

Alex turned to her at once, then crouched beside her. '*Agape,* what is it?'

If she'd thought that term of endearment hard to hear before, it was nothing compared to now that she had confirmation he didn't love her. She offered him a tight smile, hoping it was reassuring. 'I'm just—I'm fine,' she said, her eyes skittling away from him and towards the doctor, who nodded professionally.

'I should have these results by tomorrow.'

'Tomorrow?' Alex stood, turning to face the doctor, hi

shoulders squared. 'That's too long. Send them to a different lab, I don't care what it costs.'

The doctor's expression was one of patience, as though she'd heard that before. 'I will put a rush on them,' she said politely, then turned to face Tessa, 'and call you when I have the results.'

Tessa nodded her thanks and went to stand, to accompany the doctor to the door, but her legs were still wobbly and she swayed a little, so Alex rushed to her, placing a strong, commanding arm around her waist, holding her against his side. Little electric shocks flooded her. It felt so good to be touched by him, to be felt by him, she just wanted to stay there a little longer, to take strength from him.

'I'll speak to you soon, Mrs Zacharidis.'

Beth, standing by and watching, eyed the couple. 'Do you want a coffee, Tess? A muffin?'

Tessa didn't feel like anything, but she nodded, because she felt as though Alex was about to explode.

When they were alone she went to pull away from him, but he held her tight, right where she was, staring down at her thoughtfully for several seconds, before swinging her into his arms and carrying her, cradled against his chest, from the studio.

'What are you doing?' she demanded, looking around despite the fact they were alone.

'Fixing this,' he said through gritted teeth.

Even though it was cheating, she let her head rest on his shoulder, and she listened to the beating of his heart, the proximity giving her the strength she needed. But when he stepped out of the building and approached his car, she knew she had to assert her independence once more.

'Alex, I'm serious, what do you think you're doing?'

'I told you, fixing—'

'Nothing needs fixing,' she denied. 'Beth will—'

'I will call her and explain,' he insisted as he opened the

front passenger door to his car, helping Tessa in. She was too exhausted to struggle. He came around to the driver's side quickly and looked at her as though reassuring himself of something, then started the engine with a dramatic roar and pulled out into traffic.

It took several blocks before Tessa realised they weren't moving towards his home, and several more minutes to recognise where they were going. Her insides clenched as his helicopter came into view, and suspicion began to form.

'No.' She shook her head, the idea of being back on Epíneio a torture she couldn't withstand. After all, the island was where she'd realised she loved him, that she'd always loved him.

'Yes,' he muttered, killing the engine and coming around to her door. When she didn't move, he unbuckled her seatbelt then lifted her from the car, carrying her once more towards the helicopter.

'Damn it, Alex, I can walk, I'm fine.'

'Just let me do this, for God's sake.'

She startled, the tone of his voice pulling at something in her heart. She hesitated a moment and then nodded. Epíneio scared her but there was something about Alex that worried her more than she was scared, something about him that seemed…shattered.

'Thank you.' The words were dredged from the depths of his soul. Only once they reached the helicopter did he set her down, holding her hand to help her up then coming around to the pilot's side and taking his own seat. She buckled in while he adjusted the controls and started the rotor blades spinning, then they were up, Athens shrinking into a model city before her eyes.

From time to time, Tessa was afflicted by travel sickness and her exhaustion translated into nausea, so as Alex expertly piloted the chopper towards Epíneio, she pressed her head against the headrest and closed her eyes, dozing in the streaming sunlight until he set the helicopter down and gently tapped her knee, waking her. She looked at him, nothing making sense for a moment, and then she sat up straighter, her heart bolting as she saw the island.

Somehow, the place was even more beautiful now. Her heart twisted and yearned for something that was impossible.

Tears threatened and she dug her nails into her palms to stave them off, but when Alex came around to her side, she suspected he knew how she felt, because his jaw tightened and his face bore a mask of concern.

'I'm fine,' she reassured him. 'Please, stop worrying.'

His response was to take her hand and help her down from the helicopter, but before he could lift her again she shook her head. 'I'm okay to walk. Please, Alex, don't fuss. I just fainted a moment, it was nothing really.'

'It's not…it's not just that you passed out,' he said, shaking his head, silencing whatever else he'd been about to say. He tugged on her hand lightly. 'Come inside.'

She nodded, but with each step that brought them closer to the house she felt as though a piece of her was breaking off, so before they reached the delightful doors she stopped walking and stood completely still, staring at it. 'I don't know if I can do this,' she said, the words strained.

'Oh?'

She threw a quick glance at him, reminding herself she'd said she would never burden him with her love again. He'd been honest about his feelings all along, it wasn't his fault she'd broken the terms of their arrangement.

'It's complicated,' she said finally, the words halting.

'Is it? To me, it seems very simple. Here, we were happy. And I have not been happy since. Have you?'

She almost rolled her eyes. 'This isn't real life, though. We were happy here because it was a holiday. No, a fantasy.'

'Was it? Was loving me also a fantasy?'

Her heart squealed but her mind flicked to life. Perhaps that was a way to let him off the hook? She could lie to him and say that yes, everything she'd felt had been a fantasy, none of it was real. But she *couldn't* lie to him. Not about something so important.

'What I wanted was an illusion,' she said carefully, eyes roaming the house now, frown on her lips. She was unaware of the way Alex stared at her, nor of the way his own mouth turned downwards.

'Then come inside to rest for a time. Eat. Drink. Swim. You have been working too hard.'

'I love my work.'

'And it will still be waiting for you, or you can use the studio here.'

'How would you feel if I ripped you out of your office?'

'If I looked as dead on my feet as you do, relieved,' he muttered, throwing her a warning glance. 'Do I need to carry you the rest of the way?'

She was here now—the only alternative to going into the house was insisting he fly her back to Athens, and that filled her with a bag of cement. 'Fine,' she agreed mutinously. 'I'll go inside.'

But it was like stepping back into the past. The last time they'd left, they'd both presumed they'd come back again soon after, and the house had that feeling—as though it had been left quickly, everything still exactly as it was. Her heart turned over in her chest as she walked deeper into the living room, her pulse going wild as memories flooded her.

'You were happy here,' he said quietly, moving to stand behind her. 'I like seeing you happy.'

Her eyes swept shut, because she heard what he wasn't saying. He didn't like seeing her hurt. He didn't like knowing he'd hurt her. He was terrified of turning into his father and worried their marriage was going to dissolve into that same awful merry-go-round of fights.

She turned to face him, needing to reassure him. 'I'm happy in Athens too,' she lied.

'You're avoiding me,' he said flatly. 'You hide from me at home. You leave any room I am in. We have not had a conversation in over a month. Do you want a divorce, *agape*? Because I would accept that—I would accept anything—rather than seeing you like this and knowing me to be the cause.'

Her pulse hit a crescendo and her eyes stung with unshed tears. 'Do *you* want a divorce?' She volleyed the question back to him.

Alex's eyes flared to hers, something deep in their irises. She held her breath, waiting, her nerves stretching to breaking point. Finally, he shook his head. 'That is the opposite of what I want.'

She exhaled slowly, nodding. 'It would be bad for my father.'

His eyes were shielded from her by his long lashes. 'That's true.'

Had she been hoping for a denial? Her heart thumped. 'I'm sorry if what I told you the other week made things difficult for you,' she said quietly. 'It won't happen again.'

'Don't.' His voice rumbled towards her. 'Don't apologise. Your love was a gift. That you wanted to share that with me will always be meaningful.' He paused, drawing in a deep breath so his chest lifted and fell. 'I haven't been honest with you, *agape*.'

She flinched at the term of endearment.

'Do you remember the art show you had in Florence? Around your twenty-first birthday.'

Of course she did. It was only her second show, the first having garnered so much praise she'd been given a huge venue just down a lane from the Uffizi, at one of the most prestigious private galleries in Europe. 'What about it?'

'Stav was so proud of you. He spoke of nothing else

for days.' He angled his face away, staring at the wall. 'I said nothing to him. Nothing that would lead him to think I'd been thinking about it, and you. Nothing to make him wonder.'

'I don't understand.'

'And then, I went to the gallery. I flew there especially, telling myself I was simply curious, that my interest was natural. But why didn't I tell Stav? Why didn't I go with him?' His voice was laced with self-condemnation. 'On some level, I knew that my feelings were wrong. They were so much deeper than I could ever admit to. I went, I saw, I was blown away by your talent, and then I left, and told no one.' His eyes bored into hers with fierce intensity. 'You are so clever. Gifted. And then you stopped.'

She turned away from him, his words chewing through her resolve and causing hope to flicker to life—but hadn't she told herself hope was a wasted force?

'I was terrified,' he admitted gruffly, his words spoken to her back. 'I have been so determined to avoid love, all my life, and very specifically to avoid loving you. For as long as I've known you, there's been something between us, something I've fought to resist.' She closed her eyes on a wave of pain. 'To have you offer it to me so bravely, so beautifully, even after what I've put you through, was over-whelming. On so many levels, this is wrong—I have told myself this is wrong, that I couldn't have you.'

She let out a small cry of hopelessness, for the pain he'd put them both through.

'I wanted to avoid hurting you, with all that I am. I wanted to avoid hurting you as my father hurt my mother and then I had to watch you disappear from me, fade away into nothing, your face pale, your eyes haunted, and I have known it is my fault. Everything I dreaded most came to pass regardless of how I tried to avoid it.' He dropped his head forward, rubbing the back of his neck. 'I was so angr at myself, Theresa. Whenever I replayed that conversation and heard what I said to you, I wanted to shake myself. Why couldn't I admit to you that I was scared of the love you were offering?'

She made a gargling sound, moving now to the sofa and sitting down. The support was a godsend. 'I knew you felt that. You didn't need to say anything.'

He crossed to her and knelt at her feet, just as he'd done in her studio. 'But since then I have felt a thousand things, and none of them made any sense until today. I could not understand why my chest was hurting and my mind was singularly obsessed with you—where you were, what you were doing, how you were feeling. Memories of Epíneio, of your smile, your laugh, of being here together, tormented me at all hours of the day and still I didn't understand. I knew only that I'd had something special and lost it. That I'd lost you. Suddenly, I was going through the motions of life without feeling that I was actually living.'

Her eyes stayed on her knees; it was impossible to look at him.

'And then today, when your friend called and told me you'd passed out, I had no idea what had happened, or how serious it was. But in that moment I would have struck any bargain with any god for you to be okay. I couldn't face the prospect of living without you, *agape,* because no matter how hard I have tried to fight it, I love you, as absolutely as the stars are a part of the sky, I love you. Is it possible I always have?'

She made an uneven sound as the words burst around them, and she lifted a hand to his shoulder. She wanted to feel euphoria, but doubts plagued her. 'Please don't feel you have to say this. I really am okay, Alex. I'm not dying. I'm not even sick. I've just been pushing myself a bit too hard. If this is guilt or some weird sense of responsibility talking, then shelve it. I'll be fine.' She jutted her chin defiantly, desperately needing him to understand. 'I'm not your mother, and you're not your father.'

'No. We're our own people, with our own lives to lead. I get that now. There is no one kind of marriage, no one kind of love.' He leaned closer, his thumb catching her hair and pushing it behind one ear. 'And I know you will be fine, my darling, but I won't be. I have been miserable since that night, and only today have I properly understood the reason.' His eyes scanned hers, truth in his face. 'I love you. Just as you said, this is not a sudden love, it is a love I think I have felt for a long time. The night of the funeral, when we came together, it wasn't just grief. It was because I needed to make love to you, the only person on earth who had the power to make me feel better—the person who has been, for a long time, my other half.'

Her eyes parted. 'The way you reacted—'

'I was terrified,' he said quietly. 'When I was with you, I felt whole. I felt better. Like the best version of myself. One night with you and I felt everything I'd always believed torn away from me, violently, and I wasn't ready.'

She shook her head, eyes sweeping shut. 'You were so final.'

He paused, obviously weighing up his next words with care.

'There's something else, something I should have told you sooner.'

She held her breath, bracing herself for whatever was coming next.

'Your brother was very protective of you.'

She expelled a cross sigh. 'We've discussed that.'

But Alex continued as though she hadn't spoken. 'He knew you had a crush on me, and if he caught me so much as looking in your direction he would warn me away. He would joke about it, but we both knew he meant every word. I was older, too experienced, not right for you. To have slept with you right after we buried him…can you understand how I felt? I was so ashamed of myself, so angry that I'd betrayed Stavros in that way, and I lashed out. It was wrong, and it was far from an accurate representation of my feelings. I pushed you away, but not because I didn't care about you. That was never why.'

Her eyes sparkled with tears.

'I love you,' he added, simply, when all more grandiose forms of expression seemed unnecessary. 'And I am going to keep you here until you understand that.'

She laughed. 'I think I understand already,' she blinked her lashes, 'but I'm happy to pretend I don't, just for tonight.'

'A few nights,' he bartered, then, before she could demur, he lifted a finger to her lips, silencing her. 'At least.'

She nodded, her heart bursting. 'That sounds like heaven to me.'

Much later, with their feet in the balmy water of the Aegean, the sky dusky pink and orange, Tessa's phone began to ring. She lifted it from her back pocket, frowning at the unfamiliar number, then swiped to answer.

'Hello?'

'Is this Theresa Zacharidis?'

She smiled up at Alex, her heart full to the brim, because she really *was* Theresa Zacharidis, in every bone of her body, and all the cells of her heart. 'Yes indeed.'

'It's Dr Baros.'

'Oh, hello, Doctor,' she smiled, having forgotten all about the incident in her studio that morning. Truly, it felt like a lifetime ago.

'I've just seen the results of your blood tests—'

'And everything's fine?' Tessa pre-empted.

'Well, yes…' The doctor hesitated. 'Only, I think I've discovered the reason you fainted.'

'I've been pushing myself too hard,' Tessa supplied.

'Perhaps, but that's not the sole reason.'

'It's not?' She wrinkled her brows, ignoring Alex's concerned expression. Then, to placate him, she put it on speaker. 'Doctor? Alex is here too. I've put you on loudspeaker.'

'And you're happy for him to hear this?'

She looked at Alex, nodding. Whatever concerned her, concerned him too. They were partners, a pair. That was how it would always be. 'Yes.'

'Then congratulations. You're pregnant, Theresa.'

Tessa's knees wobbled beneath her, and Alex made a strange sound, his eyes shining, and then he smiled, the biggest, most genuine smile she'd ever seen, so there was no doubt in her mind as to how this news affected him. For her part, it was as though lightning bolts were firing all through her body. She was coming alive in a way that made her feel that her seams might burst.

'Pregnant,' she repeated, shaking her head in wonder.

'I take it this is a surprise?'

'You could say that.'

'Have you had any other symptoms?'

'Well, the thought of food has made me feel absolutely nauseated for about six weeks.'

The doctor laughed. 'That explains it.'

'I can't believe it.' Tessa shook her head, smiling from ear to ear.

'You can come and see me tomorrow, to go through the prenatal information…'

'I'm not in Athens right now,' Tessa murmured, squeezing Alex's hand.

'We will come back immediately,' he interrupted.

'It's not urgent.' The doctor's smile could be heard through the phone. 'Everything looks fine. Your blood tests show as great, in fact. Iron, Vitamin D, everything looks to be perfect. Only try to find something you can stomach the idea of eating—for the baby's sake.'

'I will.' Tessa nodded.

'And book an appointment some time in the next fortnight. We'll do a scan and go over things in more detail.'

'Doctor? Can you tell how far along I am?'

'It's difficult to say without doing a scan, but going from the level of hormones in your blood I'd say around six weeks.'

Tessa thought her heart might burst. 'That makes sense,' she smiled serenely, disconnecting the call a moment later and looking up at Alex.

'Does it?' he repeated, with wonder.

'I think it happened on our last night here, in the pool. It was when I knew, without a shadow of a doubt, how much I loved you.'

He tilted his head back and laughed, then wrapped his arms around her waist and lifted her into the air, spinning her around then slowly sliding her down his body, kissing her when their faces were level. 'You had no idea?'

'None,' she promised. 'I've been so distracted...'

'And at least I know now that your food aversion wasn't sparked by my awful behaviour.'

She shook her head, not wanting to tell him how hard his rejection had hurt. She leaned closer, lifting up onto her tiptoes to kiss him, as everything in her world clicked into place.

'I love you,' he said, and they were the three most beautiful words in the world, because they were true and right and always would be. She held him tight and loved him back, with all her heart, her soul, and every single piece of her, for all time.

EPILOGUE

SECOND CHANCES IN life were a gift, not a guarantee, and Alex and Tessa knew that deep in their bones. They'd been given a second chance and neither was willing to waste a moment of it.

Epíneio became not just a haven but also a home, a place for family to gather and celebrate, to be together, to make loud, happy memories, and also to remember. Stavros was spoken of so often that he felt very much a part of their lives, and when his namesake was born, eight months after Alex and Tessa recommitted to one another on Epíneio, it was with the certainty that little baby Stavros would always know about his uncle.

Orion and Elizabeth visited as often as his health would allow, and when he became too weak to travel to the island, Tessa, Alex and baby Stavros visited his home in Athens. He lived to see Stavros turn one, and Tessa's belly grow round with their second baby, to witness her first art showing in years, to marvel at her talent, and to recognise her finally, fully, as the woman she'd always been destined to become.

When Orion died there was grief and sadness, and so much heartache, but there was also hope and joy, because his life had been long and lived with meaning, and just as they honoured Stavros, they honoured Orion, and kept his memories with them always.

A cottage was built for Elizabeth on Epíneio, and after the birth of their fifth child Alex and Tessa were ever grateful to have a doting grandmother on hand to help care for their children, and to allow them the freedom to occasionally travel as a couple. For as much as they loved their children—and they did, with all their hearts—their family of seven had begun as two, and the love of that pair was something special and beautiful that each wanted to celebrate, whenever they could.

There was no contract that could contain their love, no term or agreement that could bind them more than the agreement their hearts had made, secretly, quietly, a long, long time ago.

Alexandros Zacharidis was not a man to make mistakes, and as it turned out he hadn't.

* * * * *

COMING SOON!

We really hope you enjoyed reading this book.
If you're looking for more romance, be sure to
head to the shops when new books are
available on

Thursday 29th September

To see which titles are coming soon, please visit
millsandboon.co.uk/nextmonth

MILLS & BOON

MILLS & BOON®

Coming next month

THE KING'S CHRISTMAS HEIR
Lynne Graham

Her cheeks were pink, her striking eyes downcast as she disconcerted him by reaching for the pen and scrawling her signature on the document that Dario had given him.

"You shouldn't sign a legal document without your own lawyer at hand to represent your interests," Gaetano remarked tautly.

"That's your world, not mine," Lara parried in a tone of scorn. "I don't require a lawyer to tell me I want to be free of you. You have disappointed me in every conceivable way, Gaetano –"

"I regret that you feel that way," he breathed curtly.

"No, your only goal is that I sign this form so that you can shed any responsibility you might have for me as discreetly as possible. That doesn't surprise me but I'm angry on my son's behalf!" Lara countered, throwing her head back. "He is an innocent party here and you didn't even look at him at the park!"

"You're trying to say that your son is also... my son?" Gaetano framed in open disbelief.

"He's sixteen months old, Gaetano. Who else could be his father?"

Continue reading
THE KING'S CHRISTMAS HEIR
Lynne Graham

Available next month
www.millsandboon.co.uk

MILLS & BOON

THE HEART OF ROMANCE

A ROMANCE FOR EVERY READER

MODERN

Prepare to be swept off your feet by sophisticated, sexy and seductive heroes, in some of the world's most glamourous and romantic locations, where power and passion collide.

HISTORICAL

Escape with historical heroes from time gone by. Whether your passion is for wicked Regency Rakes, muscled Vikings or rugged Highlanders, awaken the romance of the past.

MEDICAL

Set your pulse racing with dedicated, delectable doctors in the high-pressure world of medicine, where emotions run high and passion, comfort and love are the best medicine.

True Love

Celebrate true love with tender stories of heartfelt romance, from the rush of falling in love to the joy a new baby can bring, and a focus on the emotional heart of a relationship.

Desire

Indulge in secrets and scandal, intense drama and plenty of sizzling hot action with powerful and passionate heroes who have it all: wealth, status, good looks...everything but the right woman.

HEROES

Experience all the excitement of a gripping thriller, with an intense romance at its heart. Resourceful, true-to-life women and strong, fearless men face danger and desire - a killer combination!

To see which titles are coming soon, please visit

millsandboon.co.uk/nextmonth